E

William Breton was born i̶ ̶L̶o̶n̶d̶o̶n̶. While dividing his life principally between Britain and North America, he has travelled widely in out-of-the-way parts of the rest of the world. He has worked for both government and industry in advanced computer systems and communications, including Soviet traffic analysis. When not engaged in writing his next novel, his favourite pursuits are history, the early movie business, and fly fishing.

WILLIAM BRETON

Ten Days to Zero-Zero

This edition published 1994 by
Diamond Books
77–85 Fulham Palace Road
Hammersmith, London W6 8JB

First published in Great Britain by
Grafton Books 1989

Published in paperback by Grafton Books 1990

ISBN 0 261 66429 8

Set in Times

Made and printed in Great Britain

To Teddy
. . . at Forli

1

Mount Hood, Oregon

Jack Lowel's left hand betrayed him. His footing crumbled. He heard the safety line *zing* as it whizzed through the piton's metal eye – one body-length, two, three . . .

At four, the rope stopped him, with gravity's thud: but his heart hammered, his goggles fogged. This snow could kill, and he felt his age. Forty-seven wasn't over the hill for climbing; the Swiss Eiger had been nailed at fifty-one, but there was more ego than good sense in taking the lead after your third decade. It was the first rule he gave the other greying go-getters who signed on for the rafting trips and rock traverses he and his partner, Sam Wong, arranged for them in what had started as a retirement hobby and become a growth industry.

He heard Wong's shout of concern below him and waved back that he was all right. Just lay the groundwork, Lowel now told himself. Be the Grand Old Man of the mountain; leave the jazz to the kids with two whole hands. For a romantic fool with one and a half, just getting there should be enough.

The peak, shaped like a whale's blowhole, was only 200 feet above him. As he looked up, a black B52 from his old flight at Yakima crossed effortlessly, high and silent. He started labouring again. An early summer had zapped Oregon with a streak of days that fried the inland sage brush at the roots and turned the coastal rain forest into an incendiary device. At the 11,000-foot mark, where the

7

only vegetation was yellow lichen on black igneous rock, the surface snow embedding it froze to green glass overnight then became brown mush with the sun. Already he felt it on his back, making his sweat stream like the gases escaping from the fissures all around the peak.

He heaved his way through them, and was there.

'The roof of the world,' he called to Wong, as his baby-faced partner came up to the end of the rope. 'Jesus, what a view!'

He took out the last hand-rolled cigarette he had allowed for this small celebration. For himself, the irony of smoking and climbing made as much sense as the rest of life: for the white-water graduates, rolling his own was part of the Lowel Legend they were buying. He lit up and enjoyed it.

'That roof cliché has been used before, and those killer sticks are definitely gonna getcha.' Wong flopped his squat bulk on the blowhole's edge. 'Let me have a drag.'

Lowel passed across the flattened tube of coarse tobacco. His friend inhaled, coughed, grinned. 'Lung rot feels so good. Why did I ever quit? And I'm not really arguing the view when you can see to the coast.'

Lowel took back his soggy weed. 'Further than that, Sam. Rainier's visible.'

Marking Seattle to the north, beyond the Columbia which was now getting the sun, it reflected from a helicopter clearing the river's gorge.

'And Shasta,' Wong pointed south, 'that's even further – not forgetting your namesake, little old Three Fingered Jack. If you've ordered a ride home, you antique bastard, count me out.'

His partner grinned again, at being blessed with ageless oriental features and all of six months younger! The lower triple peak Wong indicated was almost hidden by Mount Jefferson, past Warm Springs. This side of the town, the

8

helicopter was closer, but Lowel ignored it. Choppers weren't happy at altitude.

'I wasn't forgetting,' he said. 'Excuse me a minute, Sam.'

He butted the cigarette, knelt down, and took the wreath out of his pack. Blue cornflowers and red poppies, twined on green juniper: Bergitta's favourites. He could hear her saying it, laughing at him as they stood here, looking south as he was now, and putting on her mother's lilting Norwegian accent that he loved. She asked him, 'What is that one over there, the diamond shape by Yefferson?'

And he said, 'Three Fingered Yack.'

And she said, 'From Yakima. That's my boy!'

Fifteen years ago, that snappy conversation. After his Air Force days were finished, and he was looking for more exciting things to do than sit in a hangar waiting on twenty-four-hour alert for the end-of-the-world gong. Things like piloting CIA bullets and her Red Cross bandages into Biafra, with no moon and only a couple of oil drums flaring to mark the African runway – until one went out. And when they were safely down, and for no other reason, he asked her to marry him. Her instant reply was –

'Jack, sorry to intrude, but we do have company.'

Lowel looked up from the flowers, so brilliant a reminder in this crisp world. Almost before he had known it, then and now, his time with Bergitta was gone; today was the first stabbing anniversary of her death. But in spite of loss, somehow life went on. Below him, the chopper was just clearing the final haunch of the east face, the throbbing of its rotors, echoed and amplified back from the volcano, sounding like a forced last gasp.

'Tokyo tourists,' said Wong, 'OK. But if it's those Rescue assholes – !'

'I don't think it's either, Sam.'

The helicopter was marine gloss green. A marine in

9

fatigues stood in the open hatch below the main gear-housing. The noise of it became a physical pressure; on the steepest parts of the slope the lighter chunks of lava began tumbling from the ice, then snow, then yellow dust in a cloud from the sulphur crust around the crater vent. The machine touched down, barely enough to bend its undercarriage. The marine in the hatch had a bullhorn to his mouth, but the roar still overwhelmed it. Lowel tapped his ears and shrugged.

'. . . One . . . you . . . Lowel?'

Now the words were loud enough, but a trick of acoustic doubling carried half of them away. Lowel nodded, slapping his chest.

'. . . with us . . . please.'

The marine signalled towards the hatch. Lowel shook his head, spreading his arms. His pilgrimage wasn't complete until he walked down.

'. . . At once . . . direct order!'

Wong's mouth framed an anatomically impossible reply. Lowel softened it with the universal wave-off sign. Thanks but no thanks.

A second marine appeared, holding a rifle. The bullhorn roared, '. . . order . . . President . . . United States!'

When you can't fight them – and you've played all-night poker with the official just mentioned, and your late wife was his sister – you climb in through the hatch. To show he had a mind of his own, Sam Wong bent to retrieve their climbing rope, still engaged by the pitons. The second marine made a more impatient gesture with his rifle barrel.

'Leave it,' Lowel said in Wong's ear, 'for next time.'

The chopper seemed to fall backwards rather than lift off. The braided nylon rippled up past the hatch to the summit of a volcano that only slumbered, and a trace of red and blue receding with Bergitta's accent into his memory.

2

Lowel noticed the toll of Daniel Galbraith's election as America's leader from the first moment of their meeting. The new crow's-feet at his brother-in-law's eyes, the small down-lines forming by the corners of the mouth, the muscle contraction becoming a habit of the cheek, the grey encroaching in the celebrated palomino shaded mane of hair.

'Jack, you son of a gun!'

'It's good to see you, Mr President.'

Which was the first time he'd ever said that, Lowel realized – Mr President. He hadn't seen the vibrant, smiling man who faced him since Bergitta's funeral, just before the cliff-hanger election, eight months ago, but he'd known this Chief Executive on a Dan–Jack basis nearly all their lives: from prep-school shyness, through the Air Force Academy's football play battles with Navy, at Annapolis, to the mess in Vietnam where Lowel lost two left fingers on CIA mountain station, while his boyhood companion commanded a patrol boat in the Delta – neither one a restful job. With time out to be best man at each other's weddings they shared the intense excitement that only comes in war, even the price it exacts, their common injuries. That Delta patrol had cost America's new leader the lower part of his right arm. In public, Galbraith wore a useless dummy covered by a dark leather glove; away from the zoom lenses, as

11

now, an unornamented prosthetic miracle of bio-med engineering that even shuffled cards. Its owner dropped his good arm for a moment on Lowel's shoulder.

'A fine pair of crocks; we can't shake hands. But before we start, Jack – I have to say again, about you losing Bergitta . . .'

Dan Galbraith had been not just her brother, but the closest friend to his only sister. And for Lowel, looking now at one brought a stabbing reminder of the other. The same hair as hers, the same hazel eyes; the same resourceful, courageous heritage of Norway, and Scotland, moulded by ranching the American South-west . . .

The pause which he had come to accept always followed that exchange of sympathy was longer than usual. Camp David seemed the right kind of place for it. Now, Catoctin Mountain was the escape from the boom-mikes of the White House press pack but, for students of history, these 5,000 acres of chestnuts, eastern oaks, and aspens began their association with the American presidency as a lovers' hideaway, a trysting place for Franklin Roosevelt and his mistress, Lucy Rutherford.

'The grief merchants tell me the first year is the worst,' Lowel said. 'I'm through that, and there's someone over in London – a woman both of us knew. Jacqueline Campbell, she's been a real help.'

'Good man,' said Galbraith. 'Let me get rid of this crowd – then we'll walk.'

The crowd was the Secret Service bird dogs, edgy as ever behind their sunshades; a young naval aide carrying the Button Box, with its miracle radio-communications electronics for launching/preventing global nuclear war; and the Secretary of Defense, a super hard-nose leftover from the previous administration. The President waved them all off with his prosthesis. Lowel said, 'That thing's a lethal weapon.'

'The only one I've got. The first year in this job,

you're a paper tiger. Since I scrubbed the last of his Star Wars game, "Captain Hawk" over there has been after my balls.' Galbraith laughed, tipping his head with undisguised contempt towards his glowering Cabinet officer who took a pace forward to follow them before the Service bird dogs closed around him. The young aide with the nuclear Button Box looked unhappy. 'Just keep it warm, son,' the President called back, 'but don't hatch anything without me.'

The entourage was left behind. Except for its bird life, the forest was silent. They came to a clearing by a cliff edge, marked off by a few stones. 'For us history buffs,' said Roosevelt's latest successor and one-time Rhodes Scholar, 'there's the old cabin site where F.D.R. and Lucy thought they were keeping it secret from that bulldog of morality, J. Edgar Hoover. For me, the air up here helps keep the Agent Orange in my central nervous system from completely taking over.'

'You still have trouble from that exposure in the Delta?'

'Only when I need to think and breathe at the same time.' Galbraith smiled ironically and held up a Medicalert bracelet on his sound wrist. 'Being a crock, at least I can promote a good cause. Jack, you know I wouldn't have flipped you here if it wasn't in the national interest. Even on Mount Hood you must have heard the press buzz about a "Final-Final Summit"?'

'For the global Zero-Zero Agreement,' Lowel nodded. 'My in-flight copy of the *Post* said there's a rumour.'

'It's now fact. You're the first to know: one hour ago I got off the phone to the other side – their First Secretary. I haven't eyeballed him yet, but we've read each other's books and have a good relationship by phone; as good as you can have through the interpreters. I should have taken Russian post-grad at Monterey, like you; that would really put me one up when we go to the mat.'

13

'Real zero-zero?' said Lowel. 'Total dismantling of ICBMs?'

'Plus our last strategic bombers and cruise, that's the stake. Take a look.' Using only the artificial fingers of his prosthesis, Galbraith fished a paper from his shirt pocket, unfolded it, and passed it across. 'You can see, since the first fifty-fifty chop, with subsequent ten per cent per year reducing, we've hardly pulled a tooth out of the dragon. With the acceleration I've proposed and he's agreed to, we'll go down in a single grand slam. There'll be a bilateral peacekeeping umbrella of five ballistic subs, with joint crews from each side, and we're still nailing some last details with Britain and France –'

'Hold on. That was *joint* crews?'

'If we can do it in space, we can do it underwater.' Galbraith replaced the working paper in his pocket. 'And not just to get some chance of real peace on earth: it's the only possible goddamn way we're going to climb back from this economic Black Hole that bunch of Hollywood has-beens dug us into. So when the other side made it a dare, "Go to Final Stage Dismantling in six months" – I said Fuck it, you smooth-talking bastard! Ten days! Are we on?'

'It sounds like those straight-stud all-nighters on the Mekong.' Lowel smiled, but this poker-playing President had to know the political reality of bluffing a Soviet leader who could outbid PR from Madison Avenue. As they passed the horseshoe pit installed by that other high stakes river gambler, Lyndon Johnson, Lowel asked, 'You really think you can swing it?'

'I have to. Already I'm being compared with F.D.R. by certain elements in our national life, as "That new cripple in the White House".'

'Jesus Christ, Dan, they elected you as a goddamn hero.'

His brother-in-law shrugged. 'The electorate has a

14

short memory. But scrapping the last missiles *will* happen – even though between Captain Hawk's Jesus Freak pals on the Right and the loony Left, my political margin is going to be one pussy hair on the vote! And I can handle our military –'

'Can the other side handle his?'

'That's half the big question. You can imagine the heavy breathing his Red Army pigshave haircuts must be doing. It's bad enough on our side: without their nukes, for the first time since World War Two my Joint Chiefs will have to come out of their closet and rely on straight fighting ability and asswipe.'

Galbraith laughed sarcastically and stood looking at the magnificent view to the west over Hunting Creek. East, in the trees, the sunglassed Secret Service bird dogs were sniffing.

'And the second half of the question?' Lowel said.

'Our Intelligence – I use that word in quotes – Community, which is where you come in. And I know why you walked from that line of business, after Iran, giving up your crack at the top. I respect you for it, but on my Intelligence front I'm facing a real stonewall crisis. *"Work with Russia?"* Those CIA grey flannel con artists at Langley are going to have to change the habits of a lifetime and actually speak to people they've been at war with forty years! Your former associates are so out of their heads over losing their slice of the Budget pie, just this morning they tried scaring me off with some nympho, set to poison *both* me and my opposite number in the sack!'

'So I'm here because you're looking for a stand-in.'

Lowel kept it light but, when Bergitta's brother turned back from the spectacular view to rejoin the world of politics and his Secret Service, he wasn't smiling.

'Woodrow Wilson had Colonel House as his pinch-hitter backstage, and J.F.K. used brother Bob – but the

Kennedys just had Jimmy Hoffa and Castro against them. Until the First Secretary and I sign that paper, every spook in the world is going to try and stop us. Already CIA has a crank note promising bilateral "Death in a novel way"!'

'Against both of you? With poison?'

Galbraith shrugged. 'Langley claims some kind of horror toxin was stolen last night from a local Beltway cancer lab, by a woman. Apparently there's a videotape. My oldest friend, I can only say if the bastards are opening with Lady Borgia, you're here to prevent international Hallowe'en.'

The threat was just another presidential assassination crazy, Lowel thought – although the military-industrial forces on both sides of the Iron Curtain with a vested interest in preventing the breakout of world peace were real and sane. The probability of the threat wasn't the issue. The stubborn yet impulsive man who was apparently its target was not only the nation's Chief Executive: he was Bergitta's brother. Lowel knew that he was too old and too rusty for making any change to global politics; but for her sake and that memory on the mountain-top, if there was an outside chance of lessening the risk to Dan's life, then he could not refuse.

3

No antidote! . . . the sign was the first thing that registered on Lowel as he entered the bronze-tinted glass doors of Paracel-Tech Incorporated. The building was one of the cluster of leading-edge laboratories spawned by the defence industries ringing Washington, all hoping to make it first with Superconductors or X-ray lasers. In the case of Paracel-Tech, the silver bullet was Oncogenetics, a cure for cancer through gene manipulation.

> HANDLING MONOCLONAL AGENTS
> RICIN, ABRIN, MODECIN, VOLKENSIN, VISCUMIN
> LIFE THREAT MAXIMUM

The scarlet signs with their black skull-and-crossbones were everywhere: Oncogene Cloning Area! Cytochemicals Present! Active Hybrid SV 40! Sarin Bonding! He recognized Sarin as a variety of nerve gas – it didn't need the police cordon in the deserted company parking lot to keep any sane human being out of a death zone like this.

'Halt!' A unisex figure of medium height, dressed in a white bunnysuit and helmet with visor hood, stepped forward. 'No entry. The building's cleared. We're closed for total decontamination.'

The voice was male and slightly muffled through the fabric of the helmet. A pair of suspicious eyes in steel-rim glasses was visible inside the visor.

'I have a pass.' Lowel produced it and said to the anonymous figure, 'I'm told you have last night's incident on closed-circuit video. Where is your head of lab security?'

'Taking leave out on the Coast. I just got back myself from vacation this morning, to get hit with a toxic alert, and do stand-in.' A hand sheathed with a surgical glove took the pass and held it up for the shielded eyes. 'More CIA! You people ought to co-ordinate. And you'll have to suit up if you want to come in.'

The figure led him past the multiple warning signs to a door marked Change Room. Inside there were shower stalls, clothes lockers, and a body-sized chute to the disposal bin. A stack of fresh bunnysuits, each polywrapped, was beside it. The lab security stand-in took the top packet and handed it over.

'Watch the sign.'

'Which one in particular?' Lowel asked drily.

The gloved hand pointed at:

PHYTOTOXIN DIVISION – SUPER CAUTION!
AVOID ALL CONTAMINATION WITH WALLS AND FLOOR!
FOREIGN OBJECTS FORBIDDEN!

This latest hair-raiser was posted in duplicate on each one of a pair of airlocking sliding glass doors. On their other side Lowel could see a second pair, and then lab counters stretching away under fluorescent lights. As he pulled on the bunnysuit, the red-eye lens of a mini-cam watched him from the ceiling.

'Not much place for privacy,' he remarked.

'Only in the showers,' said the security staffer. 'They should be included as well, but the damn union won't let it in the contract. You can view last night's tape from the monitor booth – across the Clean Room.'

The man stepped towards the glass doors of the airlock.

They slid open. Wearing the protective suit and helmet was already claustrophobic. Despite himself, Lowel felt a crawling ripple up the spine as he followed through the hissing curtain of disinfectant air maintaining a climatic barrier against lethal poison. Inside the airlock, his ears popped: the space was kept at higher pressure by humming pumps. His guide turned to the right, away from the Clean Room with its counters, and exited through another set of doors into a passage lined on both sides with interior windows. Beyond them, rows of glass cases had top-hatch openings and blue-black neoprene gauntlets hanging inside like the chopped-off arms of corpses.

'The glove boxes seem to spook visitors more than the signs,' said the security man. 'Here's the booth. I'll load the graveyard-shift tape for you, but I don't want to sit through it again.'

'Sorry,' Lowel said, 'you'll have to. I'm going to need scientific translation.'

The television monitor in the booth showed a high-speed blur, then settled as a black-and-white image of two suited unisex workers, seated back-to-back at opposite counters. Each had their hands in the gauntlets, manipulating pipettes and petri dishes inside their glove boxes. The one on screen left had a sign, Monoclonal Agent Volkensin; screen right was labelled Viscumin. The worker at that box kept staring up at a digital wall clock: the time, Lowel noted, was 02.37.

'What are monoclonal agents?' he asked his reluctant adviser.

'Exocet missiles in the bloodstream. We're bonding super toxins with the nerve enzyme, acetylcholinesterase. That's Martin working with the Viscumin,' the security man added, 'our highest power plant-poison: one molecule on the skin and game over for the lymph system. But bonded, it can home in and nail individual cancer cells.'

'And this Martin was a regular employee?'

'They don't come any more regular than Harold. A virgin PhD from Brigham Young, Utah. He's been hitting graveyard too long – his father has cancer – the only trouble with Mormons as employees, they don't know when to quit work and go play.' The man's voice tightened. 'Here's where things start.'

The other technician on monitor didn't have a play problem. It got off its stool, crept up behind Harold Martin and tickled his back. Harold Martin jumped about a foot in the air and headed for the showers. The anonymous worker followed. The television picture focused on a spot of tile floor a modest six inches away from the shower-stall openings. Two discarded bunnysuits were tossed out by hand. One hand had masculine dark hairs on it. The other was smooth, and unmistakably feminine.

'What ID on the woman?' Lowel asked.

'The file says foreign – German, but top credentials. She was taken on in my absence, as short-term replacement for Helen, who's away on maternity – see there!'

On the screen, a nude female back and buttock slipped out of one shower . . . and into the stall next door. Five seconds later a bar of soap shot out, followed by a naked Dr Harold Martin, aged about late twenties and heading like a scalded cat with a hard-on straight for the airlock doors. The soap slapped up against them. In a Keystone Kops scene Martin skidded, trying at the same time to hide his genitals. The woman was chasing him with a newspaper. Her exercised body, of average height, might have been thirty. Her hair seemed blonde. Her face was hidden from the camera. Martin pointed frantically from the newspaper to the 'No Foreign Objects' sign – which action meant releasing his excited genitals to view. The airlock doors opened.

'Like watching Ruby shooting Oswald,' said the security staffer, 'after Kennedy – when you know it's going to happen . . '

20

There was a terrible fascination, Lowel agreed: a voyeur's compulsion to keep watching. Afraid to tackle his nude female nemesis, Martin was backing away. The woman reached forward tauntingly and cupped his groin with the fingers of one hand, while the other waved the newspaper. This morning's *Washington Post* with the Dismantling Zero-Zero headline. Martin grabbed it, and recoiled, covering himself – but the woman was on him.

'All over him!' the lab security stand-in exclaimed. 'She's like a fucking python – but watch the glove box!'

No more Keystone Kops. Martin was backed flat against the Viscumin box. One hand slammed the newspaper on top of it. The woman's head was at his crotch. Martin's head went back, the veins in his neck stood out. The woman's head pulled back. Martin grabbed her hair and yanked down, desperate to keep her at a critical juncture.

The virgin PhD was too far gone in sex to notice science, or delicate equipment, or the presence of lethal poison all around him. Or that the woman with him had never for one moment stopped noticing.

'Her other hand!'

Lowel had already seen it. The woman's other hand was in one of the black gauntlets. Behind Martin's back she took a scrap of newsprint in through the glove-box loading hatch, dipped it in a dish, withdrew it . . .

'Now!' said the security staffer.

Martin's buttocks convulsed against the sharp edge of the counter. Then the poisoned newspaper fragment touched him. Once, on his left thigh, just below the hipbone. At the same moment the woman turned aside, revealing a small white hourglass shaped abdominal scar, at her groin, half hidden by blonde pubic hair. Harold Martin slumped to the floor beside the rest of the forbidden newspaper.

'My God,' Lowel said. He had seen sudden deaths too

21

often in his career, but they were slow motion compared to this.

On the monitor, structural damage from the toxin was instantaneous and massive to body tissue; the vice-like pulmonary arrest was shown through the dark coloration of extremities. The young male body of this human guinea pig lay extended at its point of climax, the look of shocked guilt frozen on its guileless Utah features. His ruthless former partner's face never once came into view of the camera – which must have demanded extraordinary mental awareness under the circumstances, Lowel thought.

Disengaged from her successful experiment, the woman calmly slipped into a fresh bunnysuit and helmet. Using the glove-box gauntlets, she transferred with exquisite care the remaining contents of the open dish of Viscumin to a sterile one; sealed it: separated the affected sheet of newsprint, sealed that also within a double-walled stainless steel carrying-case, removed both through the hatch of the glove box, went back into the change room, discarded her suit to the incinerator chute, and dressed.

She wasted no further glance on the naive remains beyond the sliding doors – she had what she came for. But on her way out of camera range, she paused to look down at the remaining *Post* disarmament copy crumpled in the burn bag under the 'No Antidote' sign. For that brief moment, her eyes scanning the Summit headline were still hidden, but to Lowel her body language was unmistakably a climber's, going for the top of Everest.

4

As the stalled traffic on the Beltway was left behind, and the landing pad at CIA came up to meet him, Lowel considered the purple stamp on the laser-printed document the President had passed to him on take-off from Camp David. Stamped so far above Top Secret, this sweeping and absolute authority meant God's Eyes Only! to the Intelligence trade; but the magic paper was valid and would shield him only for the same length of time as the Disarmament challenge. Ten days. After that, by the law covering Presidential Findings, as these exotic documents were called, the competing politicians in Congress had to be fed details of any covert Black Operation the same way the Colosseum's lions got raw meat: with human flesh.

The chopper hit the pad with a suitable shudder. And the boys at CIA weren't wearing grey flannel any longer: the man crouching from the down draught was in three-piece, pinstripe, banking midnight-blue. His hair, which he tried vainly to control, was flaming red. His name was Murphy, and when Lowel last had dealings with the Firm the man was making a slot for himself at the trough by exaggerating the threat the armed might of Grenada posed to the security of the United States.

'Deputy for anti-Terror, now.' Murphy shouted it too loudly, the rotor whine had died. 'Better hustle, cowboy, the Director has only fifteen minutes available for your call.'

23

'I'm grateful.'

But the redhead was still too busy with his coiffure to detect irony. As they rode down from the roof, the Deputy for anti-Terror adjusted a kisscurl in the gold-fleck mirrored walls of the elevator. The height of sixties chic, Lowel always thought the headquarters building must have been designed for Conrad Hilton. They crossed the marble lobby with the brass insignia set in the floor, and the stars for lost agents set in the walls. Too many of them, and too many lost friends. Too much public incompetence and political flash-dancing. It was why CIA was no longer the real backstage force in Washington, but only the decoy to take the fire of the Congressional investigators, and the far Left demonstrators the President despised.

The latest Director of the Agency was from the other side of the political track: a sixty-eight-year-old former Alabama judge and hard-line commie-basher, given the job as another part of the price for this new Administration keeping its hair-line vote. From the moment Lowel was introduced by Murphy, it was obvious that the old Director disguised his hostility to the young President's men with an excessive use of southern charm.

'Why, Mr Lowel, sir – a pleasure, a pleasure. Sit down right here and tell us how we-all can accommodate you in this mysterious task it seems our young President has seen fit to delegate on a relative's broad shoulders.'

'Thank you, Director, I'll use this other chair if you don't mind.' The deep leather seat Lowel had been offered appeared at first glance to give the best view of the cool planting of shade trees in the central court, but in fact got hit by the full force of the late afternoon summer sun. He took a brocade upholstered alternative that stood next to a set of monogrammed golf clubs leaning against the Director's inlaid and gilded Louis XIV desk – courtesy the Old Masters floor at Bloomingdales. Murphy moved towards the leather chair, thought better of it and remained standing. Lowel ignored the jab about being Galbraith's relative and tossed the ball back to Alabama. 'There's no mystery on my side, sir. The President has merely asked me to run interference for him against any roadblocks that may show up between now and his signing the final ICBM Dismantling Pact.'

'If and when, Mr Lowel, if and when. As my granddaddy used to say, there's many an egg gets away from the nest of a wet hen.'

The Director laughed, and Murphy laughed. Lowel looked across the golf clubs and said, 'As you're so short of time, sir, you'll want me to come to the point. What probability level has the Agency assigned to this morning's assassination threat?'

The Director looked at Murphy. 'Nil,' snapped the redhead.

'Which is to say,' drawled his superior, 'the incident was reported to the President in the course of my routine morning brief, but only because the night duty officer was inexperienced and slipped it in there in an excess of zeal. There's no hard indication whatsoever this woman's lethal activity is aimed at the executive level of our government. Let's just say, Mr Lowel, on behalf of the Secret Service we watch all the "exits in our basket".'

There was another one-sided heh-heh for this sourmash humour. Lowel said, 'I'd like to see the basket. May I have the duty officer's file?'

The Director stared. Murphy stared. The former's Jack Daniels' drawl got even slower. 'Well now, I'd like for you to see it, Mr Lowel, I surely would, but that document is what we call – and you-all will have to excuse my memory for slippin' – what do we call it, Murphy?'

'System Nine, Director. And things have changed as well, I guess, since Mr Lowel's cowboy days. By Act of Congress the document is only releasable now by the system custodian to names on the system access list.'

Murphy glared. The Director studied his golf clubs.

'Then put me on it.'

The sun had moved from the leather chair. Murphy was being boxed in. Sweat beaded the red hair. The Director was still shadow-boxing.

'Well now, Mr Lowel – '

'I have Finding authority to override the Act, sir, but I have to report to the President when I use it. I'm sure when the time comes for reconfirmation you won't want that.'

The job of directing CIA pays more than a southern judgeship – even allowing for a generous cut from the speed-trap fines. The incumbent of the office said, 'I do see I'm late for my meeting with the House Committee people. Murphy here can rustle you up the custodian first thing tomorrow morning.'

'I'll be airborne tomorrow morning, sir. I imagine the file is in your office safe. I'd like it now.'

There was a stand-off silence. Lowel removed the Finding document from his pocket and placed it on the desk. The old Director did a Jack Benny routine with a pair of bifocals. The Finding's purple stamp was vivid in the sun. Murphy took this chance to get out of it and moved so that he was standing directly behind Lowel's shoulder. Lowel picked up the document. The Director stared over the top of the bifocals with a death penalty stare, then opened the centre drawer in his desk and withdrew a circulation envelope tied shut with red string.

'Thank you, sir.' But the old man's offer was hardly generous. Lowel was forced to lean across the desk to take the envelope. He unwound the string and withdrew the report. There were three both-sides pages, which he studied – determined to ignore Murphy's hostile breathing down the back of his neck. He put the report back in the envelope.

'And you still feel that your duty officer's target analysis is invalid?' he said to the Director.

'Folk tales, Mr Lowel. Fairy stories. We get them by the bushel basket.'

'Then I thank you again for this one. I'll return it after I get back from my Moscow meeting with Berov.'

Lowel stood, which bumped him into the redhead, who finally exploded, 'Berov! That little red fag? After accessing our System Nine? Over my dead body you cowboy ass–!'

'In my experience, Mr Murphy,' the old judge said drily, dropping his southern corn, 'clichés are seldom effective threats of punishment. There are more certain remedies in law for this retired gentleman's flagrant disregard of current security regulations.'

And outside the law. As Lowel walked from the building, the memorial stars for the betrayed left behind told him that.

5

Second day:

Morning rush, Moscow

A man with a dog was no longer an unusual sight in Moscow, but taking it to work in a taxi still raised eyebrows – particularly, Kliment Berov thought, when your dog was an aristocrat like Mischa, with his collie's grey Merle colouring and rare blue eyes. Except on emergency occasions, Berov took a cab to work for two good reasons: it stopped American electronics from listening in on private conversation, and seated in the backseat anonymity of a stinking Moscow taxi – a stench that wrinkled a dog's fastidious nose – a policeman can take a better pulse of the city and its visitors than he could in an official car. The sight of one of those black sharks cruising at high speed with their curtains drawn inhibited spontaneous behaviour. This morning, riding out with Mischa to watch the new arrivals landing at Sheremetyevo, Berov was trying as always not only to see his nation's capital through the fresh eyes of an outsider, but to sense her totality with an outsider's heightened senses.

'The first impression, Mischa my love: Moscow must still seem monolithic to outsiders.' These glacial grey apartment blocks still appeared to march past as uniformly and anonymously as the military divisions in the anniversary parades. And the people of Moscow, these lazy workers repairing the crumbling apartments with this slow thud-thud that pricked the collie's ears and came from pneumatic drills pressured by hoses themselves only half patched up; these patient masses queuing for shoes or Lenin's Tomb, they still seemed one people, stolid and resigned as cattle. 'Until you look at the faces, Mischa . . . surely, looking at our faces the outsider must realize we Muscovites are individuals as unique – given half a chance as bloody-minded – as himself?'

The dog's banner tail wagged affirmation. Now, with *glasnost*, the people had that chance. Openness. The proof of it was visible everywhere. On Gorky Street, just past, where the shouting prostitutes in their grubby white thigh-boots hustled for tricks, 'And because of our still endemic housing shortage, Mischa, for taxis to hustle them into, which is why our taxis stink!' Or here, out at the airport, where in the cafeteria, between delayed internal flights, the flagrant Georgian cardsharps lifted 10,000 roubles from the wallets of independent grocers heading home to the Crimea with the week's new *perestroika* free-market take.

Enterprise and openness – even in those places the outsider could not go: places where, against the old guard's rigid opposition, one man, Berov's master, was standing a century of doctrine on its collective head. Or what would surely be most surprising of all to an outsider, the fact that there were individual, open-minded human beings within that vital organ responsible for state security which outsiders still thought of with their sudden shivers as the KGB – but which these Russian faces staring in at his beautiful beast called, with a mixture of humorous contempt and necessary fear, Kousin Georg.

An open-minded individual like Mischa's owner, the monster's new Chief.

'Stop here.'

Berov directed the taxi driver to the spot of kerb left conveniently vacant between two Intourist buses, a viewpoint which put the back seat window in line with the inspection booths for external arrivals from the West.

A British Airways widebody was just floating in over the anti-tank memorial at the end of the runway.

'Mischa, love, we've timed things well – my friend will be another ten minutes. Buy yourself coffee,' he added for the driver's benefit.

'For you too, comrade?'

Berov shook his head. After a look at the unlucky blue-eyed dog, and a couple of false starts, the driver entered the terminal through the one sliding door whose photocell was working. Berov took out a cigarette and lit it with a wooden match: an old-fashioned gesture, but he was an old-fashioned man. Lighters, he had found, 'Always run dry without warning when you most need them, Mischa, whereas matches are there to be counted in the box.' And their fumes helped with the unpleasant smells encountered in a policeman's daily life – which was also why he used domestic cigarettes with their harshly pungent tobacco rather than the insipid Pall Malls and Players his colleagues imported to display the privilege of their position. His doctor complained, but Berov ignored that. As the writer Pushkin said, Death is on its way regardless! Enjoy small pleasures while we may . . .

The collie sat up and poked his alert snout through the cab window. The first visitors were approaching the Immigration officials. Berov observed the usual looks of apprehension. The lead group was mixed European led by a pig-necked German already shouting.

'And our target, Mischa.' Taller and heavier in person than the statistics on his dossier, the object of Berov's morning ride appeared relaxed, with no sign of the urgency that must be propelling him, and surprisingly alert given the length of his journey. A terse smile was crossing his face.

'Hah! Our German loudmouth has been taken aside for questioning.'

Lowel was next. In accordance with earlier instruction,

the official wasted no time. The American President's brother-in-law had only a carry-on bag slung over his shoulder, and apparently no greeting party from their Embassy. As though by instinct, he strode straight to the one functioning door, then paused a moment, squinting into the bright light of the sun. His greying hair, Berov noted, unlike most men from Washington, was not dyed. His glance skimmed Berov's taxi, the Intourist buses, looking for an Embassy car? No. Lowel hailed a cab.

'A man after our own heart, Mischa.' By prudent arrangement, the other vehicle was already taken. Berov's driver returned, wiping coffee from her lips with the back of her hand. In a cloud of brown diesel, the bus pulled out as a black Cadillac flying the Stars and Stripes screeched in.

'My friend did not arrive. We shall offer that visitor a ride.'

Berov pointed. The taxi driver's eyes briefly flicked her rear-view mirror. 'As you wish, comrade. And my regrets about your friend, but I knew our luck was too good when we had this spot open at the kerb.'

Lowel was having the same thought: no matter how often he came to Moscow, and whether it was political freeze or thaw, the climate could change overnight; paranoia was part of the landscape. In the 'free enterprise' chaos of vehicles circling for position outside the terminal, the cab parked quietly at the centre was a sore thumb. Something new was that it had a woman driver. Even more so, that she had a touch of style. A shaved poodle hairstyle, an Italian leather jacket and Polo shades.

'Meester! Vantink taxee goink Metropole Hotel?'

The female driver's tourist hail demolished any further chance of coincidence. Cigarette smoke wreathed from the nearside passenger window. Lowel realized that he was being observed in the kind of game Russians

31

loved – were addicted to! – but the Embassy limo was homing in. Getting snared by the US State Department's prissy meddling was a greater risk.

'Da,' he said to the cabbie. 'Metropole suits me well if you're sure your other fare will not mind.'

'He suggests it, comrade.'

The driver's surprised relief at getting a fluent Russian answer and her fare in advance didn't smell KGB, even if her snazzy clothing did: but the guy in the back? As Lowel reached for the door – huge teeth trapped his hand! The shock was momentary, the dog's long jaws gentle, and it wore a plaited, cornflower-blue collar that matched its eyes. Bergitta's colour. Lowel smiled.

'Good! Our Mr Lowel likes you, Mischa my love.'

'I had a collie–shepherd cross as a kid. I'm glad to meet you, *Gospodin* Berov.'

And he did like dogs, but Lowel's smile was for the spook conclusions jumped to in the dark of the upside-down world of intelligence. The National Security Agency's giant antennae, which eavesdropped on the limo radio-phone calls of Kremlin wives doing their grocery shopping – and their husbands' lunch-hour pre-game warm-ups with their mistresses – had established this dog's owner as 'Confirmed homosexual: back-seaters recorded with steady gay, identity "Mischa".'

In the flesh, this seldom-seen mystery-man who had just been made Chief of all Soviet Security, was shorter – his head a good six inches down from the cab roof, almost completely bald – and slighter, not more than 140 pounds. His face was narrower, rectangular, and cleanshaven: in the rare archival photographs, it had always been covered by a Lenin beard which brought everything to a point –

The Embassy Caddie was sliding to a halt behind him. A typical buttoned-down State 'gofer', switched from his regular duties of fetching the ambassadorial coffee and Kleenex, jumped out, waving. Lowel vaulted into the cab, over the dog's startling blue eyes. The gofer ran back in panic to the Caddie. The taxi took off. Inside, Berov had a firm handshake and an interrogator's eyes. 'If you wonder about my beard, I received chemotherapy recently, for a thyroid problem. My eyebrows came back first, but I had grown used to looking naked, or perhaps it seemed the time a man makes changes in his life. With your late wife's death, for which I'm so sorry, I have the feeling you can understand?'

'Yes, thanks.' But the reference to Bergitta caught him off guard. Berov wasn't a conventional opponent – and as he thought that, he thought, Christ! 'Opponent' is exactly what I told Murphy to stop thinking.

The taxi squeezed into the morning rush. As usual, half the Red Army was out on manoeuvres, hustling T70 tanks on vast transporters, but there were also far more new cars on the road. And more accidents. A small green Lada did a U-turn immediately in front of their cab and smacked straight into the side of a flatbed truck. Except for the Army in its reserved lane, everything halted.

'One of the more unfortunate faces of our new capitalism,' Berov observed. 'We now have the private ownership of all classes of vehicles, but not the self-discipline to guide them.'

'Stop lights would help.'

'I doubt it, Mr Lowel. You must remember that red has always been the colour of celebration in this country.'

Berov accompanied his reply with a mournful smile and the offer of a cigarette. Lowel shook his head. 'Ah yes. Like a cowboy, you make your own. My conceit is wooden matches – and for my doctor, low cholesterol.' The Russian struck a match and lit up. His fingers were the amber of a chain smoker. The cab's roof lining was the same colour. The interior filled with purple fug. The collie lay on the floor with its sensitive nose between its paws. Lowel reached for the nearest window handle, which was missing. Outside, the flatbed had skewed into the Army lane, knocking out one of the tank transporters which ended up angled in behind their taxi.

'In the bad old days,' Lowel said, 'your official lane would at least have solved this problem.'

'It still does for certain of my colleagues – but for you and poor Mischa, my factory cigarette annoys, I'll put it out.' Berov did so, at the same moment closing the glass screen behind the cab driver. 'Time passing need never be time wasted, Mr Lowel. Why don't we use this time to see whatever it is you have come such a long way to show me?'

The bulbous spires of the restored churches made it obvious, Lowel thought, yet it was always a surprise to be reminded how Byzantinely oriental this apparently European nation was in its expression.

'I didn't come over to show it just to you,' he said.

'You certainly did not come to share it with your Embassy.'

Berov gave his mournful smile again in the direction of the Caddie, trapped like their taxi, half a mile back in the traffic. Beside them, an Army redcap bellowed furiously at both the crumpled Lada and the innocent flatbed. The T70 behind their cab had snapped a holding chain on its transporter. Two other MPs signalled for heavy aid to the rear of the column. Lowel removed the circulation envelope and handed it across to Berov.

'I have a Russian translation as well, but I figured you'd want to start from the original.'

Berov nodded, unwound the string with his nicotined fingers, and withdrew the envelope's contents. The pages were reversed. He turned them over, skimmed past Incident Nature, Assailant's Instrument, Place, and Method, and at the next heading, without further comment or attention to the bedlam in the Army column, began to read.

BACKGROUND OF AGENCY CONCERN

On 28 September 1978, the 263rd Pope of the Roman Catholic Church, John Paul I, was found dead in his bedchamber. Death was announced as heart failure: no autopsy was released. Because of the short duration of the papal reign, only 34 days, and the late prelate's publicly stated anxiety about certain Vatican financial organizations, considerable speculation was generated in the world press. As these financial irregularities had sensitive links to elements in the United States, the Agency was asked by the Chief Executive to conduct its own investigation.

Item: The papal bedchamber was normally attended by three Sisters responsible for such tasks as changes of linen, drawing bathwater, laying out night attire, etc. Two of these nuns were middle-aged and had been longstanding in their duties, while the third, much younger, had only been employed for approximately one year. The morning *after* the Pope's demise, the body of this younger nun was found in her room: her cause of death – determined as an overdose of barbiturates, presumably taken to assuage guilt at her failure, by being absent from his bedside, to provide prompt medical aid for John Paul – was again not released by Vatican officials. The Agency ascertained from other reliable sources that the sum of $200,000 had been paid out of Vatican account 71206 to an operative named in Italian only as — .

Item: A file search of Agency archives produced a cross-reference with the Greek — . This code-name was linked as 'Possible' with the death of the Orthodox Archbishop, and former President of the island of Cyprus, Makarios, one year earlier, 3 August 1977, again of apparently natural causes.

Item: Of greater significance is the notorious 'Umbrella' assassination of the Bulgarian, Georgi Markov. Occurring 7 September 1978, this took place precisely three weeks before the Pope's 'heart failure'. The latter was also the definition finally awarded by the British coroner to Markov, subsequent to his death, four days after his attack. The chemical agent used on this occasion was a pellet of Ricin, implanted in the victim's

35

leg while he was standing at a bus stop on Waterloo Bridge, in London. A young woman was observed by Markov, 'with an umbrella, in the bus queue behind me, immediately before I felt a sharp stabbing pain in my leg'. He had been the subject of numerous East-zone threats, one of which stated that he could expect 'Death in a novel way!'

Item: Nine years later, in October 1986, immediately prior to the Icelandic Summit on Disarmament, the Agency was informed of an *identically worded threat* made against the President of the United States, to be carried out in Reykjavik. Anti-whaling groups were active in the area at the time, but no assailant was located. However, mutual recrimination between Soviet and US protection staffs contributed to the breakdown of negotiations, presumably the threat's aim.

Item: 28 September 1987, and two months prior to the so-called Second Summit, the name — was linked to an apparent food-poisoning of the First Secretary of the Soviet Union. Although the subsequent second meeting was also delayed – and almost aborted – the incident was denied by the Central Committee which stated that 'The First Secretary's absence from public affairs was no more than a well-earned and overdue summer vacation'!

Berov was an incurable smoke addict, Lowel realized. Still locked in concentration, with a series of reflex actions the Russian removed his vile-smelling Balkans from one inside pocket, the wooden matches from another, lit up, stroked his dog's head, inhaled deeply, tapped the report on his knee – oblivious throughout to Lowel and the madhouse activity of the Army. So was the female cabbie, who seemed to be asleep.

Outside, by brute force, enough civilian cars had been elbowed aside to bring up a rumbling armoured crane that dwarfed even the tank transporters. It was operated by a woman who looked like the weightlifting champion of all Soviet forces. The collie, tired of the floor, climbed over Lowel and his master, and sat on Berov's unused seat belt to grab some fresh air from his window and stare at the weightlifter. Berov's hand patted affectionately, but his mind was back in the report's pages.

ASSAILANT BIOGRAPHY

Who is this woman we must now assume is poised for her third attempt against the world's two most important Heads of State? Although her present identity is unknown, her maiden name is almost certainly Maria Panos Meliti, and she was born in the northern provincial village of that same name, on the Greek border with Yugoslavia, 17 April 1956. Her father, Panos Meliti, was a professor of organic chemistry at the University of Athens; her mother died during childbirth. The professor did not remarry, and his daughter was raised first by a succession of nursemaids, then in the Orthodox Convent of Apostolic Mercy near Koropion, south of Athens. The Mother Superior records that, 'Her principal interest as a child was her collection of caged insects and lizards.'

At sixteen – and for a convent 'now far too sensuous, wanting to wear her jet-black hair down to her hips! And academically precocious to the point of brilliance' – Maria embarked on a dual undergraduate degree, beginning to study organic chemistry, under the tutelage of her father, paired with her other favourite subject, biology. She was also exposed to her father's politics. Panos Meliti had his first Communist affiliation as a partisan during the Second World War; he continued with the Party after it, while at the same time becoming an outspoken exponent of Enosis, the political union of the island of Cyprus with Greece.

In 1974, Professor Panos Meliti was caught in an internal squeeze play between the constantly warring Cypriot factions, which culminated in the coup ousting Archbishop Makarios. In an act of mistaken retaliation, Meliti was denounced to the Greek Colonels as a threat to their crumbling regime. He was executed 24 November of that year.

His daughter immediately left Greece for West Germany. (This choice of destination was apparently for no other reason than a love affair with a fellow student she had known in Athens.) She enrolled for her Master's degree in organic chemistry at Heidelberg, where she met 'Red Hans' Baer, the leader of the northern cell of the Baader-Meinhof terrorist organization. Taking the gang name 'Black Maria' – from her waist-length

37

hair – she became Baer's mistress and was involved in three anti-Nato bombings. She also adopted the gang's bizarre penchant for tattoo markings (Baer's – which only became visible in the 'mooned' or spread posture – was an 'Eye of Zoroaster' surrounded by flames, within the cleft of his buttocks!). His mistress had a small red hourglass, the distinguishing mark of the lethal *Latrodectus mactans* female spider (aka Black Widow), tattooed beside her pubic mound.

Her lover was arrested in the following spring, again through betrayal – like her father – by a gang member. Baer hanged himself in prison one month later. Maria Meliti cut short her hair, had her abdominal tattoo surgically removed by a physician in Bonn, abandoned her studies and dropped out of sight. On the first anniversary of her lover's suicide, his former prison guard was found dead, of 'heart failure', in his parked car. The guard had been unmarried, but a wreath left at his funeral was signed: 'From the Widow!' In German, *Von der Witwe!*

The dog sensed it first: the silky guard hairs of its blue-grey coat stuck out with an electric charge of tension that tingled the back of Lowel's hand. The animal half stood, cramped between Berov and the cab window. The Russian pushed the collie down absent-mindedly, intent with re-reading. Their cab driver was still asleep in her front compartment. The dog whined. Lowel turned his head – and caught the cabbie nodding almost imperceptibly at her side window. The massive crane operator nodded back. A shadow fell across the glass behind Berov. Lowel said sharply, 'Look at the crane!'

'Army morons,' the KGB man grunted.

The collie scratched at the door. Then at his master. There was an ominous creak from wire rigging. The sound of a cable stretched to breaking.

'Berov! The boom angle is too low! On your side! Get out!'

Lowel lunged for the door – in time to see that the female cab driver was already gone through her window like shit from a goose. Now Berov understood. Grabbing the report, the small man slid over the seat. The crane motor was grinding for an impossible load. Berov fell out on the pavement.

'Keep moving!' Lowel shouted. 'The guy wire is going!'

'I can't. For Mischa.'

The collie was half in, half out. Its front legs were down on the asphalt but its back right foot was still up on the seat, tangled in the seat-belt harness. The dog's spine arched and twisted as his front feet scrabbled in desperation. The blue eyes that stared for Lowel's help were human. Voices on all sides were shouting. He reached inside the cab and grabbed the animal's plaited collar. The twanging of the wire overhead was like a woman screaming. He lifted the dog's hips. The belt was stuck at the buckle. Something overhead began moving –

'Gotcha! Now go, you blue bastard!'

The collie was gone. So was the cable. A snap. Then a whipping *hiss*. Lowel made the home-base slide of his life.

On the sidelines, Berov held his dog, and moved his lips, but the words were lost in the echoing crash of ten tons of steel boom crushing the matchbox chassis of a Soviet-built and rusted Fiat taxi.

One of the crowd voices exclaimed in Boston English, 'Avoiding this sort of mess is why we send a car! The Ambassador is already waiting, and now you'll have to change your clothes!'

The buttoned-down coffee gofer from State was staring in exasperation at Lowel's pants. Both knees were gone from their slide across the asphalt. The dog and his owner were looking at the remains of the taxi. There was no sign of its fashion-conscious female driver. The little Russian said, 'For Mischa, I cannot thank –'

'Forget it,' said Lowel. 'Accidents happen in the best families.'

'Not in ours, my friend.' Berov scribbled a few words on the envelope flap of the Agency report. 'I shall find the woman. At this address, when you can.'

6

Forenoon:

Moscow

'The definition of a red elephant is . . . a new American Embassy in Moscow – you know, comrade: the empty one that comes for 50 million dollars with unlimited bugs, and the Winnebago wagon for the Ambassador in its garden!'

Lowel heard this Muscovite chestnut five times before his breakfast was finished in the new Embassy's cafeteria. The gofer from State was not amused. 'Nor is the Ambassador! Having to conduct his affairs in a trailer is a gross insult to a major power!'

In the airy world of diplomacy, no doubt, but to someone on the ground the Ambassador's 'electronically secure' quarters were hardly primitive. Two over-sized mobile homes had been flown out from California by a previous US Administration, and joined together, minus wheels, in a pleasantly landscaped corner of the compound. The two halves had been modified before departure by Hughes Aerospace with all known methods of radiowave screening and with décor in pastel leather by Mario of Beverley Hills.

The Ambassador himself, thickset and short-haired, was a career man, not a political crony, and so walked a fine line between sound advice and promotion. Like all professional diplomats, he knew that rules for this purpose were made to be followed by the hierarchy of his Department – and constantly shattered by undisciplined spooks like Lowel who were dumped on him from half a dozen intelligence empires.

'It's customary, Mr Lowel, as I'm sure you know, for arriving Government personnel – even for a relative by marriage to the President – to call at the Embassy for a pre-briefing *before* they make any contact with the other side.'

'I do know, Mr Ambassador, and I apologize, but with the Treaty deadline imposed by the President – like taking Concorde to come over – it's a question of time.'

'With our State Department responsible for any treaty, most particularly one which has innumerable sensitive aspects and opportunities for things to go awry, that's surely all the more reason for strict following of procedure.'

Lowel acknowledged this frigid stand-off with a nod. The junior gofer had been left outside. The two men were alone in the Kremlin Phone Booth, as the innermost compartment of the Moscow security unit was called. It was windowless and presumed completely safe, but the history of electronic counter measures is: a counter-counter always comes along. Nothing said on Soviet soil could be considered 'safe'.

'When the President goes head to head,' Lowel answered, 'normal security practices get streamlined, but I have one question – you had a car at the airport but I hadn't sent word I was coming in. How did you know?'

The Ambassador gave a terse smile. 'Your branch of government must make mysteries from molehills. My senior military attaché received a priority message from our London Embassy, with your flight-time arrival, ordering a car.'

'London? My flight had nothing to do with them.'

'We call it Embassy housekeeping,' the diplomat said primly. 'You changed at Heathrow. We need to keep tabs.'

The Ambassador produced the message as proof. The routing instruction was the military Nato net, not diplomatic, not even in code, the world could read it – as Berov undoubtedly had. The name of the originator for this giveaway was absent, but it wasn't hard to guess: 'Captain Hawk'. Lowel still had the mental picture from Camp David of the Secretary of Defense glowering at his Commander-in-Chief, who had scathingly scrubbed the Star Wars holy grail.

The Embassy's chief housekeeper stood up and checked the perfect crease in his trousers. 'Military liaison, Mr Lowel, is always our most delicate area of operation with the Soviet Union, so please be more prudent for the remainder of your time here. I need hardly remind you of the unpleasantness that would have been generated for us if you had been flattened – even accidentally – by a Red Army tank.'

Lowel didn't slapshot the obvious rejoinder. Berov's female cab driver, and her disappearing act, was no accident.

He walked to his next rendezvous. Things were different in the Soviet capital: rationed vodka, private restaurants, colourful clothes, less fear of a camera when tourists tried to take Russia home on video. But much seemed the same. As he passed the yellow walls of the KGB's notorious gaol cum headquarters flanking Dzerzhinsky Square, a city worker changing a burned-out streetlamp glanced over his shoulder towards the restored church of St Basil, then swiftly crossed himself before he walked in front of the gaol's massive door. Warding off the Evil Eye! Seventy-five years of atheist realism, Lowel thought, but peasant superstition still crops up even in the urban population.

He halted to double-check the address Berov had scribbled on the report envelope. It wasn't part of the headquarters complex. A crude plan sketched an alley

43

running behind the gaol towards Kuibyshev Street. Half-way down, second on the left, was an even narrower lane, in tsarist days a stable mews. Two women street-sweepers wielded brooms and a hose, but the smell of urine and a patch of overnight vomit pervaded the air. Like Sisyphus rolling his rock uphill, the anti-booze campaign obviously had some way to go – and good luck! At home, Lowel thought with a wry grin, Al Capone was all we got to show for Prohibition.

One of the sweeper-women smiled back shyly with silver teeth. The unmarked door beside her was finished with peeling brown varnish and set into the featureless back wall of a four-storey building. It was the only door. Lowel opened it.

Inside, a small stark hall, also mainly shades of brown. Another old woman, this one eating a stuffed onion roll, at a concierge's desk beside a shabby service elevator. There were no guards. Lowel gave his name. The woman kept munching and pointed three fingers. Lowel got into the elevator, which sighed heavily, then lurched upwards. After a lifetime of frozen war, it was hard to evade a certain unease in the pit of his stomach. The elevator stopped with a jerk, two inches below the third-floor sill.

Another shabby hall, this one in dirty greens with a lino floor that was cracked along the edges. He crossed it to another single, poorly varnished door. A black-painted knob had too much play in the handle when he turned it.

Another Russian game. Like their red-cheeked dolls within dolls, this room was a deliberate contrast with the grimy corridors outside. Stark and white, with a wooden floor, desk and chair. Except for the collie, Mischa, lying on a blue blanket that matched his collar and eyes, this secret policeman's room was a monk's cell.

'It was not food-poisoning that affected our First Secretary in 1986, but a minor brush with hepatitis. You shall see the personal physician's diagnosis. Your last position was with the National Security Agency – they haven't paid any attention to the CIA and its wild adventuring for years. Why should we believe one other word of this Trojan Horse report?'

No 'Hi!' – or 'Thanks for my dog'. Only these accusations that fired from Berov like a machine-gun's frontal attack.

'I'm not denying that Langley has been off-base with too many of its calls,' Lowel replied, 'but the Trojan Horse was a legend. With this report, their homicide is fact. I've seen the videotape. A woman with abdominal scar tissue was the killer, and the Viscumin–Sarin polypeptide is missing.'

The little Russian scoffed. 'Your nation's leading contribution to western culture is celluloid acting. A doctored videotape is child's play. *Habeas corpus*, produce the body!'

Lowel tried to keep his temper. 'Harold Martin's corpse is on its way home to a father with cancer, in Salt Lake City.'

'No doubt,' but Berov's sarcasm belied it. 'I should have said, produce your Black Widow. Wait here.'

The KGB Chief went out through a white door that was almost indistinguishable from the wall behind it, leaving Lowel with the collie, and to reflect that this was how it must have been for Churchill and Roosevelt meeting Stalin on the morning after one of their all-night toasting sessions – to find Ivan the Terrible standing-in for kindly Uncle Joe! As if to make up for his master's harshness, Mischa tapped Lowel on the knee with a grey paw, offering with it a gnawed slipper that had chunks of its soggy fleece lining missing. While he was thinking about Berov's switch, and wrestling with his dog for this

45

unprepossessing object, the white door reopened. A firm voice beyond it said, 'Please enter.'

The next round of Soviet new-style confrontation. By the time Lowel had released the slipper, dried his hand, and walked through to the other side of the door, he found himself at a psychological disadvantage for it.

The man who was changing Russia single-handed was seated in front of him. The desk the First Secretary sat behind was twice the size of the old ham's at Langley, and there was no question of this one being from Bloomingdales. The magnificent desk was centred on the long axis of a rectangular room that could have contained a tennis court, but instead appeared to hold those items too valuable for display in Leningrad's Hermitage Museum. Maybe because of the curious way the familiar purple birthmark was placed on the Secretary's forehead, like a lock of hair falling towards his right eye, or maybe because of the unmistakable aura of power and ability that emanated from him, or maybe because of the furnishings – or because of the whole damn shitaree! as Daniel Galbraith would say – Lowel had the feeling of being brought face to face not with the top gun of Soviet Russia, but with Napoleon at Versailles.

'Good day, Comrade First Secretary.' They shook hands under a huge Rembrandt of a Flemish burgher writing in a ledger. In private, the Secretary's grasp was solid but swift: no five-minute pressing-the-flesh as he did on his street walkabouts for the evening news photo opportunity. Lowel pointed at the priceless painting: 'If I may say, in such surroundings it would seem more in keeping to use an earlier address – possibly, Your Excellency?'

The Secretary smiled. 'If I may say, it is sufficient that an intimate friend and relation of an American president can address a servant of the Russian people so well in his own language. Be seated – you too, Kliment Klimentovich – and tell me why he sends you, Mr Lowel.'

The smile matched the handshake, genuine, and quickly over, and there were no old-judge games with the seating arrangements. Lowel sat where indicated, immediately in front of the Russian head of state. His security chief – who had to be something closer, from the location of Berov's sanctum, and being addressed in front of a foreigner by his patronymic – took the chair at right-angles to both of them, the interpreter's position. Or an interrogator's. Lowel reached for his incident report envelope. The Secretary made an impatient gesture.

'I have the paper's content. I want your words.'

'President Galbraith is determined that nothing shall prevent both of you from signing the final Dismantling Agreement,' Lowel said. 'I think there is valid evidence that a successful intervention could be made – and will definitely be attempted. I regret that your security adviser doesn't seem to agree. He talks instead about legends.'

'I share Berov's opinion.' The man at the desk exchanged this bluntness without any show of emotion. 'The link missing from your evidence in that envelope is the force behind it. An assassin like this woman is only a functionary hired to implement the policies of others. Who are they?'

'With so little time, what does that matter? Catherine the Great said, "When one faces a *coup d'état*, the first priority is to chop off the hand that holds the weapon. The head comes later." Comrade First Secretary, with the greatest respect, few countries have had more opportunity than your own to know the value of Catherine's advice.'

Lowel stopped, afraid he had been too blunt, but his formidable debating partner suddenly laughed. 'Stalin also had a saying, Mr Lowel. "When a man says 'With the greatest respect' – then I know he's asking me for a holiday in Siberia"!' The glimpse of humour vanished just as swiftly as it came. 'You admire my furnishings, but without knowing their reason. I surround myself with our past to remember at all times that despite our political philosophy, at heart we are *not* a new nation as your America is. We Russians are a people whose modern-day collective drags a thousand years of history and legend as a ship in a storm drags an anchor. And one day, legend tells us, the land shall be ruled by a man with the mark of the devil.' The Secretary tapped the disfigurement on his forehead. 'Blight and plague will befall us, and after our fields are scorched and beasts die from water that has become undrinkable, there will come ultimate calamity – unless our country finds salvation through the act of a woman. Your face shows what you think, Mr Lowel, but think again, and you may recall the name Chernobyl.'

In spite of the image of the streetlight worker crossing himself against the omnipotence of the KGB, this very morning, Lowel was thinking of another place-name. Scorched fields and dead beasts from a melted nuclear reactor have to make you wonder whether it *is* just blind coincidence that those stumble-bum bastards at Langley have come up with a Lady Borgia at this precise moment in East–West history.

He held up his left hand and said to the man with the disfigurement on his brow, 'If I can speak as someone with a similar problem – or compared to my President's arm – First Secretary, your birthmark is nothing. You could have it removed in a couple of hours with a surgical laser.'

'Then our citizens would say I was trying to hide from history. Understand: these are the same people who never forget that in my first months of office the cruise ship *Pride of Lenin* sank in the Black Sea, with 500 souls, half of them children and women.' The Soviet leader touched the report envelope: 'If I concede that, notwithstanding this document's coincidental timing, there are groups on

48

both sides with the strongest motives for aborting our elimination of intercontinental missiles, what do you and your President want me to do about it?'

'What I want,' Lowel said, 'is a postponement of the meeting – but as that isn't in the cards, I'll settle for a last-minute change of venue.'

For the first time the Secretary showed impatience. A frown appeared below the birthmark. ' "Last-minute"? Your President has reduced the time to barely a week! Just before you arrived, by telephone call, we had agreed to release a communiqué for your news programme tonight that the final site will be Geneva.'

'Security must have advance knowledge.' Berov, who had been silent throughout, addressed his superior. 'To screen hazards, nine days is minimal for a foreign location.'

'So change to a domestic one,' said Lowel.

'You'd meet us inside our own borders? Not on neutral territory? For so sensitive a mission as this agreement?' The small KGB man shrugged with sarcastic disbelief. The Soviet leader stared at Lowel for a long moment.

'Where?' he asked flatly.

'If this final meeting,' Lowel answered, 'is to eliminate the tensions of the past fifty years, as much as it is to dismantle its weapons, then hold it where people say the Cold War started – at Yalta.'

After the American left his office, the master of modern Russia sat on for some moments alone, in silence except for the ticking of an antique ormolu clock. Beside it, his gaze settled on a small photograph which was lost among the great works of art: above their signatures, the black-and-white faces of Stalin, Roosevelt and Churchill stared back at him with all their vested interests of the past. Today's world has a different focus, and the war has changed. Today's battle is for investor confidence in a nation's economy. Even Marx admitted that utopia must wait for tomorrow.

He pressed a buzzer on his desk. Berov came back into the office.

'First Secretary?'

'Kliment Klimentovich, I have to accept such an American poker challenge, even though Washington's report bringing in the woman is transparently a diversion to bluff us for just this purpose. And let me add, your departmental predecessor's excuse of "hepatitis" to explain my absence from an attempted food poisoning will not have been accepted by a man like this Lowel for a moment! One thing is certain: after that previous "illness" and before the eyes of history – ' he pointed at the photograph – 'a similar incident must not occur at Yalta. If an American president, seeking peace, was killed on Russian soil . . .'

He stopped. Even the catlike face of Joseph Stalin seemed to flinch at that unthinkable conclusion.

Round three of his negotiation, Lowel discovered, was to be with Berov – switched back again to Nice Guy and Dog. After his icy performance in the First Secretary's office, the little Russian resumed his mournful Slavic charm, insisting on lunch at one of Moscow's new *perestroika* gourmet restaurants.

'Low cholesterol. For my Mischa's sake, the taxi incident, please, this has to be done.'

The collie went with them and received a doggie-dish of greasy Stroganoff from the free enterprise owner, a Carpathian like Kliment Berov.

'Werewolf country, to you in the West. His parents, as my own, were Uniat Catholics, which is how I got my name of a saint – but then Stalin started as a priest!'

The Carpathian owner produced a reasonable chicken salad and an excellent white wine. 'From the cellars of

Prince Vorytsin, comrade, as you ordered. Of course, on the house.'

'The wine comes from Yalta,' said Berov, raising a glass. 'It seems appropriate, and I admired your nerve in making this historic gesture. Let us drink to the hope that so will your brother-in-law, the President.'

'Let's hope.' Lowel drank. The collie grinned at its master's irony. The Carpathian brought a bowl of fresh water for the dog and three kerchiefed violinists from werewolf country to provide a curtain of noise.

'To allow us a moment of freer conversation,' Berov said. 'Mr Lowel, I have not been entirely frank.'

'No kidding.'

The violin trio swooped closer. The small KGB chief spread his hands in an ironic gesture. The collie sniffed them. 'Mischa wants me to make amends. There are three ways. First, I may be able to confirm your "Black Maria" Meliti's connection with Hans Baer, through sources in East Berlin. Second – '

The lead violin player interrupted with an extravagant flourish of his bow, just grazing Berov's shoulder. With a ferocious growl, and a single grey-streak blur of motion, his dog came up, and out, ears flat, blue eyes blazing, from beneath the table. His seven-inch jaws clamped shut on the delicate wrist of the terrified player.

'Thank you, Mischa love. Stop now.'

A KGB man's best friend wasn't just a pretty face. With a last growl the collie let go, but the hair was still up on his ruff. The musician's face was white with shock, but the only sign of the attack on the man's wrist was six small red indentations in the skin. Berov snapped his fingers. 'Keep playing. Not so close. I was saying,' he added to Lowel, as though nothing had happened, 'a second item that you probably know is a junior protocol official in the White House, a middle-aged bachelor, who has just become involved for the first time in his life with a young woman.'

'I don't know,' Lowel said. 'What name?'

'Castilio.'

'I'm booked for London tomorrow morning, to meet their Prime Minister. I can't fit in Washington.'

'Our friend can, Mischa, with our third small help, can he not?' The collie bowed again, before settling back under the table. 'In two hours,' Berov explained, as a silver pot of thick Carpathian coffee arrived, 'for certain privileged guests, Aeroflot is inaugurating its first transatlantic supersonic flight.'

7

The Soviet challenge to Concorde was wider, faster, and half as chic. In their national effort to one-up the West, the Russian *haute couture* fashions on the inaugural cabin staff were all swirling capes and huge fur hats, which made safety equipment demonstrations look like something out of a Salvador Dali work of art. The food was magnificent, but Lowel was still stuffed from his Carpathian lunch. He spent the first hour sipping tonic and wondering about Daniel Galbraith's response to his special agent's ad-libbed change-of-venue ploy: he had sent the word on Yalta via Mario's decorated trailer at the Embassy, before departure from Sheremetyevo. The next three hours he slept, missing a split-screen movie of the Bolshoi Ballet jiving to a USSR hot rock group . . .

He woke to find himself landing at Dulles, nine-thirty in the evening, DC time. A chopper was waiting for him as requested, rotors turning: thirty minutes later he was inside the White House at the Secret Service duty desk.

'Call up the file on a protocol staffer,' he told the night officer manning the domestic system computer. 'Last name, Castilio.'

'Yes sir. Toulouse-Lautrec, you bet.'

'That's what they call him around here?'

The night man nodded, punching keys on the terminal. 'Not kind, but it fits the image. Short, prissy, and president of the Potomac Heights Art Club. Here's his file.'

Lowel studied the screen. Twenty-five years' service, no defaults. Promoted to third assistant just last month. Half his life in the same job, and no change of address: Number 17, Thirtieth Place.

'J. Edgar Hoover lived on Thirtieth,' Lowel said to the night officer. 'Not even a traffic ticket on Castilio. What else do you know about him?'

'He lived with Mom until she died this spring, and he likes painting naked ladies – models. One just shacked up with him to save on rent. The stewards say he's been boasting about it. Before that he used to eyeball the hookers bending over outside the railings on the South Lawn when he drove home.'

'The woman he's living with, what else does he tell the stewards about her?'

'I don't know, sir.' The night man drew back stiffly. 'Gossip isn't part of the service.'

'Sure,' said Lowel. 'Get me the steward on duty.'

An out of breath, overweight Filipino, first generation from Manila, arrived. He gossiped. 'Miss Janice. Oh, she very nice lady. Mr Castilio take her doggy bags of Venetian Chicken. She think he fantastic.'

Lowel said, 'That's what he told you.'

'I see. She look at him love crazy.'

'How did you see? Did you visit with them?'

'Me visit Mr Castilio residence? No way. I see here.'

'He brought the woman here?'

'Sure. Lovely lady.'

'When?'

'When she lovely?'

'When did she visit the White House.'

'Oh, *si*. Today – I meaning night.'

'You saw her, here, this evening?' Lowel demanded. The steward nodded. 'Tell me exactly what she looked like.'

'Lovely – I meaning brown hair. Little white gloves.

Black eye-glasses. She say "I am so blind without them."
Mr Castilio say, "Janice, my dear, you should use contacts
like I do." In the Oval Office.'

'Hold it,' said Lowel. 'Castilio wears contacts, or he
had this woman in the Oval Office?'

'Both things. He gives her paperweight George Washington. She holds his arm like church. Everybody do,
when they come first time. "The Mr President's own
chair. The Mr President's own pen," you know.'

'Check it with the gate!' Lowel snapped at the night
officer.

The answer was yes.

'Castilio got her in on a privileged visitor's pass,'
said the Secret Service man. 'It's normal routine when
the first family is away at Camp David.'

'Come with me.'

Lowel moved at a rush along the passage to the Oval
Office. His feet sank into the deep blue pile of the carpet. The pictures of the Fathers of the Nation looked
down from the walls. He threw open the double doors.
The office was normal, undisturbed: the Great Seal, the
models of the USS *Constitution* and Galbraith's Delta
gunboat. A cupboard of embossed stationery and freebies
for visitors. Every item as familiar to the occupant of the
Oval Office as his old boots. And with a single drop of
Viscumin on them, any one of these items could kill at
a touch.

'Seal the room,' he ordered the night officer. 'Then
call the Chemical Weapon Incident desk at the Pentagon.
Every inch of the office is to be checked for the presence
of this toxin.' Lowel wrote the name of it on the back of
an Aeroflot brochure and went to find himself some special trick tools and an unmarked car. Thanks to Berov's
co-operation, he could stop this second-rate Mata Hari at
the start: whoever she was.

* * *

The woman known as Janice to John Castilio sat on an artist's posing stool behind him. Except for a tiny hand towel of an unpleasant, light purple colour that draped her breasts and a pair of small white cotton gloves to the wrists, she was naked. That did not disturb her. She had learned to regard her body unemotionally, impartially, as a weapon to be respected and kept in peak condition. Sex was a crude weapon compared to the sophisticated arsenal provided by modern cellular biochemistry, but human nature didn't change: in the real world sex was still the most effective means of delivery. Getting to the target.

The little protocol clerk was ten feet away from her, standing in the bathroom of the house that he had lived in all his life, brushing his flossed teeth, and sniffing one last time beneath his arm for dangerous smells. Sex *was* dangerous. Sexual attraction happened instantaneously. Connections of the most intimate nature possible formed between people who would never think to become social friends, or business colleagues. Sex happened in the wrong places, against good advice or common sense. These reasons were why she used it. Sex allowed her as many disguises as there were human foibles. Sex allowed her to be here with this Washington target tonight, or in England, just as close to another, tomorrow.

The first target of her current mission, a man repressed for a lifetime, living out his solitary fantasies in coffee-table picture books on art, had required only her placing an ad as a life model, and then offering him the chance of a lifetime: *to have a nude model of his very own.*

He sniffed the other armpit, although he had showered once already, before the Art Club meeting earlier that evening –

'But as I constantly have to warn the junior foot-men, Janice, you can never be too careful with personal hygiene! Particularly when meeting Europeans.'

Europe. She noted the added tension the word produced in his high-pitched voice. He put on a fresh pyjama jacket and did up all the buttons. As he got the top one in the wrong buttonhole, she called casually across the passage, 'Will you be away long in Europe, Mr Castilio?'

Her target removed his contact lenses and rinsed them in his prepared saline solution while he answered, 'I hope not, Janice. At the time of the tsars it was fashionable, but since the Communists took over, I gather they've ruined the resort like everything else.'

'You sound cross, Mr Castilio. I've ruined what?'

'No, no! The city of *Yalta*!'

So simple. She had what she came for. Time to disengage. She slipped down from the posing stool, allowing the towel to drop. Now she wore only the little white gloves, which reminded her target of the portrait of his mother in the hall.

'Yalta.' The protocol clerk repeated the name with an edge of annoyance. 'As if the place hasn't caused enough trouble in this century! What those oafs at State never seem to understand when they make these last-minute changes, why I absolutely *insist* on being given advance notice, it takes my incompetents on the Household Staff three days just to replace the room instruction labels on the presidential luggage! But my dear – ' he hastened to add – 'of course I'm not cross at *you*. Have you seen my eyedrops, by any chance?'

She watched him place a soft lens on his right index finger, touch the lens to his open eye – contact. It was in safely. And the other one.

'Try looking on the small table, by the mirror, Mr Castilio.'

'Thank you, Janice.'

As his neck flushed red she could read his every thought: How close she was to him. *Nude*.

'How foolish of me, my dear.' His voice squeaked, in

little puffs. 'The bottle was there all the time. It must be the excitement of the moment. To have a model of one's very own . . .!'

She watched as he unscrewed the bottletop and squeezed the rubber on the dropper. The liquid climbed the tube; he tipped his head up. His pink face in the mirror saw her. *Nude*. She smiled, encouraging him to take the plunge – that instant of icy cold on the eyeball! The clear plastic tube was in line, against the light. He barely had to touch the rubber bulb. One drop formed, refracted. Her target said to her smiling face in the mirror, 'Any minute now . . .'

She froze. The lights of a car swept by the bedroom window. Stopped. Switched off. She flattened herself against the wall and glanced out at the cul-de-sac. Illuminated by a street lamp a male figure was locking the door of the car with his right hand. His left rested on the roof: two fingers of the hand were missing.

'All done, my dear.'

The male psyche was so predictable. The damaged man approaching outside the house would go through his surreptitious entry routine with that unrecognized, built-in contempt all men felt subconsciously for a female opponent. The current target in the bathroom was smiling at her with that ridiculous mixture of masculine pride for the tiny bravery of risking the cold drops and the uncertain greater danger of what was going to happen next in the bedroom.

She had just enough time to show him. To show both of them.

Lowel knew the area well: not only Hoover, Lyndon Johnson used to live with his personal secrets on what was then an unfashionable fringe of Georgetown. Now, at quarter to midnight on a weekday, Thirtieth Place was deserted. Only one house on the corner showed a light.

A Siamese cat reflected green eyes outside Number 21.

While he let his own eyes get accustomed to the dark he took the special trick items from the glove compartment – flashlight, Colt 7.62, lock pick, and a small unit like a pocket calculator – and put them in his jacket. There was no sound when he got out of the unmarked Secret Service car: the door and seat buzzers had been disconnected for this kind of operation. The Siamese had climbed onto the warm bonnet of the car: the rest of the street was still oblivious.

He walked two houses east, to Number 17, and up a cement path to the front door. It was locked. He listened at the mail slot. No sound came from inside the building. A secondary path went left, through some shrubs to the garage. It was a drive-under, taking up part of the basement. The door was a new one; there was no handle, it must open electronically.

He walked around to the back garden. A light shone through curtains at an upstairs window. The rear door was locked as well. He went back to the garage.

He took the trick calculator black box from his pocket and aimed it at the darkened garage door. Its first function was to detect the presence of a wired burglar alarm. A green LED bulb said negative when he pushed the button. The second function was smarter. Starting at the low end of the spectrum and working upwards, the box was designed to emit a series of signal pulses covering the limited range of frequencies used by all electronic door openers in the United States. On the fourth pulse the box gave a low-toned beep. He pressed the button again. A red LED flashed on the unit. The door of the garage began to lift. When it was barely three feet off the ground he ducked under and reversed the direction. The door wound down. He stood in total darkness.

He exchanged the black box unit for the flashlight

and switched it on. Nothing happened. The Secret Service hadn't checked the fucking batteries – but he should have! He took out his lighter and flicked.

An eight-year-old beige Chrysler K, waxed as an apple and scratchless, was parked over a clean drip tray, on enamelled concrete. There was also a folded ping-pong table and a cat's litter box with a poop-scoop. The resident of Number 17 didn't take chances: all four doors of the Chrysler K were locked. Three painted concrete steps at the front of it led up to another locked wooden door. The mechanism was a Yale which Lowel opened with the pick in about ten seconds. He grasped the Colt and moved forward.

The basement beyond was black, and smelled of coal dust and oil. A rumbling hum, with an eerie high-pitched squeal echoed between bare concrete walls. The house was built in the days before insulation saved money. The humming noise came from a furnace fan left on permanent recirculation as a primitive form of air-conditioning. The furnace was a huge forced-air relic which had been converted from coal at about the time the Arabs jacked the price of oil through the roof.

The basement stairs were painted plywood, with non-skid strips glued to the treads. Keeping close to the sides to limit squeaks, he climbed them and emerged in the kitchen. The smell changed to old sink and burned milk: a pan of it, and two half-prepared cups of chocolate were on the stove. The fan noise rumbled out of an adjacent grill opening. From this point on, a series of wallplug night-lights had been thoughtfully provided at frequent intervals. The third plug was even better: a rechargeable Black and Decker floodlamp. He exchanged his lighter for it and listened for breathing, or other bedroom noises.

Nothing. The first room outside the kitchen had been the invalid mother's last bedroom: scuffs from a wheelchair marked the walls and door. Presumably because the windows faced north, it was currently a studio for a small talent. Examples of the real thing, Monet and Lautrec, were tacked up to be copied: *Woman at Her Toilette, Nude Dancer.*

More important, an easel.

He stepped across to look at it. The floor squeaked. He stopped. No reaction elsewhere. The easel supported a portrait –

Of a murderess? Was this her? Somewhere in this dark and silent house was a poisoner waiting for him? Even at this moment was she watching – ?

He fought down the irrational thoughts. The portrait was useless. A study of a woman's back, which meant no evidence of any abdominal scar. The model was seated on a posing stool with her left breast and buttock cleft prissily draped by a lavender-hued towel that clashed badly with the skin colour. The hair was medium length, dingy brown. No face. Faces were way beyond this artist. One hand, rendered out of scale, wore a little white glove.

He left the studio and followed the wallplug lights past a dining–living room, with a framed White House menu collection and autographed portraits of six presidents, to the main stairs. They were carpeted with a patterned runner, held down with tarnished metal rods. The air was musty, with a trace of cheap perfume. His grip tightened on the Colt. He began climbing.

The hum from the fan grew fainter but was still audible. Just before the top, the stairs widened at a landing. A bathroom opened off to the left. Contact lens solution, a bottle of eye-drops, false tooth cleanser, and a glass, but no teeth. No pantyhose hanging in the tub. The place was bachelor immaculate.

On the right, off the landing, was a spare bedroom. The dark oak bed was made up but hadn't been slept in. A brass paperweight with the White House logo and a package of similarly embossed envelopes were discarded in a waste basket. The paperweight was stamped Made in Taiwan.

Back on the landing a slit of light showed below the final door. Four more steps. He took them and turned the handle.

The body of John Castilio was in monogrammed 'J.C.' cotton striped pyjamas, lying on a comforter obviously quilted by its mother. The feet were together in polished oxblood slippers. The left arm was draped across the body's chest. The right arm was on the mahogany bedside table, next to the phone. A tabloid newspaper, open to the tits-and-ass centre-page, was spread with the ads for escorts and phone-in sex. The receiver of the phone was in the body's right hand, clamped in its fingers.

Someone was talking. Lowel wasn't going to bring any part of himself in contact with that earpiece. He bent cautiously, to listen. A harsh female voice said sternly, 'You bad, bad boy to call me – !'

His female opponent was not second rate. Whether she was called Janice, or Maria Meliti, the clever cold bitch had done it letter perfect. Just one more middle-aged heart attack victim of lust at a distance. Under normal circumstances, Lowel thought, the discovery wouldn't raise an eyebrow in this town. He wondered how close he must have been to catching her – but that kind of wondering leads agents down the road to booze and madness.

He saw a second bottle of eye-drops, half hidden by the phone. The most obvious method for administering the toxin, taking advantage of everyday routine. Had *she* just stood there, watching, while her victim put the poison in his own eye?

Lowel felt his spine crawl at the thought. He was used to facing direct threats, not this kind of carnival midway horror. He made a note for the forensic lab to check the drops. As he left the bedroom to get the autopsy wheels in motion, before his flight to London, the recorded voice in the bedroom was beginning to describe the kind of maternal punishment that any guilty party calling its number obviously wanted, and knew it deserved.

Lowel walked down the first four stairs to the upper landing. The smell of perfume had faded, but the rumbling fan hum was louder, coming out of a floor-level vent. There was a different smell, unpleasant, maybe oil fuel. The hum suddenly deepened, as though the overtones had been re-enforced –

Exhaust!

That was the smell. He charged down the rest of the main stairs, the hall, kitchen, second stairs, basement, concrete steps. In the light from the Black and Decker lamp the garage held only the ping-pong table and fresh catshit in the box. The locked Chrysler K was gone.

On the driveway outside lay a discarded pair of women's white cotton gloves. Whatever their wearer's name was, she had killed precisely as she wished. And he hadn't stopped her.

8

Third day, afternoon run:

Gatwick–London

Lowel was stuck with Gatwick Airport after British Airways to Heathrow found 'We have a slight technical problem' with the ageing Concorde and diverted it to Antwerp, because UK Air Traffic Control was 'working to rule'. So was Immigration when he finally landed in Britain, via short-range prop-driven commuter.

Gatwick was chaotic, the London tabloids their normal hysterical.

> ONE WEEK TO GENEVA DISASTER!
> ZERO PACT PULLS LAST FANGS FROM BRITISH LION!

At least they still thought it was Geneva. He went for a pay phone and found the only one working in the whole massive complex was in the command of an Indian matron in a crimson sari and a lot of gold jewellery.

Lowel wasn't prepared to cut life short with a wrong-side kamikaze run up to town by hired car, and decided on British Rail. He was buying the ticket when, without warning, a shadow swept across the platform, followed by a whistling, roaring howl. Like everyone else, he looked up and saw the giant bat shape of a US Air Force B1 supersonic bomber mock his crawling progress as it screamed westwards at low level and the American taxpayers' expense. A poster on the platform, with the same dramatic image, said 'Farnborough Air Show! Wings

From Round The World!' Grounded, he sat back in a grubby first-class non-smoker to endure the half-hour trip on the Gatwick–Victoria express.

He felt that he was travelling in a vacuum: efficient or otherwise, civilian transport cut him off from the worldwide military communication links that might tell him some answers to the questions mounting behind him as he moved forward: whether the Oval Office was clean of poison, proof that Castilio died from the stolen toxin –

What *She* wanted from Castilio.

Already he found himself using that mental capital letter for Her, whatever her name was. And what she looked like: not her body, but the face that went with it. The ice-cold mind and nerve that –

'Hae your ticket.'

A black conductor with a Scottish accent waited impatiently. The train was whipping through Coulsdon, red-brick row houses and their jammed commuter parking lots that must need a Houdini to spring them at the end of the day.

'Is there a phone on board?' Lowel asked as he showed his ticket.

'At the far end. Watch yon boofay!'

The conductor nodded brusquely in the direction of the retreating car park. The buffet was a scruffy cart pushed by a tired woman; its sandwich selection was the same on both counts. Lowel bought one anyway, then squeezed past to discover that the phone only used a Telecom credit card, which he didn't have – but a businessman who did had just found it didn't help.

'Buggered,' the man swore. 'What's this bloody country coming to, tell me that?'

'There'll always be an England,' Lowel offered, with a neutral smile.

'Not much longer with the present sods in office. My God, if we could just have old Maggie back!'

65

Britain's last election had been as pussy-hair as Daniel Galbraith's in the USA. The result was the first Labour government in nearly twenty years, but with a minority in the House of Commons: it was sustained only by half a dozen Independent votes, and led by a Welshman called Powys, who had been at Oxford with America's current president.

The train was slowing; dingy Clapham slid past. The great chimneys of the old power station loomed up, and then the famous river of history – which was gone again before a disappointed New Zealand tourist couple on the other side of the aisle had time to register its presence.

The huge marshalling yards of Victoria Station engulfed the express. The din and rush of thousands of arrivals and departures did the same to the New Zealanders. Lowel aimed the bewildered pair in the direction of a Tourist Information booth, then headed for the nearest goddamn phone that took cash and worked.

He found it in the exit from the Victoria Arcade, a rounded tunnel which amplified voices, footsteps, taxi horns and buses into a single wave-like roar, almost drowning out the dial tone. He pressed the receiver closer to his ear and dropped a coin in the slot. He was pushing the third button for the Chelsea exchange when the intuition which had kept him alive so far flashed its mental warning light: the Maggie-loving businessman with the Telecom card had been on the flight from Antwerp!

And was still around. The man's back was half turned at the entrance to the Arcade, but now Lowel was sure of it: the Englishman had boarded the commuter plane last minute in Belgium. Which meant the son of a bitch had been told to be there. Which meant that British Airways' 'small technical problem' was ordered from high altitude in Whitehall.

Which meant SIS. The British Secret Intelligence Service. Lowel finished touch-toning, heard one ring, two, three –

'Hullo?'

The voice he hoped for. Jacqueline was at home. He hung up and moved further along the row of phones to the next one that was functioning. Before he was through calling his second number, the SIS tail was an equal distance closer, within earshot. Lowel hit the last button and asked loudly, over the roar:

'Tower Inn?'

The earpiece said, 'The time in ten seconds will be – '

'Do you have a room available?'

'– half past two.'

'Thanks, hold it for Lowel. I'll be right over.'

He broke the Talking Clock's connection and went out to the taxi rank. The line-up wasn't bad and he had no luggage. The fourth cab to turn in took him aboard. The SIS had its own transport: a black Rover hiding behind a Number 44 double-decker bus.

'Where to, guv?' the cabbie asked.

'Hampstead High Street – and go by way of Covent Garden, not Tottenham Court Road.'

They pulled out from the station. The Rover slid in behind them. When they were past the Palace, on the Mall, Lowel handed some notes through to the cab driver and said, 'Approaching Covent Garden I want you heading east on Long Acre. When you get to the tube station entrance at the corner of James Street, slow right down but don't stop. Then keep north with your fare light off until you run out of cash. Understood?'

'It's your lolly.'

One more nutter Yank! The cabbie shrugged. Lowel checked his watch. Three o'clock. Already the traffic was building for the afternoon rush, but the Rover was holding in the side mirror. They turned off Charing Cross Road at

Leicester Square, and passed Garrick Street. The dome of the Opera House. Four more blocks, only a couple, the cab slowed – too much! Stop lights on their corner went red.

He looked back. The Rover had a Fortnum's delivery van between them. On the sidewalk, a fire-eater from the Plaza plunged a flaming sword down his throat. The cab started accelerating again. Lowel pushed down his door handle . . . the underground sign was level with the cab . . . just passing . . . he jumped.

'Wotcher!'

The driver shouted. Brakes squealed as SIS caught the play. Lowel dived past the fire-eater for the tube station entrance. It was split in a Y:

CAUTION – DEEP LIFTS OPERATION – EXIT ONLY

The deepest elevators in London. They had doors front and back. To his left, the exit passage was choked with passengers disembarking from the depths. Business people with uniform City briefcases and furled black umbrellas. Immediately to his right, an equal number of the same types jammed up against the folding doors trying to board for descent, but the last half of the down herd wasn't going to make it. The SIS tail was running towards them. Lowel forced his way left, through the bodies leaving from the back of the elevator, around the corner. The exit safety gates scissored shut. He plunged, the gates caught his jacket, someone said, 'Stupid bastard – can't you read?'

One of his pockets was slightly torn, but as the lift dropped below floor level, and he left the SIS agent behind, Lowel felt the same juvenile but intensely pleasant self-satisfaction as he had when he puffed his way up to the top of Mount Hood.

The small achievement at least restored some of the polish to last night's rusty performance in Castilio's garage. Hidden underground, a passenger minding his own business could ride to any point he wanted in Greater London. He waited at the bottom of the shaft, ready to stroll aboard when the Piccadilly line swished in with perfect timing. One minute to go, according to the illuminated sign.

The crush kept building. Most in dark blue pinstripe. There were no traditional bowler hats any more, and a third of the pinstripes now wore skirts. He moved through the crowd away from the exits towards the far end of the platform, where the air was fresher and the chance of a seat got better. The unique smell of ozone from the high voltage in the tracks mixed with bunches of cut flowers held by several commuters. He felt the draught quicken on his face and the rails start to rumble from the approaching train, and then the headlights flashed around a corner, rocking and swaying like a drunk dragon. He was still clear of his SIS tail. He stepped a pace to the rear –

Something whacked the back of his right knee. Involuntarily, the tendons gave way. The object twisted between his shins. He lost his footing, began to fall forward. The train's lights rushed onward. The platform lip was in front of him, smeared with wads of gum. His hands grabbed for a last chance at the concrete. A howling blizzard of candy wrappers, dirt, and theatre programmes swept around him. He kicked out frantically to free whatever was still trapping his feet . . . and saw an umbrella with a gleaming tip drop down on the tracks, to be crushed as though it had never existed.

'My dear chap. Are you all right?'

Concerned British voices surrounded him. Helpful hands supported him. As he got to his feet he saw the back of a woman behind him. In an Italian-styled, white-leather coat, headscarf, and Hollywood dark glasses, she was using his own smart-ass vanishing trick.

9

Old Chelsea

Lowel had always loved this part of London with its
tucked away gardens. There was privacy. Seven minutes'
walk to the tube at South Kensington, first stop Harrods
– for those unfortunates who didn't own one of the Jags
and Maseratis parked nose to toes along the kerbs! There
was grass, and shady trees, in a locked railed garden for
the au pair girl and the children.

The au pair closest to the railings was the same height
and weight as the woman on the platform at Covent
Garden. He watched this one running after a brightly
coloured ball that her charges had lobbed into some
bushes. A blonde, natural runner, long strides. Speed
was on his mind: it wasn't possible for the Janice in
Georgetown to get to London any faster than he had
himself, by Concorde.

Unless *She* was on board the aircraft with him!

Or the flight diversion. Could British SIS have routed
Concorde to Antwerp just to let her jump ahead of him?
Crazy. He was still too shaken from the attack to think
clearly –

A taxi horn blasted. He had to pause for the stop light
at the corner of Old Church Street, and was joined by an
old couple out of Agatha Christie: a man in his seventies,
with 'General' written all over him, and an aristocratic
ancient Lady walking the inevitable Scottie dog. When
Lowel asked them to confirm his destination, it launched

their favourite hobby: gossiping.

'Yes, Mrs Campbell is in the corner.' The old woman nodded at her companion. 'You know, Brigadier, with the wisteria, beside me. I've advised her repeatedly, since her divorce from that oafish husband – the awful flying type with the moustache and noisy car – I've said, "Have it pruned, my dear, or the frightful pigeons will be there"!'

'Hmph,' the Brigadier grunted. 'Brutes still are, Lady M. Should be open season on 'em, year-round with a twelve-bore.'

The stoplight changed. Their trio moved onwards to the mews, backing onto Carlyle Square. After his experience on the underground platform, it obviously was open season, Lowel thought, looking back at the au pair girl making another catch. She wore a yellow poncho for the inevitable London rain. Wet weather gear was logical, but in a sea of pinstripe navy why would an anonymous assassin want to stand out like Sophia Loren or Greta Garbo?

'She was left her house by her father,' the Brigadier added to the gossip pot. 'Long-hair of some sort, from one of those Balkan places where the Serbs and Croats butcher each other. Our Mrs Campbell was Sibenik before the marriage, like the port in Hercegovina. Mother was English, good family apparently.'

'Oh, she was,' Lady M agreed, as they entered the mews, 'but the mother died before Otto Sibenik bought his corner shop and so she was never part of their life here. Their daughter's terribly bright, a degree in *linguistics* of all things, from Cambridge – and then to become a helicopter pilot for British Petroleum! Young women today are a never-ending surprise.'

'Divorcing her husband wasn't,' said the Brigadier. 'Saw that coming a mile off. Teddy Campbell was the sort of conceited young fool who thinks good looks and sporting ability make up for losing inherited capital! She's well rid of him.'

71

'I blame the marriage going wrong,' Lady M said, in a conspirator's stage whisper to Lowel, 'on their constant separate travelling. She only got home last night from another four weeks in the Canadian Arctic!'

'Nonsense,' declared the Brigadier. 'From what I hear at the Club, things went sour because, as a bloody pilot, the gal can knock the socks off any man!'

The impressive Mrs Campbell's house was a three-storey conversion, tucked away in the mews corner. And the pigeons were there, a pair of them nesting over the front door, among the wisteria flowering all around the first-floor windows. The house walls were freshly painted white, the front door lacquered green. The lion's-head knocker was gleaming brass, with a definite squint in one eye from a flaw in the casting. He put his hand out to thump it – when the door opened, and she was there.

'Jacky!'

'Jack!'

They both laughed, as they did every time they went through this Abbot and Costello routine. He said, 'Mrs Campbell, you must be turning psychic.'

'Not quite, Mr Lowel, but the phone rang when I was in the garden, and I had a feeling. Did you call?'

'Almost. There was a small problem at Victoria I needed to solve.'

'In your usual capable way, I'm sure.' She pushed a wall-mounted trio of red light-buttons in sequence. 'If we stand here any longer the burglar alarm will call the police, or the Brigadier and Lady M will break their hearing aids – come on in.' Jacqueline smiled and took his arm. 'The bloody alarm is a menace, but Lady M is a pet, really; we keep each other's spare keys.' The security light-buttons turned green. Before the front door closed behind him, Lowel saw that the old tongues in the mews were wagging again.

72

He dropped his carry-on bag in the hall and followed Jacqueline through to the large living room that looked out on the walled garden at the back. Behind his hostess, the sun shone in across a small balcony with tubs of flowers.

'You look great,' he said, 'but you've changed your hair.'

'You don't like?'

'It's fine. Just different, being short. Blonde suits you.'

'Blonde, Jack darling, makes it easier to hide the grey. And nothing looks more like growing old than a pony tail, when a woman has reached that certain age.' She kissed his cheek. 'Tell granny your plans for London while she slings you a beer.'

He relaxed into a deep armchair upholstered with red trumpet vines and crested blue birds. 'No firm plans yet.' He took out his makings, and tapped tobacco from the pouch along the paper. 'I'm only here long enough to check in at the Embassy.'

'If you keep breathing that Bull Durham, sweetie-pie, you won't be anywhere much longer.'

'Dropping animal fats was my concession to growing old,' he said, with his most persuasive smile. 'I'll add quitting the weed, cold turkey, if you'll come with me to Greece.'

'Damn!' The bottle-opener she was holding dropped with a crash on to the glass top of the sideboard bar. She recovered it and said, 'I mean, Jack, I just got home last night; I've been away for a month.'

'So Lady M told me. I'm not leaving until tomorrow, and it would only be a day and a half, that's all I can spare, but I don't speak the language and you do.' He tossed the half-rolled cigarette into the waste-basket and gave her the pouch and papers, with his most encouraging smile. 'The offer holds on the no-smoking.'

'That's certainly a step in the right direction.' She

73

put the makings out of his reach, on the sideboard, and poured his beer into a tankard with a North Sea oil-rig etched on the side. 'What part of Greece?'

'South of Athens, and up by the border, that middle slice near Thessalonika. I'm checking out a biography. If it wasn't important, I wouldn't ask.'

'Thank you, sir; very gallant, I'm sure. Some guys would do it for a lady's company.' As Jacqueline passed him the tankard, she asked, 'Would this biography be a lady?'

'Not in my book. Make the flight reservations for Mr and Mrs in your name; we'll change mine at the counter.'

'For one moment you had me scared. I thought I was going to be lumbered with Teddy again.' She picked up the beer-bottle's cap and dropped it into the waste-basket. 'Or was that name-changing a proposal on the fly?'

He said, 'I think we only make that kind of half-baked proposal once in our life.'

'Sorry, darling. Stupid Jacky wasn't thinking.' She kissed him lightly on the back of the neck. 'Bless Bergitta's memory. You arrange your Embassy. I'll fix our Greek getaway.'

When the America of Teddy Roosevelt trod softly and carried a big stick, the US presence in London made itself felt from Number 14, Princes Gate – the palatial home of J. Pierpoint Morgan, with the noble heads of Red Indians carved above the windows staring forever across the tiny prairie of Hyde Park. In the old days, Lowel could have strolled. To get to the modern Embassy nerve centre designed by Saarinen, in Grosvenor Square, he took the tube again, surfacing this time at Bond Street, and walking past Claridge's Hotel and the spot on the sidewalk where Adlai Stevenson died. The latest casualty was an illegally parked Austin Mini having a yellow steel clamp

74

locked around its kerbside wheel. Just beyond the Mini, Lowel came to the statue of Franklin Roosevelt, and the shadow of the great eagle on the roof of the Embassy, with its thirty-five-foot wing span, swept down on him.

So did a black Rover. As he walked towards the entrance, the car pulled away from the kerb ahead and cruised past on the opposite side of the Square. It was too far to see the occupants, and there had to be thousands of black Rovers in London, and British SIS could keep a much easier and full-time watch on its senior ally using a long-range surveillance camera looking over F.D.R.'s bronze shoulder from any one of the bedroom windows of the Europa Hotel. He entered the Embassy.

The Ambassador for this diplomatic plum posting was a friend of the Administration: unlike Moscow, no coffee gofer here was wasting time. The marine guards snapped Lowel straight through to the chief of station for security, a sharp black called Dawson, who came running down the staircase from the second floor.

'Mr Lowel! We had a chopper for you at Heathrow, but with the damn country on strike no one out there reported your change of flight. The President has been waiting for your call in Hi-Burst, the moment you arrived.'

The secure room here was in the heart of the building, with lead shielding in its walls and a line that communicated space-age fashion, both video and audio, in lock-and-key coding condensed and transmitted in micro-second bursts.

With the door closed, Lowel initialized the system, then keyed:

'Mount Hood hot for Delta One.'

Without perceptible delay the screen flashed back: 'Delta hot for Mount Hood. Commence call.'

In a space of ultimate privacy, headsets were redundant: the unit was hands-free. He addressed the two-way speaker mesh:

'Lowel here, Mr President.'

'I see you. How about me?'

'Looking good, sir.'

The digital image from Washington was Kodak clear. So were its frown lines.

'For my conservative opponents, Yalta makes one hell of a jump on the ante. I take it shifting there *was* your bright idea.'

'Yes sir. Things were stalling. It seemed a way to break the jam.'

'Tell me – and for Christ's sake, if we're paying for this high-tech intimacy, leave off the rank!'

Lowel described his first encounter with Berov and the accident with the Red Army. Galbraith grunted. After the session with the First Secretary's concern for his birthmark's association with the devil, the image in Washington tapped his forehead.

'The Mark of Cain doesn't sound like he's made any firm sale with his military. How "accidental" do you rate that collapsing boom?'

'Zero. But it took a lot of organization,' Lowel said, 'and there was no reason for the Red Army to think I'd be with Berov in his cab.'

'The Red Army has five divisions of organization just in the Greater Moscow zone, but I agree: I don't think the play was set up for you. I'm assessing it the Generals against the KGB.' The President touched a paper on his desk. 'This Typhoid Mary report of CIA: if we ignore the Chernobyl red herrings, did your dog lover or his boss give us anything concrete on female assassins?'

Lowel shook his head. 'On the food-poisoning episode in the summer of 87, the Party line is still "hepatitis". Berov told me while we were eating lunch, "Your widow and her heart attacks are a coincidental mixture of natural cholesterol and Langley's overheated imagination." '

'What isn't coincidence in your goddamn business?'

A look of exasperation came from Washington. 'I got here this morning to find right after my office was sealed by you, last night, for no poison – some third-ranker in protocol had a cardiac.'

'The Oval Office was clean?' Lowel asked. 'The chemical weapons people found no toxin?'

'Only a carton of fossilized cottage cheese left from Nixon. And my protocol chief should have been told immediately about that death. He'd assigned this Castilio the baggage-handling arrangements for your change-over to Yalta.'

'Castilio knew about Yalta?' And as he said it, Lowel thought, That's what She wanted!

'Yeah – and you don't have to draw me story boards in red ink, either.'

'Yes sir. What I do have to tell you: Pathology hasn't confirmed, but I'm betting Castilio wasn't a natural cardiac.' He described the episode at Thirtieth Place. 'Mr President, I'm saying for the record: if Castilio proves positive for Viscumin, you should not go on.'

'That's exactly what those Hallowe'en bastards want,' Galbraith replied grimly. 'We're steaming full ahead. At least I have one piece of good news; it cost half our gross national product, but the French have agreed to come on side.'

'Getting France sounds more like a Second Miracle of Lourdes,' Lowel said, 'but you may not be in for smooth sailing with Britain.'

He covered his British Airways flight change and subsequent SIS reception. Daniel Galbraith rubbed the elbow of his wounded arm while he listened: 'It's raining here. This goddamn thing always plays up with a change of weather, and you're right about the UK. Prime Minister Powys called me: he's been having bigger trouble with his Intelligence bastards than I have. "I ask you," he said in that Welsh accent of his, "what else can an honest socialist expect? When his spies are all recruited from the same Old Boyo net!" Listen, Jack: Powys despised my inherited cash at Oxford, but he drank my beer – and his vote in Parliament on their dismantling comes up tomorrow. My Welsh friend needs whatever help we can –'

SYSTEM INTERRUPT

flashed on the screen. The fail-safe image from Washington went black. The Embassy lights went out, leaving Lowel in the dark.

10

Evening calm:

Chequers

The power failure was comparatively minor: the BBC said so, for the Driving Home show. 'Only the inner London districts of Bloomsbury, Soho, Marylebone, and Mayfair are affected. A spokesman for the Electricity Board reports that a defective transformer at Euston sub-station is the cause.'

Lowel caught the British understatement as he climbed into another marine helicopter, this one courtesy the US Ambassador. Half the commuting population of southern England had been affected. No traffic lights for the rush hour, no escalators or deep lifts for the tube – no bloody subway trains!

'Our Hi-Burst link is immune to local power glitches,' shouted Dawson, the black security chief of station, as the rotors began to whirl. 'The goddamn Brits must have some play going on. I'll chase the FBI Lab in Washington for the autopsy on that protocol death and route the order for sex-screening White House personnel – you just watch your back!'

Lowel waved. The helicopter lifted, providing a magic carpet over the chaos of London's streets, and then more peaceful Harrow, with the stone buildings of Winston Churchill's old school. The wooded ridge of the Chiltern Hills appeared. Amersham passed, then two army camps, followed by a stone-age chalk figure carved into a hillside. Thirty miles north-west of the capital, at a brick manor house set in a park, the chopper began its descent.

Chequers was given to the British nation in 1921, by Lord Lee of Fareham, as a Camp David style retreat for future prime ministers. The house was Elizabethan, sixteenth-century, typically Tudor, archetypal English. For leaders like Churchill, who had his own perfect country home at Chartwell, the gift was of slight value. Besides, knowing that the Luftwaffe had it listed as a target, 'Winnie' switched to Ditchley Hall, near Oxford, Lowel recalled. Post-war prime ministers valued Chequers more – and it was still a target. After the Irish Republican Army bombed the Conservative Party Conference at the coastal resort of Brighton, the name 'Chequers' was no longer shown on revised British road maps.

'A futile precaution, Mr Lowel, let me tell you! Any terrorist who can read has only to visit his nearest lending library: their copies are always out of date!'

The present tenant of Chequers threw back his head and laughed. Prime Minister Powys was a short, stocky man, with the sonorous voice of a born orator and a thick mass of black hair that rolled in tight waves back from a broad forehead. His eyes were deepset, as dark as his hair, but with a humorous light in them that dared the world to do its worst to the son of a blacksmith who had risen on nothing but merit to be the kingdom's chief minister.

'I'm sorry I have to break your weekend,' Lowel said, 'but the President told me your time was short and he wanted me to give you my view of things in Moscow.'

'Your brother-in-law told *me* that you were saving himself – and the First Secretary – single-handed from the clutches of a Lady Borgia. I must say, Mr Lowel, your "Black Widow" makes my hooded gentlemen of the IRA seem a pale threat indeed!'

The British leader laughed again, and gestured towards the woods surrounding his house. A ring of troops in camouflaged battledress was almost invisible against the foliage.

'At least there's no doubt that you face a real threat from Ireland, Prime Minister. I'm trying to confirm something the Soviets say is only a phantom of the West's imagination.'

'Well they would say that, wouldn't they? I always take a stroll at this time of day; come along and let me show you the park.'

Right on cue, an armoured Safari Wagon, with two plainclothes guards, detached from the trees and rolled slowly forward. With a sharp look of annoyance, Powys turned his back on the security forces and strode off as briskly as a man with stubby legs could, across a paddock of sheep and grass, towards a nearby hill. Lowel covered the same distance with half the movement and recounted his experiences with Berov.

'A strange reaction from Moscow,' Powys observed, 'but collective human nature is a curious phenomenon on both sides of the Iron Curtain. We try to save humanity from itself by removing these fearful armaments of Terror, and half the planet rises against us in a paroxysm of fear! Are you familiar with the purpose of a kissing-gate, Mr Lowel?'

The Prime Minister had stopped where the paddock wall was broken by two half-moons of rusting iron. Within them a gate rotated on a central spindle. Powys waved Lowel forward, then clinked the metal shut behind, trapping his guest in the leading section. 'Now you see one principal of operation: if you are a country lad walking your sweetheart, with the gate in this position, the quarry is fair game.'

Lowel said, 'Prime Minister, it's not the first time in Britain I've had that feeling. From the moment I left the Soviet Union I've been under SIS surveillance. With respect, I must ask: was it done with your knowledge?'

Powys stood silent for a moment, his hand drumming on the iron rail, his gaze staring at the peaceful Buckinghamshire countryside with its magnificent beech trees and rolling hills. When he turned to face Lowel, the Welshman's eyes had lost their good-humoured defiance: they showed the pain of a man betrayed by his friends.

'Not with my knowledge, Mr Lowel, but nor can I say to my surprise. Though it grieves me to admit the fact, much of the security force of this country feels itself diametrically opposed to my government, but then I'm sure you're already well aware of that. I can't imagine why they should have taken it upon themselves to "surveil" you. I certainly do not excuse it, but their heightened zeal may be partly the result of a recent threat against my office. Forgive me, I've been keeping you imprisoned.'

The Prime Minister swung the kissing-gate forward. Lowel stepped out. Powys followed him through and suddenly smiled. The Safari Wagon and guards were stopped by the obstacle. The Prime Minister broke into a chuckle. 'Now you see the other purpose. We shall have some privacy. My sheepdogs are forbidden to harry me on foot.'

Powys began climbing a path with a signpost pointing to Loombe Hamlet.

'What kind of threat?' asked Lowel, pacing behind.

'My dear fellow, such notes are never specific. Attack on one's family, letter bombs, military intervention at Whitehall. Fear is always greater when left to the victim's imagination.'

'But this fear did come by a written note?'

'Two days ago. It seems I may expect death "in a novel way".'

'That was the precise wording?'

'It was. Though hardly original.' Powys gave a quick

laugh over his shoulder. 'To the recipient, death is always novel, I fancy.'

'I'd have to agree with you there, Prime Minister. I assume that your security advisers explained why there was special significance in this particular threat?'

'They did. The Belfast Orangemen's Anniversary Parade takes place the day after tomorrow. If you were in London, you may have noticed that government buildings have been placed on "Black Alert". Can you imagine a greater contrast with such urban horrors than this?'

The path had emerged from the trees into an elevated clearing. Behind them, encircled by a one-lane country road, Chequers sat in its Elizabethan gardens. Ahead was Loombe Hamlet, a cluster of quaint shops, steepled church, ivied manor and stone cottages.

'The calendar heart of England,' Lowel said.

'And so it is – but the real England! Genuine emotions, mixed-up feelings, honest confusion, but always an ingrained belief in fairness and hard work. This is how a leader of free people should be able to pass among them. Not surrounded by those armour-plated monstrosities and machine-guns the cloak-and-dagger merchants of Whitehall insist on. Come and meet the other kind.'

Powys grasped him by the arm and led the way past a duck pond and sign, Beauchamps Manor. 'Our Grande Dame's residence – pronounced Beecham – but don't let that minor snobbery confuse the issue. Mrs Hughes-Beauchamps may resemble a dinosaurish dragon, but she has saved the little church single-handed from dry rot with her money, and in the war she saved two children from a bombed house in the blitz. Her father was Indian Civil Service. She doesn't like the Japanese.'

The object of the Prime Minister's mixed admiration was a tall old woman with a military posture, huge chest and thyroid eyes. She was shouting instructions at an overweight, red-faced clergyman, getting out of a Toyota.

'Vicar has his problems. High blood pressure, as you can see, and Mrs H-B demanding personal daily Communion! And the man's a socialist, in an age that thinks the welfare of our fellow man has died – but it hasn't, and won't, not as long as I have anything to say about it. Mind you, I was brought up evangelical chapel. Now this is who I really want you to meet.'

Britain's leader stopped at a tiny cottage with roses and bottleglass windows. A sign said, 'Winkey's House: Cream Teas.' The doorway was so low that even Powys had to duck. Inside, a small plump woman, with pink cheeks, early forties, was setting out cups and saucers.

'Mary Morris, meet my friend Mr Lowel, from America.'

'Oh, Prime Minister. Oh, gosh. From America. Like my friend Sarah.'

Lowel said 'Hi' and shook hands, after a blushing Mary Morris had wiped hers on a pinny covered with cutesy cartoon Shetland ponies. She behaved like a schoolgirl, he thought, but her eyes were those of a lonely and ageing woman. They explained the happy-times photo beside her, of a child and donkey, labelled 'Me and Winkey'. Beyond the window a white sports car did a tourist crawl through the Hamlet: a Maserati, distorted by the bottleglass.

'I was just about to get the loaf out for your special for tomorrow, Prime Minister.' Mary Morris mopped her face, looked despairingly at the retreating potential customers in the car, and gestured at an antique oven, all at the same time.

'I mustn't stop you, then,' Powys told her. 'Not only does your delicious bread taste like my old Mam's, you cut a loaf too, just like she did, in Wales. Like second childhood it is, Lowel, having Mary here provide my little picnic snacks! Come along.'

The Prime Minister laughed, crinkling his eyes, and plunged back out through the low door in time to meet the armoured Safari Wagon. Like Congressional 'good old boys' pressing the flesh Down South at home, the trowelled-on Welshness was a politician's act, Lowel realized, but the human interest bit seemed genuine. The next part of the game was hopping a stile for the narrow path to Loombe Hill. With a totally frosted expression, the guard at the wheel reversed the Safari Wagon and headed home for Chequers the long way round by road.

'Good riddance! What a waste of the taxes the Mary Morrises of this country scrimp and save for. There's a woman brought up to think mummy and daddy, and ponies, and home, would always be there – of course, the parents divorced messily, all the money went down the sewer of the stock market – but she's picked up the pieces on her own. The little people. Salt of the earth, they are. Sit down.'

At the top of the hill a bench was placed for the view. Powys sat to admire it. Lowel joined him and said, 'Prime Minister, I think you should read the underlined part of this report.'

He took out an abstract of the agency background on the Meliti woman and passed it to his companion. The British leader read as swiftly as Kliment Berov had, but with only one eye on the paper. The Welshman's other eye was constantly observing natural history features of the hillside. The Maserati was cruising past the bottom.

'Mr Lowel, I take your point – if we may excuse the unfortunate pun – about the similarity to this long-ago "umbrella" stabbing on Waterloo Bridge. But now, that Pipestem Orchis, on your left, do you see? Alas, today such a sight is truly rare.'

The flower grew in a small colony of tiny crimson blooms on delicate white stems. More calendar art – if the observer ignored the US Marine Corps chopper, and the Special Air Service camouflaged troops, and a second Westland Sea-Fly armoured helicopter parked in a paved yard behind the 400-year-old stables. The Maserati had stopped to snap a picture of them.

'England is beautiful, Prime Minister, but the same threat in four separate episodes can't be ignored.'

'My dear chap, you are wrong there: Wales has beauty! – England is merely pretty.' As Powys stood up, the gleam of Celtic humour had returned to his dark eyes. 'Now then, as far as this threat to me, and our security reception committee accorded you, the beast of suspicion is best grasped by its horns. Sir Herbert Maxwell is my head of SIS. I'll instruct him to see you in London, the moment you return. Let us say, one hour: allowing for the uncertainties of travel.'

They walked down the hill to the kissing-gate. The armoured Safari Wagon was waiting beyond it. Lowel went through the gate first, the Prime Minister followed. He was hooking the latch when the white Maserati started up again and came out of the shadows.

A woman was driving: she wore Hollywood glasses and a headscarf.

It was too far to run. Lowel jumped on the Safari Wagon's outrider ledge. 'I need the licence on that car!'

The Brits were sharp. The spare man jumped off to stay with Powys. The Wagon driver floored it. The Maserati saw them coming and accelerated.

'No good this way,' said the Safari driver. 'Blocked by the stables.'

The Maserati vanished again behind them, heading south along the narrow road encircling the estate. 'East!' said Lowel.

'Got you. Hang on.'

The Safari Wagon went hard over to the left, half airborne from grass hummocks. The roof of the Maserati

86

was a white blur, barely visible above the hedge walls separating the paddock from the road.

'Jesus, sheep!'

The Wagon's horn blasted. A flock of blackface went in all directions. Lowel saw an apple-tree coming, just in time to duck. A side-mirror above his head got torn off. Three spotted fallow deer bounded upwards. A wooden gate was closed in front. The Safari driver said, 'Going through.'

The top of the Maserati was 500 yards west of the gate. They were three hundred. The Safari Wagon's tachometer was red-lining. The last fallow deer didn't make it. The body was hurled aside by the Wagon's snowplough armour. The gate followed it in a crashing tornado of splintered wood and deerguts. They were past the stone wall. Turning –

The Maserati made it first by inches.

There was no licence plate on the rear bumper.

'Keep following her!'

'She can do one-eighty.'

'Not with those cows.'

A herd of Jerseys, coming home for milking. She had to stop.

She didn't. Her fluttering scarf touched a hide, but the Maserati went between the two lead animals as fast as twelve cylinders on overdrive could take it, and still climbing.

'*We won't make it!*'

The Wagon's brakes smoked and screamed. The terrified cows bellowed.

'I can still take her in my chopper,' Lowel shouted. 'Head back to the paddock.'

They two-wheeled in a circle, and crunched west over the gate and deer carcass. As they got to the apple-tree with the mirror, he saw a flash of flame ahead, by the stable yard. It was followed by a puff of black smoke.

Both came from his helicopter, just below its rotor blades. Three seconds later his eardrums caught the blast. So much for using the United States Marines.

'Thanks anyway,' he said to the Wagon's driver, and when he met Powys: 'I think I'm going to have to allow more than an hour for reaching London, after this uncertainty, Prime Minister.'

The Welshman's pugnacious jaw was set firm. 'You shall take my own machine. The Sea-Fly will have you at the Horse Guards landing zone in forty minutes. My personal pilot is first class.' The British leader squeezed his guest's arm reassuringly: 'With Commander Teddy Campbell in the cockpit, I can't see you in safer hands!'

11

Jacqueline Campbell's former husband had the clear gaze of a man who cheats at cards – and the frank smile of one who'd been allowed to get away with it too long. Lowel had met several specimens of the breed: until this moment, he hadn't met Campbell. As the pilot came forward with his hand out, there was no way of telling whether Jacky had informed her ex of this friendship with another male.

'Mr Lowel?'

'Commander.'

Lieutenant Commander, to be precise: there were only two and a half stripes on the pilot's shoulderboards, not three, but Teddy Campbell didn't waste flying time with false modesty. Instead, the pilot waved cheerfully at the scorched housing of the US Marine chopper, and said in a piercing English accent that belied his Scottish name, 'Sorry about your bus. Our mechanic found a turbine blade had sliced a fuel line – spot of luck you got here in the first place. The PM tells me you're bothered for time. No probs, old boy. We'll make it Horse Guards in thirty, or a case of Mumms!'

The Sea-Fly was nimble, and Campbell was good at his job. They picked up forward speed almost as rapidly as a fixed-wing machine, climbing at the same time with the minimum rate to keep them just clear of the kissing-gate and Loombe Hill.

89

'Sandwiches in the box if you're peckish,' Campbell said over the headset circuit. 'The PM's favourite – tongue and chicken with crusts *on*. A lesby female in the village makes 'em, just like his old Welsh mam!'

The Morris woman's tea-shop and the other clustered buildings in the Hamlet were already in dusk as the sun sank behind their screening trees. The churchyard was sombre. So was Lowel's mental state. He was being hit by a major attack of self-doubt. It wasn't just a matter of checking flashlight batteries: he was too old; you can't just walk back in. With every stage of this business he was a step behind, instead of anticipating and getting in front. As for intuition! He'd fallen for the oldest dodge in the book: spotting the obvious, while the real threat stays in the crowd. In his career days, intuition would have gone on red alert the first time a car went slowly in the vicinity of a prime target, even in a tea-shop.

'Sure you won't, old boy?'

Lowel shook his head. British Rail's 'boofay' effort had been enough for one day. The sandwich-box beside him was autographed 'Mary' and decorated with a red Welsh dragon. Each sandwich inside was nested in a crinkle-edged doily.

'Don't mind if I do.' Young Teddy grabbed without looking, and began munching. Lowel decided that his pilot hadn't heard about him from Jacqueline – with his open flyboy personality, there would have been some sign of overt aggression.

'If you'll be moving on from Horse Guards,' Campbell said, between bites, 'I could call ahead for a car.'

Lowel was willing to bet the champagne that his next ride was already on order. It was going to be almost impossible to shake his British opposition – and that was the craziest part of this operation, which started with lecturing Murphy against the convention of regarding Moscow as the enemy: now he was faced with America's oldest and closest ally behaving as the main opponent.

Hyde Park and the sunset gleam of the Serpentine were below. The traffic surrounding the park was back to what passed for normal evening congestion in the narrow streets of central London. Teddy polished off the last sandwich and tipped the stick; they banked towards St James's Palace. At one end of the gravelled Parade, toy soldiers were drilling. The lines of men marched straight towards the blank wall of a building . . . then at the last minute, reversed direction. At the same time Campbell reached to start his hover procedure.

'I'll change my mind,' Lowel said. 'Go for Westminster Bridge. You can let me off directly.'

'A bit sudden, old boy – ' the pilot shot him a glance and pulled back on the control – 'But never mind the reason why . . .'

. . . Ours but to do or die! The motto of the late British Empire. Buckingham Palace swept beneath them. The flag-mast on its top was vacant, which meant the Sovereign wasn't in London. As the Sea-Fly cleared the building, a black car was turning in through the mounted Horse Guards on sentry duty each side of the archway entrance. A case of Mumms to a sure thing:

The car was a Rover.

As the sound of the helicopter from Chequers faded, back in the dusk of Loombe Hamlet the woman who had been Janice, the artist's model, for a lonely protocol clerk last night in Washington was now the next target's new friend Sarah, a senior airline flight attendant from America. The friendship had been formed instantly, in the showers, following an Old Girls' hockey match which was part of a school reunion. School reunions were another sure bond and perfect cover. Memories fade after twenty-five years: faces were younger, or older; they had braces on their teeth, or pigtails; their hair was blonde instead

91

of dark – but just mention the good times, or the bad teachers, and it all flooded back.

'Like awful Miss Snow, the Assistant Head, with her moustache and horrible black gloves and smackings. Gosh, Sarah, what a hugely impossible time it seems since then.'

The middle-class, middle-aged British voice coming along the low-beamed passage from the tea-shop's kitchen had a little-girl quality: flustered, excited, almost over the edge. Sexuality comes of age in school, with puberty – especially in the closed confines of unisexual private schools. Smackings and tears, and making up. The voice's owner had probably never been truly happy since, but there was no room for compassion during a mission. The voice was a target, nothing more.

Stretched out on the ruffled bed in the chintzy ground-floor bedroom under the picture of Winkey the donkey, and the quaint dovecot on the tea-shop's gable, for this target the woman who was now Sarah wore only knee-length, polished riding boots and shiny black gloves.

'You know, I'm all goosey!' said the voice from the kitchen. 'I simply can't help it. Thinking about you kissing me again, in that marvellous way . . .'

The tea-shop's owner would never have the nerve to say what way. 'Sarah' swung her lithe, nude body off the bed. Two long strides carried her across to the doorway so that she could observe the activity in the kitchen. A fresh loaf of brown bread was being taken from a spot on the shelf marked with a tiny Union Jack. She snapped, 'Aren't you through yet, bitch?'

The target jumped. 'When you pretend to be cross, in your growly American, you frighten me. With your gloves –'

'Ready to belt your limey ass. So hustle it!'

'Yes, Sarah. Sorry. You know, it was wonderful at the reunion, but to be totally honest I didn't really remember you, but of course you being five years younger, and you look *ten*!' The target finished cutting the bread slices, leaving the crusts. 'It's how the PM likes it. Talking of which, he had another of you Americans visiting him. With a damaged hand, poor man.'

'Oh yeah?' She lounged in the doorway and said casually, 'What about the guy's hand?'

'The left one had lost two fingers.'

So what had seemed probable in Washington was confirmed in Britain: despite her precautions, and arrangements for decoys, she must now accept that she herself was targeted by a specific opponent. It was always a male – like the men who commissioned her to solve the problems they created but then couldn't handle in their little-boy Intelligence games, hobbled as they were by the useful hang-ups that masculinity imposed. What she dreaded in the lonely moments of solo operation was to find herself facing another equally dedicated woman.

'Otherwise,' the tea-shop's owner continued, taking down a waxed cardboard box marked with a red dragon, 'he was sort of Gary Cooperish. I didn't catch the name. If you'd arrived sooner you could have met. Oh God, Sarah, standing like that you look incredible . . .'

The sandwiches were pressed tongue, from the local butcher, and the target's own cold roast chicken slices. 'Sarah' crossed one booted thigh over the other and said, 'Keep your eye on the knife, babe.'

'Jolly right.' The target giggled. 'You know I used to get up early and bake *his* loaf on the same day, but it gave the dear soul indigestion. Now they sit overnight – but I leave the key to the larder door outside in the cracked teapot, on the top step, behind the geraniums – so his personal messenger can pick the box up without waking us in the morning.'

'Great.'

The target signed the dragon-box lid 'Mary', placed

the sandwiches in crinkle-edged paper doilies, slipped them into the box and closed the lid; double checked the absurd teapot-key, and larder-door; gave one last glance at the spotless kitchen counters. The church clock struck.

'Goodness! It's time for evensong.'

'Get your fat butt in here this minute, or it'll be swansong.'

'Sarah! The window! Mrs Hughes-Beauchamps could hear you!'

Blushing furiously, the current target rushed from the kitchen to the oblivion of sex with her booted, naked lover. The woman known as Sarah bent the first knuckles of the two left fingers of her left-hand glove, and stared thoughtfully for a moment at the truncated leather outline. Men with mutilated or missing hands, or facial birthmarks, would be even more determined to prove their masculinity against a female adversary. She lifted her eyes away from the glove, in the direction of the vanished helicopter carrying her damaged male opponent.

The new headquarters of British Security appeared in the gathering dark, ahead of Lowel. The place was a twenty-storey concrete modern, built in the post-war architectural era that obliterated many of London's finest old stone buildings left standing from the blitz of Hitler. The architects called this particular slab-sided nonentity Century House. The civil servants found that too exotic for a building to administer spies. The official name for the Intelligence spider's web was agreed, in committee, to be:

GOVERNMENT COMMUNICATIONS BUREAU

The letters were painted on a new landing pad, installed with cash saved when the same Whitehall visionaries cancelled a proposal for a director's residential penthouse.

'In the immortal words of our Permanent Under-Secretary,' Teddy Campbell explained, as the Sea-Fly went into hover, ' "Too James Bond!" '

The roof was deserted. Lowel climbed down, squashing the now empty sandwich-box. Abruptly he recalled the food poisoning 'hepatitis' episode against the Soviet leader. 'A security tip for the next week,' he shouted through the hatch to Campbell. 'Put the Prime Minister on a strict diet: don't let him eat anything in flight. And thanks for the ride.'

'Any time, old man. I'll try and starve the PM. You might say Hi to my former lady wife, when you see her.'

The Sea-Fly whisked tail up and out past the guard-rail of the building, leaving Lowel to consider how easy it was to underestimate the British character.

A painted yellow pathway flanked with cat's-eye reflectors led from the landing circle to a door into the building. Modern fire extinguishers had five buckets of sand next to them, below a sign, 'In Accordance With Board of Trade Regulations'. He was about to open the door when the welcoming party caught up with him: a red-faced commissionaire, with medal ribbons on his uniform, late sixties, led the charge; and behind him, a younger version of Teddy, from one of the military intelligence departments, in civilian clothes and a bad temper, shouting somewhat incoherently.

'We sent a car, damn it! Specially! Are you Lowel?'

'No landings without Fire Party advisement in advance!' the commissionaire contributed.

'Yes, I'm Lowel.'

'Sir Herbert's waiting! He hates being kept waiting! Specially by –'

The young MI man stopped short of the word *Americans*.

'By car from St James's,' Lowel observed, 'he would have been kept longer.'

95

'Well, yes. No – I mean, bloody hell, you'd better just follow.'

'Roof entry is unauthorized without signing-in.'

The commissionaire puffed his medals. The young MI snapped, 'I'll sign him in! Give me the damn roof log.'

'The roof log is removed for night hours to the lobby.'

Lowel was tired of playing pig-in-the-middle of this stand-off. Exhausted. It felt like a month since he'd left Moscow. 'My President has directed me to meet with your Prime Minister. Mr Powys has sent me personally to meet your superior officer. Unless you want an international incident, I suggest you take me to Sir Herbert first and bring the log up for signing later.'

He started walking to the nearest door marked EXIT.

The commissionaire barked, 'Yes sir!' and saluted.

The MI said, 'I say!' and followed.

On the top floor at least, the act was Peter Sellers, not James Bond.

When Prime Minister Powys had complained to Daniel Galbraith about the Old Boy network of British Intelligence, although it was true that an apparently never-ending stream of upper-class traitors had been exposed, or quietly pensioned off, the Welshman could not have meant to include the current head of the Security Service.

Sir Herbert Maxwell was created a knight by the Monarch on the final recommendation, before leaving office, of her previous prime minister. The Iron Lady had shared Herbert Maxwell's solid, lower-middle-class background, his escape from it by the relentless pursuit of higher education, and his unswerving loathing for the popular press – except on those occasions when it could be usefully manipulated, such as election campaigns or the Falkland Islands.

Lowel had crossed his path twice, before Maxwell's

promotion: once in Washington, at a bilateral brain-storming of the Iraq–Iran problem, which solved nothing; and earlier, when the Royal Navy and Britain desperately needed American satellite intelligence to sink the Argentine cruiser, *Belgrano*. Now the UK had its own bird in orbit, with some circuitry the British refused to divulge to their Nato partners.

As he entered Maxwell's office, Lowel wondered whether that circuitry had cut short his Hi-Burst private chat to Washington. Standing inside the door was the 'businessman' who had tailed him from Antwerp to the deep lift at Covent Garden.

'Very good, Ryder. That will be all.'

Maxwell gave his subordinate a curt nod of dismissal. Without formal introduction, the tail had a name. The office door closed on Ryder. The man who gave him his orders came out from behind a desk, hand extended in friendship.

'Jack Lowel. Getting cover of the *Belgrano* operation. I remember. Good to see you again.'

'You too, Sir Herbert, and congratulations on your title.'

'Thanks very much.' Maxwell's voice still showed its bluff Yorkshire origins. 'The title impresses my shirt-maker. I don't have time for such nonsense. Sit down. A drink? Coffee?'

'Coffee would be great.'

It was waiting: on a tray, with one cup and saucer in plain white china. The tray was on a low table beside the only spare chair. The chair was angled to get a view of the Thames and to throw an artist's clear north light on the person sitting in it, while keeping Maxwell's face in shadow. This was a man who had plenty of time for the smallest details – and who could have refused his title if he wanted to.

As Lowel was filling the cup, Maxwell said abruptly,

'I'll be blunt, Jack. That's my way – I don't know any other. I've just had words with the Prime Minister, and after hearing him out I told him plainly what I tell you: with this spider woman and her poisonings, you've built a house of cards on nothing. I can't speak for the Pope's death, or Vatican politics, but Georgi Markov was done in here by two male Bulgarians, plain and simple. No female we know of went near him on Waterloo Bridge – for that matter, no trace of plant toxin was ever found in his body.'

Throughout his speech, the SIS chief's grey eyes never blinked or left Lowel's face. It gave an impression of complete conviction and must have taken years of training to achieve.

'I wouldn't say the first umbrella stabbing on record in the West was exactly "plain and simple", Sir Herbert. And it's true that with the forensic techniques they had available in '78 your pathologist couldn't *prove* Ricin as the toxic agent. But he sure as hell found the pellet – diameter 1.53 millimetres, with two channels of 0.3 – it was still embedded in the wound.'

'Not having your North American trick for total recall – of what you'll forgive me for saying, Jack, are often irrelevant minutiae in a case – I'll just observe that "bullshit baffles brains" more often than otherwise. I wouldn't place much money on potted biography, if I were you.'

Maxwell used first names only to make his bluntness even rougher.

Lowel said, 'Berov, in Moscow, has agreed to check the Meliti woman from their side of the Wall.'

'Has he indeed! Then you have more faith than I, that the leopard can change its spots.'

Lowel was exasperated with this do-or-die cold warrior, but he kept his reply level. 'Obviously, Sir Herbert, we have to be cautious with the Soviets, but in this case the threat is for all of us. I'd just ask that if you get any leads from your investigation of the latest escalation made against your own Prime Minister, you'll tell us immediately.'

'That goes without saying.' Maxwell stood up and ushered him to the door. 'One final small question, Jack: when you use the plural, I take it the meaning is yourself and your relative by way of the marriage bed?'

'The President of the United States,' he responded sharply. 'Sure. Who else would it mean?'

'Forgive me for jumping to the wrong conclusion' – the head of British security fixed Lowel with a repeat, unblinking, man-to-man stare of slate-grey Yorkshire eyes – 'I thought you might be meaning that other lady with a Balkan background, who I'm told has just bought tickets for herself and her divorced husband on the Olympic flight departing at 05.00 tomorrow morning, from Heathrow for Athens.'

He had not expected to keep his association with Jacqueline private for long, but SIS could not have picked it up so soon unless her house was already under surveillance before his arrival. The only way for that to have happened was from his chance remark of her name to Galbraith at Camp David. Someone in the crowd around the President must be working for Britain.

'If we're having this free and frank Allied co-operation,' he said tightly to Maxwell, 'try screening your female employees for one with a white Maserati. And keep the bitch away from the House of Commons.'

12

Fourth day:

Greek getaway

Lowel and his personal translator disembarked from their Olympic London flight at Eleniko Airport, to be met by an ominous declaration from the Greek Minister of the Interior.

**WOMEN OF ATHENS LOSE SEXUAL PASSION
THROUGH POLLUTION!**

In the West Concourse's central plaza a midsummer Mediterranean noon sun blazed down on the lurid headline and the travelling globe passing by it. The East Terminal had been closed indefinitely by a bomb threat; the baggage handlers in both buildings had taken a spontaneous day off to demonstrate the Thousandth Year of Vengeance against the hated Turks; the thermometer above the locked Money Exchange was stuck at 37°C, and the air conditioning had aborted.

'Could be worse,' Lowel said, pointing at the thermometer. 'If that thing is telling the truth it's only 99° Fahrenheit. We got our drachmas changed at Heathrow –'

'And I'm not from Athens?'

Jacqueline smiled at him over the Passion headline. He smiled back, and for a moment they were just like the million other tourist pairs feeling that special sensual thrill of not just being away from it all in a new country, but the anticipation of following the footsteps of Ulysses and Byron to the Isles of Greece, and letting go with uninhibited love on some silver-white sand . . . Until the Exchange wicket beside them clanged open and the thermometer hit 42°C in a single leap.

'What I was going to say, Mrs Campbell: we'll butt out of this hell, if you can rent us a car.'

Hertz and Avis were all taken, but Hellascar had a Polaroid photo of a blue Honda Accord with only one collision mark visible to the eye. A sign behind the counter said, 'English Spoke'. The young woman in front apparently didn't. Instead, she explained in a rush of Greek, 'I am standing in for my sister, and by our late mother's memory the Honda is brand new having only received the wound leaving the garage for the first time in its life this morning!'

While the girl told this string of white lies, a swarthy moustached thug, who looked as though he should have been away in the mountains with a rifle and bandolier slung over his shoulder, lounged behind her and played with the buttons on a solar-powered Sharp calculator, at the same time glaring at both visitors under beetling black brows.

Lowel could never be just another tourist in this country. He had first met the Greek secret police when they worked for the Colonels' Junta, and the only difference with the modern socialist version was that in those days, when they didn't like someone, they were more obvious in showing it. That grey-eyed Yorkshire bastard, Maxwell, had decided to spoil the trip: there was no point in saying so, and doing the same for Jacqueline.

Her use of the language cut a snarl of red tape, but it still took a quarter of an hour to get past the list of special charges: 'The girl says it's thirty drachmas extra, per kilometre, if we're going to be over 4,000 kilometres, but only twenty if we aren't, and we have to specify, God knows why. So are we?'

'Koropion is about forty miles one way,' he said, 'some running around to find the convent, the same distance return. That's less than 500 kilometres.'

'We're not going to be driving north?'

He shook his head. 'No time. We'll drop the car back here early this evening, fly up to Thessaloniki tonight, hotel over, and hire another one there for the run to Meliti first thing tomorrow morning. Ask her to make the second U-drive reservation now.'

The undercover cop in the background scowled as if his mother had been accused of prostitution, but the young Hellascar girl was delighted.

Jacqueline said, 'She says nothing is easier to oblige.'

The literal translation of that was another fifteen minutes – in the incredible heat and noise; however, their hotel arrangements at Thessaloniki got thrown in as a bonus. The bandit spat on the floor of the booth and, with one last look of sullen fury in their direction, walked out.

The Hellascar girl smiled apologetically, tapped the 'English Spoke' sign, and said, 'You honeymoon understand. Ees boyfrien', who not wants I work Day of Vengeance for no love. You like radio?'

Lowel shrugged, 'Not if it takes another half hour.'

'She says, it takes another 1,000 drachmas, and you plug it in yourself.'

'To hell. You drive. Let's go.'

He flipped his translator the keys and turned away. The Hellascar girl reached under the counter and produced a Walkman with a lighter-plug adaptor. She handed it to Jacqueline and said, 'In Greece, honeymoon must be have music. Good love.'

Forty minutes south of the brown smog of the Greek capital, they found 'Koropion – Sister City To Athens Georgia'. It was logoed on a sweaty T-shirt, topped off by a Nazi Luftwaffe Field Marshal's hat. The person in this costume was resting his considerable bulk in a strained canvas deckchair, with an Uzi chopped-off automatic rifle leaning against one leg. A complex of blue-roofed tourist retirement villas behind him was surrounded by a white brick security wall, guarded further by a barrel metal gate with drop-down spikes in the entrance paving. The English section of the bilingual sign above his head was PARTHENON ESTATES.

To Lowel, the sign should have had 'Colonels' Retirement Home' written on it. Jacqueline pulled the Accord to the side and stopped with the passenger window in line with the barrier spikes. The Uzi's owner flipped his belly sideways in the deckchair and said in an accent with a weird overlay from the sister city of the American south – or a CIA training in Virginia: 'You all better believe him, Mac! Condo Phase One, she all sold out.'

'I don't want to buy a villa,' Lowel answered. 'We're looking for a convent school for girls.'

'Oh yeah? You all like to find our young girls?'

The retired Colonels' houseboy ran his fat hand suggestively up and down the Uzi's barrel, and his red-streaked boozer's eyes both ways across Jacqueline's breasts, and smiled in an unpleasant fashion –

She lashed back in a storm of Greek which got the slob out of the chair, up on his feet, saluting his Luftwaffe cap and pointing to a small white church next along the road from the estate. She took off spitting gravel. When Lowel looked back, the man was still saluting and bowing after them, in the middle of the duststorm.

'For future reference,' he said, 'what guidebook phrase did you drop on that bastard?'

'How easy it is for a man to be parted from his most treasured possessions, if a Greek woman has a sharp knife and two strong brothers.'

Jacqueline laughed and turned the Honda up the lane

beside the church. A bungalow of concrete blockwork had been built behind it, on a foundation of old stone. The priest was out, but a motherly woman in the usual black was his housekeeper and knew more local secrets than the Church or the Colonels.

'Our town was destroyed completely by the Germans in the war,' she explained through Jacqueline. 'After our men were taken away to be shot, nothing was left standing.' She pointed at the 'Parthenon Estates' with massive contempt: 'Where the Sisters of St Spyridon had their school for young girls is now houses for new Germans to take all their clothes off on our beaches. This scandal is what it is to be Greek! – but I ask you, is this justice?'

Jacqueline commiserated. Lowel asked through her, 'This school was post-war; we're talking the early sixties. Maybe they rebuilt?'

After a brief exchange, Jacqueline said, 'They amalgamated. There's a community on the coast road, she says another forty kilometres. Do you want to drive?'

'I want to save time.'

To his surprise, they weren't being followed. On the coast highway traffic was light enough to check. There was nothing but a film crew in a van, shooting some background local colour. Passing it, Jacqueline got the Honda up to a hundred, in miles per hour.

'Going back to those guidebook phrases,' he said. 'Can an only child, like you, have two brothers?'

'Before she was born, she can. In my case, it was one half-brother. He was killed at the age of four, with my father's first wife, in the inter-partisan struggles when Tito came to power.'

'I'm sorry.'

'There's no need. I was born in England.' At an intersection with a sign pointing to the coast, a vividly crude mural on a billboard showed a bloody clenched fist holding a rifle above an Orthodox priest being roasted on a spit. 'The Deacon Athanasios,' Jacqueline explained, swinging the Honda in the new direction. 'He was cooked by the Turks in 1821 at Alamana, near Thermopylae, where the Spartans were carved up by the Persians in 480 B.C. Blood feuds and memories go on forever out here, and my father's Balkan experiences must have been equally terrible, but thank God, and my English mother, they never meant anything to me.'

'Good,' Lowel said. 'While we're disposing of the awkward questions: did you happen to call your ex-husband yesterday?'

'No.'

'And he didn't call you?'

'Why should Teddy do that?' She glanced sideways.

'Maybe about me staying overnight in Carlyle Square.'

'Jack darling, I haven't spoken to my ex for more than a year. But if we had, and if he dared to question my housekeeping arrangements, you can rest assured his bloated naval ego would get such a flea in its – damn!'

She slammed the clutch and changed down, but not before there was an unpleasant bang from the Accord's back end. The road had switched to rutted gravel. They stopped to check the damage. The exhaust was dented but intact. A peasant piling sage plants onto a donkey in an adjacent field paid no attention whatever. Beyond him, three dark green cypress trees grew out of the columned ruin of a temple. Beyond that was the sapphire blue of the Aegean Sea.

They stood silent, watching, looking . . . knowing that something was starting between them which didn't need words. For reasons that had nothing to do with motoring skill, and were older than the temple, when they went back to the car, Lowel took the driver's seat, and she sat beside him.

Around the next corner, he understood why the Greek

105

secret police didn't need to follow to know his destination.

Rising from the sea was a towering pinnacle of black basalt rock. At the top of the pinnacle, clustered like swallows' nests cemented to the walls of a barn, the buildings of a convent clung 300 feet above waves that lapped with deceptive tranquillity at the base of the column. A causeway connected it to the land. The distance of separation was roughly a quarter of a mile. Vehicular traffic was blocked by stone pillars and a heavy chain. A vineyard and vegetable garden flanked the road's dead-end. Nuns in black cultivated and pruned, heads down, in the fierce late afternoon sun.

Lowel stopped the Honda. Jacqueline went across to a nun snipping shoots off clusters of half-formed green grapes, growing on a wooden arch above a locked gate, behind the causeway chain. Greek letters were carved into the arch. Lowel recognized enough college maths symbols to get the Saint's name, Spyridon. The nun gave Jacqueline a long, searching look. At sea, a naval vessel cruised hull down on the horizon: a reminder of the Fleet mega-death the arms race had built up in the Mediterranean playground. Jacqueline returned.

'Bad news, Jack. Modern parents aren't prepared to have their little angels cut off by winter storms when they're supposed to be jetting to Switzerland for Christmas skiing. The sisters don't teach any more.'

'But they did?'

'Until 1969.'

'That's ball park.'

He started to the archway. The nun with the shears called out sharply. Jacqueline grabbed his arm. 'You can't go in. From here, it's strictly ladies only.'

The forces which stuck these buildings in their impossible location didn't work on logic. Reluctantly, he primed her with his Meliti question list.

'You'll be all right up there?'

106

'Honey, it's a convent, not a brothel. I wouldn't have missed this trip for the world.'

The nun took out a massive key and unlocked the gate. Jacky kissed him, and he watched her walk through the arch with that long easy stride from the hip he found such a turn-on in a woman. The worker nuns left the fields and followed. The nun with the key locked the gate.

Odd man out. He looked at the giant sundial formed by the pinnacle and realized that, with zonal differences, in about another hour Powys would be rising in Parliament to support the Dismantling Agreement. No thanks to Sir Herbert Maxwell. There was a sudden loud blast on a siren.

The warship was much closer, heading straight for the beach with a creaming bow wave and the sleek killing hull of a destroyer. Suddenly it wheeled hard to starboard, racing east, parallel to the coast. The splash of colour on the flag at its stern was British: the Royal Navy's White Ensign.

He moved to one side of the arch for a better view. As he did so, a helicopter whirled in over him, ground level. A Sea-Fly, like Teddy Campbell's but this one had Greek military markings. The pilot at the controls leaned out for a closer look at him through standard dark glasses – and wearing a light cotton blouse. Lowel realized the pilot was a woman.

The chopper rabbit-holed the arch and dipped below it, following the causeway. A moment later the air shook with the immense concussion of naval guns opening fire.

And he had put Jacky in the middle of it.

He vaulted the wall next to the arch and found himself running along a path made of paving stones, laid dry without mortar and worn in two channels by the passage of uncountable female feet. The sea was a few inches lower than the top of the causeway: scraps of weed and a feather moved in the opposite direction, into the shadow cast by the giant basalt needle. The destroyer fired a second salvo. The helicopter was zeroing straight in on the top buildings of the convent.

He slipped on some weed. Water was covering a depression in the paving. And the rate of tidal movement wasn't geometric, but logarithmic. Dependent on the slope of the beach, it could rise a mere few inches up a cliff in the same time that it raced a mile across flat sand.

Now it was racing. The sea floor was level on both sides of the causeway. In the next depression ahead the advancing sea slipped forward like a filling bathtub, swirling in great eddies around the pinnacle. He plunged forward and felt the current grabbing his ankles, calves, thighs. It was as though a giant rubber band was tightening around his waist to pull him backwards.

Fifty yards more, but each stride took greater and greater effort. Now the rubber band was trying to drag him under. Thirty yards, and he didn't think he was going to make it. If his feet gave way he would be carried –

A cable! It came down on posts from a landing. With both hands he grabbed it and hauled himself from the water. The guns went off again in a rolling thunder. He rested on his knees, gasping. When he looked up, he saw that his efforts had hardly started.

A deathtrap staircase, hung together with paste and toothpicks, clung to the rock. Eight hundred and thirty-seven swaying and exhausted steps later, the stairway ended. He found himself at a gatehouse, built in the same terrifying manner. There was a bell. Green with age, and a crack on the rim, but it had a rusted chain, and when he pulled it, the clapper struck the side with a resounding *clang, clang, clang* –

On the third stroke, he heard footsteps running. Jacqueline's face appeared at a grille.

'Jack?'

'Thank Christ. You're all right.'

And then he saw the figure standing behind her. A woman wearing sunglasses and a male British Royal Air Force uniform.

'Of course I'm all right,' said Jacqueline Campbell. 'Greek TV are shooting a war movie – we passed them on the road. But for heaven's sake stop ringing that bell. It's bad luck. The nuns only use it for drownings!'

The British wartime connection reminded him of the impending arms limitation vote in their House of Commons. He took his hand off the chain. Powys was going to need all the luck he could get.

'On certain momentous days in England . . .' Britain's present Prime Minister recited aloud, as he walked with his despatch box of red Morocco leather from his panelled study at Chequers towards the helicopter waiting for him in the stable yard, beyond the fragrant orchard '. . . On days like this there is a feeling in the air which is shared by all the United Kingdom's people, no matter our political divisions; from the time we wake up in the morning until the great event has run its course, and by evening become part of our island nation's history.

'Like that day in 1649 when Cromwell took over Parliament in order to sever a stubborn man's head from a King's shoulders, and so prove the supremacy of the Common People. Or the day that Winston Churchill stood here, inside Parliament, fighting Hitler with words on the wireless from the bombed House of Commons, because in 1940, after Dunkirk's defeat on the beaches, words were the only weapons left in Britain's arsenal.

'Or this day which, half a century later, dawned so bright and clear, with a skylark singing as it wound its way upwards from the meadow: a day when the time has come for Britain to prove its greatness once again by voluntarily relinquishing her hard won and dearly bought, independent nuclear deterrent forces, which in five minutes flat could have wiped Hitler and all his works from the face of the earth –'

'Good afternoon, Prime Minister.'

His pilot, young Campbell, looking as spick and span as his machine, was saluting him. Powys returned the politeness with that casual gesture which had become so much a part of his public image that all the country's television comedians used it to get an instant laugh of recognition. What a battle it was going to be, when he rose in an hour, before the cameras that had been especially installed for this occasion, to begin the debate.

'*Mr Speaker – !*'

'Mind your step, sir.'

'What? Ah – thank you, Commander. I always miss that middle one.'

For some reason known only to its designers, the Sea-Fly's entry steps were higher top and bottom. One of our typical British muddles, Powys thought, as he entered the fuselage. The Russians would have all the steps crudely 'higgledy-piggledy', in his old Mam's phrase: it was inconceivable that American technological design should be other than uniform. But dear old muddle-through Britain –

'Your buckle, sir.'

'Yes, yes, boy. I've got it.' The damned seat-belt. 'And much good it may do if the noisy thing above our heads stops whirling.'

'No problem there, sir. She'll just feather us down.'

The optimism of youth. Young Campbell was giving thumbs up to a ground crew who had their backs to the very spot in the stable yard where yesterday's wrecked American machine was still standing. So much for American design! Powys had once ridden in one from the lawn of the White House to Dulles Airport: with its massive size and duplication, two pilots for even the most routine occasion, the glossy monster was a marvel of the Pentagon – yet such gargantuan precautions had not prevented the assassinations of American presidents.

The orchard leaves began to tremble, then bend, then recede below the windows on an angle, as the small yet nimble Sea-Fly, typically British, carrying just himself and young Campbell side-by-side, lifted off with a minimum of fuss.

The guest house side walls of the convent were cemented to the rock, but the structure itself hung out over the sea, supported only by the gnarled trunks of two ancient trees used as diagonal cantilevering beams. The all-woman film crew's helicopter, naturally, had departed for the night, before Lowel's exhausted arrival at the clifftop. The woman in uniform had changed to a Greek actress in jeans. The RAF officer she was impersonating had been the only male exception ever granted by the Order of St Spyridon to live inside the convent, after the fall of Greece in 1941.

Lowel was stuck outside – in a cage 300 feet above the sea – because a boat would defeat the will of God, according to the gatekeeping nun. 'The community shall, of course, provide any stranger so separated with bedding and food. The tide will have made God's turn by four in the morning.'

A novice brought a platter of fresh fish, boiled lupin seeds, and sage-smoked kid. Jacqueline was allowed to stay and share it with him. She said encouragingly, 'On a clear road, we can be at the airport in Athens by six, and on the first flight out, in Thessaloniki by eight.'

'And no hotel rooms. That'll save the White House a dime.'

'A nickel,' she smiled. 'I only booked one hotel room. Let's eat.'

The young novice acted as a chaperone, with eyes

averted, on the safe side of a locked gate. 'So tell me the score on Meliti,' he said to Jacqueline as they started their meal.

'There isn't any.'

'No picture?'

'No nothing. The Mother Abbess showed me their attendance records herself, all the way back to 1925. There were dozens of Marias, but no girl with the surname of Meliti ever came here.'

'Maybe the spelling was wrong.'

'I checked all variations. All the young girls in Greece have long hair. One or two collected butterflies, but they weren't either beauties or academically brilliant.'

'What about their fathers?'

'I grasped at that straw. Several were killed by the Nazis, but none by the Colonels' Junta. Jack, believe me, my dear, and I'm terribly sorry, but in fox-hunting parlance, as that fool Teddy would say, we've drawn a blank cover.'

He had expected it – but refused to believe it without checking the books for himself. She brought them down from the convent library. Nothing was missing, except his target's attendance. The chaperone novice exchanged the books for his bedding. Jacqueline kissed him on the cheek. The novice turned scarlet. The gate clanged shut again. Without even one of his hand-rolled Bull Durhams, he was going to be gaoled in solitary until morning.

It was a divine judgement, he decided, for his coveting another man's ex-wife.

With young Campbell as his sole audience in the Sea-Fly, Powys had concluded the run-through of his impending speech. The most significant of his life. Even if he played Parliament with the virtuosity of a chapel organist, like his late father, three votes were the most he could hope for as majority.

'Passing Amersham, if you'd like your snack, Prime Minister.'

'Already?'

It didn't seem possible. Nor the thought of eating. Ten thousand speeches he must have made, and still his stomach rebelled – yet the sandwiches that Campbell was offering did look tempting, and the dear little woman went to such trouble. The salt of the earth, women like Mary Morris. He had enjoyed showing her off yesterday to Daniel Galbraith's chum . . .

'Sir?'

Campbell was still holding out the box with its Red Dragon rampant on the open lid. Each sandwich doily was carefully sealed.

'Not for me, Commander, but please help yourself.'

Campbell had the grace to grin; they had played out this tune as often as 'Land of My Fathers' by the Welsh miners' choir. Harrow School was approaching: what a distance there still was in this country between its classes . . . yet they could all share the enjoyment of an honest homemade sandwich. And damn his stage-fright stomach! Powys mentally recited a favourite verse from *Alice in Wonderland*, the Mock Turtle's song: *Will you, won't you, will you won't you, will you join the dance . . .?*

'I think I will, after all. What has she got for us this morning?'

'Your usual, sir. Chicken, this side. Pressed tongue, on that.'

'Are you sure? It looks the other way round to me.'

'I could always check, Prime Minister.'

The pilot grinned again. The Thames gleamed in the morning light.

'So you could, Commander. Well, go on then. A horse brass to a farthing, that one's tongue.'

The pilot's skilled fingers reached to unwrap the closest

113

doily. Powys's stomach perversely now felt like a sandwich. He looked forward to grasping it by its edges, easier to do with the rough crusts left on. And knobbly enough to crunch, yet small enough to pop in whole. A high-speed train was following with them, he noticed, down below, along the Oxford–London line. Campbell looked closely at the handwritten doily label.

'Your horse-brass wins, Prime Minister. It is tongue – oops! Sorry, sir. Security warning. Better not.'

Inexplicably, infuriatingly, just as Powys was about to take the chicken, his damn fool of a pilot yanked the box away, and scrunched closed the pressed-tongue doily in his hand.

Lowel lay awake in moonlight that cast shadows from the window bars on the walls of his cage-cell. In the long hours of isolation he had been thinking very little about his global mission and a great deal about his personal relations with Jacqueline Campbell. But when each of those hours struck on the convent clock, it reminded him of Bergitta. Since her death he had not allowed himself to sleep with a woman. The mental barrier was partly from respect for his late wife's memory – but if he was honest, it was also because he feared the pain that would come if he formed and then lost another deep attachment. His earlier pretended fear of divine judgement was just dodging the question. Inevitably the psychological barrier would have to be broken: he just didn't know how.

The last hour stopped striking. The guesthouse creaked. With only those two old worm-eaten beams holding the place up, every slightest breeze rising on the cliff-face had the threat of a hurricane.

'*Jack?*'

'Jacky?'

He heard her throaty giggle for their Abbot and Costello routine. And then he noticed, as she glided forward from the doorway, through the moonlight, that except for a bundle in her hand, and an icon crucifix on a thin gold chain around her neck, she was naked. He felt a lump in his throat, and a stirring in his groin. He tried to fight it, then relaxed. Nature had her own way of repairing psychic damage. He said in a hoarse croak, 'I thought this was a convent, Mrs Campbell, not a brothel.'

'Shhh.' She touched the icon and whispered in his ear. 'It's the nuns' namesake, St Spyridon. The head dragon gave me one, as an open warning against sin.' She slipped onto the sheet beside him. 'For God's sake get rid of those awful boxer shorts, only be quiet or the old trouts will hear us.'

Which wasn't easy, as they clung to each other on the edge of a cliff, surrounded by sleeping virgins, and tried to stifle their laughter – which got worse, the more her hands pretended to be helping with his shorts, but only succeeded in getting them hung up on his single-minded and totally humourless cock.

'But are you protected?' the organ's owner asked in a last rational moment.

'I'm wet as a herring,' she replied. 'I can't wait any longer. Just stuff it in.'

. . . After which graceful exchange, they lay together, breathing more calmly. Nothing seemed to have been stirred up on the virginal side of the gate – even when he rolled, or rather fell, off her and the whole guesthouse shook, and she said, 'Another shattered illusion. I thought just for once I really had felt the earth move.'

She gave a lazy smile and traced his eyebrow with a finger, then shivered suddenly and hugged him close.

'It's OK,' he told her. 'I'm not going anywhere before next time.'

'Sorry. Just someone walking on my grave.'

'I've had the same feeling.'

He kissed her mouth and then her breasts, to take

115

away whoever was doing the walking, whether it was Bergitta's shadow, or her ex-husband's, passing in that moment between them. His hand traced her belly and felt her inner muscles contract spasmodically below his cupped palm.

'What's this?' he said. 'Appendix?'

'Teddy passed on one of his little Caribbean adventures, a roaring PID – pelvic inflammatory disease. They had to go in and clean it out. I'm always protected, Jack darling. I'll never have children.'

The scar gleamed pure silver in the moonlight. It looked too small to have such huge consequences for a woman. He tried to ignore the voice in his head reminding him: Langley used this recognition feature for their profile of an assassin. Once again he attempted without success to fathom the female mind that could so coldbloodedly use the closest possible link between two humans as her weapon. Only another woman could truly understand his opponent's thought processes and probable next moves. But could he break security by taking Jacky into his full confidence? Should he?

That decision, and his pursuit, could wait till morning.

'If it's any help at all,' he said to her, 'you can have me full time, if you want, when this week is over.'

'It is a help. Bless you.' She stroked his hair, drew his face to her, and kissed him on the lips, as he felt the special flesh between her thighs slide over his, already open, seeking . . . 'But what I want this minute,' she said, 'is that next time.'

The causeway was exposed ten minutes ahead of the nun's prediction, by morning twilight, at 03.50. He was at the wheel of the Honda by 04.10. Jacqueline, in the passenger seat, leaned her head on his shoulder. The convent, with its pinnacle, was gone behind the basalt cliffs five minutes later, but its memories came with them.

'The car-hire girl got it half right,' he said. 'We had good love in Greece, even without our honeymoon radio.'

'We could have some music now, if you don't mind *hasapiko*.'

'Whatever. It plugs in the lighter.'

Jacqueline reached behind the seat and retrieved the set. 'No it doesn't.' She held up the radio cord: the plug was missing. ' "This is what it is to be Greek!" – but Jacky fix.'

His attention was on the road, waiting for the secret police ghost to come in on their tail. Somehow, with the casing of the lighter removed, and a nail file from her handbag, Jacky did fix. A rock station on the FM band fenceposted from poor reception as the Accord wound through the hills. She turned the dial and got a clear signal of mournful Balkan soul with tambourines which went without commercials for forty minutes until he merged into the Athens freeway, and the tambourines took a break for the five o'clock news.

'Making good time.' He had to raise his voice to compete with the guttural Greek of the announcer. 'And traffic is still easy, we'll hit that flight to Thessaloniki.'

'Jack, pull over.'

'If you need to go behind a bush –?'

'For God's sake! *Please*.'

He slammed the Honda to the verge, with all four disc brakes grinding. It wasn't just the tone of her voice. In the rear-view mirror, her face was stricken. Out of the radio gabble, the Greek announcer said the unmistakable words, 'Prime Minister Powys Great Britain.'

Lowel had heard that tone of voice all those years ago, when a US president was shot in Dallas; and he still had boy scout illusions.

'When?' he asked Jacqueline.

'Last night. They crashed into a train. And children –'

117

She began to cry. He held her close. 'Jacky, tell me the rest of it: what crashed?'

'His Sea-Fly,' she said between furious sobs. 'The rest is they've already dumped all the blame on my poor stupid fucking ex-bastard Teddy.'

13

It was no consolation to Lowel, as he comforted Jacqueline Campbell for the loss of a man she had once loved, that protecting Powys was not his responsibility, or that he had warned Sir Herbert Maxwell to take the threat seriously, or that the Yorkshireman's SIS, through a Whitehall public relations mouthpiece, was attributing 'this terrible accident to pilot error'. The reality was that 'death in a novel way' eluded all the apparatus of Britain's Security, to strike down the President's Welsh ally and friend, and because of that, the crucial vote in the British Parliament had failed, and because of that, the Zero-Zero Summit on total dismantling must also fail.

He sat in the rented Japanese car at the edge of the Greek freeway, with an English woman beside him, and while she regained her composure he tried to decide what to do next.

'Sorry, Jack.' She checked her appearance in the make-up mirror on the visor, then gave a wan smile and a squeeze of his arm. 'I've been a cow long enough: you'll want to make your next move. How can I help?'

'Change your House of Commons vote. After Powys's death, there won't be a hope in hell for the Agreement.'

'But they didn't vote,' she said. 'Parliament has adjourned until the State funeral, the day after tomorrow.'

A klaxon horn blasted. The Honda rocked from the slipstream of a passing container truck. The morning

119

traffic was heavier. The driver of a panel van, with a logo of a winged Hermes carrying flowers on the side, cut in suicidally close and gave Lowel the finger. A bilingual sign above it showed an exit for Athens Central. The ex-Colonels' secret police pals were back on the job. As he put the Honda in gear, and began easing off the shoulder, the Hermes van came with him.

'Finding the fastest goddamn way possible for us to go north,' he said to Jacqueline. 'That's how you can help.'

The centre of the town of Meliti was a square full of shorn sheep; with a town hall on one side and, facing it, an establishment called *Cafeneion Van Flit*. A portrait captioned 'Amerika General Freeing Greece From Albania Reds' hung over the heads of the coffee drinkers, backgammon players, and sheep-shearers sitting at tables outside. The bandit undercover thug from the Athens car-hire was at the table closest to the portrait. Lowel saw that the picture was a blow-up of a US Army glossy black-and-white, corner date-stamped October/49, that must have been hand-painted some time later by a drunk church artist on his day off.

'James Van Fleet never looked so good in *Life*,' he said to Jacqueline. 'Let's try city hall.'

They threaded their way across the square between the pens of bleating bald sheep and the rank-smelling, heaped piles of filthy fleece. In one corner, a dog with a distant trace of Berov's collie was herding sheep, one by one, through a ramp to be slaughtered. At the centre of the square, a man's frock-coated statue with its base plaque obscured by the wool, and most of the rest of it by pigeons, gazed north with a corroded eye. One of the arms on the multiple signpost pointed in the same direction to YUGOSLAVIA BORDER 5 KILOMETRES AND BROD.

A street opening in line with it revealed snow-capped mountains ranged behind the old buildings of the town. Lowel had gone a few paces past the sign when he sensed that Jacqueline was no longer with him. He looked back to see her staring at the peaks.

'They'd be a fine climb,' he said; 'I wouldn't mind coming back as a civilian.'

'Not the mountains, Jack. The name. My father told me that his family originally came from Brod. I've never even seen their pictures in an album, but just across a border like that, you feel a strange sort of tug.'

She caught up with him and, with the sheep pens out of the way, they walked on arm-in-arm to the town hall. Inside, they found a painted hand with its index finger directing them to *Arkiv*. The archivist was a middle-aged male with a thick Macedonian dialect and breath that stank worse than the bales of wool outside his fly-specked window.

'Birth, marriage, or death?'

The man asked this via Jacqueline, at the same time leaning forward across the counter. She recoiled, protecting her nostrils with a hand.

'Birth,' Lowel replied through her, 'the year was –'

'Ten drachmas,' said the archivist. After pocketing the coins, he took down a maroon ledger from a shelf and opened it. 'Year?'

'1956. And the month is –'

'Ten drachmas.'

The procedure repeated through April, and 17th, to: 'Name?'

'We want Meliti.' Behind her hand, Jacqueline added to Lowel, 'Have another ten ready for the Maria.'

But the baksheesh routine was broken. The archivist made an expansive gesture that took in first the worn office furnishings and then the grimy window.

'This is Meliti. All is Meliti.'

Jacqueline explained: 'No, her name was Meliti. She was the daughter of a Professor Panos Meliti.'

'You want Panos Meliti?' The archivist gave a sigh that would have tarnished silver and walked out from behind his counter past the index-finger sign to the town hall's front door. He made another sweeping gesture. '*There* is Panos Mario Meliti!'

Since the nuns of St Spyridon, Lowel had been sure it was coming: but not as such a wide-open April fool. The archivist was pointing at the pigeon-shit statue.

'Our town's most famous citizen!' The official plucked a gaudy pamphlet off a display rack of tourist literature and presented it with a theatrical flourish, and last rapid-fire stench, to Jacqueline. 'Also, Macedonia's greatest actor, born April 17, 1856, dead with all his family at the hands of the butchering Turks, in 1904, the cost of this tragedy to our nation . . .'

Had an obvious price. The archivist's own hand was still waiting.

Now Lowel was leaving the Greek interior, none of the ex-Junta's cops seemed to give a damn how he did it. When Jacqueline bribed a one-toothed Meliti taxi driver with triple pay to race his dilapidated Hugo chariot through the mountain gorges against the sun, no one followed.

They made it alive to the lakeside town of Arnissa, three minutes early for a train that got them in to Thessaloniki by four that afternoon. Their Olympic direct flight for London was scheduled to depart at eight in the evening; allowing for airport clearance, they had two hours to kill. He was only thinking of finding a coin-op shower; it was her brilliant idea to make use of their previously reserved hotel.

'Let me at least try and talk them into it,' she said. 'They'll charge your card anyway, for a no-show.'

'At the height of the season? Good luck!'

But as though to apologize for the trip's fiasco, Greece opened its doors – or the Makedonia Palace did, in exchange for their passports, with a third-floor front room that had complimentary bottles of the best retsina, twin His and Hers bathrooms and a magnificent view of the Bay. Jacqueline smiled.

'I was wrong about the White House getting this for a nickel, but at least we don't have to flip for the tub!'

'We could live here a week for what it costs to polish the cabin door handles on Air Force One,' he said. 'Go ahead with your bath. I'm going down to the desk for any newspapers in English, and catch up with the world before I tear Langley apart with my bare hands.'

'Couldn't it wait?' She took his left hand with its missing fingers. 'In an hour from now, Jack darling, the cruel world won't let you go.'

She was right about that. About most things, he thought, watching her competent pilot's hand gently stroke the scarred roughness where his own abruptly ended. Her unique mixture of optimism with that hardheaded appreciation of reality had an appeal he could not put into words.

'Sure,' he said, 'for one hour, Jacky, it can wait.'

They went their separate ways to the His and Hers showers and he stood under the deluxe massage nozzle to let the pulsing jets of water strip off the tension as well as the grime of constant travel. Over the sound of the shower he heard her humming one of the all-alike bouzouki tunes from their honeymoon radio in the Honda. He thought of her surprise nude visit in the moonlight to the convent guesthouse – and got an instant raging hard-on that tried to smash its one-eyed way through the shower curtain.

Leaving the water running, he slipped out of the His enclosure and into Hers, with three wet footprints as the only evidence of passage on the expensive carpet . . .

Her back was to him, legs apart; her face tilted up, her eyes shut. He stood for a moment, watching the rivulets running down her tanned shoulders, following the lithe contours of her muscles, before forming a tiny vortex disappearing into the white cleft between her buttocks. He took half a pace forward: without warning thrust through, between her thighs, and up –

'*Wet as a herring!*' . . . he said in her ear, and felt her startled inner flesh respond, and open, then squeeze around him . . . 'Wasn't that the expression?'

The world began intruding while they still lay in relaxed exhaustion on the satin sheets of the king-sized bed, and the horns of the traffic for the evening rush came in through the open French windows from the balcony overlooking the esplanade beside the bay. With the noise of reality, he looked at this extraordinary woman lying beside him and made his decision.

'I need your help, Jacky.'

'I thought you'd never ask.' She fingered the icon crucifix on the chain around her neck and said with a lazy smile, 'When it comes to no sin, old Spyridon seems to fall down on the job. But thank God, my sweet Jack, you don't.'

'Thanks for the compliment, but not that kind of help – although maybe it is, in a way.'

When they were dressed, he took her out to the balcony where the traffic sounds could mask their conversation from any of the Greek Colonels' left-over bugs. He told her fully about the Meliti file, and the sexual poison killings in Washington, which had now been duplicated in Britain, and his pursuit of a female phantom; and finally, the near impossibility for him, as a man, to understand and so predict the workings of such a ruthless female mind.

'Like the whore with a heart of gold,' said Jacqueline, at the end of it.

'I don't follow.'

'All men think sex is something women should be grateful for – whether you think it or not. Don't try to understand, Jack darling. I owe it to poor bloody Teddy. Of course I'll help.'

At which point the phone rang. Reluctantly, he answered.

'We regret to disturb,' said a voice with a too sleek, Latin lover accent, 'but you will wish to know the hotel has been advised that extreme airport security measures have been imposed. Accordingly, guests with flight bookings should arrive there with as much time as possible before boarding.'

'Thanks. We can be gone in fifteen minutes. Arrange my bill and order a car – a limousine, please, not a cab.'

'But naturally a limousine.'

The voice made it seem as though cabs were only used for taking out the hotel garbage. At the lobby desk they met the voice's Latin owner, a young man with the same excessive regard for his hairdo as Red Murphy. But the bill was ready, with Lowel's passport.

'Five figures for two hours!' He signed off the outrageous billing slip and said to Jacqueline, 'I guess it won't hurt if we don't do the conversion.'

'You could say that about a lot of things, Mr Lowel.' She gave him a lewd wink and asked the young Latin, 'My passport too, please.'

'But naturally, Madame.' With an ostentatious flourish, the desk clerk took it from the drawer and rifled the document's pages long enough to show who was boss in these situations . . . then handed the passport across, 'With our hope that you have had a relaxing stay with us, Madame, this afternoon.'

'Heavenly,' she said, and as they walked out to the limousine: 'Snide little shit.'

The airport of Greece's second city was hell. The Greek Army ringed the terminal, and mountains of baggage were stacked up outside the doors. After running the gauntlet of robot bomb-detectors and prowling sniffer dogs, passengers were being allowed inside single file. Lowel paid off the limousine and said to Jacqueline, 'Keep your fingers crossed that this is only more "What it is to be Greek" – and not for vowing a thousand years of vengeance to the Turks.'

A passing paratrooper didn't find that funny. The barrel of his automatic gestured them both crudely into line for the sniffer dogs. Forty minutes later, at the luggage mountain, having only a single carry-on each didn't help: the officials devoted the same amount of time to one item as they did for a French family loaded down with plastic sacks of Acropolis paperweights and white-skirted police dolls. On a clock overhead, time was starting to count: another hour had gone by.

'Passports?'

Things might speed up. This point in the procedure had two wickets for officials – but only one was manned, by a short squat female with black butch eyebrows and cropped blonde hair.

'At least we know our Meliti file doesn't have a kisser like that one,' he said with a grin to Jacky.

'My chauvinist pet, if you think sex only traps with a pretty face –'

'You!'

Jacqueline had held out her passport as first in line, but the woman was pointing at Lowel instead. He handed her his document. She took it with a grunt.

'American?' The butch blonde looked at the embossed eagle of the US national seal as though it was a vulture eating week-old carrion. She didn't like his photo any better, picking at the edges with a tool like a dental scraper to check the glue.

126

'Russia!'

Here comes trouble, he thought – but just to be awkward, his recent Soviet visa stamp pleased her. With the kind of smile the Bitch of Belsen must have given her human-skin lampshades, she returned his passport.

'Now you!'

Jacqueline offered her blue-black folder with the gold Lion and Unicorn, which got another vulture treatment.

'British?' The blonde stared at Jacqueline with a look of open disbelief, mixed with a sexual component that was barely more covered. 'Where you were born?'

'In London.'

'Where in London?'

'The maternity department of St Thomas's Hospital. That was on the third-floor west, at that time, I believe.'

The blonde accepted the third-floor sarcasm at face value and frowned her way, a page at a time, through the rest of the passport as though searching for something specific. A television monitor next to the clock showed their direct Olympic flight with only ten minutes to boarding.

'Where your parents were born?'

'My mother was English.'

'And father?'

'A British subject.'

'But born?' The blonde held the passport pressed open in front of her with a thick hand and looked up at Jacqueline.

'He was born in Yugoslavia.'

'So! And you have been in Cyprus!' The woman slapped the passport page.

'Two years ago, yes.'

'In the so-called Turkish State of Cyprus?'

'As well as the Greek state. I had business in both sections.'

127

'And in Turkey this following year.' The woman pointed at the stamp on the next page.

'I'm a pilot. You can see, I travel all over the world.' Jacqueline touched the passport. The blonde grabbed it back.

'You travel. Then you know entry to Greece is criminal with Turkey.'

The monitor showed five minutes to boarding. Jacqueline began an explanation in Greek.

'You speak Greek? Go there!' The woman shouted the last command, summoning two security police, guarding a closed door behind her booth.

Lowel stepped in. 'I'm an official of the American government. I can vouch –'

'Jack, don't. It'll only make them worse.' Jacqueline turned to him, as the guards approached. 'I've been through this hassle a dozen times. There's no urgency for my leaving. I can talk my way out for the next flight. You have to go on.' She gave him a kiss on the cheek and pressed an object into his hand. 'A key for my front door, when you can use it – just be sure to remember the bloody burglar alarm.'

'Next!'

The blonde barked. The guards closed ranks. The door opened in front of Jacqueline. She turned to him with the usual brave smile. He called, 'Good luck!' with the usual moral support. The shuffling line of anxious fellow travellers had the usual half-pleased, half-scared-shitless look: She's been grabbed. We're saved!

Until the last moment before take-off he hoped that Jacqueline might make it with him but, when she didn't, he took refuge in the press instead. The first-class cabin had that day's *Times* from London and New York, plus half a dozen other major papers: by the time the flight reached altitude over the Adriatic he was successfully immersed in their versions of events since Powys's death.

The Prime Minister was lying in state in Westminster Abbey; at least his remains were: Lowel was only too well aware how little would be left of a human body from the combined effects of collision and fire. Following their last use at the hands of the pathologists, Lieutenant Commander Edward Campbell's remains weren't getting a state funeral, but would be transferred from the forensic lab in North London for a private burial in a small churchyard near the family home in Kirkbeam, in the Scottish county of Dumfriesshire. Campbell's professional reputation had already been laid to rest by the press which had leaked the information that since his recent divorce the pilot had taken to drinking heavily in the local pubs around Chequers and had skipped his last physical.

The 'novel death' threat hadn't leaked – but that must only be a matter of time. Under the guise of grief speeches, the jockeying for leadership in Powys's party was already intense, and the other side of the House of Commons wasn't sitting on its hands.

'British signing of the Dismantling Agreement,' according to the *New York Times*' editorial page, 'is still the focal issue on both sides of the aisle at Westminster, and in this country as well, dependent as Washington and Moscow are on the so-called second-tier nations' acceptance of and participation in the larger treaty.'

The *Washington Post*'s concern was '. . . mounting right-wing opposition in the United States to the concept of bi-national crews aboard ballistic submarines'.

The tabloids put it more bluntly:

According to this flying-saucer version, the Soviets already had remote-controlled surplus subs permanently anchored to the deepest parts of the ocean floor: '. . . they will stay there forever, five miles down, loaded with ICBMs which can be upgraded by super deep-sea vehicles the Kremlin has secretly been designing for the job!'

He pitied Galbraith, facing such bullshit.

'Would you care for our wine list, sir, before your meal?'

A cabin attendant was waiting with the list. Her full mouth, with a slight smile, reminded him of Jacky, stranded – and then the little voice in his head said, Is this what *She* looks like? Before he also remembered Jacqueline's caustic warning about the male habit of automatically linking sexuality with facial attractiveness.

'No thanks,' he told the attendant, 'but you can tell me if we're on schedule.'

'A few minutes ahead, sir, we're crossing Venice now. We should land at Heathrow in about one hour and a half.'

'So I could make a call on the Euro-cellular net?'

'Yes, sir. If you don't have your own instrument, the booth is located at the front of the cabin.'

'Great, I'll use it.'

'I'm going up to the cockpit. I can show you if you wish.'

The girl's smile widened invitingly, indicating a longer trip together might be possible in London Town. Tits and ass, before Viscumin on the mouthpiece! Or just more chauvinism on his part? The phone was beside a window with a spectacular sunset view of the advancing Alps. He got through to the Embassy switchboard on his first try and asked the duty operator to arrange a car to meet his flight.

'Certainly, Mr Lowel. I'm glad you called. We have an important message –'

'Not over this line,' he said sharply. 'Send it in writing to Heathrow.'

He hung up the unit. No one else wanted it, so he stayed for a while to stretch his legs and watch the Alps turning from gold to purple, then he walked back to his seat and made a switch from what was undoubtedly a perfectly normal plate of roast pheasant to last-minute grilled trout. And then made an equal fool of himself from straight black coffee to tea.

They began their descent over Orleans, fifty miles southwest from the city of light which was Paris in the gathering dark. The Channel was cloudy, and England was raining on Summer Time. He set his watch back for the last hour change and obeyed the girl with the nice smile when she told him to be a good boy about landing.

'Thank you for flying with us on Olympic, sir. Please do so again.'

Because the cabin girl hadn't poisoned him, he gave her a farewell grin and charged head down through a cloudburst for the next round of British bureaucratic mayhem. But Heathrow performed flawlessly: all the servants were civil. He was through in ten minutes flat. Dawson, the black chief of security for the Embassy, was waiting beyond the barrier.

'When I told the switchboard kid to send the message in writing,' Lowel said, 'I didn't mean you.'

'That's no problem. How was the trip?'

Dawson knew enough not to spill an important message out for the world to hear. They began to walk towards the entrance. Lowel replied as casually, 'Good, as trips go. It seems a hell of a lot longer than forty hours since I left. I'll swap you my carry-on for the print-out.'

131

'This isn't in print.'

Dawson's face had that shit-in-the-fan look, meaning things were fluid. When the same look got down to Embassy drivers, heads had to be rolling! This driver opened the rear door. Lowel got in. Dawson followed and closed the door. The limousine began moving.

'OK,' he said, 'let's have it.'

Dawson cleared his throat, and touched his tie. The limousine emerged from the canopy in front of the terminal; the rain beat on the car roof with a relentless drumming. Lowel had to raise his voice above it.

'Come on, man – it's no sweat if I've been fired. I'm not even on pension.'

'Not you,' said Dawson. 'Mrs Campbell.'

'Jacqueline was on our payroll? I don't believe it.'

'In a luggage bombing. She was killed. Jack, I'm so sorry.'

14

Night:

London

Action was the only antidote to grief, yet in one of the darkest hours of his life Lowel found himself not back home in Oregon, where he could beat the living hell out of his body on white water or the slopes of a volcano, but locked in a sealed room in London, where all he had to do was think . . .

About this Hi-Burst message from the President, demanding an immediate return call; about what was behind a cryptic diplomatic note from the Soviet Embassy wanting the same thing in polite language; about why Maxwell had refused to send over the SIS investigative reports on the Powys crash; about what bastard in Langley –

Finally, it was impossible to think of anything but Jacky.

The key she gave him lay on the Command Room desk in front of him, and he remembered her smile, as she looked back at him. . . remembered her humour, in those clashes with nuns and petty officials, when his reaction was to blow it by playing tough . . . remembered her toughness, when the Greek macho beer-belly with the Uzi at Koropion got verbally sliced up – by a woman! And he remembered her woman's body, taking the initiative in bed but, in the shower, agreeing to surrender . . .

Agreeing to be with him for the rest of his life.

Tears burned his eyes. He slammed his head on the desk, pounded his fists to block out the image of the luggage-bomb exploding –

Action! He went through to the adjoining bathroom. He filled the basin with cold water and stuck his head in it so long that he would have held it there longer, to end everything, except that reflex took over.

He came up again, gasping.

Action. He dried his face and went back to the desk. He took out the Presidential Finding with its purple stamp of *carte blanche* approval. He broke the circuit on the electronic door lock to permit access. He punched a button on the speaker phone.

'Dawson, are you there?'

'Yes, Mr Lowel.'

'Come in here, please. I've cleared the lock.'

Dawson entered with the caution of psychiatric personnel dealing with a dangerous patient. The Embassy's chief of security still had that How do I break it? look on his face.

'I want to take certain steps. Read that.' Lowel pushed the Finding across the desk. 'And drop the mister, stick with Jack.'

Dawson gave a terse smile of relief at not having to control a nutcase. He read the Finding and returned it.

'Any question about my authority?'

'Not by me, Jack.'

'Good. Then here's step one: get hold of Maxwell at SIS. Tell him unless he wants the Intelligence Mutual Co-operation Treaty between our countries rendered void by the President tomorrow morning, I want an appointment at his Century House office in one hour, and when we have it I want the complete file on Prime Minister Powys's crash. Clear?'

'One hour is going to be midnight. Otherwise clear.'

'Let me worry about Sir Herbert's beauty sleep. Step two: from any of our military units in Britain, I want a pair of choppers that both work. I want them guarded and operational twenty-four hours, with back-up flight

134

crews. I want them for six days, starting now, and for my exclusive use.'

'That's clear. Also easy.'

'You haven't heard step three. I want a B1 bomber on the same terms.'

'That ain't easy.' Dawson's expressive face got its psychiatric look again. 'There aren't any of those supersonics in the British Isles, and the ones outside are booked in on strategic air alert.'

'Correction,' said Lowel; 'there is one here. It's at Farnborough for the Air Show, and I doubt that SAC lets it fly payloaded.'

'It's your Finding. Do I really want to hear step four?'

'More than I want to have to say it. And you can refuse, because this isn't covered by that piece of paper. I'd like you to return Jacqueline Campbell's body to this country for me. She doesn't have any family. With her former husband's death, I'm the only –'

He stopped. The action engine had run out of steam.

'As far as I'm concerned,' said Dawson, 'that request has the force of law. I'm sorry to press, Jack, but will you want a church funeral? Burial?'

He realized the engine that drove his emotions wasn't just out of steam: it had frozen solid. 'She was a flyer,' he said. 'She wouldn't want to be grounded. Cremation, please. No religious ceremony. I'll take her ashes.'

'You bet.'

Dawson squeezed his shoulder and left the Command Room. Alone once more, Lowel was prepared to act, but what fuelled him now must be ice-cold reason: because if it took love, the machine inside him would never run again.

Daniel Galbraith was attending a July Fourth gala, and so was unavailable on Hi-Burst, which was fine with Lowel: from here on, the only safe communication across the

Atlantic was going to be face to face. His first priority in London was Maxwell; the Soviet Embassy could wait. The message panel in the Command Room flashed 'Chopper Ready'. He went up to the roof.

The rain had stopped. The air over the old City was crystal clear and still not completely dark, so close to the longest day of the year. For him, this was the longest – he forced the intruding thought down below the surface. Dawson had carried out his instructions. The first of the helicopters he ordered was already on the roof; the second hovered over the lawn behind the Embassy, lights winking. The combined beating of their rotors made the whole building vibrate. He flipped a coin: tails. He ordered the landed chopper off and brought the second one in, then boarded it. If there were going to be any more 'incidents' organized by third parties against his aircraft, they were going to have to be psychic to pick the right one!

The two machines flew in tandem, eastward, past the cross on top of St Paul's. On a longer flight he would have ordered changes of station, turn and turn about for the lead, but this hop was too short. They swung in an arc, leaving Tower Bridge with its necklace of lights to port, then crossed the river. Approaching his destination, for the pilots' training, he reversed the take-off procedure, sending in the other chopper first, and at the last minute landing himself.

The reception on the roof of the Government Communications Bureau was businesslike this time. The medalled commissionaire that went with the 'Century House' and 'I say!' bullshit had been put back in the closet. Ryder, the burly tail from Antwerp, was waiting alone by the circle of blue lights surrounding the red-lit cross that marked the landing pad at night. The rain had stopped, but large puddles went up in spray as the first of Lowel's newly acquired helicopters set down. The second stayed on hover until he was safely disembarked.

'Ryder,' said Ryder, stepping forward with his hand out. 'I'm told we're back on the co-operation track.' The Englishman indicated the paired armed choppers by nodding his head. 'Frankly, I'm glad to hear it.'

'Me too,' Lowel answered. 'And I got your name our last time around.'

'All I got was a rocket up my arse from Sir Herbert, for your deep lift dodge at Covent Garden.' Ryder grinned and put on a North Country accent: 'Master had to break dinner wi' Royals. He in't best pleased, but you'll know from last time's bark, yon's worse than his bite.'

Not taking 'last time's' threat against Powys seriously was fatal. As Lowel left the roof he wondered whether Ryder's new frankness was the man's way of indicating civil war inside SIS over the Prime Minister's death. When they reached the top-floor office, Ryder stayed clear of the battlefield by waiting in the hall.

Inside the office, the head of British security was wearing evening dress and his Yorkshire granite expression. 'We don't take kindly to blackmail in this country, Mr Lowel. Diplomatic or otherwise. You may sit down.'

He took the same chair as before. With no sun glare off the Thames, there was no disadvantage; both their faces were equally illuminated from the lamps in the room. He said, 'If you mean my message about cancelling the Co-operation Treaty, Sir Herbert, it was a statement of fact. Refusal to exchange information on possible assassination attempts against either country's leadership negates the Treaty under clause one.'

Maxwell grunted, 'Nitpicking over legalities is for our lawyers to decide.'

'Not as far as my President's concerned.'

The Yorkshireman's pale eyes did their unblinking

routine. Lowel stared back. The silence between them got longer. Maxwell's knuckles whitened.

'I have the crash file, Sir Herbert.'

Ryder's appearance at the office door broke the stalemate.

'Well put it here, man,' his superior snapped. As the folder was exchanged, he added to Lowel, 'You'll find no more evidence in this of poison plots than you did in Greece.' Maxwell's voice became gruffer. 'And you have my deep sympathy for that personal tragedy – but we didn't plant the bomb for your lady, if that's what you're thinking. Unlike your maniacs at CIA, we don't go off half-cocked in this country.'

'Jacqueline –' he felt something twist in his gut as he said her name – 'there is obviously no connection whatsoever between Mrs Campbell's death and the response of any branch of the United States government. Frankly, Sir Herbert, I don't see either the logic or relationship of our present problems in your last remark.'

'Are you trying to tell me that Langley's setting up a will-o'- the-wisp biography that almost exactly mirrors Mrs Campbell's was mere coincidence?' The Yorkshireman leaned back in his chair with a look of open disbelief. 'The "logical relationship" is the same as it was between young John Kennedy calling for a nuclear moratorium with Russia in 1963 and ending up four months later with a CIA operative's bullet in his head. That's what you people in Washington are really after, with these crocodile tears for Powys. You want to say, SIS did it! – and then your new Sir Galahad can cut off the missile supply to British submarines, whether Parliament votes for the Dismantling Agreement or not. Well, sir, read to your heart's content and tell your poker-playing relative: it won't wash.'

With which extraordinary diplomatic speech, Maxwell stood up and walked out, leaving Lowel seething with the open file, and Ryder open-mouthed.

'Strewth!' he exclaimed, as the door slammed. 'That's one for the book. Jack, you must believe, I'm deeply sorry –'

'Don't bother apologizing. There's enough paranoia on our side, although the thought of SIS complicity in Prime Minister Powys's death hadn't occurred to me before Sir Herbert said there was no evidence of poisoning.'

He began to read the file. Ryder came across and sat on a corner of the desk. 'It doesn't say there's no evidence. If you'll look at the bottom line, the way the forensic people phrase it is, "not possible to be conclusive yet".'

What the experts said before the bottom line was '. . . Had the recovered lymphoid tissue been in a normal state, the presence of Viscumin in molecular quantity would currently be determinable through the process of microscopy known as immuno-cytochemistry, using the enzyme, horseradish peroxidaise. However, given the severe charring of the sample, further testing with ELISA (enzyme-linked immunosorbent assay) will be required and it may never be possible to be conclusive.'

'Without getting in over our heads on their ELISA,' Lowel said, 'one question: whose tissue are we talking about?'

'The Prime Minister's presumably.'

'I didn't know Powys had a chopper licence.'

'Ah,' the light began to dawn for Ryder. 'You mean the pilot, Campbell.'

'Sure. I don't see any test for the presence of Viscumin in his body.'

'If Forensic didn't test him,' Ryder said grimly, 'heads will fall. I'll get right on it.'

'Good. Where did the incident happen?'

'This side of Amersham. About halfway from Chequers.'

Lowel remembered the area roughly: the two army

139

camps, Harrow School, Teddy offering him the box with the red Welsh dragon –

'The in-flight sandwiches,' he said to Ryder. 'I warned that goddamn Campbell. A woman made them daily, at a tea-shop in the village. Her name was Mary something; it was written on the box.'

'Mary Morris,' Ryder answered, checking a list in the file. 'The locals all got security vetting because of the PM's country walks. It says Morris is lesbian but harmless. The village grande dame living next door, Hughes-Beauchamps – that's Beecham – doesn't like little Miss Mary's choice of girl-friends much. Revving their sports cars after hours. She told the vetter she has pictures to prove it. Without knickers on, I shouldn't wonder!'

'A white Maserati,' said Lowel, 'the day I was down there. I told Maxwell to check it.'

'He never mentioned.'

'There's a whole pile Sir Herbert hasn't done. I'm going to see these women.'

'At one in the morning? Three, by the time we drive out there. It's none of my business, but it must have been one hell of a terrible day. What about some sleep for you?'

'Lying flat on my back in the dark isn't going to help with anything,' Lowel answered. 'But thanks for the thought. And no driving. I'll collect you here on the roof at 06.00.'

Ryder escorted him up to it, adding a final reminder. 'Heading west out of London on a working morning, tell your pilots to look sharp filing their flight plans. They can do it now if you want; we're on Data Link with Heathrow.'

'Fine,' Lowel said. 'Now point me at the Soviet Embassy.'

The piece of England that belonged to Russia was located in the genteel collection of Victorian mansions known as Kensington Palace Gardens, off Kensington High Street, west of Hyde Park. The noise by-laws of central London forced Lowel to ground his helicopter fleet and go by car. A choice of a standard Chrysler and a battle-plated Lincoln, with drivers waiting, and engines running, was in the Embassy's underground garage. He flipped his coin, got heads for the Lincoln, and took the Chrysler.

It swept him silently under the branches of the lime trees and glided to a halt among the mass of diplomatic licence plates parked at the kerbs. The Russians were located at Number 13. He told his driver to wait and walked to a pair of impressive iron gates where he had to wake an unimpressive, sleeping Soviet guard.

'I'm here to see your Secretary for Cultural and Artistic Affairs,' Lowel said in Russian.

'*Da*. Certainly. Who are you?' The guard must be a man, but he had the startled eyes and high cheek colour of a kid of eighteen.

'Lowel.' He spelled it out. The kid-guard wrote it down laboriously, one cyrillic capital letter at a time.

'And your nationality, comrade?'

'American. The Artistic Secretary wants to see me. I don't have his name.'

'Comrade Strelnikov. You are sure he wishes to see at – ?' the kid checked his sentry-hutch clock – 'now is 01.45?'

'I'm sure as soon as possible.'

'Takes one moment.' The kid turned to an intercom, but added over his shoulder, 'There has been party, if you understand?'

Meaning everyone had toasted themselves blind under the table. In Lowel's experience, such occasions were the Red Inquisition's most wide-awake moments. Sure enough, the kid turned back, looking greatly relieved.

'Artistic and Cultural Secretary will meet you in lobby, comrade: please to wait.'

An electronic lock on a side gate clicked open. Lowel

passed through and on up the sweeping drive to the mansion. The next armed guard was well over legal age and let him into the building with the usual Russian look of suspicion for foreigners on their own foreign turf. The lobby had a traditional winter landscape of a three-horse troika hung on the right side for conservatives: for the progressives, a Chagall of two rustic peasant lovers surrealistically screwing in space was on the left.

'Mr Lowel,' a deep voice said in English behind him. 'Boris Strelnikov.'

Kliment Berov's man of culture in Britain was six-three and brick shithouse. He walked across the lobby's Astrakhan carpet and extended a size 14 hand.

'So sorry to have kept you.'

'I'm sorry for the hour.' Lowel shook the huge hand and felt his own carpal bones rearranged. 'Your message said meeting was important, and I have a full day ahead.'

'The one behind you has been more than full already. Shall we talk where Sir Maxwell and SIS can't listen?'

The KGB art-lover opened a door beyond the Chagall. Inside it there was a second door, faced with an anti-microwave metallic grid. Strelnikov ushered Lowel through this to a space like a radio studio without a mike. When both doors were shut, the massive Russian said, 'Mister Coffee?'

A percolator with Joe Dimaggio's signature was plugged in on a Plexiglas table. Lowel filled a cup and took it back. Nature was finally taking over; his body was starting to run down. He said, 'No Maxwell. Let me see Berov's message.'

'Not in writing, and no names. This is information only, for your head.' The Russian gave a wide smile, as though he had granted a favour.

'I can't hack riddles at two in the morning,' said Lowel. 'Feed it straight.'

'OK. Straight is, one: screening arrangements for

Yalta are already in place. Two is: the man with the dog wishes to meet you the day after –' Strelnikov corrected himself – 'with the time, this now means tomorrow, in Berlin. Three is: a man with red hair visited Athens before you. Four is: deepest condolences are extended for the tragedy that happened later in the north of Greece. Five is: exercise great care yourself.'

The Secretary for Cultural Affairs finished his warning with another beam of satisfaction. Can it be true? Lowel wondered. Murphy was in Athens?

'Which side of the Wall?' was the question he asked Strelnikov.

'Mr Lowel, with *glasnost*, there is no wall.' The huge Russian gave his broadest smile yet. 'But your meeting will be in the part of Berlin we used to call our own – before the Four Power Agreement came to an end with the suicide of the Nazi criminal Rudolf Hess.'

'I can make it sometime tomorrow in East Berlin,' Lowel said, 'but tell the man with the dog he'll have to be patient because I don't know yet exactly when I can be back on this side of the Atlantic. Thank him especially for his point four. On his last one, I'm already looking out.'

The US Embassy driver was looking totally pissed off when Lowel returned to the tranquil normality of Kensington Palace Gardens. The man stood under the moonlit lime trees, staring in disbelief at the shadowed front end of the Chrysler.

'Some joker's put a fucking boot on,' said the driver. 'Excuse my language, but with diplomatic plates! And at this time of night! What the hell's going on?'

Speechless, the man gestured at the Jags and Porsches under the No Parking signs, but all safe at the kerbs with their diplomatic owners' immunity from prosecution.

'I just went for a leak, down to the public john, and

143

take a boo at the sports job by the corner.' The driver pointed at an illuminated GENTS casting a faint glow through the grime of its glass across a sleek car bonnet half hidden by the plane trees. 'I was only gone a minute, I swear. Well maybe a couple. And now look at this!'

Lowel moved forward. The front left wheel of the Chrysler was locked in one of the yellow steel clamps ordinarily used to nail less privileged traffic offenders. The driver squatted and spat in disgust.

'Bloody –!'

The next word was gone in the reverberating blast of an explosion. Silence followed for a timeless moment. Then the rattling of yellow metal shrapnel raining down on the sidewalk. Then moaning from the driver, alive, but already in shock. Then the squealing of Pirelli oversized radials, as a white hull raced by the shattered Chrysler. Sprawled on the paving stones, half stunned, probably saved from death only because of the blocking body of his driver, in the moonlight, Lowel still made out a D and 33 on the rear licence plate of a Maserati.

And the person behind its steering column was a woman.

15

Lowel woke with the shock of disorientation that came from sleeping in strange surroundings, after taking a knock-out pill. The chief of security's concerned face was looking down at him. Dawson's dark skin was accentuated by the white walls and ceiling of the Embassy's sick-bay.

'How are you feeling?'

'I'm OK.' He sat up and realized that was a relative statement. His body felt as though it had spent the past four hours crushed at the bottom of a football huddle. 'How's my driver?'

'You know head wounds. The MO says only fifty-fifty, and if the poor bastard does make it, his family may wish he hadn't.'

'His family. Jesus Christ.' Lowel swung his legs off the cot. The ceiling light fixture and the eye chart on an opposite wall did slow half circles, then stabilized. 'Did we get anywhere with the licence plate?' he asked Dawson.

'We didn't, but your new SIS buddy did. Here's the owner's address. I guarantee you won't like it.' The station chief passed across a motor-vehicle search pink slip.

Lowel read the address aloud, '58 Knightsbridge, SW1. I can see it means money, but we knew that from the car. What kind of money, is the question.'

'Francs,' Dawson answered. 'That address is the Embassy of France.'

145

Lowel's head was throbbing. 'France came on side for dismantling before I left Washington. The President had just got the word in person, from Paris. For the French to renege by taking me out at this stage of international relations would be crazy.'

'I'm no diplomat,' said Dawson, 'but these are the same folks who brought you a blown-up Greenpeace yacht in nuke-free New Zealand. From a national image point of view, that wasn't exactly sane.'

Lowel walked stiffly through to the sick-bay head for a pee. The French secret service, like its political masters, for years had had what would be diagnosed acute mental illness in a single individual. The government in France had been operating with a schizophrenic split between a succession of right-wing premiers and leftist presidents. Or vice versa. One thing was certain, he concluded, as he flushed the john, for all parties in Paris, a France without nuclear weapons would be short on *la gloire*.

He went back to the sick-bay door and said to Dawson, 'The woman I saw driving the car – when you say, "same folks", do you mean she was also involved in that Greenpeace bombing? Do we have an ID?'

The security chief nodded. 'Jeanne-Marie Claron. The press calls her "the woman who got away". She directed Sûreté operations in the South Pacific from Tahiti. Part of the deal that was cut between Paris and Auckland was her name never shows up on a court subpoena. Ryder at SIS says she showed up in London the day you left for Greece.'

'Which was the day Prime Minister Powys died.'

'Yeah,' said Dawson, 'but no tie-in there. Brit Immigration swears Claron didn't land at Dover until after his crash.'

Which would mean she could not have been the woman in black sunglasses at Chequers. But she drove a Maserati. 'Everything misfits too goddamn neatly,' he told Dawson.

'Have my choppers ready on the pad, in ten. I'm going to soak my head in a shower. Did Washington send anything on that autopsy of the protocol death?'

'Not yet.' The station security chief paused. 'Jack, there's one other thing: Mrs Campbell's body, I'll have it here in London by tonight. I've arranged private cremation for tomorrow.'

Dawson left. Lowel turned on the shower . . . and the memory of their last afternoon's His and Hers in Thessaloniki flooded back. He shut off the hot tap, but the sudden stinging shock of cold was no help.

The crash site where the late Prime Minister met his death was just west of Amersham. Lowel's machine went into hover above a set of railway tracks beside a hill: Campbell's Sea-Fly had gone down at the entrance to the adjoining tunnel. A narrow country road passed over it. The stone parapet and tunnel-facing were blackened by the fire.

'Some kids were train watching when it went in,' said Ryder grimly.

The zone was still marked off with yellow police ribbons. The kind of ambulance chasers that like watching the body-count in freeway chain-reactions were satisfying their morbid curiosity from the closest possible distance up the road.

'We maligned the forensic lab about Campbell,' Ryder continued. 'They did perform a tissue analysis, but apparently his corpse was even more badly burned than the 85Prime Minister's. So much so that his family asked to have what was left cremated in London, rather than the churchyard burial they had planned for Kirkbeam. There was a memorial service, but nothing official.'

'How about the French reaction to their Jeanne Claron involvement?' Lowel asked, as his paired choppers moved on.

'Not to worry.' The SIS man gave a tight smile. 'Paris can scream diplomatic immunity, but we'll keep her bottled up in their Embassy. For the next five days, that bitch is out of play.'

The Stone Age chalk figure cut into the hillside near Chequers appeared. Then Loombe Hill and the Hamlet. Lowel ordered his helicopter fleet to land on the golf course behind the church. The red-faced socialist clergyman that Powys had liked was standing outside his church door, looking as agitated as last time. They exchanged polite English good mornings.

'We'll hit the tea-shop woman first,' Lowel told Ryder, 'then the other one, what's her name.'

The Vicar was waiting to serve Mrs Hughes-Beauchamps her personal, daily, Holy Communion. With two other parishes to serve, he certainly would not have done so for one old woman if she hadn't provided the new heating system, restoration of the stained glass in the eastern window, and now the altar roof. The sexton's wife had spoken out most strongly on the matter . . .

The clock in the tower above his head struck quarter to the hour. The dragon of the parish was never late. He carried the bread and wine to the altar from their overnight storage on the shelf in the sacristy where, despite her complaints, the sexton's wife always set them each prior evening. Now the early morning sun streamed through the renewed eastern window, turning the silver goblet gold. A cuckoo sounded its clear summer call.

Preparations for the parish summer fête were making his days even more than usually hectic. There was still no sign of Mrs H-B. The Vicar decided he must serve himself.

Mrs Hughes-Beauchamps had been woken rudely, but in ample time, by the wretched noise of the odious helicopters landing on the golf course beyond her manor garden. She always left her shuttered bedroom for the bathroom at half past six, precisely. The half-hour allowed sufficient time to purge her bowels, with the nightly aid of herbal tea, to dress, and then walk to the church as she had every day without fail for the last fifty years. Except, she reminded herself, as she searched with the aid of the sunrise filtering through the shutters for her spectacles (which should be by her cigarettes or the dratted telephone on the bedside table!), except on those two occasions in the war when beastly German bombs prevented trains returning her from London –

'Got 'em!'

Her specs. The first thing she saw with them was the photograph of Mary Morris with her 'friend'. That sort of female had been unknown to Mrs Hughes-Beauchamps before her wartime chairmanship of a Women's Institute committee on the care of young landgirls. One in particular, a Canadian naturally (the next worst thing to being American!), had exactly the same corrupting look as this 'Sarah' woman, without her dark glasses, staring at the miserable Morris like a poison-adder at a mouse. Since Parliament made such revolting behaviour the law of the land, it did not surprise Mrs Hughes-Beauchamps that today's police weren't interested in a mere picture of such goings on!

She put on her slippers and crossed slowly to the bedroom door. She had told the foul National Health doctor a hundred times: her hip replacements might be free, but they never worked properly first thing in the morning! She turned the door handle.

'Damn and blast!'

Swearing did nothing. The handle wouldn't budge. But her bowels did. She could feel them rumbling. A simply appalling situation. She tried the doorknob again. Nothing. She broke wind – and as she did so, detected another odour, less familiar. Terrifying to an old lady living alone.

Smoke!

She went to unlatch her bedroom window and shout 'Help' at two stupid men who were walking from the helicopters, past her garden, towards Morris's absurd 'Winkey-Donkey' tea-shop.

The window had been barred from outside and would not open.

The hand-lettered sign hanging behind the distorting bottleglass in front of Lowel said 'Closed'. The low front door of the tea-shop was locked. When he knocked, no one answered.

'Let's try the back,' he said to Ryder.

They walked around the cottage and found a stone step at the rear. A delivery of milk and cream sat on it in a wire carrying basket. The back door was also locked. He ran his hand along the top of the wooden frame for a spare key and found nothing.

'Too subtle,' Ryder said. 'It'll be in the teapot.'

One with a broken spout and cracked lid, behind the basket. The key was inside. Lowel opened the outer door. There was a scrubbed pantry with a slate counter, and a larder. Loaves of bread sat on a shelf. A gap on the shelf was marked with a miniature metal Union Jack. A painted green inner door was shut.

When Ryder opened it, the sickly sweet smell of death met them.

Mrs Hughes-Beauchamps tripped over her slippers on her frantic way back to the telephone. The smoke wisped steadily under her locked bedroom door. A sound accompanied it, like the scratching of giant cat's claws.

Fire!

Crackling, snapping at her rosewood furnishings that came back with her father from India. On the floor, the smoke was thicker, already choking. She scrabbled forward, found the bedside table, hauled herself up, grabbed for the receiver. The instrument tumbled down with the ivory cigarette holder and stupid photograph of the 'Sarah' female in a clatter beside her.

'Operator! Operator!' she shrieked at the earpiece. Realized it was her own mistake – 'Fool! You must dial 999! Operator! Operator!' The flames were louder. Something was terribly wrong with the receiver – no dial tone.

The phone was silent. Terror loosened her bowels.

'Please God,' she prayed, 'help me!'

'Preserve my body and soul . . .' the Vicar repeated from the Prayer Book, as he meekly knelt to receive Communion for himself, '. . . And everlasting life –'.

He became conscious of a sound that seemed to fill the church, louder than his praying. A strange whooshing in his ears: the sound, he thought, was surely like that mighty whirlwind which swept through the desert of Sinai to scourge the offending Israelites of Moses who blasphemed against His commandments with their polluted golden idol.

'The blood of our Lord Jesus –'

Miraculously, even as he spoke, the light from the east window changed from gold to the flickering scarlet crimson of the wine of the cup! The Vicar trembled in exaltation, his hammering heart raced, the pulse of his own blood pounded against the temples in his head. After a lifetime of service, he was to be granted a vision!

'Drink this, and be thankful . . .'

The wine touched his tongue.

The quaint rustic kitchen behind the green pantry door was deserted. So were the small flountsy-chintzy parlour and the tea-shop itself.

'The bedroom,' said Lowel.

Followed by Ryder, he walked along a low passage with windows looking towards the golf course. Another closed door was in front of him. Beyond it, the corpse of Mary Morris was lying face down on its frilly bed.

'Christ,' said Ryder, unfastening a window. 'I'll let some air in.'

The stench was bad. The time of death was at least forty-eight hours ago, Lowel decided. The bedroom always reflected the character of a house-owner most closely. Mary Morris was surrounded by a needle-point *Aphrodite Rising from Her Bath* prize from Girl Guides, a silver-framed *Love from Mummy and Daddy* of her divorced parents, and a tortoiseshell frame of the donkey wearing a cute straw hat.

The woman herself was naked. One brutally unattractive buttock showed a discoloured welt. A schoolmaster's leather punishment strap was draped across it. The strap handle was still grasped by the corpse's rigored fingers. Other paraphernalia hung in an antique wardrobe. The set-up of exploiting human weakness was the same as Washington, with Castilio.

'Don't touch anything else,' Lowel warned, as Ryder threw open a second window. 'If she died from the toxin, we're on borrowed time already. Just keep your fingers crossed the old woman at the manor really does have a picture to show us.'

'Not bloody likely! Look over there!'

Ryder pointed. Through the window, a column of smoke rose above the elms screening the rest of the village. In a clear blue sky the smoke was the yellow-grey that came from the old wood of antique walnut furniture, and sixteenth-century elm roof-rafters; the kind of Agatha Christie structure someone called Mrs Hughes-Beauchamps had to live in.

The two of them raced from the cottage. Already a warbling siren was sounding an alarm. As he came out of the elms, Lowel saw flame from the roof-ridge and a figure briefly in the smoke at an upstairs window.

'She's still in there!'

He headed for the manor's main entrance. The hammered iron of the handle was too hot to touch. He tore off his jacket, wrapped it around, and tugged.

'It's no good, Jack!'

He felt Ryder grab him. They fell backwards on the grass. The roof collapsed with a roar. The liberated flames swept up to meet the summer sun. If there had ever been a photograph of a female poisoner, it went too.

Emergency vehicles filled the village green and the churchyard; the whole population was out in the High Street. Two policemen arrived to keep good British order with bullhorns.

'Keep back! For your own protection, ladies and gentlemen, please!'

'SIS.' Ryder showed a pass that got a salute and allowed himself and Lowel inside the cordon. In another ten minutes the building was a gutted ruin. The outer walls of the house were still standing, like a false front on a movie studio lot, but the green creepers that covered the Elizabethan timbered brickwork were shrivelled brown, and the climbing roses that twined through them had fallen away and now blocked the front door like loops of barbed wire.

Three firemen with blackened faces stumbled back through the door, arms raised for protection against the thorns and the heat.

'She's a cinder,' one of the men gasped. 'Poor old girl must have got herself trapped upstairs.'

The crowd *oohed*. 'Not to speak ill,' said a thin-faced woman, wearing a plastic post-office badge, 'but she smoked like a chimney, and that's a fact.'

'The shock did for *him*!' A shorter, fat woman dabbed

153

a grubby handkerchief to her eyes, while at the same time managing to look past it for a glimpse of the body. 'I told my husband, his blood pressure may have been too high but –'

'Your husband, madam?' One of the cops had exchanged his bullhorn for a note pad. 'And who might you be?'

'I'm his wife. I mean the Sexton's. I said to him, "You can't tell me!" Without *her* getting that personal Communion every day, Vicar wouldn't have had no heart attack. Never!'

The Sexton's wife looked to Lowel for confirmation. An ambulance was turning out of the churchyard behind her and into the lane leading to the High Street. He shouted at Ryder, 'This may be our chance for a live one!' Ducking the police cordon, he ran forward. Ryder followed. The ambulance lurched over a gutter. The blue light above the driving compartment began flashing. Lowel vaulted a privet hedge flanking the lane and waved his arms. The ambulance halted. The driver said, 'If you're looking for a free ride to hospital, mate, that's the way to get it.'

'Security,' said Lowel. 'While you're driving your patient, we'd like to talk to him.'

'Talk all you want, mate.' The vehicle stopped. Lowel moved to the rear doors. The driver stuck his head through the front window and added, 'But if you get an answer, it'll be a bleeding miracle.'

'He's unconscious?' Ryder came in on the tail end.

'No, chum. He's cold. I know it was a massive coronary, but I'm just Regional Pathology pick-up this morning.' The driver pointed back at the church. 'The local doc's still inside; any more questions, that's who to ask.'

Lowel said to Ryder, 'This coronary has to go to Forensic in North London with the Morris woman. Can you stay with them – and see that the Lab people know what to look for this time?'

'Wilco.' Ryder climbed into the rear compartment. The siren howled. The crowd in the High Street parted then, as the ambulance accelerated, closed in again for a hopeful last glimpse of sudden death.

The local MD was sitting in the front pew, with a briefcase balanced on her knee, which she was using as a desk while she filled in a form. As Lowel entered the church, the doctor looked up from her paperwork with obvious distaste.

'Already? You insurance lot don't waste time. The carpet isn't dry and you're fighting the claim.'

'I'm not in that line of work.' He showed a Nato identity card. The doctor didn't look any happier.

'I don't know why the statistically predictable high-risk death of an overweight, overworked clergyman should bring us closer to being part of an American police state.'

She was overworked herself, he realized. Mid-thirties, off-blonde hair coiled up behind her head in a plait, glasses, and a reasonable figure that must have been sensational when she was a carefree twenty-one. She stared back at him with a cool professional gaze, equally appraising of his own defects. When her eyes took in his thickened waist and missing fingers, he suddenly thought again, Is this what *She* looks like . . .?

His phantom was certainly a professional. He said, 'You mentioned the carpet being wet. Was it from –?'

'My God, you people really do play cloak and dagger.' The doctor put away her form and snapped the briefcase lock. 'In this case, your "victim" was serving himself Holy Communion. Wine was spilled, not blood.'

The silver chalice was still lying by the altar. The wine had soaked into the threadbare carpet, but the colour of the wool was deep red and the stain scarcely showed. A silver plate had crumbs on it. The mind that was carrying out these damage-control operations, Lowel thought, was incredibly cool under pressure, and leaving nothing to chance: if the chain-smoking Mrs Hughes-Beauchamps had escaped death by burning and made it to the church as part of her regular daily routine, then the toxin would have killed her. It could have been administered to the old woman – or this innocent clergyman – either way, wine or bread. Or both.

'Anything else?' the doctor asked impatiently.

'Only if you could tell the police to come in, when you leave.'

With a last hostile glare, she walked out. Lowel listened to her clicking heels on the flagstone slabs fade away, and felt sorry for her. He looked again at the stain in the carpet and wondered how easy it was for molecules of Viscumin to become part of the air.

'Sir?'

One of the policemen had entered silently from the grass, through a side door. Lowel indicated the Communion vessels.

'This area could be contaminated with a toxic chemical. Until SIS return, the church must be sealed. No one in or out.'

'Yes sir.' The policeman eyed the stain. 'May I ask how toxic?'

'Sure,' said Lowel, 'you can ask. Just don't touch.'

He got back to the golf-course to find his chopper fleet under attack. A groundsman who must have been ninety was standing in a bunker of flawlessly smooth sand, while angrily waving a wide wooden rake at the crews of both aircraft. The old man had string tied around the knees of baggy corduroy trousers that looked even older. The threatened pilots looked amused.

'I tell 'ee again,' the old man shouted, as Lowel came up, 'Links Rules be clear as brook water. Members only, and none of they Bob Hope electric carts on my sand!'

'That's OK, Pop. We're running on gas turbine.'

The senior chopper pilot winked at Lowel. He tried to unruffle the feathers by saying, 'If there's been any damage to your course, I apologize, and the American Government will pay for it.'

'All you Yanks think on is cash!' The old man waved the rake in a circle that threatened Lowel's head. 'I tell she this mornin' when her offers it – the first time I levelled my sand, and her steps in it, afore the fire at the manor. "Lady," I says, "apart from no women never should have let be members in the first place, you keep your damn Yankee dollars! 'Tain't a matter of money, in this country, 'tis rules!" '

The flight crews were laughing. For Lowel, the target of the old boy's rage was no joke. He said to the groundsman, 'You're a hundred per cent right about the rules.' And added casually, 'I guess this woman before the fire must have been a new member of the club.'

'No member at all. I said, her were foreign. We filled our quota on foreigners by two Germans last April. With she snappin' orders and wearin' black knee-boots, her were just like 'em bloody Nazis.'

'But you said before that this woman was American?'

'Her talks like a Yank, and her spends like a Yank, and her looks like a Yank – you tell me, whatever your name is.'

'Jack Lowel.' He put his hand out. The old man stared, then abruptly his face cracked in a grin that showed two brown stubbed teeth, top and bottom.

'Well I be danged.' He shook hands warmly. 'My wife's people on her mother's side was all Lowels, and three of 'em was Jacks.'

Lowel said, 'So now you tell me something: how does an American woman look different from a German?'

'All leg and no bum, Jack.'

Which got a fresh round of guffaws from the flight crews.

'Anything else?' Lowel asked.

'Corn colour hair in a scarf and film-star dark glasses afore sunrise.'

'And did you see where this movie star came from? How she got herself out here to your bunker?'

'By lane through from manor. But her car were parked yonder –' the groundsman swung his rake first at the church then, as the senior pilot ducked, 180 degrees towards the clubhouse – 'that's why her was crossin' my sand. Hussy was parked in manager's own spot, Jack, bold as brass, can you believe 'un!'

'A white sports car?'

The weathered face split in another grin. 'You Lowels is a sly lot. I had feelin' all along you know'd she.'

He patted the old man on the shoulder and gave a thumbs up to the flight crews.The turbines whined, the rotors began turning. He boarded the senior chopper without flipping a coin. As the helicopters lifted off, and their combined down draught sprayed half the old groundsman's perfectly raked sand out of his trap onto the green, all Lowel knew for certain was that, with Jeanne-Marie Claron and her Maserati barricaded inside the French Embassy, there was at least one woman too many wearing headscarves and dark glasses, and driving white sports cars around Britain.

It was time he started moving faster.

16

Transatlantic

Flush on warning! . . . The capacity to take off within ninety seconds of receiving an alarm was the chief
design characteristic of the B1 strategic bomber. That
specification was demanded for the B52's successor by
the Kennedy administration in 1963: now, decades later,
Lowel watched it happen.

As his helicopter touched down at Farnborough, beside
the bomber, its three-man crew raced from a standby hut
across the tarmac to their aircraft. Barely pausing, the
flight engineer punched a yellow-arrowed button located
on the hull, immediately behind the bomber's nose-wheel
struts. Within seconds all four turbofans were alight and
howling. Before Lowel had stepped off the ladder into
the fuselage, the B1 was rolling. By the time he took the
ejection seat purposely left vacant by an absent fourth
crewman, the nose-wheel was already off the concrete.
As he snapped the last strap of the built-in escape harness,
Farnborough was behind him.

The computer display in front of him showed that
120,000 lb of roaring afterburner static thrust was hurling
the bomber aloft with the force of a rocket. The G-force
from the acceleration squashed him as flat in his seat as a
stamp on a letter. His lungs and circulatory system were
getting the same treatment. He saw his face reflected in
the glass of the small rear pane of the flight-deck window:
his cheeks dragged down, his eyes pouched, he looked

like a hundred-year-old version of the B1's reluctant third parent, Richard Nixon.

'Not too shabby,' a laconic Texas voice drawled on the intercom headset. 'Two minutes forty from scratching our ass to the English Channel – another five and we'll be flying. When Lady G lets up, you can take a front seat, Mr Lowel.'

The force of gravity eased enough to let him turn his head. They were flying already; on a corner of the display, the Mach reading hovered at nine-tenths the speed of sound, roughly 700 miles an hour. He unstrapped and changed places with the co-pilot.

'We have to make our big bang over water,' the B1's commander explained, as Lowel got into the Second's seat beside him; 'if we don't, all those Limey chickens between Southampton and Land's End stop laying together. Otherwise, I guess things are just as dull around here as they were in your SAC time.'

'You know about that?' He didn't make a habit of referring to his Strategic-Air days. The pilot shared an ironic grin.

'It ain't every morning we get pulled out of an international show just to flip a civilian nobody to Washington for breakfast grits with the President. A man has a certain natural curiosity. There goes boom one.'

Inside the hull the only evidence of the sound barrier was a slight tremor. Lowel said, 'If you've got something as old-fashioned as a one-time pad on board, I want to get a message to the White House.'

'The old ways are still the best ways, lots of ways. Second –' the aircraft's commander looked over his shoulder at his junior – 'pass us all an OTP.'

One-time codes were still the most secure means of converting plain language into a secret. His message was brief: 'See you, sweat box, NSA?' In a couple of minutes he found and converted the alphanumeric substitutes needed. He handed the encoded signal to the co-pilot and destroyed the one-time leftover in the flight-deck shredder. The Second typed in the symbols on the Hi-Burst Link terminal, which encoded it again . . . and only seconds later the machine replied through its operator: 'Accepted and verified. Answer will follow.'

For Lowel, the flight was Santa Claus and a candystore rolled up in one. He recognized pieces of equipment like the Link and the decoy flare launch-tubes, that hadn't changed, and others that must be distant relatives of the Singer-Kearfort doppler, or the Hughes forward-looking infra-red that were just being developed when he left his first career in the high-performance world of Strategic Air Command. Behind him, each of three internal bays could take six Cruise Missiles, with hardpoints for eight more under the wings, and if that wasn't a suitable payload the straight bomb lift was sixty tons –

'Talking of old-fashioned,' the B1's commander picked up their previous conversation, 'with this Zero-Zero loony tunes shit apparently really going to come off, I don't reck-on Rockwell's gonna be selling too many of these beauties from Farnborough or anywhere else. After taking twenty years to finally get 'em in the air, it does seem a crying shame to scrap Baby for Miller cans. Stand by boom two.'

Twice the speed of sound was only a psychological barrier: 1,500 knots, just another blip on the display. Except for a developing luminous pale pink glow at the wing tips, there was no response from the bomber to the further demands made on it. In one part of his mind, Lowel shared the pilot's disappointment for this obsolete mechanical marvel. Divorcing your mind from the reality of what you were doing, and where you were going with what you were carrying, that kind of schizophrenia had been the first design characteristic of the human components of SAC from day one.

Disappointment was too weak a word. Bitterness and

savage resentment were the emotions being felt by men like 'Captain Hawk', the Defense Secretary, and the Air Force generals and Navy admirals seeing their bomber and missile empires laid as waste as the day before yesterday's ruins of Ancient Greece. If the number of women in dark glasses with white sports cars was any measure, the mental states of the hidden empires of the free world's intelligence communities were no more stable.

And *Her* mental state . . . ?

With Jacky gone, he was forced again to try and understand what kind of a woman could get close enough to a man – or another woman – to observe their most intimate personal kinks and habits, yet remain so detached that she'd do it only to kill them in the most efficient manner? He took a pencil and scratch pad from his flight-suit pocket and sketched a rough flow-diagram of the dates and travel movements that had to coincide if the phantom he thought of as *She* poisoned the Morris female in Britain and the two men in Washington . . .

'Boom three,' the pilot's voice intruded on the headset, 'but don't tell the folks back home. Congress thinks our wings were clipped to Mach 1.6 after we were cancelled the first time round by Bible Jim.'

Any faster, Lowel thought, as he put away his flow-chart, and the wing tips wouldn't just be glowing. The pilot's old-fashioned military cynicism for all politicians struck a nerve that was already twanging. President Jimmy Carter had been a good and decent man, seeking peace for the world, but when *he* scrapped the B1 – for what seemed the last time! – the Soviets took that as just another green light for Afghanistan. For all the First Secretary's outward charm, it was only America's advanced war-toy technology, and the cost of trying to catch up with it, that had brought such a tough Russian to face high-rolling Dan Galbraith at the wind-down table.

'Command, Second: Hi-Link's calling.' The co-pilot's

162

crisp Midwest voice broke in. 'It's one-time back, for personal decode, stand by.'

The Hi-Burst screen flashed five-figure groups of random numerals and letters. The co-pilot depressed a key that had them printed on paper tape, which he handed to Lowel, who consulted the decode side of his one-time pad. The White House answer translated as 'Delta One sees you.'

'Excuse me, sir. We have to get off a wind-drift package at apogee, for the new Geophysical Year.' As Lowel was shredding the rest of his paper, the navigator reached past him and pulled a red T-handle on one of the decoy flare launch-tubes. A slight whoosh of compressed air was the only indication that anything else had happened.

'There goes our high point,' drawled the B1's commander. 'Make the most of the view, we'll be braking for the Potomac in forty minutes.'

The sky was below them at this altitude. Above was black heaven. For an instant Jacqueline's free spirit seemed at his side: what a kick she would have got out of this space-age trip . . .

'We'll change the point of landing,' Lowel said into his headset. 'Use NASA's facility at Goddard, but don't call them up yet.'

'You're the boss, Boss.' The pilot looked sideways at Lowel. 'If you're tied in with those moon-walkers, maybe you could rustle a favour and put my name down for Mars?'

'I know a couple of people, and I'd be glad to, but no guarantees.'

'That's life,' said the Texan. 'Goin' down through boom two.'

The real world was coming back. The rolling arc of the horizon began to flatten. A bright line in the north-west deep purple was the edge of Nova Scotia. His Hugo taxi hair-raiser with Jacky through the Greek mountains from

Meliti couldn't do it, but this B1 chariot had fulfilled one of man's oldest dreams and outraced the sun.

The Goddard Space Flight Center clock read 08.10 when Lowel's State-side chopper lifted him past it and out over Road One heading east from Fort Meade, centred between Washington and Baltimore. The nine-storey brown concrete building dominating the complex that loomed up ahead of him had a more folksy name for the thousands of civilians who worked in it.

The headquarters of America's truly secret service, the National Security Agency, was called by the locals SIGINT City. For outsiders the first word meant Signal Intelligence, which was what the organization collected from sources as diverse as Kliment Berov's Moscow taxi or a charge-card transaction at the nearest branch of Sears. Or any other branch, or credit transaction, or taxi anywhere on earth. NSA heard everything and, unless otherwise instructed, the banks of super Cray computers in its basement forgot nothing.

As Lowel approached the mass of golf-ball and star-fish antennae on its roof, he saw that the presidential helicopter had touched down before him. Accompanied by his inseparable young naval aide carrying the nuclear communications Button Box, Daniel Galbraith stood by the pad, tight-mouthed and squinting as the rotor storm from Lowel's machine blew his thick mane of hair in all directions. The visible Secret Service bird dogs surrounding him looked as though they wanted to shoot the chopper out of the sky on spec. The President waved the bodyguards aside and strode forward. Lowel saw he was wearing his functioning prosthesis, not the useless dummy glove. Galbraith's welcome was 'I let you off the leash five days ago. Since then, you've changed the venue for signing the Agreement to Soviet territory entirely on your own; the man I particularly asked you to help is dead; and when

164

I try to find out from London what the hell's going on, I'm told my special envoy – and my late sister's husband – Mr Jack Lowel's fucked off to Greece for a dirty weekend!'

Galbraith tossed his head to get the hair out of his eyes. The look coming from them could boil water. The young Button aide showed increasing embarrassment. The bird dogs scanned the NSA compound, pretending they hadn't heard a word.

'Well, sir?' the Chief Executive demanded. 'What have you got to say for yourself?'

'You'd better have this back.' Lowel reached into his pocket and withdrew the Finding with its purple stamp of authorization. 'You're right, Mr President. I've achieved absolutely nothing. My only recommendation is that, for your protection, you abort the signing – no, I guess I have one other suggestion. On future occasions if the national interest is at risk, stick to your professional advisers: don't employ someone just because they may have been a friend.'

He held out the Finding.

'There's no "may have" about it.' Galbraith thrust the paper away with his prosthesis, then waved the device in the direction of the Secret Service. 'Do you think I could get a straight answer like yours from any of this crowd? People in Washington wouldn't walk out on their pensions if I showed them the Beltway was the Yellow Brick Road. Jack, I don't know what it's been like on your side of the Atlantic, but since Yalta hit the papers it's been shit on wheels over here.'

Lowel put the Finding back in his pocket. 'I figured it must be rough when I saw you weren't wearing the glove.'

'Yeah.' Galbraith rubbed what was left of his elbow. 'Cosmetics for the photo ops are the least of my worries. I'll have less chance of re-election after Yalta than a eunuch in a harem getting tail.'

'That bad?'

' "Red Sucker Play of the Century" is one of the milder headlines. The only thing Yalta means to the hard Right is Joe Stalin stealing eastern Europe from Roosevelt, and putting up Churchill's Iron Curtain. And the minority senior member on the Senate's Intelligence Committee got a leak from nowhere of our lady's possible assassination attempt. In order to placate all their howling about another Pearl Harbor, I've had to beg on the Hot Line for the other side to allow us to airlift one of our redundant armoured brigades from Berlin for guard duty on Soviet territory! He's ignored the insult and OK'd – but enough of my troubles: you must have something better, or you wouldn't have spent half the Air Force budget to bring it over.'

'We need to talk,' Lowel agreed, 'but not out here.'

'You don't trust this bright blue sky?' Daniel Galbraith looked up at the starfish antennae and laughed. 'Old pal, you're back in harness all right. Paranoid, in less than a week!'

They began walking to the brown building. The workforce of SIGINT City was as excited as any other medium-sized town at getting a presidential visit, but the discipline was tighter, and there were definitely no photo opportunities. The drug store in the building's shopping mall had a Kodak sign, but carried not one roll of film. Beyond the Kodak sign a huge mural of toiling workers, which would have been at home in Red Square, filled a wall. The NSA seal, of an eagle with a skeleton key in its claws, was set into a mosaic floor.

As the public official elected to represent the eagle was crossing the seal, an elevator door opened: a small man wearing a brown three-piece suit, and nicknamed 'Pixie' by his classmates and subordinates, rushed out. The rest of the world called him Admiral Sweeting. The Director of the National Security Agency had an intellect whose superconducting circuits only began to warm up at the level of post-doctoral research at Livermore Labs and Princeton.

'Mr President! On behalf of all our NSA family, our warmest possible welcome! And, as head of the family, let me add my personal deepest apology, sir, for not being at the pad to greet you fittingly on landing!'

This excessively effusive pixie greeting was accompanied by the warmest bubbling pixie smile from under the coldest pair of rat eyes Lowel had seen since bargaining with a Mountain People village leader to spare the life of a Vietcong infiltrator.

'Apology accepted, Admiral Sweeting. I'm not here for ceremony, just to use your family sweat box. This is my personal oldest friend.'

The President shook the pixie's tiny hand and winked at Lowel over its bald head.

'Indeed, indeed! I surely recognize him, Mr President.' The pixie smile was flashed in Lowel's direction – while the rat eyes, of palest grey, coldly compared Lowel, in the flesh, with the holographic laser image already on file in the computer brain behind them. 'But may I suggest a more suitable location than our sweat box? My ninth-floor office quarters are equally secure from prying ears and offer considerably greater comfort to other parts of the anatomy.'

A pixie chuckle accompanied this generous offer which the President declined by following Lowel into a down elevator.

'Thanks for the kindness, Admiral, but if my oldest friend here wants the sweat box, I guess we'll have to suffer. Don't let me hold you from your family business.'

'Not at all, Mr – '

The door slid shut on the rest of Pixie's answer. The village leader, Lowel recalled, was wearing exactly the

167

same expression when he reached his decision: the Cong infiltrator was spared his life . . . but not with his skin. The poor bastard's flayed live body was turned over in exchange for CIA mountain station providing the village with two dozen laying hens.

The sweat box was a tube within a sphere. The outer sphere was composed of a honeycomb matrix calculated to trap all wavelengths: from the deepest pipe organ note, rumbling below the audible threshold of human hearing, to the electronic bat squeak of super UHF. The inner tube had the dimensions of, but somewhat less comfort than, a deep-sea diving decompression chamber. Both units were sealed by bank vault doors.

Lowel turned the locking wheel on the last one, shutting out the Secret Service – and even the anxious young naval aide who was furiously spinning his radio dials to prevent the building's static from limiting his nuclear-button reception. The effect of the vault door's closing could be described as injurious to the health of anyone subject to the mildest form of claustrophobia. A sign by a monitoring and control panel advised:

SELF-CONTAINED BREATHING UNIT
STRICTLY NO SMOKING

'At least I'm going to be spared those home-rolled Bull Durham lung tanners of yours,' said Galbraith. 'Believe my Surgeon-General and quit cold turkey. Am I striking a nerve?'

'Someone else gave me the same advice. I already stopped.'

Lowel gave the locking wheel a vicious last twist, but Jacqueline's voice in his head would not stay out . . .

'I'm glad to hear it.' The President settled himself into a breathing vinyl chair. 'This home-sweet-home of Pixie's brings back my last spell in an attack sub. Did you notice, Jack, he's got a head like one of those golf-ball antennae on his roof? With Sweeting's brainpower in that diameter, we could conquer the universe.'

All Lowel wanted now was his makings, left behind in Jacqueline's flat, to jolt himself out of remembering with a killer hit of nicotine. Denied it, he said, 'I wouldn't want to be in the Admiral's family, and he couldn't run human agents on the ground in enemy territory, but he's the best qualified man for this electronics job – which is the principal reason I suggested we use his facility. NSA has to be the one military-industrial empire that doesn't see itself in danger of cutback after dismantling.'

'No argument there,' Galbraith agreed. 'Our need for satellite verification will make his golf-balls more important than ever. And you're off the hook for Yalta. History will approve. Now run the rest of your ugly pictures.'

Lowel ran them: from the diversion of his first British Airways flight at Antwerp, to Prime Minister Powys's possible poisoning by the lunch-box sandwiches, versus Sir Herbert Maxwell's stonewall of SIS uncooperation; to CIA's apparent matching complicity in a thirty-six-hour wild goose chase through Greece, with Jacqueline interpreting; to day five's flight back to London, and last night's car bombing by the Frenchwoman, Claron, outside the Soviet Embassy in Kensington Palace Gardens; and finally the village deaths this morning.

'You predicted international Hallowe'en,' he said in conclusion, 'and there have been eight deaths so far, but except for the first worker in the cancer gene lab – and with CIA's behaviour we can't trust that one either – I don't have confirmation of Viscumin toxin on a single count.'

'I make it seven deaths.' Galbraith had been ticking them off with clicks of his artificial fingers. 'There's the lab worker, and Castilio, Powys, his pilot, sandwich-woman, old lady, her clergyman. Have I missed one?'

'No,' Lowel said, 'I left an incident victim out of the summary. Jacqueline Campbell, my interpreter, was killed in an airport bombing. At Thessaloniki. I went on ahead of her to London. Because of her ex-husband's death, and my personal involvement, at first I saw a tie-in, but the incident cause was unrelated, Greek–Turk nationalism.'

When speech stopped in the sweat box, the psychological effect of its isolation seemed to make the sound of a human heart audible. His oldest friend stared at him for a long moment.

'My secretary got a call from your partner, who was worried for you,' Daniel Galbraith said at last. 'I told her I was too busy to take it. Jack, that dirty weekend remark I made to you outside – I've been a prize shitheel . . .'

Bless old baby-faced Sam Wong for caring, Lowel thought. The heart sound was a filter bellows, he realized, running behind his chair on alternating current, sixty cycles.

'No, Dan. Thanks for the apology, but you were right. If I hadn't gone to Greece, I couldn't have stopped Powys being killed, but I would have been on the spot with SIS for their autopsy procedures. Now the British will almost certainly vote against your Agreement.'

'I may be able to swing them a little on that,' said Galbraith. 'I'm going over there tomorrow to address Parliament, at the invitation of the interim Prime Minister. It's the French involvement that throws me. Their President is so far out in right field, the people at State call him Attila the Frog, but he gave me his personal guarantee there'd be no reneging. Are you absolutely sure about that car bombing?'

'Nothing's absolute in this business. I'm sure I got blown flat on my ass by the blast. I'm sure I saw a woman driver and the French Embassy's address on the getaway vehicle's registration.'

'But if that woman is holed up in Knightsbridge, and she's also the poisoner –'

'She can't be,' said Lowel. 'I think there are at least two women – each being run against the Agreement by one of your allies' intelligence departments: this Greenpeace bomber, Claron, from the Sûreté, in Paris; and another one out of some closet of Maxwell's, backstage at Century House. *If* there is a poisoner, she must be a third agent, and as to who's running her I don't have a clue.'

Galbraith said grimly, 'You've got a phony, bullshit dossier out of Langley.'

'Yes, I've got that.'

'And you have my full authorization to tear the balls off that senile Alabaman son of a bitch running it. Go in there and let's have some blood on the track.'

'I can do it,' said Lowel; 'I intend to. And the same here at NSA, and over at the FBI but, after Powys's death, what about you?'

The reason for this pause was different; the oppressive silence was the same. The air in the sweat box appeared to have measurable weight, making it difficult to breathe.

'The possibility of danger to me personally, we just ride out,' Galbraith replied, loosening his tie, 'like we do with the gun crazies. It goes with the territory. But a successful threat against my Office, before the seal goes on the Agreement, is unacceptable. Short of not showing up in Yalta, I'll do whatever you tell me.'

'Be random.' Lowel eased his own collar. 'Except for your House of Commons speech, you announce nothing more in advance to anyone, and that includes your personal security staff and closest advisers. For the transatlantic trip you take Air Force Two at the last minute. You have all your food tasted, and the drinks –'

'Unacceptable.' Galbraith rubbed a bead of sweat from his right temple with his good hand. 'No leather-neck kid in my Marines is going to die while I stand by and watch him. I'll switch helpings of scrambled eggs, and coffee mugs – that's random.'

'Let's hope so.' He felt his own skin starting to prickle: not just from lack of nicotine. Four hours' sleep in the last fifty was getting to him. 'What were you planning after the visit to London?'

'A day off, at my forebears' place in Scotland. Now, it's going to have to be France, to wrestle Attila.'

'Which would leave us one day before arrival for the signing. You could spend some of that time with your relatives. A Scottish castle isn't a bad place for security –'

'*Getout!*'

'Say again?'

Because for a second it didn't sink in. That it was two words –

'*Out . . .*'

Just one word now: gasped, by Galbraith. Sweat poured down the President's ashen face.

'Dan, what's wrong?'

No more words. Galbraith hit his good wrist with his prosthetic hand. The medic alert bracelet from Camp David. At the same instant a red warning sign on the monitoring panel flashed:

FREON CONTAMINATION

IMMEDIATE EXIT

A klaxon went off with the terrifying shock of a smoke alarm at night, deafening in the confined space of the sweat box. Galbraith's breath was more alarming: a desperate, rapid-fire panting. Lowel flung himself at the first locking wheel, on the inner door . . . to find that he had smashed the wall beside it.

His own motor co-ordination was failing. He scrabbled along the wall, got both hands on the locking wheel and tugged . . . *tugged* –

The arrow, fool!

172

A sharper part of his brain pointed out that he was trying to rotate the wheel in the wrong direction.

'The goddamn right way now!'

He said it for Galbraith's benefit – but his previous action had tightened the wheel further. Cursing his left hand's missing fingers, he twisted with all his strength.

'It's starting!'

Spinning. So easily that the wheel threw him to the floor. When he got up and tugged the door open he fell again, hitting his head on the leg of a chair. Above him, Galbraith, sitting in it, eyes closed, was inert. Lowel slapped his face, 'Dan! For Christ's sake! Come on! *Come on!*'

No reaction. He stumbled to his feet, got his arms beneath the President's shoulders, began dragging Galbraith towards the second locked door. The air was no fresher for opening the first one. The haloed lights on the monitoring panel flashed like Christmas in a drunk tank. The klaxon wail split his head.

'Second wheel, Dan.'

His voice sounded tee-hee, a cartoon chipmunk's. The panel lights came into focus showing HELIUM added to the lethal mix. When his arms let go, his friend Daniel Galbraith dropped like a sack.

'Open, you fucker!'

Designing the sweat box was someone's cosmic joke. It took the last chunk of his mind what seemed like an hour to realize that on this outer lock the rotation arrow pointed in the opposite direction. By the end of which time the sweat on his palms made them skid down the polished locking wheel in an arc, dropping him again on the floor beside his friend, the President.

The Christmas lights winked cheerfully. Lowel stared at the Leader of the Free World and giggled. For some reason, hearing his own giggle made him furious. The still alive part of his dying brain observed this abrupt switch in reactions with detached interest. Sitting on the floor by President Dan, backbone braced against a corner wall of the sweat box, old pal Jack watched a pair of huge clown feet brace in the opposite corner.

'Your feet, Dan . . .?'.

His own! Immediately after this incredible stupidity, his rolling eyes latched on to the presidential old school tie. Suddenly, a pair of sweating gorilla hands were playing with it –

Wrong! His hands were ripping the Annapolis tie off the Chief Executive and frantically winding it as a bandage on the locking wheel rim. His rage was as icy now as the wheel under the fabric felt to his shivering skin. This fury easily allowed his freeze-dried hands to rotate the wheel in the right direction, and pull the second vault door open.

As the mass of it toppled him backwards, and something called OXYGEN rushed in . . . outside, a round pink pixie face was mouthing concern for, 'Mr Pres –!'

The precious oxygen came too late to stop this wave of blackness rolling over Lowel. As he went under, the pixie's flat grey eyes, he remembered, were the colour of death.

17

Lowel sat in another sanatorium reading the bottom line lower-case print of another eye-chart on another white wall: 'o – t – i – x – m – z.'

The NSA medic grunted and tapped his knee with a hammer . . . This round of kick reflexes still worked. The doctor scratched the sole of his patient's foot and got curled toes; shone the little light at the pupils of his eyes . . . then grunted again.

'Anything left in there?' Lowel asked, pulling on his sock.

'You look as though you need sleep, otherwise you'll do.'

He needed to get even – starting with the man in charge of this latest medical establishment, Admiral Pixie Fucking Sweeting. He tied his shoe, put on his jacket, and walked across to the next compartment. Daniel Galbraith was still on the bed, resting against pillows and breathing oxygen through a mask connected by a flexible hose to a blue-labelled outlet.

'You've got more faith in these walls than I have,' Lowel said with a smile.

The President set aside the mask and returned a wan grin. 'My Service bird dogs took the first drag. Any future sweat-box conversations, line up one of those coal-mine canaries for this old crock.'

'I'm ordering electronic sniffers for gas and explos-

175

ives. They will be installed in all your cars, aircraft, and accommodation, effective immediately.'

'Thanks, Jack – and not just for your reorganizing. I'm told things were goddamn close.'

Galbraith held out his good hand. Lowel gripped it with his own.

'You know what they say, Dan: you can't keep a good crock down.'

'I won't be, much longer.' The President released him and took back the oxygen mask. 'They want me sidelined for another half-hour, then, if I can pee straight, it's back in play. Will I see you at the White House?'

'You'll see me sometime.'

'Keep in constant touch.'

Lowel nodded, to indicate a need for verbal caution. Behind their charts for a patient's eyes, these sanatorium walls had the keenest ears in the world.

Sweeting's ninth-floor office had corner windows which gave a magnificent view of the Maryland countryside and the Agency's garbage removal operation. Having to dispose of more waste paper daily than the output of Disneyland East and West combined was this secret empire's greatest physical challenge. Shredding technology couldn't cope: huge sealed warehouses held light-years of yesterday's useless information, waiting under top-secret classification to get on the conveyor belt ride to the knives. Furnaces that could run an ocean liner the size of the *QEII* belched the remains of the stale secrets through stacks many times higher than her funnels – but not high enough to avoid spreading a pall of gloom over the complex when the wind was in the wrong direction.

Lowel walked in to find the Admiral staring moodily through his expensive bronzed glass at a cloud of brown fug.

'It's a scrubber problem,' said Sweeting. 'We've gone

to the Hill five times and Congress still won't appropriate. Our planned maintenance schedules just can't keep
up – but good heavens, Mr Lowel, after this morning's
horror story with our Freon recycling unit, I hardly need
to tell you that!' The head of NSA turned away from the
unpleasantness of his command view and immediately
switched on some pixie cheer for his visitor. 'Coffee?'

'Forget it. If you want to keep your job past lunch,
get a better line than maintenance failure. I've just come
from the President.'

The Admiral's eyes never had been cheery: the laser
intelligence behind them took only a micro-second to
measure their opponent and conclude he wasn't bluffing.

'I want the job, Lowel. Tell me the President's further
requirements.'

'Blood on the track, was how he phrased it. For public
consumption, you can blame this morning's sweat-box episode on obsolescent equipment. If your microwave trawl
records for the period immediately before it don't show
an intercept of my message via B1 to the White House
when I inspect them, I guess the President may buy the
excuse as well, but I won't.'

When Sweeting bargained for his life in government,
a heightened flush on the tips of his pointed ears was the
only pixie thing about him.

'What would you buy?' Sweeting asked, with a narrow
look.

'The total resources of your hardware, to analyse all
transatlantic airline ticket purchases for the last six weeks,
and compare them with a passenger profile and schedule
parameters I'll give your chief operator.'

'Mr Lowel, I'm anxious to co-operate, but our Congressional mandate specifically excludes any surveillance
whatsoever of domestic microwave traffic. If by accident
we may happen to have trawled some, we destroy it.'

A trawl, in the electronic scanning of space, had the

same sense as it did for ocean fishing: scoop up whatever was out there, indiscriminately. Sorting for species and gutting them came later, in comparative leisure.

'I don't have time for bullshit,' Lowel said. 'Aside from the small point that you do in fact trawl every microwave in the US – if you want strict legality, all airline corporate material goes offshore by satellite, for processing in the Bahamas and other parts of the Caribbean to take advantage of Third World slave labour.'

'At this critical juncture we can't possibly risk down-sizing our Soviet trawl surveillance. I suppose we could allocate one Cray Super Two mainframe.' Sweeting added grudgingly, 'Switch it off the Chinese. It would take days to make a dent in what you're after.'

'I want the answer within twenty-four hours. The chances of the Russians launching a first strike overnight are a damn sight longer than the President's patience. You will allocate however many Crays I can count when I get down in your basement.'

Seven was the number finally decided on after discussion between NSA's Chief Operator and Lowel. The most powerful computers on earth sat in neat booths, colour co-ordinated to match their casings which were a trendy restaurant pink and grey. The super machines stood a little more than head high, each one rising out of a circular skirt of cooling fins, like a park bench fitted around the trunk of a tree. The rest of the basement was a jungle of exposed wiring harnesses and insulated coolant pipes marked with flow arrows and prudent warnings.

IN EVENT OF MELTDOWN – THIS WAY AUSTRALIA!!!

'Fucking clowns,' said the Chief Operator, 'there's nothing radioactive around here. It's what comes of

178

hiring twenty-year-olds; the wetware burns out faster than the hardware in this business, Mr Lowel.'

The head of the clowns wore a hamburger happy-face name-tag, 'Ronald McDonald', and didn't look thirty himself. They were in a booth which had only terminals and printers installed, one for each computer. The 'wetware' programmers had given them names like HOT TITS, HARD-ON, and FRED FLINTSTONE.

'The first generation of the Super Two,' explained the Chief Operator, tapping Fred. 'I don't ask why the others – and I'm suggesting we go with seven systems because that's as many as we can run using today's software in parallel processing. If we went linear, we could use the whole suite, but that wouldn't give any capacity to cross-link. OK?'

Lowel said, 'I have the feeling this isn't something I can get too many second opinions about.'

The Chief Operator nodded agreement. 'We used to like having a lead time of five years over the civilians, or the Reds; now that's maybe only three against the Japanese.' He pulled out a scratch pad and a luminous pink felt marker. 'What you're after is passengers in the air, per hour, domestic, that's 130,000 average . . . and transatlantic in summer, about the same . . . over a six-week period . . . which gives . . . 2.6 times ten to the power eight.'

'That sounds one hell of a number.'

'That's why we're here.' Ronald McDonald smiled. 'Anyway, not so big: with rounding, your search ratio is 1 in the population of the United States. What's our trawl target?'

Lowel had known his odds were long, but this made it seem useless. One un-named, un-fingerprinted, unseen human out of 260 million, and he expected an answer overnight!

'The target is female,' he replied, 'age between twenty

and forty. Hell, maybe fifty, with the way women exercise these days. She travels alone –'

'First class? Don't mean to interrupt the flow, but First cuts the traffic by two-thirds.'

'I can't say that. You can assume she takes regular direct flights – no special holiday rates, with tour stopovers for shopping or weekend Club Med – now that I think about it, given the time constraints she might well go Concorde.' He passed the operator the chart he had sketched aboard the B1. 'Within these dates, she could have commuted London–Washington two, maybe three times each way. There might be a connector tie-in to Greece, and her nationality could be Greek, or East German, but that would only show if you get far enough to cross-reference with the US Immigration visa-check system.'

'And if we do?' asked the computer operator. 'What does this jet-set babe have for her physical parameters?'

'Median height, median weight, median length hair – maybe blonde. And she has a scar on her groin. Otherwise, I'm sorry to admit, I haven't got a clue.'

'Don't sweat it. Being median ain't so bad in this business. Scrub male, old, young, tall, short, blind, and assistance in boarding, we're down to no worse than 1 in 50 mill. And if Immigration ever did a body search, we have a great program label.'

Ronald McDonald grinned again, scribbled with his pink felt marker on a yellow stickit tag, and applied it to a terminal next to HARD-ON.

The clown chief's tag read:

TWAT SPOT.

Lowel hit the FBI next. The headquarters building named after the father of the Bureau of Investigation, and personally designed to be Edgar Hoover's fortress against corruption in the nation's capital, had its own helo pad and was strategically located halfway between Fort

180

Meade and Langley. It was also next door to the White House. As Lowel passed by to the south, he observed that Daniel Galbraith must have peed straight enough for medical release: the presidential chopper had returned to the lawn beyond the Rose Garden.

Wilson Q. Elricks, the nation's current top policeman, was a lifelong academic, not a cop. He had been president of a midwestern Catholic university, with a background in family law, when he was plucked out of it by the previous administration, who expected a crackdown against Gay Rights activists and abortion mills as a fair return on investment. Instead, they were saddled with the first FBI Director in history who insisted on seeing both sides of every socio-criminal cause and question – and then doing what his militant Protestant wife told him to do about it.

'I have to admit, Mr Lowel,' Wilson Elricks said when his office door had closed and his visitor was seated, 'I still find these sexual entrapment cases, such as the ones in the priority investigation you asked for from London, particularly distasteful. I get it all the time with Enforcement officials posing as prostitutes, for example.'

'I'm sure you do, Director.' Lowel indicated a file on the desk. 'Is that your investigation?'

Wilson Elricks nodded unhappily.

'And is it complete?'

'It is. You're welcome to use my office for your perusal.'

'At such short notice, on both counts, I'm grateful and impressed. The President will be, too.'

'I doubt that, Mr Lowel.' The reluctant boss of the FBI looked unhappier than ever. 'When our nation's Chief Executive is informed of the amount of sexual irregularity we found among his domestic White House staff, I doubt that very much.'

Which showed that Wilson Q. Elricks was not as closely in touch with presidential attitudes to morality – sex – as was the dedicated founder of the Bureau: by the time of his death, Hoover had three locked filing cabinets on the subject, in the corner hall between his toilet and his office. The stuff in this White House file was small potatoes: one wife-swapping between butlers, three mistresses on the payroll with doubtful typing skills; the inevitable closet homosexual working in the food preparation side and being blackmailed by his lover because of the AIDS scare. Pathetic, not shocking.

Like the sad little life of John Castilio: the file showed being a slave to an invalid mother, and telephone sex. Lowel tossed the page aside impatiently. If the Bureau hadn't dug out anything more –

The autopsy. It was attached by mistake, with a used paper clip, to the blackmailed homosexual's file sheet.

. . .Castilio's cadaver was transferred to J.E.H. Forensic, where, using ELISA procedures developed at Leeds University in Britain, a full range of tests for plant toxins was conducted.
Results were:

But even finding the word ELISA again gave Lowel some sense of progress. He turned the sheet to get:

. . . Abrin, presence negative. Modecin, negative. Ricin, negative. Volkensin, negative. Before continuing with the results for Viscumin, a word on scientific procedure is in order. The presence of toxin is determined by measuring the colour intensity of enzyme substrate in solution, against a graph. Caution should be used in considering this comparison as laboratory results have only been obtained using animals as test samples. To date, regrettably, human subjects have *not* been used. The graph information is therefore a guide: it is not absolute.
TENTATIVE CONCLUSION:
Although no toxin was present in the victim's eye drops, as suggested, a compound was found in cadaver lymph node tissue, with molecular weight 68,000 daltons; consisting polypeptide A-chain and B-chain, with trisulphite linkage as would be expected for Viscumin. The chart colour was also within

tolerance – *however*, the glycoprotein receptors were *not* the binding lectins expected, but instead resembled those naturally occurring in the demoic acid of paralytic shellfish toxins, habitant in Japanese and Eastern Canadian sea-water. It is likely (though again not absolute) that death occurred from administration of a recombinant-bonding amalgam, hitherto unknown, prepared from these two poisons.

For possible administration,

See Addendum:

Lowel paused first to bless the memory of J. Edgar and his megalomaniac dream of the best crime lab in the world. He ignored the caution; 'absolute' was just the usual technical experts covering their ass.

. . . From the absence of enzyme acetylcholinesterase within nerve junctions of cadaver muscle cells (lung and heart), and the corresponding presence of acetylcholine, which prevents transmission of muscular nerve impulses from those junctions, it is concluded that the composite toxin has further been bonded to a nerve gas agent, probably type Sarin as used for military field studies in Britain.

APPLICATION:

Despite the absence of toxin in the eye drops, application may be direct – a single drop of the combinant liquid, possibly diffused throughout a sheet of paper. *Or*, the two agents could be kept apart, in which case reaction would only occur indirectly (i.e. when both halves were brought together – a common lay illustration would be the mixing of constituents for quick-acting super-epoxy, 'Crazy Glue').

In either case, application must be to the victim's skin. No specific area is required. The toxin composite described has no present antidote.

But did *She* do it . . .?

If yes, as usual with his second guessing of her actions, he had been wrong about the eye-drops: She never used the obvious. There had to be something, any-thing, in the FBI's file that could turn his phantom into a living woman. He set the autopsy aside and went through the Bureau field agents' sexual risk reports again.

The wife-swapping butlers were stable in their new relationships; the mistresses who couldn't type weren't – but the women were not poisoners either. One had a suspended sentence for shoplifting pantyhose; the second had just collected another traffic citation on her licence for driving over 30 in a school zone; the third was appealing a $50 fine for not scooping after her micro-poodle. All three women had current addresses and solid references.

The following page was one he had missed. Oval Office passes, in numerical order of seniority. Kolinski, Victor – a listing a third of the way down had an initial sexual preference assessment of 'probable transvestite, based on conversation overheard in Georgetown Racquet Club steam room'. That Bureau preliminary assessment was nulled when 'higher level surveillance found subject acts out "king of the singles bars" off Pennsylvania Avenue at 13th. Wears Prince Valiant "rug", metallic gold. Comes on to young Miss Lonelyhearts type woman as Mr Macho. Following recent blood test scare (negative) set up home gym and turned monk.'

Lowel found himself agreeing with Wilson Elricks: working with the grubby underbelly of human nature, the grime rubbed off. He picked up Castilio's file sheet again. The field agent's report mentioned the 'bondage type personal ads circled by victim' – and a sterling-silver string of character references: Castilio's chief in Protocol, his bank manager, the outgoing lady president of the Potomac Heights Art Club, with her glowing testimonial: 'our newly elected club president, Mr Castilio, was always so kind. Like the way he cared for his mother with her illness at the end, and that poor girl, Janice, with the appendix scar who modelled our life class and got evicted –'

Her!

With a scar. The file informant's name was Julia Teague.

His chopper landed in her back paddock, scaring the horses. In this privileged neck of the nation's capital region, there were more of them per square mile than people. The Teague residence was in strict conformance with the area's building covenant: white, mock colonial, four pillars, blue shutters, black jockey, bronze eagle. The latter was up on the barn roof-ridge as a weathervane; the jockey was down on the ground, painted cast aluminium, wearing the Teague racing colours of orange and mauve, and holding out the word STUDIO.

Julia Teague's hobby connected the house to the barn and had three huge skylights set into the north-facing slope of its shingle roof. A Dutch door, cut in half, had the top half open. Julia Teague was leaning on the bottom half, wearing a checked cotton shirt, sleeves rolled above her elbows, and smoking a pipe. Which was when Lowel began to wonder whether he had the firm handle he'd anticipated on this witness. The odour coming from her was unmistakable: hand-raised, mountain-grown, top leaves only, Mary Jane. Julia Teague removed her marijuana pipe and said with a pleased smile, 'I know that indecisive look of a man. You're trying to decide whether to meet horses first or paintings.'

'I like horses,' he said, 'but I'm pressed for time.'

'Paintings it is. Come inside.'

The woman's Virginia voice had the self-confidence that came from a lifetime of owning acreage and introducing unexpected club guest speakers. Julia Teague slid back a bolt and opened the lower half of the Dutch door. The smell of pot and oil paints, mixed with horse shit and saddle soap, was strong enough to pour back in a jug and sell as cologne at the Smithsonian Boutique. Stretched canvases were stacked in drying bins around the studio;

185

a large wooden easel supported another beneath the centre skylight. The picture's rough backing was turned to Lowel. He gave his name and added himself to the Bureau's payroll.

'The FBI again! About our poor Mr Castilio? Goodness gracious, what on earth more can I say?'

'In your previous statement, you referred to a girl who modelled for your art class.'

'Janice, yes. But she wasn't really a *girl*, Mr Lowel. I mean she must have been thirty if she was a day. The poor thing was desperate. My husband tells me with all these computers everywhere, there just aren't jobs any more in shorthand, or whatever it is women like her used to do. My husband is senior partner in the firm Teague Lock and Associates; they're very well known inside the Beltway. No doubt you've heard.'

He sidestepped back to Janice. 'Tell me how she came to your club. Was she an artist as well as a friend of Castilio?'

'Oh no. She couldn't *paint*,' said Julia Teague. 'And I'm quite sure our president had never laid eyes on her before her advertisement in the club newsletter. He was friendly afterwards, that was the dear man's nature, and even in early summer the life class can be chilly at night. He brought along his own electric heater for her – of course, he laughed off any suggestion of ulterior motive, like charity: "Goose bumps are so difficult to do!" was how he put it.'

'In our file you state she also had an appendix scar. Can you confirm that?'

'No.'

He felt a massive let-down.

'I'm afraid I told a little lie. She had a scar, but it wasn't really from appendicitis. Much smaller and lower down. She said it was from having a mole removed that was giving her trouble with her elastic' – Julia Teague's voice broke off in feminine delicacy, then inquired – 'Mr Lowel, are you married?'

'I was. My wife died.'

'Oh, I'm so sorry, but then you'll understand . . .'

'Not exactly.'

'I mean,' said Julia Teague, 'how in *that* area a woman, well, especially a person like Janice, just can't be too careful. The unfortunate creature had clearly had herself sterilized, but to spare her feelings I left that detail out of my painting.'

He said, with his last bit of self-control, 'Does your painting show her face?'

'You want to see her *face*? Why didn't you say so at the start? I thought it was poor John Castilio you were interested in.'

A whinnying laugh reverberated up into the high loft-ceiling. Julia Teague put her hash pipe on the door-ledge and took his arm. They came around to the front of the painting on the easel. This society matron didn't have a care in the world about being busted for smoking a controlled substance in front of a G-man, but when it came to her Art she had the fearful apprehension of any creator.

'You must be honest, Mr Lowel. Now tell me truly what you think of my Janice.'

Three eyes stared sardonically at him – at least they were like eyes inasmuch as they had diamond shapes with black dots in the middle and lay on their side. Other parallelograms set within off-centred rectangles and skewed squares might add up to parts of a female body, if the viewer dropped enough LSD onto a sugar cube to float out of his own head. As a last hope, the Bureau ID reconstruction staff could give the blonde coloured pieces a try, he decided.

'I'll take it.'

'Oh, how wonderful! They do seem to be popular,' said

Julia Teague, picking up her pot pipe. 'I sold one just like it – but of course from a different perspective – to another policeman of some kind, only last week. A Mr Murphy. Perhaps you know him.'

18

This time Lowel started at the bottom. He arrived without warning and proceeded unescorted straight from the landing pad to the CIA Clerk of Records' Office in the west annexe. A young woman doing fielding duty at Enquiries didn't know him from a hole in the ground: the flush-faced senior clerk of the division, summoned at the double, did.

'Mr Lowel! A long time since we've seen you here. How are you?' The double was a slow one, barely a rapid walk, and the senior clerk puffed between each short sentence from the effort of it.

'I'm well,' Lowel answered, with concern, 'but how about yourself?'

'Quadruple bypass. Six months ago. Coming on fine. Much better than it sounds. How can we be of help?'

It sounded terrible. He said, 'I want to see two things: first, your current list of proprietaries; second, travel records for deputies and above, covering the last six weeks.'

'Mr Lowel, we're old friends. But you have no current departmental standing. These are level one search requests. I must have Director's authorization.'

The clerk looked at him regretfully; even with this short conversation, the man's face had changed from a flush to drawn and pale.

'I have authorization.' He produced his Presidential Finding. 'You can consider this an audit without notice, under the terms of CIA Review Act, para five.'

To a man serving a lifetime sentence among classified paper, the Finding was the equivalent of Moses getting the Word in stone.

'At once . . .' the clerk said, with short gasps. '. . . You can perform . . . the audit . . . in my office.'

Which was automated to the minute. The documents required were listed on a terminal, then either displayed there on the screen or, in the case of paper records, were drawn from basement bins by robot arms and passed upwards through a sealed tube to be scanned by a video recognition laser as they emerged. If the call code matched, the document was allowed to fall into human hands: if not, it returned via rotating drum to the nether world.

The clerk sat at his desk and got back his breath while he keyed in the control instructions for the search. When the terminal showed CURRENT PROPRIETARY INDEX, he said in a more even voice to Lowel, 'I can take it to the next search level, or leave now, as you wish.'

'Stay. I'm playing against time. Can we go straight in, alphabetical?'

'Certainly.' The clerk's hands waited with a slight tremor on the keys. 'Please spell phonetics.'

'Papa Alpha Romeo . . .' The clerk repeated each letter as he keyed it in, '. . . Echo Charlie Hotel – PARACEL-TECH.'

The dirty linen appeared instantaneously on screen.

| Nature of proprietary: | Medical Research Laboratory |
| External function: | Oncogenetic (cancer) applications |

Internal function:	Chemical warfare (nerve) agents

Financial status:	Preferred Shares:
	    agency wholly owned
	Common shares:
	    Agency 51%
	    Founder 49%

Agency acquisitions:	3 months
Deniable contact:	Martin, H.

There it was: just as a poisoning bitch needed a private playhouse in which to mix her new super brew, the Agency happened to have bought one – complete with a deniable human guinea-pig recruit, called Harold Martin.

The senior clerk said, 'It's touch-screen if you want to expand on anything further, Mr Lowel.'

'Line eight.'

He put his index finger out and touched Founder.

Name:	Melcham, James St John
Activity:	Entrepreneur
Age:	50
Born:	British subject, East Grinstead, Sussex
Education:	Harrow School, and Oxford, UK
Government service:	Three years British SIS
Other history:	One term Member of Parliament Resigned seat for financial irregularity, Guinness stock listing Formed Levant Trading Ltd for Iran/Iraq arms transshipments Granted US citizenship (1989)

No surprises here, either. The background of entrepreneurial corruption was exactly what the previous administration liked dealing with, and what had moved Lowel out of this line of business. The brewing company scandal had made financial waves on both sides of the Atlantic: the name Melcham meant nothing to him.

'The deputies' previous travel,' said the senior clerk, 'shall I call them up now?'

'Give me a print-out on Paracel-Tech first.'

The laser repro unit had it on paper almost before he finished speaking. The laboratory information vanished from the screen to be replaced by DEPUTY WORKING INDEX and a list of six names. The fourth name – JAVEZ, Garcia – was the only one from the old days that he would trust out of the Agency's present rat's nest.

'Any expansion?' asked the senior clerk.

'I'll take it to next level my eyes only,' Lowel answered. The clerk's brief nod conveyed complete understanding of that implication. The man walked to the door of his office at his slow pace, and said as he opened it, 'The intercom buzzer. When you're finished.'

The door closed. Lowel touched line 2: MURPHY.

Division budget title:	ANTI-TERROR
Travel warrants issued:	
Preceding 60 Days:	UK, USSR, UK
" 30 Days:	UK, GDR, UK
" 15 Days:	UK, FR, UK
" 7 Days:	UK, GR, UK

He stared at the pattern of the Soviet Union, East Germany, France, and Greece: the fillers in Murphy's recent travel, neatly sandwiched between pre- and post-slices of consultation in Britain. But what to do about it? In relation to the time left until Yalta, getting external corroboration of the who-withs and why-theres of the Deputy's movements would take forever. Taking the man out of circulation might tip off the woman; but if the redheaded boss of Anti-Terror was left in place –?

There was no easy choice. Lowel postponed a decision, made a hard copy of the travel schedule, erased his terminal entry, and called Enquiries on the intercom. When the girl that fielded them answered, he asked, 'Is Mr Murphy in the building?'

'I'll check my status board.' Longer than necessary. He crossed swiftly to the door . . . in time to hear the Enquiries fielder saying on her side of it, into an internal phone, 'Yes sir, I'm to show sign-out one hour ago. Very good, Mr Mur –'

She broke off, and looked up with a belligerent stare at Lowel standing over her. Decisions make themselves. He pressed the switchboard's alarm red button to Security, which got doors closing before they asked questions. With the first raucous clang of the bell, the Enquiries person was starting to look more like an employee concerned for her pay cheque than an active belligerent. He took the receiver out of her hand and said, 'Murphy, this is Lowel. I've ordered internal security to seal the building. Tell me what room you're in, and don't leave it before I get there. Understood?'

'If we're playing cowboy again,' Murphy's voice said contemptuously, 'bring your six-gun. I'm turkey shooting with the Director.'

Lowel passed the phone back to its switchboard operator. Further comment on her actions would be overkill; as the alarm bell kept ringing, the barrier doors automatically slammed shut all around her, the Enquiries person was only a badly frightened young woman.

'Locate the Fourth Assistant for me,' he told her. 'Mr Javez – and there's no need to check your status board. It's a working day; he'll be in the building.'

'Mr Javez. Yes, sir. Mr Lowel, with Mr Murphy, I was just following instructions.'

'Sure,' he said. 'And I'm about to remind him, for public servants that line hasn't held up in court since 1945.'

The pistol range used to be called the turkey shoot, because of the distinctive noise which came from the gobbling bellow of southern marksmanship instructors trying to make their yodelled commands heard over the amplified explosions of small-arms rapid fire. Now, the practice weapons were laser fitted, the instructors murmured, and the only sounds from the guns were crisp trigger clicks as the monochromatic beams of light stabbed out against a moving row of photo-sensitive targets. The triggers had a normal action so that the weapon 'feel' was the same as it would be under working conditions.

Three internal security guards, standing outside the door of the range when Lowel reached it, were at work, and so packed two 9 mm versions each of the real thing.

'Is Mr Murphy still in there?' he asked the senior guard.

'Yes, sir. With the Director. The instructors are segregated in the control booth.'

'Release them. No one else leaves without my order. When Mr Javez arrives, allow him through.'

'Yes, sir.' The senior guard allowed a raised eyebrow. 'That verbal order was, no one leaves?'

Lowel nodded. 'Your superior has it from me in writing.'

In this town where nobody signed for anything on paper any longer, that was enough to nail him to the cross if Yalta went wrong – and probably if it didn't!

Murphy was standing with his back turned, studiously ignoring Lowel's entry. The Director was seated magisterially, like the judge he used to be, but not on a court bench: the old man was in a converted golf cart, minus its sun canopy, that ran back and forth on electric wheels behind the firing line. One of the laser pistols was attached to a rest bracketed on the front handlebar of the cart, and raised to eye level: just squeeze and shoot. He pointed it at Lowel and did exactly that.

'I only pray the Lord Jesus it was live!' the old man shouted, as the red beam missed his target and illuminated a sign behind saying TREAT EVEN YOUR PRACTICE WEAPON WITH RESPECT. 'What in Satan's hell do you think you and that one-armed squirt on Pennsylvania Avenue are all playin' at with my Agency? Lowel, you turncoat son of a bitch, answer me that!'

With the same pinpoint imprecision, a second laser blast from the Agency's Director highlighted the polished left shoe of his Fourth Assistant as it came through the door. Garcia Javez looked concerned for the overall situation, but not surprised by his superior's specific action. He was a slim man, with the carved profile of an Inca priest rather than the rounded Chicano peasant features of his San Antonio parents.

Lowel showed his Finding to Javez and said, 'On the President's authority, you are hereby appointed interim Director of this Executive Agency, with the full powers of that office. Your predecessor is being relieved of his duties for at least the next five days, while he undergoes immediate medical examination for extreme exhaustion. The necessary testing will be conducted under strict sequestration, at the Agency's special psychiatric unit at Walter Reed. Inform your trauma team that the patient requires sedation and a helo lift –'

'In a pig's ass!' The subject of the proposed medical assistance attempted to launch himself from his mobile firing-platform before stopping it, so falling victim to the laws of momentum and inertia, via the rear wheel of the golf cart. 'Goddamn you all,' the old man said, like a tearful child from the floor. 'I can't walk. You've gone and made me hurt my knee.'

Javez said to Lowel, 'God help my wife and kids, I accept the President's order,' and lifted an adjacent phone. As the call connected he added, 'I'll include a stretcher party for the patient.'

'Never trust a spik.' Murphy enunciated it clearly, over his shoulder. 'White men in the company learned that lesson from the Bay of Pigs.'

The redheaded Deputy fired a string of six moving target heartshots with his laser. Garcia Javez spoke crisply into the phone and flushed slightly on the back of his olive-skinned Hispanic neck. The old judge hugged his knee and, while a white-coated medic arrived and jabbed the needle, made unprintable predictions of the death penalty for Lowel.

He waited in silence for the former Director's removal on the stretcher, then when Javez had relocked the door he said to Murphy, 'I won't be wasting much time on you personally, but I do have a question about your biographical report on the woman called Maria Meliti.'

'Not my report, cowboy. You were told that paper was asswipe from day one. Both the Director and myself specifically discounted it.'

'I was told,' he said, 'the biography was compiled by that night's duty officer. What was his name, and where is he now?'

'For the sake of the record,' Murphy replied, with a sneer, 'and the Congressional investigation that's going to follow this shit-play of yours, let's keep our starting-gate facts straight: if you check the tapes, at our last meeting the Judge did the talking. I told you word zero about any woman – but the originating name was Erikson, and if you want him he's in a Hercules cargo bay, somewhere between San Salvador and a hero's funeral in Arlington.'

'Is that true?' Lowel turned to Javez for confirmation.

'I can't authenticate he originated your biography, but we did lose an agent, name Erikson, in San Salvador two days ago. He was posted down by standard rotation on the Central American roster. Just after arrival,' Javez added, with a grim sadness, 'his car was crossfired from ambush, halfway between the airport and the Embassy. So far no group has claimed responsibility.'

And no one was going to, thought Lowel. There might be a false front funeral at the National Cemetery, but the man called Erikson would be remembered as no hero: just one more betrayed gold star in the CIA lobby. Meanwhile, the former Number Two of the Agency was making a production of not being affected by small-scale tragedy: Murphy shrugged contemptuously, turned back to the targets, fired from the hip and bagged two more heartshots with his laser.

'For the sake of the record that Mr Murphy's so concerned about,' Lowel told Javez, 'let it show he has volunteered his fullest co-operation with Counter-Espionage in the inquiry they're just starting. He also agrees to remain confined in their debriefing vault at Safe House One until the President returns from Yalta, or you get further orders.' He indicated the redhead's laser pistol, 'Tell his keepers from C-E they can begin by taking that toy, his badge and his office away from him.'

Which brought down the curtain on the former Deputy of Anti-Terror's cool performance.

'You cowboy cocksucker, I won't –' Murphy was shouting incoherently at Lowel's back, as he walked out of the small-arms range, and the defensive tackles from C-E came in from the passage with their straitjacket. 'It wasn't this Agency that tried to gas your bumbuddy. We don't have 50 billion going down the tubes because of his Star Wars cancellation. Me running any poison broad is bullshit. After Lebanon, not the vault! Lowel, you bastard, I can't handle close confine . . .'

197

The soundproofed door shut off the rest of it. As Lowel returned to the outside Washington world of endless buck-passing and hopeless explanations, the question of who drafted a profile of his female antagonist was academic. She existed. In the time remaining only one thing mattered:

Stop Her!

19

Moving house:

Washington

When Lowel checked by the Oval Office to dump on Daniel Galbraith that the upper crust of the nation's external security apparatus was now under virtual arrest, he was nearly run over: stacked-up trunks of Chief Executive clothing, china, insignia, and giveaway freebies were being trundled at the rush, on built-in wheels, through the backstage passages of the White House.

'Worse than a Las Vegas roadshow,' the President said as he caught sight of Lowel; 'meet my Chief of Vaudeville for State visiting.'

The person in charge of the protocol show was a former Navy chief petty officer and fellow crewman of Galbraith's with the unflappable demeanour and deadpan face of a society undertaker. He shook hands as though in sympathy. Lowel used the opportunity to request an inventory of Oval Office effects that the dead Castilio could have accessed.

'Certainly, sir. But if you want to include the rotational items in basement storage – President Johnson's doghouse for his beagles, for example – it will be a somewhat lengthy list.'

'I didn't mean furniture,' Lowel said. 'Everyday stuff. Office supplies, liquor decanters and glasses, the kind of freebies you stock in those trunks I saw going by. I want to know anything missing, even the smallest item.'

'I understand.' The protocol chief bowed himself backwards from the Executive presence in time to stop the imminent collision of a trunk labelled KENNEDY WINE-STEMS with another of LINCOLN CHINA. The latest White House incumbent seemed fully recovered from his brush with death by asphyxiation.

'Let's take five, Jack, in my version of a sweat box.' Galbraith gave him a grin, then called sharply after his former crewman, 'I want the interpreter, soonest. Have someone chase up Prince Valiant, and tell him from me to hustle his ass.'

The subject in question, Victor Kolinski, flexed again, admiring himself in his latest Danskin aerobics spandex bodysuit, in the mirrors of his personal Aurora Heights townhouse gym. Glittering emerald green, and tight-tight-tight. Man, there wasn't a vein or a muscle that it didn't reveal! Biceps, triceps, dorsals, pectorals – his chest was so developed he sometimes worried it might be almost too much; under his monogrammed, hand-sewn shirts it could look almost like female breasts.

But that was crazy . . . because right after checking his rippling abdominals his admiring eye got to the parts that proved he was all Man, with a capital M! He turned so the sidewall mirrors could catch the bulges better. And just looking made him harder, so the rim of the head stood out more under the sleek –

His concentration was broken. To his violent annoyance there was another face in the mirror behind his own. The latest bimbo's, what's-her-name?

She had already been Janice on one side of the Atlantic, and Sarah on the other: back in Washington again, this time she was anonymous. Obsessive vanity, to the point of blindness, was the sexual weapon used to get her inside this ultra private townhouse. The pumped-up mass of male insecurity called Kolinski never used his sexual partner's name. As she discovered at their first meeting last night, in the singles bar around the corner from the Executive Office Building, the interpreter spoke mostly to himself, in the mirror, using the royal plural. Men like this were repelled by women, subconsciously preferred other men, but refused to admit it, producing a constant guilt which found its outlet in anger. The only thing she had to watch was not to reveal her utter contempt for him. She averted her eyes and said diffidently, 'Hi, Vic.'

At the sound of her voice, automatically he sucked in his gut, although it couldn't be flatter, or his waist smaller. She hardly needed the extensive information in her target profile: his body language made his thoughts transparent. God, the hours he had spent! Forget the money! Thirty-five grand, easy, on the gym, lap pool, Home Master automated security system. The last item was permanently installed as part of the house wiring, inside the walls, but was worth every penny because it kept him Private with a capital P. When he used to work out at the Georgetown Racquet Club there wasn't a session some crotchbound, ironhead jock from the Pentagon didn't laugh at his 'girly' ass, because no matter how much work Kolinski put in on the bench-press his goddamn hips were still set that infuriatingly feminine bit too high.

'Do you want I should start on my back bends, Vic?'

She was wearing one of the dozen new Jane Fonda stringsuits he had bought her for a moving-in present: cut so high on the thigh in front, by the small scar over her groin, the suit barely covered the lips of her mound.

'No back bends,' he snapped. 'Give us a Jump-Turn, right now!'

'Yes, Vic.'

He didn't use her name, but the reason he had decided to keep her, he had condescended to explain last night, was that she did what she was told, pronto! 'Like now, bimbo! Legs apart!' With a high spring so that, in back, the fabric from her crotch disappeared completely up between the cheeks of her ass.

She said softly, 'Is this how you like it, Vic?'

Her head was down on the floor, looking back at him, her eyes fixed on his, while she contracted her buttocks, squeezing them together, letting them go . . .

'That's enough!'

His prick was rising in spasmodic jerks across his belly under the taut front of his stretch suit. It was something new, he had told her scornfully at the bar, Victor Kolinski having only one bimbo on tap. But when you were in the world's eye, with the AIDS thing! That was why he was having one of Washington's best private investigating firms, who did contract work for places like the CIA, check her out overnight. She had given a meek thank you, and managed a blush . . .

Now she said, 'If you want, I'm ready, Vic.'

'You most definitely are *not*! With the AIDS thing, even with one partner –!'

Even insisting on a blood test, even wearing surgical gloves and two condoms! For a man in the world's eye, it was impossible to be too careful. She watched as he checked the digital, twenty-four-hour wall clock by the sauna, figuring there was just enough time before his White House limo was due to arrive. He flipped her the rubber enema kit and baby oil, and barked – although in his excitement the House Master audio recorder picked up and sent out on the sauna loudspeaker something unpleasantly close to a hysterical female's yip, 'Bitch: when Victor Kolinski uses a woman – he wants *in* her, capital C-l-e-a-n: *Clean!*'

For Lowel, the only thing different about the White House version of a sweat box was that it had been decorated by a previous administration's First Lady with a down-home wallpaper of oil-lamps, weather-vanes, and coaching inns, to give the space-age cubicle an absurd colonial motif.

'OK,' said Galbraith, 'so how wet is the track out at Langley?'

'We won't be able to lay money on anything they have produced up to this moment.' Lowel gave a swift summary of his actions at CIA, concluding, 'I just hope you can accept my apology for the political embarrassment it's going to –'

'Screw politics!' the President exploded. 'You gave the old fart only four days on the couch? After the world-wide security hysteria he's allowed that bastard Murphy to touch off, and an agent lost in San Salvador – Christ on a crutch, I should string them both up! But at any rate,' Galbraith's flare of temper cooled slightly, 'I guess it means we're off the hook with their Typhoid Mary.'

An intercom buzzer sounded. 'Protocol speaking, Mr President: the interpreter is being collected, and the schedule is two minutes late on your departure for the United Kingdom.'

'OK, Chief, we're through.'

Galbraith moved to the door. Lowel said, 'I'm afraid we're not off the hook. The FBI Lab confirmed your junior man from protocol, Castilio, was poisoned. The toxin used was a derivative of the stolen Viscumin, and he was involved with a woman who had a scar on her groin.'

The President stood for a moment, with his good hand holding the doorknob, then he said, 'On the level: with four days to go, can you find her?'

'Maybe. If the Cray computers –'

'Jack, I said level.'

'I don't think we'll find her before you arrive at Yalta.'

'And after?'

Lowel looked into the eyes of his oldest friend. 'Then

I'd say, Dan, it depends how close in for the kill she's prepared to get.'

She was standing behind Victor Kolinski's shoulder. As just his latest 'what's-her-name', she had been discarded after he was finished with her, and after he had disinfected his genitals thoroughly. 'With our new special anti-bacterial soap,' he had informed her tersely, on exiting the bathroom, 'recommended by the Army presidential medical team at Walter Reed Hospital. Use it!'

'Yes, Vic.'

Now she watched with suitably downcast eyes as the self-obsessed ham in front of her checked his appearance yet again in the townhouse mirrors. 'All our life,' he reminded the glass, 'we've wanted to be an actor! From the moment we step out that front door this afternoon, we're on the world stage. Our clothing has to match the occasion.' His manicured hands patted the Egyptian cotton shirt and handkerchief, Italian silk socks and tie: all colour co-ordinated and matched to his Trump Tower suit and Bond Street shoes.

She saw the petulant mouth pout. He was looking at what was listed in her file on him as 'our crowning glory!' The hair. The childish expression on his face said it all. Premature baldness, what could be more unfair? A hairplug treatment had worked along the edges of the scalp but it never took on the top; and the weaving process looked good on camera, but it couldn't be washed so that was out. 'Now we're stuck with the tried and true!' Which meant a 'piece', and spirit gum. Twice monthly, her file recorded, he had one of the presidential beauticians – who also provided his Max Factor pancake make-up to hide his five o'clock shadow – tint his moustache, eyebrows, and sideburns to match. As he stroked them again she murmured, 'Your suitcase, Vic.'

She was standing with it on the landing behind him.

'Standing around in that?' She was wearing a see-through baby-doll. He threw a heavy terry robe at her. 'Cover it up.'

'Sorry, Vic. I thought you would like it.'

'She *thought*?' He was addressing the mirror. 'The bimbos we're forced to use don't have one collective thought in their heads!'

For such a man, the mere sight of a woman's body after the sexual act was repugnant. As the White House limo swung into the driveway, she thought that he was indeed going to be physically ill. He gasped out, 'You used *our* razor!'

He had a pair of them, for home and away, gold plated, with his autograph engraved and vernier controls for the blade gap. They were specially made for him in Switzerland, with black ceramic cases hand-polished in Japan. Now, with his last glance around his spotless dressing-room, he had seen the home one sitting out on the counter where she had deliberately left it, the oriental beauty of its case smeared with a stomach-turning mixture of soap and scummy baby oil.

He raised his hand to strike her – but doing so would ruin his appearance. Seething, he cleaned the razor and case, dried them with a monogrammed towel, and put them away in the cabinet beside his spare hair pieces. He caressed the razor case lovingly a last time with his finger tips, then locked the cabinet door.

'OK,' he told the mirror, 'I guess we'll do.'

On the landing again he grabbed the suitcase from her. 'Bimbo! You want our limo driver and the rest of Aurora Heights to see you?'

'Sorry, Vic, I didn't think.'

With a snort of disgust he made his last system settings for the Home Master security system: time away, time of return, rooms to be entered by staff, rooms *not*.

'Remember, the dressing-room and bedroom are strictly off-limits. The system will tell us when we come home next week if you've messed with any of it.'

'Yes, Vic. You left your pen.'

His special gold Sheaffer, a gift from his presidential employer. Further annoyed at the error, Kolinski began to slip the pen in his pocket.

'Does it have ink?' she asked.

'We don't need you to remind us.' But he checked anyway, flicking the lever. A blue-black drop formed on the nib. Touched his index finger. 'Shit! Now look what you've made us do.' He wiped the blot and snapped, 'The system will also tell you when to send out our laundry and dry cleaning. Don't forget.'

'No, Vic. Good luck!'

The target regarded her with complete contempt. 'For a world actor of our irreplaceable skills,' he said icily, 'luck has nothing to do with it – but if you must wish us something on these occasions, for next time the appropriate phrase is "Break a leg".'

'I'll remember that, Vic.'

She had made a mistake. The piece of slime leaving in the limo was not a target. Not this time. Until the right time he was just an object. While she prepared to take the crucial actions for which she had been forced to tolerate Kolinski's macho sadism, she turned on the high-definition TV set in the den . . . and found herself looking again at a more serious male challenge: her principal opponent.

On the White House lawn, Lowel watched the interpreter preceding the President into the helicopter. The scathing nickname, 'Prince Valiant', was self-explanatory. A hairstyle of fringe and full bangs, dyed metallic gold, was ludicrous on a middle-aged male. The interpreter was dressed to match, in clothes that must have cost a fortune, and made him look like a 42nd Street pimp. Purple tinted glasses were the finishing touch. The nickname had also been used by the FBI, Lowel suddenly remembered, for their Oval Office sex file: so this was the ex-king of the singles bar, with the terror of AIDS, who turned monk. The President's own celebrated hairdo blew in the down draught. He waved for the cameras – and the vain interpreter moved sideways to get himself included in the shot. The chopper lifted off on what the TV news anchor beside Lowel called portentously, 'The first leg of a journey into history . . .'

If they only knew, he thought – and thanked God, so far they did not! If the threat leaked and was added to the word Red, the pressure cooker of public opinion would kill the Dismantling Agreement. But it might save Galbraith's life. For as long as it took the dark green presidential machine to vanish westwards, he wondered whether he should spring the leak himself to the network heavyweight beside him . . .

'Mr Lowel, sir. An urgent personal call for you at the security office.'

A junior gofer running out across the lawn brought him back to White House reality. Daniel Galbraith would rather die than call it quits on achieving final nuclear disarmament. He followed the messenger back to the Secret Service control centre. A lead-sealed special courier pouch was waiting for him at the switchboard.

'It just came in from London, originator Dawson.' The female operator extended a logbook. 'Initial receipt here, please.'

He scrawled J.L. and broke the seal. Inside was a cube-shaped package in another, smaller pouch. There was also an envelope sealed and embossed with red wax. He borrowed a paperknife from the switchboard girl and slit the flap. The envelope contained a memo, but it wasn't from Dawson at the London Embassy. The letterhead was Government Communications Bureau, the SIS headquarters.

BY HAND OF COURIER

To: J.Lowel, The White House, Washington.
Subject: Post-mortem results from Viscumin.
North London Forensic reports:
Local Vicar: Negative
Grande Dame: Negative
Sandwich-maker: POSITIVE
Summary: Bull's-eye and congratulations.

Signed: Ryder

There was nothing to be proud of in the murder of a naïve and innocent woman who labelled sandwich-boxes with Welsh red dragons and little Union Jacks, and yet, Lowel admitted to himself, he shared Ryder's elation at this proof of Morris's death. Coming on top of the Castilio result, it gave two absolute dates and approximate times. He asked the Secret Service operator to put him through to the computer chief clown in the basement at NSA.

'Before you ask, the answer is no,' the senior programmer said. 'But the good news is that we've medianed your odds on the lady down to about 1 in 30 mill.'

'I wasn't asking,' Lowel replied, 'but maybe what I'm going to pass on will whittle things down further.' He gave the dates and times. 'There can't be 30 million transatlantic flight combinations which tie in like that.'

'Now we're crunching,' the programmer agreed, 'but don't hang around for me to call you back.'

'I won't be here, anyway. Relay any results to the chief of security, London station, and good luck.'

'Mr Lowel, the tiny mind of a Cray Super Two ain't never heard of nuthin' as Fred Flintstone illogical as luck.'

He laughed and hung up the phone. Things were rolling. He turned his attention to the other sealed pouch and snipped the wire bonded by the lead. On top of whatever lay inside was a handwritten note.

'Oh, by the way,' said the switchboard operator, 'we have a phone message here for you from Mr Wong. Maybe more good news?'

Dear Jack:
I'm not finding the right words and I don't see when there's going to be a right moment but, with no family over here, just thought you might want this on your side of the wide ocean.

                                                                    Dawson

Lowel didn't know . . . and yet he did. He reached into the pouch and drew out the cube-shape that filled it. The box was white cardboard with a polished surface; a container that might be used for a Harrods' gourmet ice-cream, but the logo in embossed black script read 'South Kensington Mortuary'. The label below it:

IN MEMORIAM

THE LAST MORTAL REMAINS

OF

JACQUELINE MARYA CAMPBELL

He didn't know her middle name was Marya. He didn't know what he was going to do with her ashes. He didn't know why life was the way it was, or love, or death. He said to the switchboard girl, who was looking at the note and the ice-cream carton, 'Did you ask me something just now?'

'No, Mr Lowel. Maybe you should sit down.'

The girl was lying, because now he remembered her good-news question with complete clarity. He saw that she had eyes as black as the ice-cream lettering and that there were tears in them. He couldn't handle more sympathy, not even from Sam Wong. He put the container back in the courier's pouch and slipped its handle on his wrist.

'Thanks,' he said to the girl, 'but I can't sit here. Call up my chopper please; I've got a fast flight to catch.'

The B1 went through boom one at 4 P.M., Eastern Daylight Time, climbing away from Washington and the sun at a rate of acceleration that made the overtaken Air Force Two, with the President and an hour's head start, stand still. Twice the speed of sound was achieved by the four General Electric turbofan afterburners 50,000 feet above an oil-rig colossus whose platform looked like a pinhead, 300 nautical miles east of the Bay of Fundy.

Although it was their second transatlantic flip that day, the bomber's crew had been able to rest in the interval. As the G-force lessened on his body, Lowel felt the return of grinding exhaustion. The B1's laconic commander took his numbed silence for deep thought: the senior pilot turned down the intercom and gave a mute sign to the two other crewmen behind him. For the return journey, Lowel had again been given the privilege of the co-pilot's in-front position . . .

'Don't want to intrude,' the commander's Texas drawl did so, somewhere past Newfoundland, as they were overtaking a Concorde, 'and I can't offer the goose in the ass of a good prop-job dogfight but, with boom three comin' up, I thought maybe you'd still like to hold on to the computer?'

No flyer could refuse such a compliment. The aircraft's control column poked up from the floorboards, in front of the seat, but that was the only similarity to an old-fashioned joystick. In what must now be the final modification of the B1, the column didn't move: pressure from the pilot's fingers reflected his intentions, through three axes – up, down, sideways – to be transmitted electronically and converted by computer commands to the appropriate control surfaces. In battle, pilot commands could even be sent straight into the system vocally.

But the thrill remained. Lowel held the column and pressed his fingers . . . and watched the Mach read-out creeping upwards, 2.8, 2.9, and the wing tips developing their luminous pink glow, and the black edge of space reaching down to touch the hull . . .

'Boom three!' When he said it into the headset, the crew grinned.

'Makes three in a row for aviation history.' The senior pilot pointed at a silver gleam off the starboard. 'We've just taken out Aeroflot's new hypersonic competition. The Reds are doing their caviar-run today from Dulles to London.'

'Excuse, please: apogee now.' As on their westward flight, the navigation specialist reached past and released another wind-drift package from one of the missile decoy flare launch-tubes.

Lowel took off the mike and leaned across to speak in private to the aircraft's commander. 'A great experience. Can I have one more request?'

'Anything short of dropping the big one! You're boss on this ride, Mr Lowel.'

He took the ice-cream box out of his courier pouch. The B1 commander glanced and took in the black letters on the side. Lowel opened the flap of the expended tube, placed the box inside, sealed the tube flap, pulled the red T-handle.

And Jacky was where she would wish to be: somewhere between the curve of this one blue earth and those billion silver stars . . .

His two helicopters were waiting for him on the tarmac at Farnborough. England was still raining. He climbed down from the B1 and shook hands with the crew. He gave a special thanks to the commander.

'No need, sir. My privilege. Any time.'

The pilot saluted, rare respect from a Texan. Lowel walked to the closest chopper and boarded: heads-or-tails farting around could not fool fate any longer. At 10 P.M., British Summer Time, they lifted off in a whirl of mist and set course for London. Once more the sky cleared as he reached the city, to show its old buildings washed and shining in the dying light.

He crossed the narrow Thames again, crowded not with history but tour-launches, all heading down river to take up station for the evening light show at the Tower. The choppers swung north, using the corridor between Big Ben and Buckingham Palace, where a mounted trio of Horseguards were clip-clopping home. The eagle on the Embassy roof was casting its shadow over the lawn as he came in for landing. Someone stood waiting.

He got down and stretched. A deep-throated rumbling whistle overhead was the Aeroflot hypersonic, just entering the Heathrow pattern. By the time Daniel Galbraith's horse and buggy aircraft landed, it would be tomorrow. He saw the shadowed figure was Dawson.

'Never know I'd been gone,' Lowel said, with a bone-weary smile. 'Thanks for the greeting party, but I'm hitting the sack until the President gets here.'

Instead of returning his smile, the Embassy's chief of security held out a message tape. 'I don't know why it always has to be me, Jack. NSA just sent this through.'

The tape read:

YOUR PASSENGER PROFILE MATCH ID:
CAMPBELL, JACQUELINE MRS.

20

In the bomb-and-bullet-proof back seat of the Embassy's
most heavily protected car, Lowel rode once more through
the crowded after-theatre streets of central London. The
car was a Lincoln, built to reflect the previous administration's battleship view of the world, with steel plate like
the newly re-mothballed USS *Iowa*'s on its sides and under
its floor. The Lincoln dinosaur was at Dawson's insistence:
after NSA's last-straw clown message, of Jacqueline as his
prime suspect, Lowel's mood had been damn the torpe-
does for a taxi – to take him to a black-out drink in the
nearest London pub.

'She's dead,' he had raged at Dawson on the Embassy
lawn. 'She came home in an airline coffin. You met it. On
your direct instruction her corpse was burned to ashes in
South Kensington. You collected those ashes –'

'Yes,' Dawson said quietly, 'I collected the coffin and I
delivered it to the mortuary, and before it was cremated I
even looked inside it. And the remains were female which
I accepted, from the clothing description you gave me, as
Mrs Campbell's.'

'Accepted? You had her passport photograph. All I
have in my wallet to remember is a goddamn house-key!'

'What was left, Jack, had no positive means of identification.'

And never would. From the opposition's not allowing
him to ever know whether Jacqueline was truly dead

213

Lowel had realized, as his adrenalin ran down, that someone was really trying to destroy his mind: not his ageing, clapped-out carcass . . .

The armour-plated Lincoln turned off Old Church Street. All light had left it. The mews backing onto Carlyle Square and the garden in the centre were deserted of their daytime old gossips, of nannies and kids. Within the confines of the converted stable yard, the solitary Lincoln loomed so large that it was as though the *Iowa* herself had cruised up on the cobbles.

'The local residents won't be able to manoeuvre,' he told his latest Embassy driver. 'Find a parking spot in the main street – and after that bombing in Kensington, don't leave your vehicle unattended for any reason.'

'No chance.'

The driver tapped his sidearm holster. The Lincoln reversed and turned the corner; the mews was silent except for the pigeons settling down for the night in the wisteria vine over the front door, with its brass lion knocker. The pigeons watched with cocked heads and a cautious expression in their bright eyes, while he searched his wallet for the key that Jacqueline had given him. As he put the key in the lock, the birds poised for flight.

'Stay there,' he said, 'no one's harming –'

The pigeons clattered wings in emergency take-off. A ginger cat sprang on to the step beside him, tail thrashing. The cat pushed forward; the front door moved inward.

He hadn't turned the lock.

Hair prickled on his neck. He was unarmed – but the days when that didn't matter in law-abiding Britain were long gone. The door was stopped, ajar at the width of the cat's sinuous body. He placed his outstretched hand, palm flat, against the planking, and pressed gently . . .

EEEY-AAAY-EEEY-AAAY

The burglar alarm. To go off now, after the house had already been broken into, was typical.

A shadow.

He jumped to the other side of the doorway, to see down the hall. No lights were on. In the dusk of the interior, a squat shape moving at the double – tripped. The cat yowled and flashed from under. Lowel dived, got a Nelson on one arm, twisted. The siren drowned out the intruder's screaming. He yanked the head back in a buffalo strangle, to get the face visible.

He found himself staring at the agonized features of a man meant to be 7,000 miles away, in Portland, Oregon: his best friend and business partner, Sam Wong.

'Aargh,' Wong said, or something like it. The rising doppler wail of a police car added to the already impossible din. The tyres screeched on cobbles. Lowel stopped choking the life out of his partner.

'Sam, for Christ's sake. I'm sorry.'

'Aargm!' Wong was pointing to the alarm. The security panel's red lights were ripple flashing.

'All right, then! Not one move out of you two villains.'

English law stood in the doorway. Instead of a quaintly helmeted bobby, there were three detectives: a middle-aged sergeant and two young heavies, begging for a move to allow them a real spot of evading-arrest villain-bashing.

'I'm working with SIS,' Lowel said, from his inferior position on the floor. 'Your Special Intelligence Service.'

'Go on, Yank! With a Chink? Pull another.'

'Call them. I'm Lowel. Ask for Ryder.'

Real names introduced a slight return to order. The sergeant went out to a squad car. His two juniors stared morosely, still hoping for the gasping Chinese Wong to offer them a drop of Kung-fu bovver.

'It's a Special job all right, lads.' The sergeant came back with the confirmation for his brooding subordinates, and added to Lowel, 'Sorry sir, Mr Ryder at SIS knows about you, but not this other gentleman. If he could be so kind, we need something for Divisional records.'

'Me, too,' Lowel said, as his partner sat shakily into a kitchen chair. 'Sam, what the hell got you here?'

'Your friends at the White House. I read in the paper about –'

'Pals of the White House is one thing, sir. It doesn't exactly explain how you came to be inside this one of Mrs Jacqueline Campbell's.'

The senior member of the London police wrote a note to himself on a pad. Wong wiped the perspiration from his smooth forehead with a red-chequered kerchief.

'I was killing time on the doorstep. An old lady was walking her dog and asked why? When I explained, she said she was the nextdoor neighbour, a friend of Mrs Campbell's, and had a key to let me in. If I had reset the goddamn alarm correctly instead of letting her –'

'Oh my gawd,' one of the junior heavies saw some light. 'Not old Lady Melcham again.'

'Melcham,' Lowel repeated the name. 'Would she be related to a former Member of Parliament, by any chance?'

'The city stock swindle lot? Right!' The cop tapped his forehead. 'Funny peculiar runs in the family.'

And now it owned forty-nine per cent of a CIA proprietary company, to manufacture poison: Paracel-Tech. Not by chance.

'We'll be getting on then,' said the police officer with a sigh. 'Good night, gentlemen.'

'Good night, sergeant.'

Lowel closed the door behind the police and walked back to put together some kind of show for Wong.

'Triple Scotch for both of us, Sam; the bar's in the living room, at the rear. God, I need a slug!'

'I need a weed,' said Wong, following him. 'A day like this one knocks a guy off his wagon. Loan some of your lung-rot?'

'I quit. My makings are over there in Jacqueline's

desk. Do me a favour. Take the stuff home with you and ditch it.'

He passed Wong's glass and took a stiff belt from his own. Memories in this room were everywhere. Last time she stood where Wong was now, putting Lowel's pouch of Bull Durham away in her desk, kissing his cheek, talking about her pony tail and growing old together, and slinging him a beer . . .

'I never was so hot at this, Jack. How you do it one-handed!'

His partner was shaking the shreds of coarse tobacco along the translucent vee of cigarette-paper, attempting to form it into some kind of cylindrical shape. There was more tobacco on the desk than the paper.

'Thumb on top, two fingers under,' Lowel said, 'then lick.'

Wong paused for a drink, then repeated, 'Thumb on top, two fingers under.'

The result was a flattened drainspout.

'You're moving the fingers, Sam. Keep them steady. It's all in the thumb motion.'

'It's why Marlboro peddles them in packs of twenty!' The downspout was squashed almost shut at both ends, with wisps hanging out. 'Forget the shape, man; it's the smoke that kills yuh.'

Wong grinned. Lowel took another rasping gulp of single malt and watched the ridiculously fierce concentration as his friend lifted the unsealed cylinder to his lips and stuck out his tongue.

'You'll drown it. Just the lower lip. Run it along with your thumb, a real light touch.'

Wong's was hopelessly heavy. The redness of his lip showed through the sealing edge of the paper as his stubby hand pressed it, and his brown eyes almost crossed in a squint because the point of focus was too close.

Then he toppled and fell at Lowel's feet.

He had seen enough men die to recognize death, but his intellect refused to believe it. He stared down at his friend's crumpled body, at his face. The normal, baked-almond colour of Wong's skin was purple, his mouth was slightly open, the cigarette-paper still stuck to one lip. The contents had spilled onto the carpet; the wafer of paper was immobile – although the lightest tremor of breath would have moved it.

Breath!

Shock gave way to action. Cardiac arrest! Resuscitation!

He dropped to his knees at Wong's side, grasped his partner's head, turned it upright, took a deep breath and bent his own face down –

Don't touch that paper!

Now intellect was working: cardiac arrest meant poison! The full realization hit home. *He* was supposed to be Her target.

Torn between grief, helplessness, fury, for some time longer he knelt beside his friend, trying to ignore that other emotion his instinct could not keep out.

I'm afraid of Her.

The ginger cat came back and rubbed against his legs. Automatically he scratched its head, between its ears. One was notched with scar tissue from street battles. Two old strays, he thought, alone in the vast city. He felt the vibration through the animal's lean body as it began to purr. And then to tremble. The tail started to twitch again. The cat was staring fixedly at the French doors leading out onto the balcony.

A nightbird's trill sounded faintly. The doors couldn't be fully closed. Lowel got to his feet and moved cautiously towards the windows. The curtain on the left was drawn shut. The right was halfway open. He looked for any kind of weapon. The only possibility was a Victorian brass toasting fork hanging for ornament beside the fireplace. There was no poker: the fire itself had been converted to electric imitation.

He grasped the fork and kicked the French door outward. It flew back and sank with a scrunch of foliage into ivy growing thickly on the back wall of the townhouse. The garden was dark. The balcony was small and seemed deserted. He stepped through cautiously.

Something whipped by his head.

He whirled the toasting fork – and missed a small bat by a country mile. He heard its sonar squeak. So did the ginger cat. Hunter and hunted vanished together into the London night. Lowel turned to the French door to close it; the handle had caught in the ivy. He tugged, and only succeeded in pulling a tangle of vines off the wall. He tugged again. The handle began to come free. The door swung far enough that the glass reflected the living room's interior: the chair with the bird design, and the desk where Jacky –

Something moved in the dim hall beyond Wong's body. The door of the free-standing Georgian corner clothes cabinet swinging slowly shut. On its own weight, from the slope of the old floorboards. Which meant someone must have opened it.

He jumped over his partner's corpse, raised his primitive weapon, and grabbed at the cabinet.

Empty. Except for a trace of perfume.

Like Jacqueline's – but sharper, more pungent. That slight difference carried the second jolting message of the evening. Through the whole townhouse episode, the alarm, the cops, the killing –

She was there!

Watching her target from the cabinet. He marvelled at such ice-cold nerve. Metal clicked on the spiral staircase.

He spun to his left and saw a shape slip upwards.

He turned on a bank of light switches and rushed the stairs. Now he could see where he was going, but the treads were small on narrow winders. By the time he got to the first floor, outside Jacqueline's bedroom, the shape was gone. The bedroom and bathroom doors were shut.

Which one?

Another creak above his head. He went up the next spiral flight with more caution. The top was dark. *She* was cornered.

Vulnerable in his lower position, he came around the last bend and felt on the wall for a switch –

Glass smashed. In the darkness he saw a paler square. The moon was rising. Something blocked it. A body going through a window. He charged forward, grabbed a leg – and from the other one, got a stunning, rubber-soled kick on the jaw that felled him. By the time he was back on his feet, the body was running over the roof. The hole in the glass was too small for him to pass through. He jemmied the catch with the toasting fork.

EEEY-AAAY . . .

Again! He ignored the howling burglar alarm and got out on the roof. The shape ahead of him was vaulting a parapet on to the next building. He followed and caught up a bit as the shape slowed to negotiate a mass of Mary Poppins chimneys. He saw a shortcut, to the right, and made an end-run. The gap between them halved again. She went over a second parapet. Now he *knew* it was Her, the killer bitch. And no Garbo white raincoat shit. Assassination gear: a skin-tight black tracksuit, hood and gloves. He vaulted –

And felt himself falling. The nextdoor house was half a storey lower. The wind was knocked out of him. She was still running. Her agility and fitness humiliated him, but he still had his mind and a lifetime's training. At the next half storey he was ready for it. She went over, headlong. He slowed. Just in time. He heard a metallic crash, hollow and dangerous. A man's voice shouting.

She'd made a mistake!

His quarry must have dropped farther than she bargained, on to an iron shed of some kind. He looked down.

A double-decker bus. A late night bus, with the upper floor empty. She was crouched on top of it. Some lush, stoned outside the closed corner pub, was staring open-mouthed at her. He got ready to jump. The bus began moving. Its roof was rounded, precarious, nothing to hang on to. He hesitated . . .

She sprang. Up and across to the mews' far side. The bus driver gave the finger to the drunk and accelerated. Without the bus as a vaulting horse, the cobbled gap was impossible.

She was only twenty feet away from him.

It might as well have been the distance to the moon above the elms. Wherever She was heading next, he couldn't follow.

21

Loose ends:

Chelsea

The weary London police responded by telephone this time. Was the second burglar alarm, at the same address as the last, still part of the Special job? they wondered. Lowel said it was. They said, with a detectable note of derision, they thought it might be. He gave them a description of a possible suspect. Scotland Yard replied: 'wearing all black, no facial recognition, no fingerprints, might be female, and ten minutes ago she was on top of a double-decker in South Kensington. That will be very helpful for our enquiries, sir, I'm sure.'

He didn't blame them for being sarcastic. He left the house, with the alarm definitely *off*, and went to use the more secure communications available in the Embassy's armoured Lincoln. He found it parked around the corner and rapped on the glass to disturb the dozing driver who went on the offensive.

'I saw the local gendarmes, but you said not to leave for any reason.'

'I'm not here to chew ass,' Lowel said. 'Turn on your scrambler.'

He climbed into the back of the Lincoln and punched in the SIS number. A nasal female voice answered: 'Government Communications. This is night duty.'

He asked to be put through to Ryder.

'Mr Ryder has left the building to dine with Sir Herbert at his club. I can't disturb him unless it's quite important.'

'Say Lowel's got another sandwich job for him. '

'Are you *sure* it's quite important?'

'Quite.'

Understatement was night duty's wavelength. After a short interval, Ryder came on the line. 'More trouble with the Metropolitan Police?'

'There will be unless you can help me cool it. The lady was here. I almost caught her. She left an item that has to get to North London Forensic. In private – no flashing lights and sirens on an ambulance.'

'Wilco. I'll arrange things myself. About half an hour.'

Lowel told the driver to switch off the scrambler and stay put, then he walked back to Jacqueline's house at the end of the mews. The cul-de-sac was still deserted, the front door and alarm system as he left them. Wong's body had started going into rigor: with the lower lip's contraction, the cigarette-paper had fallen away onto the floor. He didn't like the job, but something had to be done to contain the paper and its toxin.

He found a pair of lined, pink rubber gloves under the washbasin in the bathroom, and a pair of eyebrow tweezers in a drawer. The kitchen provided a boxed roll of zip-lock, alligator-textured vinyl baggies. He had no idea how effective that material was for segregating Viscumin, but at least it would stop the cigarette-paper from any further free movement. Using three chairs from the dining room, he cordoned off the section of contaminated living-room carpet. He pulled on the gloves, which were too small at the wrist to go over his hands. Slitting the cuffs with a knife got past that hurdle.

Gloved, he took the tweezers and, with more care than a stamp collector handling a mint Penny Black, placed the used cigarette-paper in one baggie, sealed the zip-lock, placed that baggie inside another, which he also sealed. He repeated the process for the packet of the remaining unused –

Was it only in the papers?

The FBI report said that the two halves of the poison could be kept apart. Like Crazy Glue, nothing might happen until they were brought together. Paper *and* tobacco!

He gave the double-zip treatment to his pouch of Bull Durham. The last item to go under wraps was the tweezers. He placed all three doubled baggies on a large stainless steel serving dish from the sideboard, and poured himself another Scotch from the bar. He was lifting it to his lips when the voice in his head said –

You are Her prime target!

She could have poisoned anything he touched. Which was a paranoid's conclusion. The bitch didn't heist a gallon jug of Viscumin from Paracel-Tech, just a one-inch puddle in a petri dish. And she couldn't get any more: she must be hoarding it like a miser, not spraying the stuff around. A drop for Castilio, one for the Morris woman – a couple surely for her helicopter sandwiches – one for his cigarette-papers: her supply might already be half gone.

As a deliberate test, he fetched a clean glass from the kitchen and opened a new bottle of single malt Scotch from the bar. He poured a solid two fingers and knocked back half of it in one go. His stomach ignited but he was still standing. He put down the glass. Although he would have liked to get drunk before his next task, it had to be done cold sober, devoid of the underlying emotion too easily brought back to the surface by booze.

Room by room, drawer by drawer, he was going to search this house, starting with its laundry basket, to see if Jacqueline Campbell's dirty linen could tell him who else she might have been.

But he began with the desk where she put his makings . . . when it came to the crunch, going straight to her clothing made the search unbearably personal.

224

The desk was a Georgian antique, walnut, with cupid's bow brass handles and keyhole locks. There were two narrow drawers on each side of the knee space, a single wide one above it, and pigeon-hole shelving over the writing surface.

The side drawers opened when he tried them and contained household bills, marked Current and Pending, plus recent bank statements and cheque stubs. The middle drawer was locked, but the key was in a glass dish of rubber bands and paper clips. The drawer held nothing but a pair of year-old theatre tickets to a comedy at the Haymarket. The pigeon-hole shelving held writing paper and envelopes, a folder of stamps, and blue airmail letter-forms – blank, waiting to be used on her next overseas trip.

There was no evidence in the desk of her past trips. The only other item of furniture in the living room that might hold something was a mahogany, glass-fronted bookcase beside the French doors opening onto the rear balcony. The bookcase was also locked, but the key was in it. Two books, covered in dust, were out of their places on the shelves. *Follies of the Rich* by Henry Hunt, subtitled *Experiences of an Englishman Building in Hampshire & Russia*, was a typical Victorian mix of nineteenth-century travel journal plus engravings of plans for everything from Gothic grottoes and thatched summer-houses to the foundations for palaces. *Sanscrit as Foundation for Contemporary Linguistics* was printed forty years ago, along with other texts on the dry bones subject. It all seemed so opposite to Jacky's flying character. The books were obviously her father's, kept on for sentimental reasons but never read.

Her father.

Suddenly he realized it: there was no other evidence of her father anywhere in the room; no framed portrait, not even a casual snap. And no mother, nor one of Edward

Campbell, her ex-husband. He did a quick walk-through the rest of the house . . . there were pictures – nineteenth-century oils of dimmed Swiss Alps, some harshly modern abstracts – but no faces anywhere.

Not even her own.

And now he remembered a scene from his last visit to England with Bergitta: they were having lunch together, the three of them, at the outside café in front of the National Theatre. A U-Like! U-Pay! strolling photographer popped a shot, and Jacqueline was upset.

'I know to Nordic cools, like Bergitta, it sounds Balkan gypsy, but look: you can see us all reflected in the glass of the café windows. My father always said it was three years worse luck than broken mirrors.'

They all had to cross fingers while she burned the picture in an ashtray. And they laughed, but in fact, Lowel thought, the only other photograph he had ever seen of Jacqueline was the one in her passport which Dawson had been unable to use for identification. He made a mental note to recover it from the security chief and went back to checking the furniture. There were several flat surfaces, corner and hall tables, but few closed storage spaces. The kitchen was clear, the hall, lower washroom, main bathroom – which left her bedroom.

He looked at the bed and remembered the convent and hotel in Greece, and wondered what the Christ he was doing to suspect the woman who gave and shared herself totally with him on those occasions.

With a cold contempt for his own actions, he stripped the bed and found nothing . . . except a lingering trace of perfume on a pillow. Her own perfume: the bottle was on a ledge of the headboard. He threw the pillow down and checked the bedside table: clock-radio, phone, a note pad with no writing on it, and no depressions in the blank surface from any earlier message. Instead of a closet for clothes, there were two more large, freestanding cabinets like. the corner one downstairs in the hall. They held clothes and nothing else. Nor did a long chest-of-drawers, except that the clothing was intimate, which made him feel filthy for touching it.

The last item in the room was a small desk under the window. He pulled down the blind and looked at the desk. It was fragile, some kind of reproduction: gilt on white, with arched legs. It was locked.

He looked for a key. There wasn't one. He went down to the kitchen, found a screwdriver, came back, and broke the desk-front open. The only thing inside it was a small packet of letters secured by a rubber band. A note underneath it in her handwriting said, 'Bergitta's last, and darling Jack's.'

He didn't think he could have despised himself more, but after he thought, *She* could have poisoned them! and hesitated to pick the packet up, he did. Underneath the letters there was even a photograph, 'Porno finale with idiot Teddy!', a candid shot, by a swimming pool, with Jacqueline herself in a torching string bikini. That shot down in flames his paranoid no-pictures theory.

But the picture didn't show her face. Jacqueline's head was turned away from the camera.

A doorbell chimed. He put the packet of letters and the picture in his pocket, closed the forced desk, and went downstairs to return the screwdriver to whoever now owned it. There were no legal papers in the house, no key to a deposit box. But Dawson might have something at the Embassy, with her passport. He opened the front door to let in Ryder.

'Lowel,' said Sir Herbert Maxwell, 'it's time you and I talked bluntly.'

The Yorkshireman strode inside and slammed the door behind him, leaving his subordinate, Ryder, on the other side of it. Lowel caught up with the head of SIS under one of the alpine oil paintings in the hall beyond the kitchen. He said, 'I thought when you referred to the President as "your poker-playing chum" our last time round, that was blunt enough, Sir Herbert.'

'And I told you when we first met, it's my nature to speak my mind, Lowel, no harm's meant. But I'll admit, on those earlier occasions I might have been a touch rough. From what I've heard since out of Washington, I underestimated your clout, and that's a fact.'

'What have you heard?'

'Don't pussyfoot, man!' Maxwell made an impatient karate gesture. 'Chopping Pixie Sweeting down to size would be enough for most blokes told to clean house. You went on through Langley like a dose of salts. If our political side got wind –'

'I'm not going to tell them.'

'Your chum the President might, when he meets our interim Leader in the morning. Put a bee in that gentleman's bonnet and I could be out on my ear by afternoon – who is this?'

Maxwell had seen Wong's body.

'He was my partner,' Lowel said, 'and a good friend.'

'I'm sorry.' Maxwell appeared to mean it. 'After Mrs Campbell's death, you're having a very rough go, and I'm not helping, but it's her I'm here to talk about.'

'Jacqueline?'

'Aye.' Maxwell continued gruffly. 'Not like this though. I'll bring Ryder and his people in. We'll continue when they've finished with your friend's body.'

There were two other men besides Ryder. They were dressed in blue denim boiler suits and carried a large cardboard packing crate by wooden handgrips, sticking out like the tips of a ladder at each end. The crate was stencilled

YOU'RE ALWAYS IN HOT WATER WITH GAS!

When the pair reached the living room they set the crate down on its side, opposite to the stencilled warning, opened an end flap and took out a black doctor's bag and a collapsible stretcher. From the bag, one of the men removed heavy neoprene gloves and face masks, which both put on. The other man asked Lowel, 'What was the method of toxin application?'

'Cigarettes. At least the makings for them. I think only the paper was contaminated, but it could also be the tobacco. I've isolated everything, in case.' He showed the baggies on their stainless steel tray, and then the chairs around the contaminated spot of carpet.

'We'll take that with us for a start.' The first man flipped the button on a Stanley knife. A gleaming razorblade extended. With a single deft motion the man cut a neat circular section out of the carpet.

The second technician said to Lowel, 'You think just the cigarette paper was contaminated – any specific reason?'

'It was the only part that touched his lip. Nothing happened before.'

Ryder said, 'Christ, Jack! You mean you watched . . . ?'

Lowel nodded tersely. The two experts rolled Wong's body onto the stretcher, secured it with straps, slid the loaded stretcher inside the water-heater crate, and closed the flaps. Only the ladder-tip ends of the handles were exposed.

'Up together, then.'

The men lifted; the hot-water crate went out through the front door and into a panel van marked Rapid Plumbing Ltd. Old Lady Melcham was watching from her window, Lowel noticed – getting the good word for her morning session with the Brigadier.

'I'll go along and stay with your partner's body at

Forensic,' said Ryder. 'What instructions are there for after?'

'By air direct to Portland. I'll arrange a US military flight and phone his family.'

Ryder patted him on the shoulder. The Rapid Plumbing van turned a circle on the cobbles, and Sam Wong was gone from his life. He closed the door and returned to the living room for more salt in the wound.

The SIS chief was standing looking out at the garden. He had opened a window. Moonlight shone in across the balcony. A bird trilled a long series of liquid notes. There was no sound of traffic.

'It's hard to believe we're in the centre of London,' Maxwell remarked, without his usual aggression. 'It must have been like this for a certain party, in the war, waiting for one of those bomber's moons to hop her over the Channel. And a nightingale in Carlyle Square, to boot.'

Lowel said, 'Are you telling me Lady Melcham was one of those wartime agents?'

Maxwell nodded. 'That's why we took on her son. The old boy net was still in operation, and much good did it do us!'

'Old girls were better.'

He was being ironic, but Maxwell said seriously, 'Women always are better. You must have found that out. People call intelligence a man's game, but that's not the way I see it. Men can go in for the quick stab, but women have that cool courage it takes for the long haul. Particularly working alone, like Jacqueline.'

So this was the salt. Half expecting it didn't stop it from stinging like hell. He said with bitterness, 'Was she working for you in Greece?'

'It wasn't kiss and tell,' Maxwell replied. 'Just keeping tabs. The personal side between you is your own.'

'Thanks. Anything else I should know?'

'You'll probably dig it out anyway: Lady Melcham is – was Mrs Campbell's maternal grandmother. Which of course makes that bastard running your CIA cancer lab in Washington her uncle.'

The nightingale trilled again out in the moonlit garden. Compared to Maxwell's grubby wheels within wheels disclosure, the bird's complex spiral of sound was clean and simple.

'Langley were so bloody sharp they cut themselves,' continued the head of British Security, 'but you can see now why they used Jacqueline's biography as the basis for their Borgia file. From start to finish, the whole thing has been to implicate us at SIS as the group responsible for the Dismantling derailment. Lowel, I want you to accept my personal word' – Maxwell's gaze reinforced his tone of absolute honesty and conviction – 'neither SIS collectively nor the late Mrs Campbell independently, had any recent dealings with her relative in Washington. Furthermore, in the time that is left before the President's final signing with the Russians, if there's any assistance our side in Britain can give to help you find out who's running the female who killed your partner, and wants to do the same in Yalta, ask and it's yours.'

Sir Herbert Maxwell shook hands with the iron grip of a gentleman; spun on his heel and marched like a Grenadier Guard away down the hall; and let himself out, closing the front door quietly, like a perfect butler. Alone in the living room, Lowel listened to the nightingale's pure melody and wondered if there was a word of truth in the SIS Chief's theatrical speech from the heart.

His own mind couldn't cope any more with the problem. And there was Kliment Berov to meet in Berlin tomorrow. He set the burglar alarm correctly and locked up Jacqueline's house for the last time.

22

Seventh day, dawn:

by Stealth, East Berlin

Lowel flew to West Germany in the starboard seat of a Stealth X-20. It was one of a pair of America's latest generation of manned fighter aircraft he had commandeered for the occasion. Perhaps the last generation, he thought. Smart missiles had made it dumb to put a fallible human at the controls of what was really just a laser-guided hypersonic torpedo: all Stealths were being banned under the final Dismantling Agreement. But Cold War habits died hard. The US Air Force four-star OIC in Britain had thrown a fit about letting his radar-proof babies go inside Redland – notwithstanding that, under the terms of the earlier agreement limiting Nato and the Warsaw Pact, the two Germanies were already being demilitarized.

As far as Lowel's Stealth pilot was concerned, World War Three was still planned to start when they hit the giant sand-trap delineating the East German border. The rule of Stealth was Silence: without a word on the headset, or even pushing a Link computer button, as they crossed the Rhine at Cologne,

ACTIVATE ALL COUNTER MEASURES

appeared reflected in the visor glass of Lowel's flight helmet. He looked past it at the brilliant sky, wondering again why Kliment Berov wanted to see him. And why Berlin? All the action had been in the West –

GO FOR HEDGEHOP

His stomach left through the top of his skull. The Stealth was plunging almost vertically.

4.5, 4.1, 3.7

a thousand feet of cloud went by with each tick of a second,

2.2, 1.8, 1.3, 1.0

and no sight of the ground –

HEDGEHOP 500

The Stealth levelled, his stomach and brain got back together and Germany was visible: neat little squares of green, with red box houses that appeared as streaks like a car's rear lights on a time exposure.

MACH 0.9

No boom. The Stealth was abiding by the sound laws of European airspace; the house-streaks were only flashing past at 700 miles an hour. At this rate, Checkpoint Charlie would come up in ten minutes. Would Berov be waiting there in a trench coat like a sixties' movie? Would he have some fresh information? Before take-off, there had been none overnight from Washington, or in Britain. Lowel was certain that Viscumin killed Wong – but he still lacked Forensic's proof of it; and NSA hadn't come back with any kind of explanation for Jacqueline's name being at the top of their trawl list; and the FBI couldn't make anything human out of Julia Teague's geometric portrait sketches.

The Elbe River. The natural barrier where Stalin and Eisenhower's armies met – and halted for almost five decades – came in as a blue streak to port: the Berlin access autobahn to starboard. The Stealth was entering the last relic of the old Four Power Agreement, the Corridor.

'Unidentified aircraft,' called a German-accented voice, 'north-west at low altitude. This is Tempelhof Tower: Who are you?'

Stealth worked. With a tone of considerable satisfaction Lowel's fighter pilot lifted his self-imposed rule of silence. 'US Air Force requesting priority anti-terrorist landing.'

'Roger US Air Force. But reduce your approach rate, please. For some reason we cannot track you.'

A brief smile was reflected in the pilot's visor. Then,

GROUND SPEED 200

At this sedate pace both Stealths touched down, side-by-side, with brake chutes snap-crackle-and-popping, and taxied away from public view to the restricted diplomatic zone of the airport.

The paranoid vibes of Moscow still started in Berlin. Whatever was left of the American presence in the city had sent a staff Mercedes, with a military driver, to take Lowel to the other side of the Wall. And that structure of post-war political division was still standing – he could see it from the Tempelhoffer Damm, but the wire and machine-gun towers were gone when the Mercedes swung him around the Mebring Platz onto Friedrichstrasse.

The crossing place of a thousand life-and-death encounters located at the head of it, Checkpoint Charlie was now a Place For Friendship. The single approach lane's unsmashable barriers and mirrors set into the paving for under-vehicle inspection had been replaced by a normal street flanked with high-school pennants of a Friendship Festival. They also festooned the hut that used to house the metal-eyed East Zone border guards who watched John Kennedy declare, 'I am a Berliner!' . . . while that other peaceful leader, Nikita Khrushchev, ordered in the bulldozers and put the Wall up. The smiling officials inside the hut were now wearing kitschy lederhosen shorts and perky hats as they greeted a visitor – but the gun-metal eyes were the same. Like Moscow, Lowel thought. This could all be put back in the deep-freeze overnight.

Yet what visitor would believe that the diminutive figure with the mournful smile, standing in bright sun, sending up smoke-ring signals of welcome from his perpetual cigarette, and surrounded by a group of laughing children petting his beautiful dog, controlled the entire freezing apparatus?

'I know how much travelling you have been doing since our last meeting,' the head of the KGB said in Russian as they shook hands. 'With Mischa, I thank you for coming.'

The cool grey collie nuzzled Lowel's sleeve with enough warmth to show that the dog might remember the hand that had saved him. He was wearing his eye-matching blue cornflower collar. The children gave the animal a last collective hug and climbed into a Volkswagen bus.

'No problem keeping moving,' Lowel answered; 'it's getting started that makes me feel my age. Do you have to pay Aeroflot, or does Mischa get a free ride on the People's Airline?'

'All citizens are equal, of course, in a People's Republic, but Mischa is still allowed the privileges due an aristocrat.' The KGB man gave his mournful smile and waved goodbye to the departing children who were waving back, then added, 'I asked you to Berlin because, through the efforts of the German Democratic Republic's security force, we have detained a person you should meet. It is walking distance, unless you would rather ride?'

'Walking's fine.'

With the collie leading, they moved away from the grassy nowhere to the left that was once Adolf Hitler's bunker, and went north across the Akademie Platz and over the bridge spanning the west branch of the Elbe by St Hedwig's Church. Economic *glasnost* was more advanced in its East German version, Lowel noted. Merchandise and customers had returned to most of the shops and restaurants that had just been used as bureaucratic filing cabinets since the war. People passing seemed more cheerful and outgoing, although the dog helped there: a man with a dog couldn't be a rapist, or a secret police chief!

'I have two particular things to tell you,' Berov said, out of random tourist conversation as they entered the broad open space of Marx-Engels Platz, 'or perhaps I could call them corrections. One is that the First Secretary did not have hepatitis in 1987, as I said earlier. A poisoning attempt was made against him while he was on vacation in Crimea.'

'Let me guess the other point,' Lowel said. 'The attempt was made by a woman.'

'I understand that you would be ironic. I should have told you, but it was not clear what power you had when you visited Moscow.'

'I thought I made it crystal clear. The President authorized me directly.'

Berov smiled mournfully again. 'There is a difference between authorization and power. Flying on Concorde may be authorized. Commandeering an Air Force and removing a director of Central Intelligence, that is power. Besides, to be fair to myself, at the time I was not convinced that the attempt had been made by a woman. Stop, Mischa, we're here.'

In the centre of Museum Island, in the shadow of the ruined Protestant Cathedral was a functional, low concrete structure with a one-word sign in German: Drinking-Water-Pumping-And-Cleansing-Station! Horizontal ventilation slits ran along all four sides. Berov pressed a buzzer at a steel door in the side closet. Lowel heard the sound of a lock sliding back. The door opened outwards, not inwards.

'Manners, Mischa. Allow our friend to enter first.'

The reason for the door's direction of movement was obvious as soon as Lowel stepped over the sill. So were the ventilation slits. Twenty-millimetre machine-guns were set up at each one. Their firing arcs covered the whole of

Marx-Engels Platz. And all the strolling men, women and children on it.

'A Stalinist relic of 1953,' said Berov, 'after the June uprising of German hotheads. Doubtless it will become part of the museum soon. Meanwhile, such a place has its uses.'

In the centre of the structure was a circular steel column, about fifteen feet in diameter. There was only a single point of entry and it was held shut by a series of metal lugs around the edges, controlled by a wheel, like a watertight hatch in a ship. Berov turned it and pulled the door open.

'Stay, Mischa. Inside is no place for a gentleman.'

The collie lay down obediently outside and put its long nose on its paws. The dog's disconcertingly human blue eyes followed Lowel as he accompanied its master through the hatch.

A man chained to a steel chair sat in the command turret – which was the function of the central column. Display boards and telephone systems were all 50s technology, meaning 40s in the eastern bloc, probably surplus from the war. The man in the chair looked as though he had been through it: bruises showed on his hands and face, his eyes were puffed. A Slav of some kind, Lowel judged, but not Russian; the man's clothes had more style.

'This person is Bulgarian.' Berov said it dispassionately, as a professor of medicine might to a group of attentive students watching an operation. 'If I tell you that he was an associate of the late Georgi Markov, you may begin to understand why he finds himself in this present predicament.'

'Waterloo Bridge?' said Lowel, with quickening interest. 'In '78? The umbrella murder?'

'Not himself.' Berov indicated the thickset subject of his lecture with distaste. 'As you see, specimens like this are not agile enough to merge swiftly in a crowd. He was a paymaster, who skimmed sufficient cream from the jug to keep himself living comfortably.'

'You mean he paid *her*?' Lowel demanded.

'So he was telling me before you arrived. Now let us continue the conversation.'

Berov lit a fresh cigarette from the stub of his present one. The man in chains flinched. Lowel said sharply, 'I don't want to be part of torture.'

'My dear comrade, nor does this person.' Berov's smile added irony to its usual sadness. 'We can spare your western conscience. Ask him a question; he speaks primitive Russian and is eager to talk.'

The man in chains said, 'Throat is hoarse. First please, drink water.'

A glass jug, with ice cubes floating, and a supply of paper cups, were on a writing ledge in front of the steel chair, but a foot out of reach.

'Wrong,' Berov corrected the Bulgarian, and moved the jug six inches closer. 'As I explained earlier: talk first, drink after.'

'If I'm here,' Lowel said, 'it's done my way.' He filled a paper cup and handed it to the man in chains. Berov shrugged. The man gulped.

'Please, another.'

Lowel refilled the cup. 'Did you see her?'

'Yes.'

'What did she look like?' He handed the water.

'Black hair, long, down to arse, is all I remember.'

'You didn't see her face?'

'She wearing mask. Like Mozart opera.'

'Did she speak? Can you describe her voice?'

'English. Cold bitch, you wouldn't fuck this one. She likes women, maybe.'

'And that's all?'

'Before next time.'

'You met her again? What next time?'

'Ten years more – nine years – '87.''

'Jesus!' Lowel exclaimed.

'As I think you suspect,' said Kliment Berov, 'this person was asked to go between on the hepatitis occasion. That is why he is here, dying to sing, and not at our Embassy by the Brandenburg Gate, where certain military factions could hear him.'

'You're saying he was a go-between for your own Army's GRU?'

'Partly. But ask him yourself. I've heard this verse already.'

'Who else did you work for?' Lowel queried the man in the chair.

'Not work. Information. I talk now, so not to be shooting.'

'He means by my firing squad at Lubianka,' the KGB Chief contributed.

Lowel asked the chained man, 'Information to who else?'

'Afghanistan rebels.'

'I don't believe him,' Lowel told Berov. 'Mojahedin peasants aren't that sophisticated.'

'Not peasants,' said the man in the chair. 'American naturally. CIA.'

'Give me a name. Who from CIA?'

'Code names. I, Blackie,' the man touched his head, 'dye then, not grey like now. He, Red.'

'He had red hair?'

'Yes.'

Murphy paid Her!

'Where?' Lowel demanded of the Bulgarian. 'Where did you meet when he gave you money for the woman?'

'First time, Rome, magazine-stand by Colosseum. Second was Airport U-drivski Greece.'

'Hold it. You met Red twice in '87?'

'No. Once was Rome, by –'

'So what year was this U-drive in Greece?'

'This year. Last week. With her also, Thessaloniki.'

'*I can talk my way out. You have to go on . . .*'

Jacky's last words to him. He could see her now, smiling at him as the butch blonde from Greek Immigration had her led away by the guards. The butch might have been a poisoner payrolled by Murphy – but Jacqueline, never.

He said with tight fury to the chained man in the chair, 'Describe the woman you met at Thessaloniki.'

'Not meet. She –'

'Bulgar bastard! You *saw* her. Now tell me!'

'I think the person wishes to,' Berov observed, 'if you release his throat.'

Lowel found that his hands were choking the man in the chair.

'Not see this time,' the Bulgarian gasped. 'Greek troops guarding airport. Red leave me money. I wait by car. She not come. I hear explosion. Then car radio; woman killed inside by Turk bomb. More water.'

He would have given champagne! This slobbering wreck in no way whatever linked Jacky to *Her*. He passed the Bulgarian a refilled paper cup. 'If you didn't know what she looked like, how do you know she was killed? How were you to recognize the woman?'

'She wear icon cross for St Spyridon. When I see, I will say English: "Are you related Panos Mario Meliti?" '

'*When it comes to no sin, old Spyridon seems to fall down on the job . . .*' She said that to him, in bed at the hotel, before she added her smiling, sensual, '*But thank God, my sweet Jack, you don't.*'

Meliti: Marya-Mario. The names interlocked like the links in the chain of the Saint's icon he could still see around her neck – but the fit of the Bulgarian's evidence was too perfect. The nuns gave Jacky the icon cross; she hadn't asked for it and couldn't have known in advance

240

they were going to hand one over. Murphy obviously rigged the operation, shooting on the wing as he went along. But did that mean he also set up this –?

'The question I ask myself,' Kliment Berov said, staring dispassionately at the man in the chair, as smoke from a fresh cigarette curled up to join the rest of the stale, eye-stinging smog obscuring the command post's steel ceiling, 'now that both of us have heard what this person has to say, is not who the woman was, but how many of her are there? If it was only one woman, even though she might also have been a close friend' – Berov turned his sad eyes at Lowel – 'and she is dead, then the threat against our leaders is over. But if another woman was planned to pass through Thessaloniki Airport at the same moment as the bombing, then the danger for Yalta is very much alive. With regret, I believe you have the evidence to support the last deduction.'

'All I have,' said Lowel bitterly, 'is a perfect frame-up of Jacqueline Campbell. There's nothing solid for any other –'

'Comrade, we have so little time, we must be entirely frank. But if you don't wish to speak about the most recent personal tragedy for you, last night in London, because we are in this person's hearing, we can continue outside.'

The KGB Chief turned the wheel to unlock the hatch. As the massive steel door swung open, the collie waiting beyond stood up and bowed deeply, to stretch its spine. The man left in the chair frenziedly rattled his chains: 'I tell truth. Woman not coming. Turk bombing –'

The hatch clanged shut on his cries. The concrete-tainted air in the outer section of the structure had a meadow freshness after the smog inside. Lowel said with a sharp edge to Berov, 'If we're being "entirely frank", how the

241

hell did you hear about my partner's death last night in London?'

'Like your NSA, my job is to hear.' Berov defused the sharp answer by patting his dog's triangular head. 'Tell me precisely how Mr Wong died.'

'By smoking a poisoned cigarette meant for me. I don't have forensic confirmation on that yet, either.'

'And when was this cigarette poisoned?'

'Probably yesterday evening.' He described the pursuit across the rooftops. 'But while I was in Greece and Washington, my makings – the papers and tobacco for rolling your own – were left in Mrs Campbell's house almost four days. The toxin could have been administered any time in that period.'

'But not by Mrs Campbell. Except,' Berov appeared to choose his words with deliberate care, 'before you both departed for Athens, and in the two days after her death. Neither of these options seems logical to me.'

Lowel's head was spinning from the changes in atmosphere, physical and mental, and the Russian's merry-go-round questions. 'You can obviously beat the hell out of a game of chess,' he told Berov, 'but OK, we both agree Jacqueline didn't do it.'

'I *said*,' the KGB Chief employed the same deliberation in his phrasing, 'a dead Mrs Campbell as your poisoner does not seem logical. Lead us, Mischa.'

The collie took them with its aristocratic grace out into the sunlight where the tourist adult masses from both sides of the obsolete Wall strolled the chequerboard slabs of Marx and Engels, oblivious to the murderous weapons aligned at the level of their children's playful heads. Berov used the walk back to Checkpoint Charlie to outline the extraordinary physical security arranged for Yalta.

'Impressive,' Lowel said, 'but are you sure it will be ready?'

'Of course. After all, we have had some experience – although on the last occasion the Soviet Union was trusted to save the lives of Roosevelt and Churchill from Hitler's Nazi assassins on its own. This time,' Berov concluded, with a half-mocking farewell wave, 'thanks to your airlifted American armour, a small iron curtain of additional defence will be in place on the board. However, as for your earlier remark concerning chess, Mischa can tell you: I have never played a game in my life.'

The collie gazed up at the sadly smiling face of its slim owner . . . and then at Lowel. The look in the dog's expressive eyes was unmistakable: if master says it, man, that's truth!

The Stealths returned Lowel to Britain, still not sure that he knew what was true about anything he had been told in East Germany. At least this time on landing he was spared Dawson greeting him with news of another funeral. On the racks outside the air base at Greenham Common the British tabloids blared:

FAREWELL RULE BRITANNIA!
DISMANTLING VOTE PASSES
GALBRAITH SPEECH TRIUMPH

His own headline would have been, Dan's Done It! Climbing into his waiting chopper for the trip across country to the Embassy, he felt a sense of pride and pleasure for his friend's accomplishment. Reading the fine print put things in their proper perspective. Sell-out and Stab in the Back covered the Rule Britannia right wing's opinion; and Triumph hardly described a left-wing majority of one – a squeaking tie-breaker that couldn't be heard over the boos when it was cast by the House of Commons Speaker.

Anyway, he thought, as the helicopter brought him safely down again at Grosvenor Square, Britain was in; which left Paris tomorrow. High politics was the President's problem. Keeping him alive on French soil was Lowel's. If *She* was really after the whole ball game – hitting the Soviet and American leaders together – then France should be safe. But so should NSA's sweat box and the tree-lined Kensington Palace Gardens. The Hallowe'en trick-artists of a dozen intelligence organizations could still strike anywhere to run final dismantling off the rails.

Even if they did not, he decided, as he walked into the ground-floor security office, Paris was a golden opportunity: the face-to-face meeting of Daniel Galbraith with the French head of state would be a dry run for Yalta.

'Where is the President now?' he asked the security desk.

'At Sandringham,' the man replied, 'the Queen's country house in Norfolk. Her Majesty's original invitation was for the President to look at horses and have a family supper, but we just got word he'll be staying on there overnight. It caused a shit storm around here. The SS people go ape over any unexpected change of plans.'

Galbraith was keeping things on the hop as he had promised. Lowel said, 'I can't think of anywhere in England safer for the President to spend the night than next door to Her Majesty's bedroom.'

'The Secret Service only remember the time some drunk climbed the Buckingham Palace fence and broke into it.'

Lowel had forgotten that episode, but Sandringham was deep in the countryside and on maximum alert. He shut the inner door of the security office and put through a coded call to Ryder at SIS. Instead he got a familiar, 'This is night duty. Mr Ryder isn't here. Can I help?'

'Not unless he left a message for Lowel.'

'The answer is yes.'

'Good. What's the message?'

'Yes.'

'I meant,' he restated with his last reserve of patience, at the end of another too long day, 'would you please read the message that you say Mr Ryder left for me.'

'I've done it twice for heaven's sake!' Night duty took an amplified deep breath: 'He told me to tell you, if you called before he got back from Forensic, that his answer to what you would want to know is *yes*.'

Viscumin killed Sam Wong. The big question was settled. He wrote out instructions for the Embassy staff sending his partner home to his family.

Breaking the news could not be left to the State Department.

He put through a call to Sam's wife, and left it at heart attack, which it was, brought on by Wong's trip across to find him. He scarcely had to lie. But he had to endure the voice of his partner's widow at the other end of the satellite, breaking up, but still managing to say, 'Dear Jack. Thank you for everything you've done . . .'

He took a shower after that and then put through a call to Garcia Javez at Langley. The old judge's replacement at CIA could feed the Bulgarian's story to Murphy. By now the redhead must have had enough time in the vault to realize that, without some plea bargaining, he was facing not just a truncated pension but twenty years up the river.

The green LED high-sign came up on the Hi-Burst system.

'Garcia? Jack Lowel calling.'

'This is Langley Switching, Mr Lowel. Hold on, please, on your call to the Interim Director.'

The LED bulbs went to flickering orange. He used the time to segregate the Bulgarian's various responses into categories: like probable, possible, and fucking ridiculous. He jotted them down on a notepad, in three columns. He was getting a pattern that formed a right-angled upside-down triangle – with practically nothing in column one, about twice that in column two, and everything else in column three – when the lights went back to green.

'London? Javez speaking.'

'Garcia, this is Lowel. I have a list of hard questions concerning that vault deposit I gave you to hold.'

'I understand. I've been expecting it. I'm only sorry you had to hear the word from someone else. I accepted full responsibility; it was my job to tell you.'

There were crossed wires over the Atlantic. He said, 'I'm just back from a same day return flip to the GDR. I haven't heard any word. You still get to tell me.' The lights stayed green, but they should have gone orange; as the pause grew longer, he said impatiently to Javez, 'Well, go ahead. Tell me.'

'I'm trying to think how to phrase this. Jack, your vault deposit isn't available any longer.'

'You're not saying you let it into the hands of a goddamn lawyer?'

'No. I'm saying since 15.00 our time – that is, an hour ago, 20.00 with you in Greenwich zone – the deposit cancelled out.'

'That's not possible,' Lowel exploded. 'You had binding instructions on cancellation.'

'The deposit cancelled itself, sir. I'm sending you a capsule statement of the account by courier, and proceeding with a full in-house audit.'

In legal terms, the rebuttal witness who could have matched the right questions to the Bulgarian's answers was no longer available. In CIA shop talk, a prisoner under solitary confinement had got out of it by swallowing a suicide poison pill. In plain language, Murphy was dead.

Plainer still, Lowel realized: he had no control over any part of this operation or the lives of the people in his care. Not in Langley . . . or London . . . or Thessaloniki . . .

Death could strike anywhere *She* wanted.

23

If Moscow always seemed under the paranoid shadow of Stalin for Lowel, Paris was still overawed by Charles de Gaulle: war-winner, nation unifier, greatest peacetime leader. Airport, bannered streets, fashionable salons all now bore his name. De Gaulle was *la gloire*: military glory was France!

'And the banner saying that,' observed the visiting American President, as his armoured Cadillac passed under it, 'is pure bull. As I'm about to remind the present backsliding bastard leading this country, France hasn't won a war since Napoleon lost his because he was short of Preparation H at Waterloo.'

The cavalcade, with its flanking black Citroëns from the Sûreté, was passing one of the famous teaching hospitals of Paris. Medical personnel stood outside to applaud and wave. Galbraith shook the famous hair from his eyes and waved back; that got a louder cheer. 'Never know who might have voting relatives back home in Boston,' was the presidential explanation for this switched enthusiasm for the French ordinary citizen. 'Parisians are the salt of the earth, Jack. Look at that priceless old guy over there.'

A small, wrinkled man in a shabby suit from the 40s, a cigarette stub in his lips, was standing under a sign, 'Verger – Costumier'. The grimy window display behind him contained a pair of beaten-up Arabian

247

Nights harem pyjamas and a few tattered ostrich feathers.

'Memories of shore leave,' Galbraith continued with a crude grin. 'In its glory days, this quarter was where they used to hold the Interns Balls.'

These days, the street was barricaded to head off one of Paris's annual left-wing student demonstrations. The cavalcade swung right, passing yet another statue of de Gaulle. Medicine and pleasure still went together in the area, Lowel noticed. A professional-looking woman from the white-coated hospital crowd was just entering the costume shop.

She saw the Cadillac slow down beside her and for a moment could not resist the normal human impulse to look at a prime target. Instead, she found herself being looked at, by her principal opponent! In spite of all her training and self-discipline, she felt a stab of shock. He sat between herself and the American President: she was close enough to see plainly the missing fingers of his left hand. He must see her as clearly, and her only facial disguise was steel-rim spectacles. After the near-miss in London, he would connect –

The Cadillac was already past, and turning the corner by the student protesters. Her fear was irrational, she put it aside. He would not connect. Men made associations to women via their bodies and their clothing: a white coat was a doctor, a string leotard was a slut. Her momentary weakness was the logical result of constant travel and unrelenting tension. Although she had trained herself to sleep on aircraft and to ignore the past, her central nervous system was not immune: there was safety in operating entirely alone, but there was always a moment like this when the pressure of outwitting the world was bound to tell. Better it did so here in the crowd. Her nerves would be steady now for the finishing kick. Not only women: 'clothes make the man' as well. Voyeurism was her weapon for Paris. She entered the decadent world of the costume shop.

Monsieur Verger was expecting her. Indirectly. After seven decades of inhaling Gauloise smoke from early morning until midnight, sooner or later all the young doctors at the local clinic arrived to prescribe the latest wonder drug for his chest, stare amazed at his X-ray pictures, and say they had never seen a plugged alveoli like his!

'Oh yes. I remember you all,' he assured this morning's young woman. He turned down the radio, which was just describing the American President passing his shop, and led the new doctor to the back of it. 'Of course,' he continued, 'it isn't like the old days. On the night of the Interns Ball, for example, the young devils all went naked, except for gold-dust paint, mixed with beer, to wash off, so they wouldn't be asphyxiated.' He laughed, coughed, and showed her the portrait collection on his walls.

'I'm told you still practise your speciality as a costumier?'

The young doctor snapped out her questions with the same brisk, no-nonsense authority that she employed to tap his chest while she listened through her new-fangled computerized stethoscope. All the best butches behaved in this way. After a lifetime of catering to their special costume needs, Verger's lungs might be plugged but he could still sniff out a butch before she was through the shop door.

' "Practise" is the word,' he emphasized for this morning's brusque young woman in her steel-rimmed spectacles. 'Like you doctors trying your medicines, matching a male costume to the female body, it's learned by doing. It's an art.'

'This picture.' The young woman doctor tersely tapped the 1933 one of Lulu in her tuxedo, pouring absinthe behind the Club Monocle bar in Montparnasse. 'You fitted her?'

'More than fitted! Hairstyle, width of lapels, shoes, masculine underwear and cologne. For Lulu and a thousand others, let me remind, I, Monsieur Verger, did it all!'

This burst of a craftsman's righteous indignation brought on a longer fit of coughing. He groped through his armoury of pill bottles and containers, and squeezed himself a generous double dosage from his latest prescription: Beclovent, an antibiotic inhalant spray. He had long since given up paying any attention to the directions on labels.

'You were in your prime with Lulu.' The young doctors today no longer wasted time on unproductive bedside sympathy. 'The point is, are you still so good?'

'Is my name not on the sign above my shop? Ask from the Quai Malaquais to the Church of Saint-Germain-des-Prés! In all Paris the reputation of Verger is –'

'OK. We don't want a heart attack. I have a fancy-dress party to attend tomorrow.'

'A party. But of course.' He smiled to himself. The butches always used an excuse like that – when what they intended was strolling by the stage door of the opera-house waiting for the lithe little ballet girls. 'This way, if you please, Doctor, to the racks.'

'I have my own costume.'

'Ah . . .' Obviously our professional young lady wore men's clothing regularly, in her off-duty hours. 'Then it will be the fitting service you require.'

'With absolute privacy.' She demanded it with a freezing stare.

'Without total discretion, Doctor, one would have no business.' He hobbled to the front of the shop, turned the key and slid the bolt, then rotated the *Open* sign to *Closed*.

'The blind as well.'

He complied, tying its string around the door handle, explaining, 'To stop its annoying habit of flying up.'

'Be sure of it. I also require your services with hair and shoes.' While he tied a second knot, from her medical bag his newest customer produced a wiglet and a pair of alligator loafers. The former was an inferior synthetic that would never have been touched by any self-respecting wigmaker in the old days; the pointed shoes were too flashy to be proper butch. 'The hairpiece is only for the colour,' she explained. 'I wish a perfect match to natural hair, in a full wig set to a particular style, with matching moustache. The shoes are too large; they must be reduced to fit.'

The hair colour was a shrieking metallic gold, like a Pigalle tart's who knew she was over the hill. The loafers were expensive and hand-sewn. 'Italian,' he said, 'yes, I can break the seams and match the thread.'

'Good. These are the clothes.' She removed a crumpled jacket, slacks, shirt and tie. As expensive as the shoes, with the same pimp's flashy taste. 'After the alterations they must all be cleaned and packed for travel; this afternoon, you understand.'

'Doctor, they shall be immaculate. The changing cubicle is this way.'

He bowed and pulled back the curtain for her inspection. The cubicle was the size of a sentry hut; a single bulb hung on a twisted lamp cord; a wooden bench faced an old Man Ray calendar and a mirror with the silver of its backing chipped off around the edges; a worn scrap of Persian carpet was in the centre of the planked floor. With a look of distaste, his client passed inside. He discreetly drew the curtain shut.

. . . And hopped around to his peep-hole – a happy

251

accident from the flaking of the mirror. Beyond the peephole now, his newest customer was peeling off her tights! Despite his earlier remarks about the brisk state of business, it was some time since a customer of this attraction had revealed all her charms in the cubicle. He reached for his modern Polaroid camera – God's miracle, which solved an old man's problem of home development, and in colour! – and pressed closer to the mirror. Facing him frontally, the doctor's medical hands stroked down her body in the familiar way of all feminine self-inspection, lingering at the hips, fingers stroking lightly inwards to the groin where she had a little scar –

Sacré! At the click of the camera, her head looked full at the mirror. Could she know? Not possibly. Yet there was such a look in her eye . . . under cover of a paroxysm of coughing, he hurriedly hid the camera and its emerging photograph beneath a cushion, inhaled a puff of decongestant, and appeared to be measuring a dummy near the shop window when his customer emerged in costume from the cubicle.

'But yes,' Monsieur Verger assured her, 'I see completely the effect you are after. If I may suggest, with the jacket shoulders – so. And the bosom' – he studied it closely: for business and otherwise – 'your present brassière I shall replace with a custom garment, for rib-cage padding as well as nipple binding, like the twenties. And now if one may just measure . . .' He took the tape and marked with chalk, then stood back to examine again . . . 'The trousers are invariably the problem. The buttocks, even with today's more athletic female figure – may one enquire, Doctor, as to your preferred choice of underpants?'

'Calvin Klein briefs.'

'Bikini style, or –?'

'Men's hipsters. I can't see that it matters.'

She stared at him with that disconcerting gaze from the mirror. 'It is always the last small touches,' he offered in swift reassurance. 'Can you leave the pair of Calvin Klein's with me?'

'Very well. Now show what you can do with the hair.'

The hair was more businesslike; there were not the overtones that went with underwear. He examined the piece provided for colour: the Pigalle tart's gold, though still ghastly, would be no problem to match. He produced his wigs' styling album for inspection.

'No, no, no . . .' her finger stabbed like a lancet – 'this one. And that moustache.'

The styles of both were what a prematurely bald and failing actor from the provinces might imagine for himself as a brothel lothario. 'I can manage the bangs with no problem, if you are quite sure –?'

'Positive. Try it on.'

The result was as frightful as he knew it would be, but fitting to her head would be easy. 'If one cuts for length, however, you will not be able to return it. And payment would have to be –?'

'Half now, half on completion is how I do everything. In four hours.'

'Will be totally acceptable, my dear Doctor.'

Lulu had this imperious way with her instructions. Awed, even a little frightened by his new Lulu, Monsieur Verger limited himself to a single peep while she redressed. Not such a sacrifice: he could look at his new picture! Meanwhile, he turned up the radio again to listen to the American President arriving at the Elysée Palace.

The Cadillac slid to a smooth halt beneath the portico. The bands crashed into 'The Star-Spangled Banner' and the 'Marseillaise'. The two great men exchanged fraternal greetings of mutual affection. Global video feeds recorded the moment.

Polite applause came from a crowd of expensively dressed invited guests, held back behind the cordons of security forces on the far side of the forecourt. Sharpshooters in paratroop battle-gear ringed the court-yard on the surrounding rooftops. Z-barrie.s, cemented into the cobbles at each archway, prevented student or Middle East fanatics from making kamikaze runs with a car-boot load of high explosives. Sûreté men, with dark bankers' suits and the mafia eyes of professional Intelligence, covered every door and window giving access to the Palace entrance. Other than an Army coup, Lowel was satisfied with the French physical security.

A gun fired. On silencer. He spun round –

'*Champagne, Monsieur le Président, s'il vous plaît . . .!*'

False alarm. Inside the main foyer, with its golden starburst chandelier reminders of the Sun King, magnums of the liquid of the gods exploded their corks in all directions. He had just switched the first glass offered to Galbraith for another, when a French voice behind him said quietly in English, 'Jack Lowel, with no fuss, step back to me here for a moment.'

He eased out of the crowd and turned. In an alcove behind the portico columns was a man he hadn't seen for seventeen years.

'André –!'

'Not so loud. The globe will hear us.'

André Dolmain was the kind of Frenchman the PR firm handling President Atteler thought he should be, instead of the ape they had for a client. Dolmain was debonair, suave, with a noble head and silver hair. The fact that for years he had made his living from killing small amber-skinned men in dense jungles with his bare hands was not immediately obvious. When he embraced Lowel, the strength of his grip still made it seem possible.

'How've you been?' Lowel asked him. 'Where have you been? I figured you'd make top gun in Paris at least a decade ago.'

'You should know careers.' Dolmain shrugged a perfect, ironic Gallic shrug. 'You hitch your wagon to a star – but it had better be the right star! Since the inglorious *Rainbow* episode in New Zealand, with which I profoundly disagreed, and now with this present gentleman in office, let's say I have been in the far reaches of outer space.'

Dolmain's tone and expression, as he looked at his national leader performing for the cameras, undercut the 'gentleman'.

'But you're still active in Sûreté?' Lowel said.

'I regret to admit. Your car bombing by that lunatic bitch Claron in London has convinced me finally to resign, but there is some business first which I am keeping tabs on here in Paris that may help you with your own female nemesis.'

'I wish!' The world's intelligence services had been turned upside down; there was no need to ask how André Dolmain knew why he was here. 'I've been chasing a shadow flat out for a week,' Lowel admitted, 'and I still have no hard proof my target ever existed.'

'You can have my word.' Dolmain drew him further from the boom mikes and strobe lights. 'In 1974, there was a final anti-Gaullist flare-up, aimed at his successor –'

'President Pompidou. But he died of cancer.'

Dolmain nodded. 'Which made the lady's mission redundant, but she had gone far enough in her plans to demand the first part of her payment. I say "lady", but then she was only a girl. Yugoslavian, linked with the Red Brigades of Italy – she was involved with them again for the Pope John Paul murder – so the anti-Gaullists here dismissed her girlish demands entirely. I can tell you for another fact that, after two of them died in considerable pain, the money owed was paid. The people who wrote the cheque are the same crowd who support our friend from Marseilles out there, all these years later.'

Dolmain tipped his silver head at the TV show, just concluding with a last round of global smiles. Lowel said, 'The time you have her starting out, '74, matches what I've been told already – except that she was Greek, and it was the Baader-Meinhof gang, not the Red Brigades. I don't see how it helps me now.'

'I have been keeping watch on Atteler's financial friends,' Dolmain answered. 'If Nato reduces its conventional army further, and France's independent *Force de Frappe* is tied to that reduction, fortunes are at stake. They have had a source of the most highly classified information inside the military Nato headquarters. The cover used for relaying messages was a computer-porn ring – the tabloids call it the "X-Net". Last night, an electronic voyeur naming himself "Angel Ears" informed a certain "Miss Cream" about the airlifting of American troops from Berlin to Yalta. This morning the man was found dead in the same circumstances as your other recent casualties in Washington and London. Returning to your initial problem of proof, old friend,' André Dolmain concluded with a wry Gallic smile, 'from the logic of my Jesuit schooling: our lady exists.'

The unexpected jangle from the shop doorbell frightened Monsieur Verger into dropping the photograph he was examining. If she had seen! His shaking hands covered the new picture and his special collection of earlier photographic treasures with a pressing cloth. Only a sepia King Tut, hung like a bull in a transparent muslin jockstrap, was left in view beside the steam iron – and that could be considered an artistic study.

'From a costume advertisement, Doctor. It appeared in *Le Figaro* prior to the Four Arts Ball in 1931.' He turned down the radio broadcast of the American President at the Palace.

'No. Leave it up.' She flicked the picture. 'What about my costume?'

'All ready for last fitting, and cleaned as you asked.' The two presidents were warmly exchanging toasts of friendship. Verger removed the hangers of clothing from the pressing rack and took them inside the cubicle.

'Good. Now get out and lock the front door. I'll call when I'm ready.'

Lulu had the same knack of always keeping him off balance; this one's cold eyes never left him as he did the *Closed* sign, the key, and the double knot for the blind.

'Total privacy, Doctor, as you rightly insist. But before you commence changing, for a minor adjustment one must first ask: are you left-handed or right?'

'Left. What on earth does it matter?'

'Only that if you should chance to find yourself in all-male surroundings . . .' He took the Calvin Klein hipster men's briefs and held them up. Viewed frontally, the crotch pouch bulged to the right. He made the slight, but crucial alteration to the segment of carefully shaped foam rubber inside the pouch. '. . . At this fancy-dress party you will be attending, for example . . .' Viewed again, the change was satisfactory: the bulge of the pouch now had a definite displacement to the left side. '. . . Certain gentlemen notice such things, and you would not want to spoil an otherwise perfect illusion. Now you may put these on. And the chest padding and shirt – not the trousers. After which I shall need to inspect carefully again.'

She allowed the old voyeur time to hobble to his glaringly obvious peep-hole, and turn up the radio to mask any noise. The two presidents, said the announcer, were now also in private, to discuss frankly world affairs. She let him see that his new Lulu was admiring herself in the Calvin Kleins. She touched the left-dressed bulge of the crotch lightly with her left hand. It jiggled. She nearly smiled!

257

'Very good, old man,' she called through the curtain. 'I misjudged you.'

'Your task, Doctor, is to heal the customer. Mine is to please.'

'I have the shirt on. You can re-enter.'

The padding was perfect. 'So it should be. Your bust measurement was within a centimetre of Lulu's. But before the outer clothes are tried, Doctor, sit on the bench, and please first check the shoes.'

She heard his leg joints crack as he knelt on the scrap of Persian carpet. The pain was worth it: her firm thighs were only inches from the old pervert's face. She allowed him to slip the restitched, Italian pimp's alligator loafers lovingly on her slim feet.

'Excellent!'

She meant the shoes, but the Calvin Kleins were even more realistic sitting down. She stood and zipped the fly. In the tight tailoring of the stretch flannel slacks, the frontal bulge looked perfect.

'Perhaps you should see the behind for yourself, Doctor? From the wing mirror? One may still be able to add –'

'It's not needed. You've given me exactly what I wanted.'

Almost. He lifted the crowning glory from the styrofoam head in the hat box where it had been waiting. The colour would always be atrocious but –

'Absolutely accurate, Monsieur! And the moustache. I congratulate you.'

She inspected herself, wearing both the hairpieces. The target summoned up his courage . . . 'To ask a great favour. If one might take a photograph, for my private theatrical collection?'

She brought back her cold, appraising stare – and then her earlier hint of a smile. 'Certainly, old man. We should record such an achievement for posterity.'

Predictably, the shock of asking, and of getting, started

the target coughing. While they both waited for the Polar-oid to develop, she reached into her medical bag.

'It's just on the market.' She passed him a spray container in an outer box with a red bar on a blue label. 'The very latest, but don't overdo it.'

There was no need for the patient to read the label. He knew the instructions for such curatives by heart. He opened the box and said in a sing-song, 'Breathe out. Spray. Breathe in . . .'

The spray was sucked into his wheezing lungs. He gave her a child's smile of naughtiness.

'Medical science is not for kindergarten,' she said harshly. 'Now read the directions pamphlet.'

With a child's petulance he picked up the box again and withdrew the inside paper. The first line said the usual boring *Knowledge of your prescription's directions can be a matter of Life and Death* . . .

Outside a pair of enormous Palace windows looking into an enclosed garden, Lowel saw more French paratroopers' steel flak-helmets among the ornamental trees. Such crack troops were useless against his present target.

From Her perspective, the Elysée office was an arsenal. A silver-gilt trolley held éclair pastries and coffee demi-tasses; on a sideboard, a carafe of ice-water, bottles of Perrier, drinking glasses, a selection of cigars and ciga-rettes; on Atteler's desk, scratch-pads, blotters, fountain pens and ink.

As the mirrored doors closed out the press in the foy-er, Galbraith fired the opening salvo. 'I know you speak excellent English and my card-playing friend, Jack Lowel, here can cut a deal in French. Monsieur le Président, I suggest you might be happier if we dispense with this other skilled person's services before she hears what I've come a long way to say. And you won't need notes to remember it either.'

Two young men for this purpose were apprehensively perched to take shorthand, on appliquéd velvet chairs. Their boss, the man the US State Department referred to as Attila the Frog, was a short, squat thug who had come to power with the money from raping the last publicly owned mile of beach on the Riviera: his newspaper monopoly blamed it – and everything else wrong with the country – on the Jews. After a moment for translation, via his effacing female interpreter, Atteler contemptuously returned Galbraith's fire.

'*Il n'y a rien* – there is nothing you could say, sir, to a President of France that he would not be happy to have his people hear.'

'Then let's open with "You're a liar",' said the President of the United States. 'After that, maybe the French people will enjoy listening in to our last dismantling conversation at Camp David, on tape.'

Between the shorthand for *liar* and *tape*, the office was emptied of all three extraneous French citizens. Atteler's phallic dockside gesture with his right fist didn't need professional translation. Without his officials he said derisively to Galbraith, 'You want to play rough ball, *Mister* President, you've come to the right guy. But also, let me tell you, a salon of Paris is no "OK Corral". Divulge your tape, and French diplomacy will cut your incoherent American foreign policy to shreds with what's left of Nato, and in Eastern Europe. Do eat some cake.'

Lowel tensed – but Galbraith defused the minefield that could be waiting in Atteler's sarcastic hospitality by ignoring it. 'Nato got used to French double-crossing when de Gaulle pulled you out of the Alliance,' he replied. 'They aren't going to lose any sleep over it today. But I'm not here to argue diplomacy. I had your word on the Dismantling Agreement, and your word can't be trusted any longer.' Galbraith pushed across one of the note-pads and fountain-pens – but using his safe dummy-hand. 'Unless you confirm your country's participation in writing, now, then when you and your latest mistress are sharing a *bidet* shampoo tomorrow morning, you can expect to find the value of the French franc like her shitniks: somewhere down around your knees.'

For a moment Atteler was speechless. The Frenchman's fleshy face reddened. Lowel passed his own pen and notebook to Galbraith, instead of those on the blotter.

'Economics is your six-shooter?' Atteler gave a short, guttural laugh of incredulity. 'I was expecting an atomic bomb! America's last economic embargo against France increased our wine sales in North America by forty per cent. Or perhaps this time, it's to be Chanel Number Five?'

The French leader picked up one of his own éclairs and stuffed it whole into his mouth. The cream filling squirted. He wiped it away with the hairy back of his hand. During this display of Gallic grace, Galbraith had scratched some quick figures in the notebook.

'Forget perfume. The left column is the approximate value of French arms sales around the world. The right is the percentage against your foreign debt. If I leave this room without your written acknowledgement of France's commitment to the Dismantling Agreement, the US Defense Department will offer your military customers our latest technology on terms not one of them will refuse.'

Atteler choked – but had not been poisoned: a crumb of pastry, caught in his windpipe, suddenly shot out. 'With your test failure rates?' he scoffed. 'You would have to give that Pentagon crap away!'

'Exactly.'

The French head of state stared at his American counterpart. So did Lowel. Galbraith had to be bluffing. After a long pause, Atteler reached the same conclusion.

'That would cost you tens of billions. And you talk of our debt, with *your* deficit?'

'It would cost me around three per cent of Budget,' Galbraith agreed, 'but that would still leave me up seven, after the nuclear cutback savings I get from dismantling – just in the first year. Fifty-one weeks before that, the French real estate market would be another Hiroshima.'

That A-bomb wasn't the one Atteler had expected. He bit his pendulous lower lip, studied the figures Galbraith had given him, then made calculations of his own: bank demand loan calls on his Riviera mortgages, Lowel presumed.

'So,' the President of France said finally to the President of the United States, 'you want me to write IOU one Dismantling Agreement?'

'Just initialling our Joint Communiqué will do fine.'

As he had for the Finding at Camp David, with his good hand Daniel Galbraith drew another magic paper from an inside pocket, unfolded the document, and slid it across the desk. While Lowel shredded the notes of both sides, plus blotters, Galbraith added ironically, 'No need to worry about the fine print, Pierre. We'll be reading it together under the TV lights on your front porch.'

The display of Allied solidarity was a triumph for satellite technology and world peace. The female French interpreter was allowed on-stage again for the curtain call. The two Leaders stood smiling, arm in arm.

Lowel stood with André Dolmain, off-camera, watching and listening, still astounded by Galbraith's poker display of brass-balled nerve. After Sam Wong's collapse in front of his eyes, the strain of waiting for another instant death by poison was telling badly on his nerves.

Otherwise, the familiar arc of flame in the sky would have registered more quickly. His eyes saw the fiery, unmistakable dip-and-dive trail of a Soviet-made anti-tank rocket streaking towards him above the helmets of the paratroop sharpshooters on the rooftops opposite . . . but his legs just stood there, holding him safe inside the shelter of the palace portico, while he watched the firestreak getting closer, '*RPG-incoming! Dan, hit the deck!*'

The words came out by themselves. And even as Lowel finally crashed forward past André Dolmain, the old instinct from those distant delta patrols made Galbraith react.

The American President's body was already halfway to the closest stone column. Lowel's charge carried him the rest of the distance. The sound of the rocket's impact-fuse detonation was muffled by a full defensive line of Secret Service bird dogs piling their bodies on top.

Their combined protective weight was almost suffocating, but not enough to stop the next sound: the familiar moaning from the wounded. In the modern non-stop war called Terrorism, as usual there were innocent civilians. When Lowel got his head free, he saw that the rocket had fallen short. The immaculate Parisian fashions on the invited visitors across the courtyard had been blown to bloody ribbons.

In front of the whole world.

24

Castle Galbraith brooded from a cliff at the head of
Dungeon Loch where the high, heathered hills above the
town of Dumfries fanned out into the lowlands of Scotland. When this branch of the interloping Welsh family
of the Barons Strathclyde first had to fight for its toehold
among the savagely resisting native Scots, the dungeons
above the lake were used full time. Today, as the most
famous modern member of the clan visited them with
his oldest friend, those cells housed longhaired Highland
cattle and the family's wine collection.

Daniel Galbraith was using the security offered by
3,000 acres of gentle pastoral surroundings for his own
stocktaking.

'You've bailed me out of being gassed by Pixie Sweeting and bombed by French students,' the President said,
with his wry smile, as they stood for a moment looking
at the rogue-eyed cattle. 'I guess we just hope poison in Yalta doesn't make Typhoid Mary third time
lucky.'

'We can do a lot more than hope,' Lowel replied.
'Poison has to be administered: which means via something needed by both you and the First Secretary, which
the poisoner has been able to come in contact with – '

'Air Force One to Kremlin toilet paper,' Galbraith
interrupted impatiently. 'That definition hardly narrows
the field.'

'It would, if you let other people run interference ahead on it.'

'I told you, Jack, no food tasters. I'm not a Russian tsar. I chose to run for office; I'll take my own chances – that's if the Cold War shellbacks on the Hill don't impeach me. After seeing me rocketed by our French ally on the evening news, my Press Sec tells me the hard Right back home are over the moon about trusting the Soviets!'

'Physical security against overt terrorism is the one area we can trust them,' he insisted. 'On the Crimean Peninsula, Berov's ratio is a thousand KGB to every dissident. And if any nationalist extremists make it through the police, they hit a full division of crack Lenin Guards – not counting our own brigade from Berlin.'

'Thanks for the handholding, but we both know the real odds.' Galbraith looked down at a Highland bull tossing its fierce horns as an old herdsman with a nose-ring stick backed it up into a section of dungeon segregated from the cows. 'Today, I'm safe here with my Secret Service and all the faithful family retainers. Tomorrow, Jack, you and your dog-loving Soviet cop stake me and the First Secretary out and wait for your lady tiger.'

But a whole day was too valuable to waste doing nothing, Lowel thought, as he drank coffee with the President's Scottish cousins in the great hall of the castle. By now his body just couldn't stop running. While the lady of the house refilled his cup, he noticed an old shire map of Dumfries on the wall behind her. Castle Douglas, Gatehouse of Fleet, New Abbey, Kirkbeam, Kirkcudbright –

Kirkbeam. The name registered, but not the reason. He excused himself and went to the security locker that, like the nuclear communications Button Box, travelled everywhere with an American President. He retrieved his special courier's chained briefcase and sat down in the castle library to go through his notes. The FBI file

265

on White House staff sex was on top: one blackmailed food fag, three typists who couldn't type, the king of the singles' bars – 'Prince Valiant' or Victor Kolinski, the interpreter with the absurd dye job.

The next document was North London Forensic's report on Prime Minister Powys and Lieutenant Commander Edward Campbell –

From Kirkbeam.

The remains of Jacqueline's ex-husband were buried there. His family lived there. With time to kill, Lowel decided to go there.

His lead chopper set him down on what seemed to be another British village green, but was called, with letters of equal billing:

MUNICIPAL MEMORIAL PARK
KEEP OFF THE GRASS
BY ORDER!

A policeman with a red-chequered band around his cap was waiting to enforce the order. He enquired politely, in a soft lowland Scots burr, 'Did you not see the sign, sir?'

'Only after it was a bit late, constable. I'm with President Galbraith's party, and – '

'Galbraith is it? Och well, that's different altogether!' The policeman saluted the name with considerable respect, then added, 'How can Kirkbeam help you?'

'I want to locate a family called Campbell.'

'Aye, well we have a fair number of Campbells in this district, though not so many as Argyle.'

'The ones I'm after just buried a son in the churchyard here. He was a Royal Navy pilot.'

The constable nodded, pointing past a square, blackened stone Church of Scotland. 'The Edward Campbells that will be. Of the Old Manse – ye'll not need to move your machine, the place is walking distance, as you can see.' A house of matching stone sat in a low-walled garden behind the church. 'A sad end to the honour of a son flying our late Prime Minister.'

Lowel said, 'Things aren't always the way they seem. If the municipality gets worried about the grass, I shouldn't be long.'

'No worry on that score, sir.' The constable looked at him with a policeman's ability to read between lines. 'If you were able to tell the family about "things", no doubt it would be a great comfort.'

'I'll do my best.'

He walked past the Grass sign and the blackened church, along a narrow lane leading to a weathered wooden gate in the garden wall. An elderly couple were working, as all similar British couples appeared to in daylight hours, bent over and weeding in a flower bed.

'Mr and Mrs Campbell?'

The pair straightened up slowly, at an identical rate.

'Yes,' they said together.

'My name is Lowel. I'd like to speak to you about your son.'

'About Teddy?' The question was doubled too, and the grief in their eyes. The husband said, 'I'll do this, Anne.' The wife said, 'No, Richard. Come in, Mr Lowel.'

He opened the gate. A herringbone red-brick path followed the curve of the flower bed to where the old couple were standing. As Lowel reached them, Richard Campbell suddenly sat down heavily on a teak bench set among the flowers.

'The heart,' he said, 'not as strong as it used to be.'

Anne Campbell looked at him and said anxiously, 'Mr Lowel, about Teddy . . .?'

'I don't have anything to say that will be an additional shock for your husband,' he assured her. 'I only met your

267

son once, but my late wife and I knew his former wife, Jacqueline.'

The couple exchanged another of their shared glances.

'Jacqueline . . .' they both said, with equal slowness.

'She overpowered him,' the old man added to Lowel.

'Tragic,' said his wife. 'I mean, coming so soon afterwards.'

Richard Campbell said, 'That bloody terrorist thing in Greece. They were like that in the war, when I was with them in the mountains. The partisans – we operated as far as Yugoslavia sometimes – once took out a bridge at a place called Brod. If they got their hands on any of the plastic explosives, you couldn't trust the mad buggers an inch! Are you going to tell us they blew up Teddy and the Prime Minister, too?'

At the end of this extraordinary outburst, the old man slumped back exhausted, while his wife stared beseechingly at Lowel.

'No,' he said to both old parents, 'I can't tell you why the Prime Minister's helicopter went down, but I can say that your son wasn't responsible in any way for the crash.' He addressed Campbell Senior. 'Did you know that Jacqueline's father's family came from Brod?'

'Of course,' the old man replied. 'Prof taught me the basics of the languages. Sibenik was one of the training staff for Balkan MI.'

'You were in British Military Intelligence?'

'Only wartime, and reunions. Haven't been to one in years.'

Lowel had the feeling of walking on quicksand. Wherever he turned in Jacky's life – old Lady Melcham next door, this gardening couple here in Scotland – every ordinary day-to-day path got twisted down into the intelligence underworld. And Sir Herbert Maxwell claimed there was no such thing any more in Britain as an old boy net!

He said to the mother, 'Part of the answer to the

crash may be in your son's effects that were sent on to you by the Defence Department. May I look through them?'

'Yes, but there isn't very much. You couldn't call Teddy a provider. It was her house and furniture, you know, after the divorce.'

Anne Campbell checked to see that her husband was comfortable on his garden bench and then took Lowel inside the Old Manse. A back room on the main floor that used to be a cold larder, with hooks for hanging game, was now a general storage space. Four cardboard cartons in one corner had Defence stickers on them.

'I was going to have the boxes moved up to the attic,' she said with a sigh, 'but here they are. I'll leave you. He doesn't like me to be away long.'

The old woman was right; a young man without a house or a wife did not leave much. The first box had books from Teddy's boyhood: editions of *Kidnapped* and *Treasure Island*, with the ink line illustrations coloured in crudely by crayon. The next box had the flying clothes Edward Campbell hadn't been wearing. The third contained unpaid bills that never would be. The fourth box had what Lowel had flown two choppers from Galbraith Castle to get hold of: a photograph album.

He lifted it out and opened it. Campbell Junior had been a good flyer because he lacked imagination – which was why he could never have made a great one: the pictures were arranged, with subtitles, strictly in the order that reflected Teddy's life. 'Me in christening dress,' full length white lace; then 'Me on first day of school', in British schoolboy short trousers, blazer, cap; 'Me in first flannel longs'; 'First time in a boat'; 'First time in a plane'; 'Getting my wings'; 'First carrier landing', thumbs up! 'First car accident', after a party, thumbs down.

'Meeting Jacqueline.'

Full face, nothing hidden. Her eyes stared at him from the picture with their quizzical hint of a possible future Jack–Jacky routine. Her wide mouth was smiling, just the way he remembered her leaving the line-up, turning and waving . . .

He took the photograph from the album and put it in his pocket. He thanked the two old Campbells and told them to ask Mr Ryder at SIS for help in restoring their dead son's reputation. The local police force was still waiting by the choppers illegally parked on the municipal green.

'Were you able to tell the family anything helpful, sir?'

'I hope so, constable.'

He climbed into the junior machine for the ride back to the castle. The marine pilot was an American Teddy, a young man not cursed with too much imagination for his own good.

'This came in for you, Mr Lowel. From NSA at Fort Meade. Plain language, but I guess maybe it's some kind of code.'

> FROM RONALD MCDONALD STOP
> TWAT SPOT GOOFED STOP
> INTERROGATIVE CAN WE TALK

The B1 made its second transatlantic run to the Goddard Space base. The clown chief of the National Security Agency's basement super-computer forces was waiting with his burger name-tag in the officer's lounge. The bomber's crew were not relaxing: Lowel had informed the plane's commander before take-off from Britain that this was going to be a jackrabbit turn around. Ronald McDonald came forward with his happy-face grin.

'Hi there, Mr Lowel. I've got the catch hanging out to dry on the Wailing Wall.'

270

The Wall was ghoul talk for the listen-proof room where the Space Agency controllers huddled when a mission wasn't coming back: to hold off from the press the astronauts' last words and names for next of kin. McDonald fed in the combinations that unlocked the room's outer door, and the inner one. Reams of fanfold print-outs were accordioned open and held up with coloured pins covering various Moon–Earth–Mars orbital recovery maps on the main wall.

'The bug's so goddamn obvious,' said the programmer, apologetically, as soon as the doors closed. 'We went off-track right after start – here in first loop, line three: single female parameter, equals exclusive alone.'

The computer expert grabbed a handful of paper and stabbed it with a nail-bitten middle finger. 'It's not obvious to me,' Lowel said with annoyance. 'That parameter was how you came up with Jacqueline Campbell: the target does travel on her own.'

'Sure, but that doesn't necessarily equate single. You could have a double purchase ticket, Mr-and-Mrs, where he's a No Show. And when you feed baby *that*, plus Aeroflot, instead of Concorde . . .' The programmer lifted up the last page of another huge paper fan. '. . . Shazam! From Flensburg Creek, Minnesota, little Twat Spot presents – !'

Mr and Mrs Litziskaya.

Lowel saw the name on the sheet and tried not to let himself think, *This is Her!*

'Keep going,' he said.

'Mr and Mrs Morris, from England, that was the first time, coming over. And here's the third one which fits our dates parameter, in between, and you ain't gonna *believe* the nerve of this – '

He could believe it. The third ticket name was Mr and Mrs J. Lowel.

'The last time,' he said to the chief programmer, 'as

Litziskaya, that was Aeroflot to London, from here in Washington?'

'Right on, man! Good old John Foster.'

He reached for a Wailing Wall phone and punched a button designated Media Hot-Line. An operator answered the first ring.

'I want FBI,' Lowel said. 'Dulles Airport. Anti-terror.'

The Senior Field Agent met him as he came out of the special tunnel leading to the airport's segregated security facility.

'It was his Frisbie day off,' said the field agent, 'so he's unhappy.' The agent knocked twice on a door with a frosted window:

INTERROGATION

The door was opened by a second narrow-tie FBI representative in shined shoes. Behind his shoulder was a scared shitless young man wearing sneakers, patched jeans, and a Grateful Dead sweatshirt.

'This is Mr Playfair,' said the senior agent.

From his reaction to the harmless introduction, every nerve in Mr Playfair's young body showed that life had given him the shaft with a name like that, in circumstances like this.

'I'm sorry you've had to be inconvenienced,' Lowel said, 'but there's nothing for you to be alarmed about.' He nodded at the senior agent who beckoned his subordinate. When both FBI men were gone from the room, he continued, 'You were the boarding clerk on duty for the new Aeroflot flight to London, correct?'

'This is my first time off for ten straight,' said Mr Playfair, in a voice that trembled on the edge of tears. 'I want you to know that, and I have the right to call my lawyer. Don't I?'

The last two words pretty well defused the kid's

272

surprising show of strength. 'Five minutes from now,' Lowel told him in a level voice, 'you can call whoever you like, but if you mention the person we're going to talk about to anybody in the next forty-eight hours, those gentlemen outside the door will put you away for the rest of your life.'

'I won't mention. What person?'

'You boarded a passenger on the flight, a woman. She was travelling alone, but she had a double ticket to include her husband. She – '

'Oh Jeez!' Mr Playfair rolled his eyes at the reversed INTERROGATION on the frosted glass. 'He never showed up. Honest! Don't let me lose my job. It's not my fault I didn't tell him.'

'You're not losing anything. You remember the woman?'

'Remember! Sir, a lady like that is not forgettable! If I hadn't heard her accent, I'd have thought she was some Pentagon general.'

'She had an accent?'

'Hungarian or something. She called me "Sonny".' Mr Playfair pronounced it, Sun-nye. ' "Vhat I tellink, you do not for-gyet!" And I didn't. But her husband never –'

'What did she tell you not to forget?'

'That she was keeping her old man's ticket, of course. So the poor mug would have to buy another. She said she was taking his to the Ritz Hotel.'

'That's all?'

'I think – hey! Was her name Litzki-eye?'

'Litziskaya. What did she look like?'

'A goddamn tank! Well, not like First Class, know what I mean?' Lowel stayed silent. Mr Playfair was forced to find words. 'She had these Soviet-type bushy black eyebrows, and an ass like that Jackie Gleason on "The Honeymooners" reruns. And no jewellery or neat

273

clothes. And this old carpet bag. You could tell she had to be loaded, and I swear she must have got her husband to cut her hair.' The young ticket agent ran a finger around his own head to approximate the cut. 'Like with a bowl, you know?'

Drawing attention to oneself was the best disguise. Mrs Litziskaya would be unforgettable in the Gucci crowd.

'How about age?' Lowel asked.

'Old. Well I mean middle. Maybe like my mother, or less.'

'How old is your mother?'

'Forty-seven. But really she looks younger – with Mrs What's-its? I guess it was more her clothes were so old-fashioned.'

'OK,' he said. 'If you remember anything else at all, no matter whether you think it's important or not, tell it immediately to the FBI agent who brought you to see me.'

'I can go?' Mr Playfair was so relieved, as he got up to walk, his legs buckled.

Lowel made himself take the step he had been dreading. He took out Jacqueline's photo.

'Before you leave, just look at this picture.'

The ticket agent glanced: 'Sure. That's her – hey, it can't be.'

25

The legal hypersonic route from New York to the Crimean Peninsula would have taken the B1 south of the European landmass, through the gateway Straits of Gibraltar, along the length of the Mediterranean, and down below the sound barrier somewhere between the islands of Malta and Crete. That would have been twice as long as the Great Circle track the bomber was currently following.

Lowel dozed in the absent communications specialist's back seat for the hour required to transit the northernmost leg, via the Greenland–Iceland–Norway gaps which cut the top arc of the circle route, like opening a breakfast boiled egg in what navigators referred to as a Rhumb Line.

He woke as the bomber's navigator beside him announced arrival at the Greenwich Meridian. Things were tense on the flight deck.

'If we sound a touch edgy in front here,' drawled the aircraft's Texan commander, 'this is the first time yours truly's had to puncture Redland's balloon for real.'

'We're already over Sweden?'

'No sir. The Volvo people have just refused permission for us warmongers to boom over their summer herd of neutral fucking reindeer. Which means we either take on their Saab missiles, hit the brakes, or detour north and go in at short notice through the Sovs' maximum defensive line at Rybachi.'

'Are you monitoring their Interceptor frequency?'

'On circuit 22.2,' said the pilot. 'From all the jab-bering, those good ol' boys must think we're a Korean civilian.'

Lowel switched the jabber through on his headset. Russian ground-control was talking to a five-fighter group of Combat Air. The 'Yanki Ghost' going balls out at Mach 3, and 70,000 feet, had been recognized first as a snooping reconnaissance 'Blackbirdski' but was now correctly, from its radiating Identification transponder, 'Bee-Vun'.

'They know what we are,' he said, 'tell them who, and ask point of entry clearance for Rybachi.'

'Understood,' replied the pilot, 'but as you're sitting in the right seat, maybe you could give them that little thrill, speaking their language.'

Surprisingly, Russian ground-control sounded pleased to hear it.

'*Spasibo*, B1 from Amerika. Thank you, but we have reply for you in English. As in our Great Patriotic War, welcome in friendship once more to Murmansk. You are cleared present speed and altitude to Arkhangelsk, Vologda, Moskva. Then reducing to subsonic between Bryansk and Kiyev; then descending at Odessa, for approach to Simferopol. We at Rybachi, and all Soviet Defence forces, hail your cause of renewed world peace with historic second signing at Yalta!'

'*Spasibo, Rybachi*,' Lowel sent back, speaking off the cuff for the happy Hallowe'en forces of the united West. 'America and her allies appreciate the new spirit of co-operation between themselves and all the citizens of the Soviet Union. We too look forward to a new era with the second signing at Yalta.'

'Then enjoy good luck, B1. From Rybachi, goodbye.'

'Well shit,' drawled Texas, 'don't anyone on board be surprised if the next thing to light up a scope is Jesus!'

* * *

The image that appeared was nothing more out of this world than the city of Archangel, on the sickle-shaped inlet of the White Sea. For all the crew's joshing response, Lowel knew that, after five decades of deep freeze, he wasn't alone in feeling a prickling surge of emotion from that warm Russian welcome. At this elevation, even more than walking the *glasnost* streets of Moscow, it began to seem possible that, in the First Secretary's own way, that man with the mark of the devil on his forehead was achieving a kind of miracle. Thank God that, in Dan Galbraith, America had a leader with enough guts to respond to the challenge of getting it right at a second Yalta.

In spite of Mrs Litziskaya . . .

Lady X: Did she enjoy inflicting sudden death? Or did she get that sudden fit of shuddering and vomiting that he experienced on the one occasion that he realized he had taken a life with his own two hands? If only he still had Jacky to explain from the female perspective, instead of being taken when –

Two days late he made the blindingly obvious connection: Jacqueline had been taken, killed, precisely *because* he needed her to help him understand the female mind. The single thing his opponent, with her built-in contempt for men, would fear in the male-dominated world of Intelligence was the brain of another exceptional woman.

'Take a good look, y'all.' The aircraft commander's voice intruded. 'Those golden domes down there mean this has gotta be the first and last time we'll be flying for SAC over the top of our *numero uno* Ground Zee!'

Beside the tiny thread of the Moskva River to the east, three gleaming pinheads were the minarets of St Basil's Cathedral reflecting sunset from Red Square. Death was different when it was delivered from thirteen miles high. Maybe that was how She did it, Lowel thought. She just changed her mental distance, like the

NSA clown programmer changing an instruction for his computer –

'Down through boom two.'

The vocally activated systems automatically compensated for the ordered lower speed. An English-speaking voice at Bryansk took them smoothly into her control umbrella. The pink glow faded from the B1's wings. Russia came a little closer. The Second World War between Hitler and Stalin was fought out with nobody watching, below Lowel on this immense Kharkov Plain.

'Down through boom one.'

And the Ukrainian capital of Kiev. The scan showed Mach 0.9. The B1 was crawling again at a mere 700 miles an hour. And unbelievably, from this altitude, with the last light of the falling sun shining sideways across them, he realized that the random lines he was looking at on the Ukrainian fields were the track-scars from Hitler's panzer tanks. No wonder fear of another war was part of the soul of this immense and frightened country. War was literally carved into its skin.

'Odessa calling Amerika B1. We have severe turbulence, Black Sea Region. Vectoring you Zeero Nye-ine Zeero, to Dnepropetrovsk.'

'Roger, Odessa. Vector 090.'

Again the flight-deck computers responded to a verbal order; this time to head due east. The bomber banked smoothly to port, its bat wings sweeping into the approaching night. Five hundred miles dead ahead, Hitler was stopped at Stalingrad: Volgograd, since the Soviet dictator's name was wiped from Russian maps and history books. A bogeyman who slaughtered millions, and no longer existed . . .

'Command, Navigator: my ECM scan shows SAM-guiding acquisition.'

The specialist crewman's voice was professionally cool, but it had that edge which Lowel would always recognize from his own days in a cockpit: that hair-trigger moment approaching the Fail-Safe point, where the enemy knows if you don't go back, you mustn't come on.

'OK, Navigator. Redland's play acting.'

The scene was Doctor Strangelove, but Slim Pickens wasn't yahooing his way to glory. The B1's commander had a Cal Tech Master's Degree in Aeronautical Science. Lowel glanced at the Electronic Counter Measures scope beside him. The oscillating pulse of radio energy was unmistakable: a Surface-to-Air Missile radarbeam had –

'Lock on, Captain!' The co-pilot's voice was full-alert. 'System Master doesn't think it's playing.'

The oscillation had ceased.

'Command, Navigator: I have beam-rider!'

A second pulse, a line of red laser light, slicing the scope.

'Mr Lowel,' said the bomber's commander, 'if we get a blip on that beam-rider, things are gonna go a little wild. Maybe you should call those boys at Odessa in their lingo.'

The Texas voice might have been about to take a leisurely siesta. Which meant the hair-trigger was down to the wire. Lowel changed his headset mike-switch and called in Russian, 'American B1 to Odessa. We have been acquired by missile battery Novomoskovsk. Please inform them of our cleared status.'

The hiss of white noise filled his ear phones. The red laser on the scope had frozen. He called again, 'B1 to Odessa . . .'

Only more hissing. The red laser was fused with the main yellow beam of the ground-missile radar. The snaking Dnepr River showed dark green on the TV night-scan.

'This is American B1. Come in –'

'*Blip, Captain!*'

The co-pilot's voice had dropped any pretence this

was playing. The amber blip of a launched missile slid smoothly up towards them along the red rider-beam. Insanely, Lowel was reminded of one of those Fall Fair booths where you measure your strength by swinging a hammer.

'I see the turkey.' The commander's laconic voice now held a tinge of amusement, maybe even disappointment, at such a Mickey Mouse challenge. 'Navigator, Command: give us some active squawking back there.'

'Navigator, Roger: all ECM to active!'

The specialist beside Lowel hit a bank of Electronic Counter Measure switches. Four parachute-shaped pulses ballooned on the scope, blocking the matching quadrants of the gyro compass. The amber blip slid towards their forward quadrant.

'Second, Command: stand by your flares.'

'Second, Roger.'

The last time Lowel saw a gloved hand reach like this for the red T-handle, it was his own, with Jacqueline's ashes. On the screen the blip of death met the forward-facing electronic parachute – and quivered . . .

'Active's nailed that little fucker,' the Texan drawled, then, 'Correct my last –!'

Active hadn't. The blip came onwards . . .

'Flares away!'

The whoosh of compressed air was the only sign of anything happening. At this speed, the flares were already a mile behind them.

'Command, Navigator: Infra-red shows flare deployment!'

A sunburst lit up the scope. The blip was dazzled. The missile diverted to starboard. Death by remote control was dead.

'O-kay,' came with a long, deep breath from the senior pilot, 'bye-bye Novomoskovsk. Now where the hell are we?'

The TV night-scan showed the Dnepr curving to head due south. The attack computer responded to the last question:

TARGET 12001: MARGANETS, ALTERNATIVE, NIKOPOL

If there were bombs in the bay, Lowel thought, the doors would be open; this would be the lip of Armageddon.

'I was only asking that fool machine a rhetorical question,' said the computer's commanding officer, 'but I like its south direction. Mr Lowel, I have a feeling we're going to take it without asking Odessa's permission.'

The last time he had been through this experience was sitting in the co-pilot's position of his first B52, after the coup that ousted Nikita Khrushchev. It had been like sitting on top of a powder-keg: all the world outside the Fail-Safe points could do then was ask questions; only a handful of men inside Russia knew the answers. This time around, he was inside, but it didn't help; he still didn't have the answers to Winston Churchill's Soviet enigma.

'I agree about going south,' he said, on the captain's circuit. 'But if this hostile action by Novomoskovsk had Odessa's sanction, we could be in trouble from the whole Crimean region.'

'That kind of trouble's what this baby was built for –'

'Command, Second: I have a new SAM acquisition.'

'Roger, Second. Navigator, give us Terrain-Following. All positions: heads down and digging!'

When a B1 dropped out of the sky, the end of the world came up to meet you. In the Stealth fighter, there was a feeling that it was just an overgrown sports car, built to take impossible corners and recover; but when something the size of this bomber took a vertical dive at full power, the human body gave in: the human mind said *This is it!* . . . but the mechanical brain in charge of the massive aircraft's control surfaces had no nerves, and no stomach. The sight of the altimeter readings unwinding at 300 feet per second was within acceptable limits for a machine. The fact that blood burst from the capillaries in lungs and eyeballs didn't matter. Long before the frail crew had bled to death, the machine in charge would pull them back from the brink.

When the red curtain drained from Lowel's eyes, the B1 was straight and level, 100 feet above the Dnepr River. There was no trace of the SAM acquisition beam; at this frog-hop level no missile blip could follow a rider. The map of Russia unrolled on the scope of the inertial system at a rate too fast for the eye to detect, let alone match with landmarks, but for a computer built to run at Mach 3 this river cruise was only idling.

'Command, Navigator: at Kakhovka, we should track overland again. How do you want to handle the approach on Simferopol?'

'That's the 64K question. What's our answer from the White House, Mr Lowel?'

A colour-graded, three-dimensional photo-reconstruction of the Crimea showed on the navigation console. The Peninsula was an orange diamond, elongated on its west–east axis. Its northern point, now only 100 miles distant, coloured palest orange for flood-plain level, connected the diamond to the Ukraine. The dark green space above the diamond to the west was the Gulf of Odessa, presumed hostile territory, circled in red. To the east, the blue circles of the missile battery forces ringing lighter-green Azovskoye More – the inland Sea of Azov – were an unknown quantity.

So was Simferopol, the airport for Yalta, lying fifty miles inland from the southernmost point of the diamond. A 4,000-foot-high barrier of darkest orange divided the two towns: the last gasp of the Caucasus Mountains in Europe, the Crimean Range, running along the whole south-east coastal diagonal of the Peninsula. When approached at low altitude from the Russian side of the hill, the two southern flanks of the diamond, guarded by the Black Sea batteries, could be considered Missile Neutral.

'Command, Navigator: passing Kakhovka.'

'Roger, Navigator. We'll hold another moment for the White House.'

'Until we make contact with Simferopol,' Lowel replied over the commander's circuit, 'there is no definite answer. Unless you think otherwise, I suggest we maintain radio silence. Alter heading east again – to take us out over water, the Sea of Azov – then reverse in, heading south-west along the north flank of the mountains to Belogorsk. If we get that far without incident, call Simferopol for landing clearance and see what happens.'

The B1 rolled so swiftly to the east, he thought the river would tear off the bomber's port wing tip.

'No point in wasting time on what *I* think,' the Texan drawled over the headset. 'The dumb machine liked your suggestion.'

A blur of lights went by below them, marking the town of Askaniya Nova, then they were clear of the Ukraine, hurtling out across the green-black water. Like the other three human and two mechanical brains on board, Lowel's total concentration was focused on the looming blue circles of the Azov batteries.

Nothing flickered. The starboard wing dipped, not quite so steeply. The B1 swung south through an arc of 135°. The orange coast of the Crimea approached again, closing rate 650 knots – was past; the orange got darker, the bomber's nose tipped upwards, the twin altimeters showed altitude rising, but the actual height above the ground remained constant. The B1's electronic brain was hugging the mountain contours. He stared in fascination: one split second of error . . .

'Command, Navigator: range of Belogorsk, twenty miles.'

'White House, Command: stand by your call to Simferopol.'

The lights of Belogorsk were gone to starboard. All radio voice frequencies were silent in Lowel's headset – but a fan-shaped beam suddenly appeared dead ahead on the electronic detection scope.

'Command, Co-pilot: we're being held by S-band radar.'

Civilian traffic control radar from an airport tower. Lowel crossed eight fingers and called in Russian: 'Simferopol, this is American B1 transiting from Murmansk with internal route approval by Moscow and Kiev; request status for landing. Over.'

And waiting . . . one second, five seconds . . . a second radar beam appeared on the detection scope, as rock steady as a missile beam-rider.

'Command, Co-pilot: locked by X-band.'

'Simferopol, this is American –'

'We have you, B1, and welcome!' Once more a Russian voice seemed to mean it, but . . . 'Our ground-control has trouble with your signal against the mountains. Alter heading away, please. Also, our strip may be short: reduce to your minimum speed of landing. Over.'

Lowel translated for the crew and asked their commander, 'Can I say, we comply?'

The bomber's nose dipped. The Texan said, 'That's baby's answer.'

'Simferopol, thank you, and stand by: B1 approaching.'

The dark orange of the mountain chain grew paler. The altitude decreased hand in hand, by computer, with the aircraft's speed over the ground. A control tower

searchlight beacon rotated in the night. Familiar thuds.
'Command, Second: Landing gear –'

Then howling wind. Chaos.

'*Christ –?*'

From the B1 captain. His co-pilot said nothing. The Second was slumped forward in his seat. Behind him, Lowel realized the small glass window by his head had shattered. A blizzard of paper and insulation fragments whirled about the cabin.

'Command, Navigator: ECM's saying we had cannon attack from a rear-closing MiG 35!'

'Lowel, Command here: with my hull integrity broken, if that fighter bastard comes back, I can't go high, and I can't go fast –'

'Captain, look to port!'

A shout from the navigator. That fighter bastard wasn't going anywhere. Through the unshattered glass, a scarlet and yellow tulip of flame lit the night sky behind the jagged crest of the mountains . . . and a calm voice said in English: 'B1, this is Mischa's owner speaking for Simferopol: continue to land your aircraft. A problem of local administration has been solved.'

The computer set them down in Russia as though nothing more serious than an administrative glitch *had* happened. The rows of Lenin Guard tanks, and mobile anti-air missile launchers lining the taxi strip could be just more evidence of a warm Soviet welcome – except for the scorch marks on the launchers and tanks' gun-barrels, from recent firing, and the flame still burning high above them on the side of the mountain.

Except for the B1's slumped co-pilot.

While the bomber rolled along the taxi strip, Lowel unstrapped, grabbed a First Aid kit, and leaned forward to check the Second's condition. Blood trickled from a flesh wound on his scalp, but the skull didn't seem to be broken.

'Landing gear . . .?' The co-pilot grunted, looking around groggily at the blue taxi lights and massed artillery sliding by the hole in his window.

'The gear worked fine,' Lowel assured him, 'you got scratched. Try and relax until we can get you checked over by a medic.'

The Soviets were prepared for catastrophe: three ambulances waited with a fleet of fire trucks at the end of the apron. Runway handlers waved the B1 forward with luminous wands to a section as far from the civilian terminal building as it was possible to get. When they gave the 'kill engines' high sign, the Lenin Guards moved one of their tank columns to block any remaining view. Two more handlers rolled out a ladder.

'In the name of world peace,' drawled the B1's commander as he opened the flight-deck hatch, 'America's here.'

The small calm Russian with the big blue-eyed dog walked forward on the concrete and looked up. Berov gave a casual salute. Mischa's banner tail wagged. Lowel stared out at the Soviet enigma and thought: I am here!

Is *She?*

26

Graveyard shift

The B1's commander was last to leave the bomber. As he set foot on the concrete beside Lowel, a field howitzer of the Lenin Guards fired without warning, point-blank at the B1's cockpit.

The collie's prick-ears flinched. The diminutive KGB Chief was unperturbed. White feathers and crimson blood were splattered in and all around the already MiG-blasted flight-deck window.

'An appropriate choice of weapon, the howitzer,' Berov said in conversational Russian, while the smoke cleared from the runway; 'named, you must know, from the Czech word for catapult. As the press will be informed in the morning, white pelicans, though delightful to look at, are a constant hazard to air travel during their nesting season in this area. I did not think that our common interest would have been served at this delicate juncture by telling the world that the original hole in an American fuselage was made by a twenty-millimetre Russian cannon.'

The Soviet's action was astonishing – but the excuse might be plausible, Lowel thought. Boeing, at Tacoma, used seagulls in the same way, for testing bird impact on jet intakes.

'But what guarantee can you give,' he asked as the Guards' howitzer was removed, 'that another of your "pelicans" won't take a similar head-on at my President?'

'You have my absolute word: all local disturbances

have been quelled; a further such episode will not be possible. From the moment President Galbraith's plane crosses our border, it will be escorted by the First Secretary's own squadron.'

'And one of ours.' He made another snap call. 'Under the circumstances, I'm bringing in US fighter cover from Scotland, right through – plus our own refuelling tankers. There won't be any signing without it.'

'Very well.' Berov indicated the two unwounded members of the B1's crew standing behind him and added in English, 'As for your uninjured pair of competent and gallant officers –'

'This one is staying right here with Baby.' The Texan commander addressed Lowel. 'While our thoughtful Russian friends are fixing my windshield, I'd appreciate it if you'd ask them to bring me out one of their mobile Alert bunkhouses. And until my Second gets a clean bill from their sick bay, the navigator will go along to keep him company.'

Berov organized the Russian side with a snap of his nicotined fingers. Lowel made final use of the B1, to transmit his American fighter escort signal. As he prepared to climb down from the flight deck for a last time, the bomber's pilot stuck out his hand.

'I couldn't find a better driver,' Lowel said.

'Put a couple of hours in on the trainer, I figure you might.' With a tired grin, the pilot released his hand, then saluted. 'Meantime, sir, don't let these peace-loving bastards palm us too many wooden nickels.'

In the lobby of the new Yalta Grand Hotel, a person called Ilyich Nev was trying at that moment to con the western foreigners leaving the hotel's Lenin Disco into selling him their tape cassettes. '*Perestroika*,' he told them, 'was supposed to solving tape shortage in Moscow, but in backwater convalescent hole like Yalta!'

He halted his spiel. A 'cool-street' broad had strolled out of the disco. Ilyich Nev prided himself on his western slang. The broad was wearing a 'down-button' shirt of expensive Indian cotton, and a suede miniskirt, so short –

He looked away before she noticed. That was when she smiled and let her eyes catch his eyes . . . as she touched a Star of David on a chain around her neck, hanging down between her gorgeous, thrust-up western breasts.

She knows I'm a Jew like her.

Unlike himself, of course, she'd been able to afford a 'job-nose'. She strolled closer to examine the ethnic dolls' concession, and he could smell her exotic perfume. He saw also that she was older than she seemed at first, perhaps even thirty – she knew what she was doing. And had some Russian. Enough to say, 'Good evening.'

'Hi. Good evening, Madame.' His English was far better. 'I speak it to you, *da*?'

'*Da*,' with that smile which made his whole backbone wriggle. Not just his backbone! 'I have rock tapes,' she said casually, picking up one of the Kalmyk region dolls; 'how much do you pay for them?'

'Dollars or roubles?'

'Dollars are illegal.' Again the smile. 'You work for the KGB and want to arrest me.' She put the doll down and half-turned away.

'Madame, no, I swear! Don't say so loud!'

'Big brother will hear? I thought he went out the window with *glasnost*.' She laughed an open western laugh, not caring. 'I've got an old Mick Jagger Live I don't particularly want.'

'Does he doing "Jump Flash-Jack"?' When she nodded, he knew he said too eagerly, 'I give you for him ten dollars.' . . . But if she said 'Yes', he could sell it for thirty!

'Sure. It's up in my room. Come with me.'

There were 3,000 rooms in the new Intourist beach hotel; the police could not watch all of them – these days they probably didn't try, with the town bursting its seams with western press for this conference –

Was *she* with the press?

Ilyich Nev felt the usual scary tension of never quite knowing. And the wriggle sensation of going with a strange woman to her bedroom . . .

Lying on the bed, she had a stack of tapes that made his mouth water.

'Bruce Springsteen to Abba – like wow!'

'You can have the Abba for nothing. You'd better listen to the Jagger, so you know I'm not ripping you off. Vodka?' She pointed at a bottle with glasses, next to a perfume flask, *White Musk*, on the table by the bed, and added, 'Or is booze still a no-no for little Russian boys?'

She laughed again, a low throaty laugh that wasn't really funny. Nor was the Big Brother five-year ban on liquor in the new shops. He said nonchalantly, 'Vodka's swell, baby. I not little boy.'

'The way you eyeballed my thighs in the lobby, I kind of wondered. Pour your own vodka, big boy.'

She bent over to locate the Mick Jagger from the tapes on the bed. Underneath her suede miniskirt, she was wearing only tiny lace-edged –

She straightened. Hastily he picked up the vodka bottle. She flipped the other tapes aside, stretched out on the bed, loaded the Jagger in the Walkman, opened the perfume. When he handed her the glass, she said, 'Bottoms up!'

'Please? I have not such phrase.'

'You have now.' She drew one long, tanned western leg lazily up beside her other, dabbed the White Musk behind her knees, and gave him the earphones. 'Listen to Jack jump.'

The tape could have kopeck-sized holes cut out of it

and he wouldn't notice. The vodka burned his throat. The beat, and her exotic animal scent, pounded in his head. She lazily stripped off the tiny, lace-edged –

'Please. I must not.'

With all his willpower he broke free and sat on a cane chair facing the door, away from the little white scar half hidden by her black curly –

To keep his mind off that female part of her, he explained about his sanatorium job: how he had to take the bloated or skeleton bodies of the thoracic-chest, cardiac-heart, and unmoving lumbar-stroke convalesents, 'Or the morons like Old Alzheimer, who can't remember anything except being was chased by the ghost of Rasputin! I have to lug them down to their canvas cots on the beach. All night, every night.'

'So leave them. Stuck in their straitjackets, your Rasputin veggies aren't going anywhere, and I'm here – Big Boy.'

He ruined it their first time. He'd never had a western woman unzip his fly and hold that male part of him. As an army helicopter thundered overhead, Ilyich Nev showed her the second time: he was no little boy!

Berov's Red Star chopper was landing in a garden. Spiked evergreen trees stood around like sentries, throwing giants' shadows. Water from a fountain in the shape of a Christmas-tree ornament blew to a jewelled spray from the rotors. A palace in the garden was a three-tier wedding cake: its walls were pink and white, with blue-tiled windows. Square towers at the corners had the domes and minarets of a Moslem mosque. This point of Europe was almost Asia.

'It's been a long trip,' Lowel said; 'where exactly am I?'

'The Alupka Palace,' replied Berov, 'approximately seven kilometres from Yalta. It was Churchill's residence at the 1945 meeting. Roosevelt stayed at the Livadia Palace, which is closer, and where the signing took place, but although that part of the ceremony can be repeated, the living quarters of Livadia are no longer available, and the location here at Alupka allows us to ensure absolute security.'

'And the First Secretary will be staying –?'

'*Not* at the Yusupov Palace. "Under the circumstances",' Berov smiled dryly, echoing Lowel's earlier remark on the landing strip at Simferopol, 'it might not seem auspicious to the western press if the Secretary slept in the same bed as Joseph Stalin. Now you must sleep yourself: we will discuss everything fully in the morning.'

No argument: he was exhausted. He followed Berov and the collie inside, and was conscious of more Lenin Guards saluting, of parquet floors and marble columns, of a huge four-poster bed in a thirty-foot bedroom. An oil painting on one wall was of a woman. After nine non-stop days of international mayhem, this floodlit fairytale palace was the end of the line.

When Ilyich Nev regained his senses, it was one in the morning and she was gone from the hotel bedroom. He dressed hurriedly and ran to the beach.

The bloated or emaciated bodies of his convalescent 'vegetables' – as she so perfectly western-slanged them! – like the old Alzheimer all lay there, with the waves of the Black Sea practically lapping at their swollen or skeleton feet and the crystal stars of the Crimean summer night over their stroke-blocked heads, and they showed no more sign of life and interest than Egyptian mummies. He began a routine head count. Fortunately, one of the other attendants had settled them down in their sanatorium pyjamas and their sanatorium kitbags of extra warm clothing, and their foul-smelling mineral water drinks, and extra pillows and –

Disaster. One female chest vegetable was missing.

It wasn't the first time. It hadn't happened to Ilyich Nev before, but with so many annual thousands of sick people, suicide on the Yalta beach was fairly common – that was one of the reasons the attendant had to stay with them all night. He was responsible. He would lose the job, and he had no training for another. This wasn't the old days; with the blasted new 'reforms' of *perestroika*, a pay cheque was no longer automatic.

He had at least to look for the missing patient.

Half-heartedly, he wandered east along the pebbles, remembering. He had never had any woman cry out like that. Prudish Russian didn't have the other English words she used! He could hardly believe that it was him, Ilyich Nev, who changed the spelling of his last name and tried all his life not be called a little Yid from Yalta, who had made a grown woman's body go so crazy.

Someone was in front of him. He could see the silhouette against the new neon sign advertising the Harbour Tours: 'Come Ride American Peace Heroine Launch Seemantha Smeeth' . . . And the glow of a cigarette: the female thoracic had just stolen away for a forbidden smoke! He wouldn't have to explain a suicide after all. With a huge sigh of relief –

'Hi, Big Boy.'

'*You?*'

With her animal smell of White Musk and her throaty western laugh – but not her expensive down-button shirt, which was off! . . . so that her neon-lit, bared western breasts banished all thoughts of his missing convalescent, as she said, 'You didn't think I was going to pass up our second, second time.'

'No. Yes.' Already her bold, manicured western fingers were shamelessly reaching, as he remembered from the incredible first time. His pants were zipped open, the night breeze made him gasp, 'Where will we – back at your hotel?'

'Uh-uh. Your beach. Slip this on.'

Under starlight, and neon, she had a rubber in her hands. Not one of the state prophylactics that could be used for a fire hose – except for the holes in it – this guaranteed western rubber was thin as a whisper.

After his trembling fingers had trouble unwrapping it, she even helped him roll it down! Using her mouth! He thought he would die . . .!

But of course he didn't.

'And for being such a good big boy,' she said, 'I've brought you a present. The Stones doing *Sticky Fingers*, on compact disc. Still sealed.'

'Seal See-deez?'

Even better than sex. He grabbed for it. Like *wow*.

27

Morning precautions:

Alupka – Livadia

Lowel woke with sun on his face to hear birds singing.
The sound and light came in through an open window.
It led on to a balcony overlooking the garden where he
landed – and beyond, to the golden water of the Black
Sea, reflecting sunrise. Behind the palace, a golden mountain, silhouetted like an enormous crouching bear, did the
same.

The natural setting was stunning, but even as he
watched, humanity intruded: a rumbling column of
white-starred US Armour from the Berlin airlift-in-
reverse swung three personnel carriers around a corner
to take up station with the Red Star tanks already waiting.
He checked his watch: 06.15, six hours before the President's arrival. He walked back into the room and found
a palatial bath with a marble tub and gold fittings. And
an impassive Lenin Guardsman holding the palatial soap
and towels.

'*Spasibo*.' Lowel held out his hand for the items and
continued in Russian, 'I'll take those, soldier, you can
go.'

'*Gospodin*, not yet. My orders are to test the water.'
The man turned both taps, let them run on his palm . . .
wetted the soap and rubbed it . . . touched each towel to
his cheek . . . 'You have a razor?'

'I brought my own.'

'Very well. You may now bathe. Good morning.'

The guardsman saluted, leaving Lowel to wonder whether the man had any idea what the consequences might have been from his impressive display of Soviet prudence if *She* had got to these items first!

He knotted his tie and found himself looking at the painting on the wall. A brass plaque was engraved in English:

Mary Herbert, from Wilton,
Wife of Prince Vorontzov.

The face in the portrait had Jacqueline's eyes – but that was runaway imagination, this was Russia, not Britain's old boy net. He went downstairs and found another solitary Soviet guardsman wearing woollen socks on his feet and waiting to die from eating Lowel's breakfast.

'*Nyet*,' he said to the guard with the first glass of tea, but he was wasting his breath.

'*Gospodin*, I have orders.'

The tea, the fresh-baked bread, and curls of local yellow butter . . . even both sealed, five-minute, soft-boiled brown eggs: he had to sit in splendid isolation in the palace's enormous dining room and wait for each approved item to be passed to his place at the head of a twenty-foot table. As the guardsman was surviving the last egg, Berov and his dog arrived.

'It seems, Mischa,' said the KGB Chief from the dining room's double doors, 'that our arrangements for our friend have proved adequate. Walk gently and we shall join him for some tea.'

The collie's claws clicked on the elaborate parquet flooring. When he reached Lowel, the dog sat without further instruction, gave two wags of its feathery tail, then gazed unswervingly at a remaining crust of bread on the table.

'The arrangements seem impregnable,' he said, 'but

the President won't use them.' He explained Galbraith's absolute prohibition against allowing human tasters to take his risks.

'What the presidential eye does not see . . .' Berov accepted an approved glass from the guardsman. 'Your friend will be unaware of the extent of our protections, but I wished you to know of them. Leave us now.'

This order was to the soldier, who saluted and tried to goose step smartly from the room – which didn't work a damn in socks!

'The restoration of the wooden floors in our heritage buildings has been an expensive and time-consuming proposition, but sometimes military zeal goes too far.' Berov called after the soldier. 'If you have no rubber soles, tell your commander to buy some Adidas running shoes, Black Market.'

Lowel wiped his lips on a tested linen table-napkin. 'Speaking of heritage, maybe you can tell me how an Englishwoman called Mary Herbert came to have her picture in my bedroom?'

'That was a different kind of testing. As you have finished eating, I shall let Mischa join us.' Berov picked the leftover crust off the table. The collie took the delicious bread as gently as an eye-surgeon – then, without tasting, swallowed it whole in a gulp. His master continued, 'Prince Vorontzov was, in the late nineteenth century, Imperial Ambassador from St Petersburg to the Court of St James in London. There he met the family of Herberts and was attracted to their daughters. When the Prince returned to Russia, he had portraits painted and sent to him so that he could make a wifely selection without pressure. He also employed an English builder, named Henry Hunt, to construct this house.'

And write a coincidental book: *Follies of the Rich!* – the dusty volume of Victorian engravings in Jacqueline's father's bookcase. Berov completed his explanation.

'Like Livadia, and Prince Golytsin's "romantic Alex-andria" at Gaspra, which are all the work of Englishmen, Alupka is only partially open to the public. The outer wings here normally accommodate sanatorium patients, but because of renovations, the place was empty, which is why the President and his party can use it at short notice. If you are ready, we shall inspect it.'

The central core of the palace was all as beautiful as the rooms he'd already seen, but the wings were institutional: an antiseptic smell still hung in the stale air, although dull green and brown paint had been freshly slapped right on top of silk wallpapers, and cheap linoleum over marble.

Physical security in the vacant wings was improved by the conversions. The ground-floor windows had been barred and the doors connecting to the central core had massive double locks. Outside, in daylight, the giant sentry trees of last night's landing had turned back into fifty-foot cypresses: the palace was ringed in fact by the combined Soviet and American troops, stationed unob-trusively but continuously around the garden's perimeter.

Lowel walked over to touch bases with the US senior tank commander. A turtle-like head, neck and shoulders emerged from the turret of the Automated Battle Center vehicle: they belonged to a six-and-a-half-foot light colo-nel, from Bangor, Maine.

'Any problems?' Lowel asked from the ground.

'Nothing that a leet-ah of German schnapps can't handle,' the colonel called down from his turret in the clipped phrases of a North-Eastah. 'We don't have much else to put things out if it comes to anything hottah!'

'How is that?' Lowel called up.

'Seems someone in charge decided to send us through from Berlin with only half our regul-ah, on-board suit of am-munition!'

The turtle's head disappeared back in the shell of the

ABC turret, leaving Lowel with a memory from Camp David: the expression on the face of Daniel Galbraith's bitter Defense Secretary; the man in charge of all the Pentagon's ammunition. Berov recited the rest of the KGB's precautions.

'No vehicles may approach or overfly within two miles of Alupka, and all necessary supplies are already on the premises, and inspected. Obviously, there are no females in either the Soviet guard units or the household staff. No members of the press or guests – of any rank, sex, or nationality – will be permitted through the perimeter to visit the President, without your personal approval. We have a choice of road or helicopter: how do you wish to go now to Livadia?'

'Let's fly over and drive back. That way I can see the layout from both angles.'

He was impressed, and reassured, by Berov's efficiency. The Alupka Palace seemed as safe a hotel today as it had been in 1945 for Winston Churchill – but Soviet appearances could deceive: the Yalta Agreement signed then, with Stalin, *appeared* to give an absolute right of free elections to Poland and the other Nazi-ravaged nations that became the East Bloc.

'Mischa, in, boy!'

The blue collie disregarded the stairs, with a single graceful leap up and through the chopper hatch. Once inside, the dog lay quietly with its noble head against the forward Plexiglas observation bubble and watched the ground recede below it.

The country on the coastal side of the Crimean Range was lush where it was watered and sparsely covered where not. From the garden that Prince Vorontzov laid out for his English county wife, with its lawns and cypresses, a winding road flanked by vineyards of stony, light brown soil led along the side of Bear Mountain – the great limestone massif that was golden at sunrise and which now,

Lowel saw, formed the main backdrop for both palaces. A garish *perestroika* billboard for free enterprise bore a two-storey portrait of the late Prince Golytsin, hustling his still world-famous wines. Other nineteenth-century relics, in the form of white villas, were dotted among spindly palms and fluffy acacia trees along the three-mile flight-path, but their gardens were not so grand. Convalescing patients, lying out on aluminium and vinyl *chaises-longues*, were scattered as thickly as the vineyard rocks.

Camouflaged troops and armoured vehicles lined each side of the road. They were clearly visible from the air but, mixed in with pines and blue-green Atlas cedars, they should be more disguised at ground level. The Mediterranean-white town of Yalta was another two or three miles to the east, flanked by its beach and a hooked harbour, but Daniel Galbraith wouldn't need to visit either before the signing.

The chopper cut away from the road and skimmed in across parkland, with a walkway enclosing an open-air amphitheatre and three ponds, which had shapes that were familiar: only hours before, Lowel realized, he had been looking at them on the B1's terrain radar.

'The ponds are miniatures of the Caspian, Black, and Azov Seas,' Berov confirmed. 'The amphitheatre holds one thousand and will be the venue for the allocated press conference after the signing. The entire park is Oreanda, Nicholas I's handiwork. Like Tolstoy, Mischa enjoys its walks, don't you, boy?'

The collie pressed its black nose against the Plexiglas, leaving a heart-shaped imprint. Figures outside, following the walkway, stared back up. As the helicopter descended, Lowel saw that most of the figures were dressed in uniform pyjamas. When the twin opposed rotors stopped howling he asked Berov, 'Isn't there anyone except the walking wounded in this neck of the woods?'

'It appears so, now, but normally the convalescents would be lost in a sea of healthy visitors. I stopped that flood three days ago – despite the screams of the Intourist organization. After Leningrad, Yalta is our most popular destination in the Soviet Union. Mischa, out!'

The collie was a perfect guide. It led them briskly along the shortest brick path, between vivid scarlet salvia beds, towards the White Palace, as the Livadia was commonly known.

'Built for the second Nicholas, and also our last,' Berov elaborated, with his dry smile. 'The main selling attraction is not the historic 1945 Conference but that the Princess Anastasia was born here, and here the Mad Monk Rasputin visited her Empress mother. I have often wished I had been given the opportunity to question the convictions of that particular man of God.'

Lowel said, 'I think I prefer the palace at Alupka.'

'I agree. This has sixty rooms approximately, fifteen more than Alupka. With Stalin, size was always more important than aesthetics – also, he wanted to impress the sick Roosevelt, and he disliked the too observant imperialist lion, Churchill. The main street in the town was renamed for your great president. There is nothing with "Winston" in its civic title.'

There were lions. Three pairs flanked the broad steps rising to the Moorish arch of the main entrance to the palace. The lions were carved from the same white granite as the flat-roofed building, which appeared more Italian than Middle Eastern. A sign at the top flight of steps ordered, 'Observe! Inner Court is copy of St Mark in Venice.' As Mischa reached it, an old man in an antique wheelchair stretched out a trembling hand to touch the collie.

'I have not had these senile patients removed,' Berov said, 'because the facilities in the region are already filled to bursting: however, for the next two days, and in spite of the glorious weather, they will remain confined within

301

their portions of the building. Since Livadia will only be used for the signing ceremony, and not for the President's living quarters, as it was for Roosevelt, this seems a safe compromise. Unless you disagree?'

'If the doors from the sanatorium sections are double-locked, like Alupka –'

'Mischa, our friend thinks your master is an idiot! Any openings through the walls dividing the conference section from the cardiac and thoracic facilities have been bricked-up solid for thirty years.'

Lowel froze. In front of a mural showing Stalin and Roosevelt and Churchill dividing up the world, in top secret, he said to the latest head of the Soviet State's police, 'Cardiac facility? Heart-attack victims?'

The big dog with blue eyes had unlocked the past in an old man's mind. He had already been thinking of the long ago, before the beautiful animal that was like the Empress's Borzoi walked by him . . . He had just been talking about the long-ago to –

Who?

He stared at all these strange people in the chairs with wheels on the lawn around him: was it a man or a woman who had asked him about –

What?

His name, probably, that was always the hardest question. There was so much noise suddenly. The ones in coats who did the looking-after were all running out of the White Palace, shouting . . . It was a woman who had asked him –

'Where?'

It was *this* woman! The young one in a coat, who spoke like a White Russian.

She had only a moment to decide. Take the wheel-chair – or turn away before her American opponent saw her? A white medical coat in Paris, and now here, was one too many, but for her next to final target there was no other disguise that she could use. The dog was sniffing in her direction, but her opponent was studying the architecture being pointed out to him by the dog's KGB owner.

'Where what?'

The drooling old Alzheimer patient beside her had suddenly come to life. To be so close to him at this moment had required a hundred brilliant moves, or lucky strokes, in the last nine days. Washington, Chequers, Paris, last night's beach target here at Yalta. On any mission she believed in the psychology of sex, and luck. Both had combined to bring her this far. She would get no second chance. As her opponent turned back from his study of the building she wheeled her patient calmly but rapidly straight past him, away from the fuss.

'Where what?' the target asked again, more querulously.

She repeated the all-important question: 'Where did you say that her Imperial Highness, the Tsarina, put down her basket?'

Using her kindest smile, she wheeled him smoothly inside his room of the palace, but all the sudden activity outside had totally confused him.

'My name is the Old Alzheimer. Why did her Imperial Highness put it down?'

The dog was moving closer. She closed the French doors to the garden and turned the key in the lock. The outside noise stopped. She drew shut the faded curtains. The room was cool and dim. The patient was safe now. She said, 'We know why. The Empress's Father Confessor was going to visit.'

'I told you he was!' He began to remember. 'Rasputin. When I was apprentice footman here – in this very room where I live now – my name was different then. I met him.'

'Yes, you did. It was a very special day.'

She smiled again encouragingly, as her file said every one must if they wanted to get the Old Alzheimer's special story.

'It was extra special because the little Tsarevitch was bleeding.'

He wagged his frail finger to remind her. She nodded. 'That was why Her Imperial Highness was waiting for Father Rasputin,' she said, 'to pray with him that God above would stop her little boy's bleeding. The Empress was standing here, you told me, between the window and the fireplace, when she put down her embroidery basket.'

'They bricked up the fireplace.' He said it with a child's pleasure: getting to the best part! 'They bricked it up long ago, after the Mad Monk was stabbed to death in the cold north. There was no need of the passage here in the warm south any longer. How could he come back through the fireplace if he was dead?'

'Perhaps they thought he might come back as a ghost.' She smiled again, wheedling for more, but it was the wrong reaction.

'Ghosts are not funny! The Mad Monk was a man of incredible magic powers.' He crossed himself shakily, with three mottled fingers. 'When Rasputin saw I was here, he told me, "My son" – these very words – "you must never touch this shelf. If my mortal body should be left inside the chimney, while my spirit is away with God our Father in Heaven, my unhallowed corpse would haunt you forever!" '

'Don't touch the shelf . . .'

She repeated it in almost a whisper. Now all the advantage was with her: the darkness that lay ahead would paralyse her male American opponent with the deep sexual fear all men felt, but could not speak, of returning to the womb. The old neuter in front of her was too far gone to have any residue of sex. An ambulance siren screamed closer, and closer, voices shouted, the dog barked – but the Alzheimer simply nodded, and smiled, and showed her exactly where to touch. Now the two of them were fellow conspirators: the only ones still alive who knew the secret. Keeping calm, she would win.

The increasingly desperate man outside must lose.

28

Noon, Livadia:

Double-checking

By the time Lowel finished making the perimeter tour
of Livadia, the kind of Soviet brute-force efficiency that
once moved Russia's heavy industry, almost overnight,
a safe thousand miles east of Hitler, had emptied the
sanatorium wings of the Palace. One last ambulance was
backed up on the grass beside a pair of ten-foot-high
French doors: two male orderlies came out through them
with a blanket-covered stretcher. A heavyset Ukrainian
in charge called coarsely to the driver, 'The fun carried
the old Alzheimer off with his pants down! Inform the
Authorities by radio: this stiff is the last one out; we're
all shut up.'

The orderlies closed the handcrafted French doors
with a kick, slammed the vehicle's, and climbed in front
with the driver. Chewing turf, the ambulance raced off
at high speed across the velvet lawn to catch the tail of
the convoy of flashing lights and sirens winding down the
road to the coast. Livadia was silent.

'It should be so, always.' Berov stared at the magnificent vista of mountain and sea, framing the former
Imperial building. 'Once, on the day the war damage
restoration was complete at Leningrad, Mischa and I had
all of Peter's Palace to ourselves, on an early morning. We
felt like tsars, didn't we, boy?' The KGB Chief stroked his
collie's soft ears, adding in a harsher tone, 'But also there
was never a stronger sense of the violation that had been

306

done to our country – mainly through our own backward weakness. This same sort of clumsy stupidity.'

Berov indicated the French doors: the ornate wooden frames had been almost as badly damaged as the grass by the orderly's booted kick, and the lock wouldn't hold. The collie nosed the doors open and moved inside. Lowel followed. This room was smaller than the other sanatorium wards at Churchill's Alupka and hadn't been coated with as much cheap enamel. The delicate pattern of the wallpaper beneath was clearly visible.

'This space for ten patients was Nicholas's German wife's sewing apartment,' Berov said, adding to his dog, 'and if our friend will watch it for a moment, we shall call for a guard from the detachment. Come, boy!'

The collie was enjoying the range of new smells from the old occupants too much; for once the animal's perfect obedience was replaced by a roguish gleam as he hunted some imaginary game along the walls of the ward. When his owner said more sharply, 'Mischa!', the dog lay down on the linoleum floor with his four legs waving, looked up, and gave an unmistakable laugh.

'It's my bad influence,' Lowel grinned. 'We'll hold the fort together.'

Berov paused, then shrugged, and left.

'No brownie points from this corner, pal,' he told the collie. 'You've hurt your master's feelings.'

The dog stopped rolling, got up and bowed, as though to say, It does my little man good – then resumed his sniffing where a puddle of something unpleasant had left a dried stain on the floor. There had been a chimney and fireplace to keep the German wife of the last Tsar warm, but that had been torn out and bricked up; large cast-iron radiators did a more efficient job for the convalescent proletariat. The collie sniffed and scratched at the chipped wainscot board marking the division between floor and wall: once that delicate moulding too, had been part of a charming

307

room, where a woman sat sewing while Russia burned . . .

'At least you didn't desert me completely!'

Mischa's owner was back with a goose-stepping Lenin Guardsman who waited until Lowel had followed the collie outside, then closed the French doors with proper respect, wrapped a chain around their brass handles, padlocked it, and stood ramrod stiff as though guarding the Tomb. Similar toy soldiers with live ammo were posted at every ground-floor door and window. The resources of the Soviet state seemed unlimited – but they weren't, or Daniel Galbraith wouldn't be arriving in an hour to sign the Final Arms Limitation Agreement.

'The guards will check with the human eye, but security of entry will be augmented by machine.' Berov pointed at video surveillance cameras installed as unobtrusively as possible within the scalloped stone tracery of the main arch. 'Furthermore, while I do not share the modern faith of electronic infallibility, all individuals on both staffs will be required to pass voice and fingerprint matching. Soviet personnel have already been entered into the system. Americans will do so on arrival at Alupka. This seems as good a moment as any to see how well the beast is working.'

They walked past the last pair of carved lions guarding the top of the steps. Behind the lions, within the building's square outer skin of weather-darkened granite, the entry changed to a curve of snow-white marble, with a fan-shaped double doorway of six-paned glass each side. Above, at the level of a second storey, was a balcony with a similar, but smaller, doorway. Five feet out from the lower door, under a leering gargoyle copied from Notre Dame, a white metal box had been installed in a niche to the right. A ruby laser, visible even in sunlight, shone across to a reflector in a matching niche on the left. As Berov touched the laser, a voice said in Russian: 'Highly Esteemed Excellency, it is a great honour to meet you. *Poznakomitsa* – what is your name?'

'That electronic excess is its first mistake,' Berov said sarcastically. 'It was only required to issue a simple good morning – *dobroyeutro!*'

'*Poznakomitsa* –' the machine repeated.

'Very well! Berov, Kliment Klimentovich.'

'*Spasibo.*' The red laser switched to green and English: 'Place right hand. Please. Inside unit. Palm down.'

The KGB Chief put his small hand into the white metal box, as instructed. 'Given its inadequacy in Russian, one can hardly be surprised by the bilingual program, but to bring those Moscow "hackers" in again at this stage would not be a step forward. Mischa, my love, let our friend by and we shall see what happens with America.'

'The system doesn't have my voice yet,' Lowel said, 'or my prints.'

'Try anyway.'

The dog and his owner exchanged a look of quiet amusement. Lowel stepped up to the red light and got the Esteemed Excellency treatment. He gave his identity. The laser went green again. He inserted his hand. The box said bilingually, '*Spasibo*, Mr Lowel. Front door Livadia Palace open.'

The conference room of 1945 was a cross between a Gothic hunting lodge and an Orthodox church. The ceiling was of curved, carved wood with diamond-panelled ribbing: the doorways were also carved, as were the windows, to resemble picture frames – that matched the actual picture frames. Carved wooden Orthodox crosses surmounted each one. The largest picture, dominating the great room, about eight by sixteen feet, showed the war leaders and their staffs sitting at a circular table: Stalin with Marshal Zhukov; Roosevelt with General George C. Marshall; Churchill with Air Marshal Tedder.

The same table was now set up in the centre of the room, with chairs around it and little national flags for the absent principals. A scarlet carpet runner formed a border. The effect was eerie, as though the men in the picture had just stepped down and walked out for a moment, putting the conference on hold. Which is what happened to the world, Lowel thought, and tomorrow men would step back into the picture and resume the road to difficult peace.

'Our friend is impressed, Mischa. But doubtless still wondering how our idiot machine knew enough to let him in.'

Lowel turned away from the table, and the picture of it, to find Berov and the collie both smiling at him. 'The voice you could have bugged anytime. I presume you lifted my prints off the doorhandle last night at Alupka, after I arrived?'

'Half right, with the voice. Your fingerprints, however, were courtesy from our initial meeting, and the First Secretary's office desk. The other room here which will be of interest was Roosevelt's study.'

Not excluding Berov's Byzantine mind, everything was of interest: the richness of the scarlet and Turkestan carpets, the incredible artistry of the inlaid parquet floors, the glass and marble seashell baths for chilling the tsar's champagne, the enormous fireplace with a canopy the shape – almost the size! – of a French château roof. The chimney must be one of the original connecting links of the palace: the collie was sniffing the down draught from the fireplace with the same keenness he exhibited for the smells beside the bricked-up one in the abandoned ward.

'Are the chimney flues big enough for someone to get through?' Lowel asked.

'In the old days. I have had a steel grid installed.'

'How about a gas detector?'

'No, but it shall be done.'

310

Berov snapped his fingers at one of the surveillance cameras, to tie off another loose end. Lowel wondered, How many have we missed . . .?

The Roosevelt study adjacent to the conference room seemed impregnable. All its openings were not only electronically monitored on closed-circuit video: telescoping carbon steel mesh filigree screens, meticulously worked by craftsmen into gilded leaves and flowers, like those for old fashioned elevators, had been installed on their inner sides. The locks on the screens, once activated from within, could only be released by dual-vocal command from both Berov and himself.

The study itself was not as physically impressive as the conference chamber but, besides being easier to guard, it was even more beautiful. The walls and ceiling were covered in blue silk studded with a silver-starred design. On the longest wall was a smaller fireplace with a square opening and a gold clock on its mantelpiece. A huge crystal chandelier was suspended in the study's centre: its facets catching light from the high cathedral windows facing onto the same view of the palace gardens as the Empress's sewing-room.

'The original signing by the President and First Secretary will be carried out here, in private,' said Berov. 'Once their two signatures are safely on paper, a repetition for the television cameras and selected print press will be enacted in the conference hall.'

Four ladder-backed wooden chairs, a normal-size square table, and a pair of mini high-speed shredders were set up beneath the chandelier. Two vinyl-wrapped blotters, embossed with a hammer and sickle and the American eagle, already faced-off against each other across the table.

'To avoid any argument over precedence,' Berov elaborated, 'there will be two documents. Each head of state

311

will sign simultaneously, at the top of one: then exchange and sign the other, at the bottom. The copy with the American signature leading will go to Moscow, for the Presidium's inspection and approval, a formality –'

'And the Russian-first to the US Senate,' Lowel said, 'for ratification, which isn't a formality, but the President has the votes.'

'So we are told.' With a sombre expression, Berov touched the American seal and gestured at the filigreed screens with their automated locks. 'And as long, my friend, as we have done our job.'

They returned to the conference room to find two military technicians sealing a pane of bulletproof glass and embedded high-tech gas sensors into the fireplace opening. An advance guard of stewards in military dress uniforms was stocking the marble and crystal seashell coolers with assorted wines from the famous Livadia estate cellars and with magnums of even rarer vintage champagne from Prince Golytsin's legendary collection at adjacent Massandra.

The television cameras for the shared global feed were also installed, facing the conference table and massive fireplace. The cameras' heavy black cables were discreetly hidden by another few miles of scarlet carpet until they snaked underneath a pair of locked and chained French doors leading into the courtyard copy of St Mark's in Venice. The two technicians carried a second sheet of bulletproof glass next door to seal the fireplace in the Roosevelt study. More soldiers wearing fatigues entered from the opposite direction, holding absurd little gilt chairs with pompom crimson velvet seats labelled in Cyrillic characters: media and diplomatic guests.

'You must have vetted the foreign press to the bone,' Lowel said. 'About how many are we expecting?'

'At last count, the number was slightly in excess of 10,000.'

He stared in amazement. Berov shrugged.

'It is not so surprising. There were 7,000 reporters for the Intermediate Treaty signing in Washington, and eight plus for the Strategic fifty-fifty at Geneva. We are prepared: only 100 passes allow entry here, and 1,000, as I said earlier, for the amphitheatre press conference which will follow at Oreanda. Regardless of their feminist outrage, no passholders at either location will be women.'

'That may stop her getting into this room,' Lowel said, 'but I can't imagine a better way to have made it to Yalta than disguised as one of the thirty per cent of a hundred nationalities in that press mob who are female. We need an immediate triple check on all media women: who they work for, why they came, where they are – and once we've found them, from here on they get a tail, with no exceptions.'

The KGB Chief nodded and, with a sign to his collie to stay, walked across to a heavyweight thug standing in a grey business suit behind the pompom chairs. Another 'not so surprising' arrival on the scene: Lowel recognized Boris Strelnikov, last week the man supposedly in charge of London's Soviet art and culture.

'My Deputy you met,' said Berov, returning. 'He already has answers to the who and why. Within the hour he expects to confirm where. We have no Russian female journalists present, in case you were wondering. And as at Alupka, that holds true also for the entire Soviet secretariat staff – bodyguards, cooks, servants, stenographers. We have even done without the services of our finest interpreter, the First Secretary's right hand on these occasions, who is a woman.' Berov looked down into the blue eyes of his dog and added in a tone that came close to bitterness, 'There can surely be no greater demonstration of trust on our part, Mischa, than that for

313

the duration of this occasion, when the leaders are alone, our head of state will be relying solely on our friend's President's man for fair treatment in his explanation of American intent.'

The drive back to Churchill's palace at Alupka, in Berov's staff car, was more scenic than by air – but there was less to look at. For the few miles connecting Alupka to Livadia, every vineyard worker and tractor, every sanatorium convalescent and sickbed, had been swept up by the Soviet military machine and out of the Crimean landscape. Only the camouflaged troops and tanks were left to blend with the pines and palms lining the route.

The giant billboard portrait of Prince Golytsin stood out like a sore thumb at the halfway mark. The tourist concession was closed. An armoured personnel carrier had been backed into the archway in front of TUNNEL TO PRINCELY WINE CELLARS. Galvanized tubs of just harvested grapes were abandoned at the side of the road. Lowel was suddenly reminded of the desolated scenes around Chernobyl after the reactor explosion: that emergency evacuation had also happened in the Ukraine. What were the local population making of this one? Did they think the American President visiting their man with the mark of the devil was the cover for another national disaster?

'*Yedlash!* Stop the car!'

Berov's driver slammed the brakes at the snapped command. A brown-skinned soldier from one of the eastern Soviet republics came lurching out of the archway from the wine cellars, swinging an uncorked bottle in each hand.

'You there! What unit?'

'One hundred twenty-fifth, comrade.' The man grinned, too pissed to feel the normal fear of authority. 'From Irkutsk – and you Russki bastards can kiss my ass.'

Lowel waited for Berov's explosion, but the small secret policeman was never predictable. He lit one of his lung-killer cigarettes and said in a level voice to his driver, 'Go on.'

The Irkutsk soldier took the staff car's departure as a personal victory – and another long swig from one of his jugs. He chucked the empty after them and collapsed against the steel side of his carrier, under the princely tunnel sign.

'Mischa, your American friend knows all about our "Yedlash ethnic" problem,' Berov said to his dog, 'but I'm sorry he had to see it in person.'

'Those things happen in the army.' Lowel pointed at the sign, 'What's the extent of the tunnels?'

'They honeycomb the region, but there is no connection from here to either of the palaces we are using for the signing. Military sappers have already tested the grounds at both for the presence of land mines.' Berov jerked his head at the drunk vanishing into the distance: 'That problem comes from the Army ignoring instructions and using non-commissioned ranks.'

The Red Army's regular practice was officers-only for battlefield exercises to which foreigners were invited, but to find enough commissioned personnel for this operation must be stretching Soviet forces to the limit. The common soldier's unreliability, on top of the missile incident against the B1, brought back the question the commie-bashers had never stopped asking:

How do we know the Reds *can* be trusted?

At the Alupka Palace, Kliment Berov provided an enigmatic answer. The KGB Chief ordered the immediate arrest of the drunk and his senior superior. For the second time in twelve hours, and as the President of the United States set foot on the Crimean Peninsula, the volcanic southern region of the USSR had no overall military commander.

29

Afternoon:

Cross-currents

Lowel watched Daniel Galbraith's historic touch-down at Simferopol, via the super-sized Mitsubishi television screen the Russians had provided for the President's use in Winston Churchill's old quarters at Alupka. As Air Force One rolled to a halt by the red carpet edged with gold hammers and sickles, the combined escort of Soviet and American fighters howled overhead in a double arrowhead salute, a band of a hundred instruments crashed into the two anthems, and the man with the mark of the devil on his forehead strode forward with a smile.

The Japanese TV was digital, split-screen. The left half of the screen showed Simferopol, with the interpreter Kolinski hogging it: the right half showed America watching. When the pool correspondent for CBS shouted his welcoming question, the whole world saw and heard it.

'Mr President! Have the Soviets explained to your satisfaction why they shot one of our planes out of the sky here last night?'

The stereo track switched abruptly to a chorus of kiddie voices shrilling Russian nursery songs. When Galbraith met Lowel on the Alupka Palace lawn thirty minutes later, he said grimly, 'Your B1 joyride and that network fucker just cost my vote. Tell me you got here in time to catch Typhoid Mary.'

'All I can tell you, sir, is that apart from open revolt in the Crimean Red Army, the Soviet government seems to have adequate physical security at Yalta.'

'Glad you haven't lost your sense of humour.' Galbraith gave a terse laugh and said to the interpreter, hovering too closely behind his right shoulder, 'My friend Mr Lowel speaks enough amateur Russian to see me by tonight. I won't need your professional translating until we go head to head at the goal line, over the fine print, in the morning.'

'Certainly, Mr President. Whatever you say. Thank you, Mr President.'

Behind his fawning manner and purple tinted glasses, the interpreter's expression had shown a flash of sadistic anger.

'Another leftover from the Hollywood crowd,' Galbraith said. Haunted by his shadow, the nuclear Button Box naval aide, he walked on towards the palace. 'Assuming your mutinous southern sector bastards won't launch a full coup in the next half-hour, and while our people from State get settled, I'm going to unload my tin hand in Churchill's bedroom. Allow me five, Jack, then you can give us the rest of the grand tour, and your low-down on last night.'

Lowel hadn't anticipated the size of the US delegation either: the convoy of incoming choppers was like a delta fire lift in Vietnam. As the helicopters' properly badged passengers poured out, he counted no fewer than a hundred State Department logos, as many again from the National Security Council, and White House protocol and personal staffs, but at least his main instruction had been followed:

Every picture on a badge was male.

It was only as he was finishing his private report and mini grand tour of the Alupka Palace for Dan Galbraith that the latest piece of the blindingly obvious caught up and struck his ageing brain with the force of a physical object.

She doesn't have to be female.

She could be here disguised as a man. Probably not among the relatively small American staffs, who all knew each other, but the situation with the 10,000 international press was once again blown wide open. At which point a badgeholder from Security said, 'Excuse me, Mr President, for interrupting, but the KGB want Mr Lowel to fly over to them right away. On the beach in Yalta. It's about some missing woman.'

He saw Mischa first. The conspicuous collie was sniffing delicately at an object lying on a patch of shingle pebbles, between his master and Berov's linebacker Deputy for Culture, Boris Strelnikov, west along the beach from the Yalta Harbour wall. The beach and a concrete promenade running beside it had been cordoned off by the Army with khaki-coloured rope.

'Next to the dog,' Lowel told his pilot.

He stepped out of the helicopter onto the concrete. Mischa drew back in disdain from the sniffed object and bounded towards him, banner tail waving. Lowel touched noses and made his way back with the collie across the pebbles to the waterline. Before he got there, the object had become a half-clothed body – but close up, the half without clothes had skinny legs and male genitals.

'I was told you'd found a woman,' he said to Berov.

'Over there.' The KGB Chief pointed back towards the harbour. 'Both bodies have been in the water for the same length of time: since about two hours after midnight. They went out on the eastern current, and then the Dnepr washed them in again. Unfortunately for our Russian image, and privacy, it was an American newspaper reporter on a tour boat who spotted them.'

'Do you have an identity for this one?'

Berov nodded. 'Its name was Nev – Nevstein on its original internal passport. When their use was abolished, it tried to drop the Jewish ending: this has been common, and perhaps understandable. Although we no longer have official anti-Semitism in this country, human nature takes time to change, as you saw from that Irkutsk oaf this morning.'

Lowel felt considerable sympathy. Strelnikov didn't.

'The yid was employed as summer temporary at Livadia, Sanatorium Number Three,' the Deputy said coarsely. 'Nevstein's job was looking after convalescents brought down to sleep on the beach. Instead, he screwed one of them. Also, he had a booze problem. It happens here at Yalta all the time. After they fuck, they pass out, and the currents get them.'

Strelnikov put his size 12 shoe on the bloated stomach of the corpse and pressed. Liquid gushed from the mouth, with a strong stench of alcohol. The collie jumped back.

'My poor Mischa, this is not at all your aristocrat's milieu.' Berov touched the animal's broad white ruff and its plaited blue collar, then stared again at the corpse. 'There is a further complication: last night this Nev was seen to fraternize with a western Jewish female photographer in the new Grand Hotel on Drazhinsky Street.'

'So where is she?' Lowel asked.

'That is the complication. This morning, no patient from Sanatorium Number Three was reported missing.'

Berov ordered his Deputy to stay and his dog to come, and began to walk east, with difficulty, over the slippery pebbles. Lowel followed, taking one pace for two, trying to control the building tension.

An ambulance was parked on the promenade near the harbour wall: a medic in a white coat knelt beside the second corpse. He looked up as Mischa stepped delicately towards him. 'Stay back, damn you!'

The collie showed total disdain in its blue eyes – and vaulted past to nose the sheeted body. Berov said in the flat voice that usually preceded firing a commander-in-chief, 'You will not object if I take a place beside my dog.'

'Yours?' The kneeling medic's face suddenly looked as grey as the stained wall behind him. 'Comrade, I thought this – magnificent creature – was a stray.'

Berov took out a cigarette. His collie, for some perverse doggy reason, sniffed the sheet with greater interest, working along the edge as he had the wall of the sanatorium ward. Berov lit the cigarette and said to the man in the coat, 'Mischa strays where I stray, which is to the farthest corners of our country where there is a chronic shortage of medical staff. Lift the cover!'

The cloth came off the feet first. They had been tanned – but now looked jaundiced. The ankles were slim, the calves the same and smooth, not even a stubble of hair, unusual for a Russian woman.

'The left knee is swollen,' the medic addressed Berov in the servile tone of a second-rate waiter offering a poor choice of menu, 'but as you see, not discoloured. The contusion must have occurred immediately prior to death, from contact with the pebbles. Comrade, as a child, I too had a delightful dog . . .'

Berov ignored the overture and exhaled. The thighs on the body were firm from exercise, but not overly muscled.

'So was there sex, before death?' Berov asked the question clinically.

Although the pubic hair was blonde, not dark as it would be on a Semitic, there was no scar by the groin, now showing below a Lady Brooks button-down, tailored shirt of Madras cotton plaid. A Star of David was on a chain around the neck. The collie was sniffing the shirt even more intently.

The medic answered Berov, 'There may have been penetration, comrade – it is not possible to say in a mature female – but if so, there is no evidence of release by the male.'

'The male corpse was still wearing a safe,' Lowel said to Berov. 'Both bodies should be tested immediately for the presence of Viscumin.'

The KGB Chief nodded, called his dog away from its preoccupation with the soaked Madras cotton, and walked up the beach to his staff car on the adjacent promenade. Lowel asked the medic to remove the Lady Brooks shirt from the corpse and pass it to him, adding the caution, 'Autopsy procedures must only be done by technicians equipped to handle nerve-gas toxins.'

After the threat of Siberia from the collie's owner, the man seemed relieved at confronting mere medical catastrophe. He made notes on a pad, placed the shirt in a waxed brown paper bag, and handed it over with a smile. 'Procedure shall be as you say, comrade – but if the prophylactic was a state product, whatever was inside will already have fertilized half the sturgeon of the Black Sea.'

Or killed them. Lowel rejoined Berov on the promenade where he was talking to Strelnikov. On the harbour wall beyond, a group of day trippers had just come off the tour boat, *Samantha Smith*, named for the little girl from Maine who wrote to Brezhnev about world peace and became a Russian heroine. The foreigners in the group craned their heads past the rope cordons towards the ambulances, hoping to see the bodies. After one quickie at the Army ropes and Berov's massive deputy, the Soviet citizens looked just as hard in the opposite direction.

'I had already made provision for a mobile forensic

facility.' Berov demonstrated more of his extraordinary foresight and efficiency. 'They expect to produce results before midnight.'

'No patient in Third Sanatorium was Jewish,' said Strelnikov. 'The dog likes your bag. What's in it?'

'A shirt from Brooks Brothers.' He turned to Berov. 'We are missing a western journalist, who was Jewish. We have a body, who isn't – and no report of any missing patient. I was watching Mischa earlier at the sanatorium: if we take him and the shirt back to Livadia, maybe he'll make something out of it.'

'Will you chase a wild goose for us, Mischa love?' The animal's master smiled wryly: the collie gave one of his laughing upward glances of apparent understanding. Berov interpreted: 'He says why not? I agree, we have nothing more sensible to follow. But you, Boris Aleyevitch,' he ordered his deputy, 'will conduct another comprehensive sweep of every sanatorium female in greater Yalta – regardless of age or physical appearance. If you find a discrepancy, I shall be having supper with Comrade Lowel at mission headquarters.'

30

Evening:

Last supper

Joseph Stalin commandeered the imperial splendour of
the old Yusupov Palace for the first Yalta Conference.
For the second, the less exotic but more hi-tech facilities
of the Party Leadership Spa had been taken over. The
building, originally designed strictly for the bosses, since
the reforms was now renamed Crimean Regional Superior
Recreational Facility and open to a wider clientele – who
had just been summarily evicted for this historic occasion. To Lowel, approaching the Soviet delegation's main
entrance with Berov and Mischa, whatever they called it,
the place looked like a cut-rate version of the CIA's sixties hotel outside Washington, but it was lavish by USSR
standards of construction.

As for Langley . . .

He tried to block the thoughts of the Congressional
fire storms which, even if a miracle took place here,
were still going to be waiting for him in Washington,
because of his summary removal and forced hospitaliza-
tion of the Agency's old director. And Murphy's suicide
in the interrogation vault.

If it was suicide . . .

'Identification!'

Another red laser beam protected this main entry.
The ID and print recognition equipment were the same as
those at the Livadia Palace, but the voice here was human:
a ramrod Lenin Guardsman, armed with a Kalashnikov

automatic, stood in front of the red beam. He compared Lowel's face to a photograph, and watched as he placed his hand in the chamber. The laser switched to green, the guardsman stood aside, then repeated the procedure as meticulously with Berov. But in typically sentimental Russian fashion, when the collie's white-tipped tail triggered the red light, the dog was granted a smiling dispensation.

'We should call you Tsar Mischa,' said his master. 'While your friend Mr Lowel has his next talk with the First Secretary, let us organize our meal.'

The surprise factor was less, and poker-playing helped, but Lowel still wasn't used to Berov's little bombshells. He knocked on the ribbon-grained mahogany door where the KGB Chief had left him.

'Enter.'

The firm voice was the same, but on this occasion the man changing Russia wasn't seated at a museum-piece desk in an office like a national treasure, but standing by a plate-glass picture window staring outwards.

'The great mystery of our Revolution,' the extraordinary heir to that upheaval observed, without turning his head, 'is why we accepted such ugliness with it. Such drabness. For contrast, come and look at Chekhov's house on Kirov Street, down there.'

The First Secretary's forcefulness made him seem taller, but he barely came to Lowel's shoulder. From the window, it was apparent that they were both at an elevation above the old town of Yalta. The scene was certainly not Soviet Russian. The streets below, where the famous writer came to spend the last part of his life, were curved, shaded with trees, and flanked by white stone houses with colourful gardens.

'Chekhov's is the one with the three small round windows by that large walnut tree.' The Secretary pointed:

'As you see, it has two different roof lines, which are not flat, but slope pleasingly – a third roof, if you count the canopy coming out towards us above the front door. And observe how it does so at an angle to the rest of the building. Mr Lowel, there is not one Soviet citizen who visits that house, who does not go away thinking it charming – and then returns to a slab-sided desert of centrally planned, concrete boxes. If I can at least begin to brighten that grey desert, and get them to demand some colour once more in their own lives – in a country that produced Tchaikovsky and Chagall! – then I could think I had done something worthwhile.'

'I'm sure history will think you've already made a promising start,' Lowel replied.

'Are you? If I were to die tomorrow morning? Without signing your Agreement?' The Secretary smiled ironically and gestured in the opposite direction from Anton Chekhov's house. A spectacular panorama of rocky cliffs and blue water, turning to sheet gold as the evening sun dropped west, spread before them. 'That Black Sea vision of nature, Mr Lowel, is only remembered, by the history you mention, for two disasters: first, as the body of water across which the British Royal Navy sailed their Light Brigade to charge in our country; and second, the spot just beyond the horizon – there, past the Swallow's Nest – where the *Pride of Lenin*, as I mentioned to you in our last conversation, went down to inaugurate my assumption of office.'

Like the Guardsman's sentimental behaviour with the dog, the First Secretary's streak of fatalism was typically Russian: but if you had to go through life with the devil's mark on your head, Lowel thought, that wouldn't be an easy trait to break! He said as a conversational filler, 'The Swallow's Nest is beautiful. I haven't had time to visit.'

'The "Last Folly of the Tsar", many people call it.'

The Secretary continued to stare at Yalta's most famous tourist attraction: a turreted mini-palace, perched like the St Spyridon nuns' convent on a rock pinnacle high above the sea. 'It never ceases to remind me that leaders are most remembered for their human weaknesses. In the Tsar's case, shortsightedness. Nicholas built that monument as an afternoon teahouse for his wife, because of its spectacular view, without realizing that tea would be impossible on most afternoons because of the wind at its exposed location.'

Another folly of the rich. 'But maybe not such an "ill wind",' Lowel said; 'the building must have generated a fortune in tourist hard currency.'

'Which we will not need so badly, once your brother-in-law and I end the arms madness. Yet already that historic document waiting for us both at Livadia is genuinely and passionately regarded by many in this country as a monument to *my* shortsightedness. My folly.' The Secretary smiled briefly. 'The Tsar's other dominant trait was pigheadedness – after the wind problem was discovered, he ordered a tunnel built to the Swallow's Nest, but larger historical events cut short that final excess.'

The sun touched the top minaret, then slid out of sight, down into the sea. Lowel waited for the real point of this strange summons. At last, as evening twilight crept towards Yalta, the Secretary turned away from the view.

'You are a patient man, Mr Lowel, and a competent one. I wanted to thank you for your efforts and apologize for our mistakes. As for tomorrow, I have considered the additional security proposals you've put forward with Berov, and I agree to them. For the signing, we shall do without note-takers – you and he can fill that function. There will be no photographers or other witnesses, and we are using only your interpreter.'

'Kliment Klimentovich told me. The President is most grateful.'

'Let us hope we shall both be, in the morning. Until then, good night, comrade.'

The Soviet leader shook his hand. At that moment, the title *comrade* truly implied friendship: not just the bored and hostile formality from eighty years of frozen dogma. As Lowel left, the Secretary had turned again to stare at the last Tsar's turrets, blackly outlined against a flaming western sky.

Follies of the rich . . . the phrase which was the title of a book would not stop running through Lowel's head. The tunnels of Yalta sounded like another bad story, but Berov had said his sappers were on top of that possible mine threat.

'Mr Lowel?'

An American voice shook him out of his reverie. With a Lenin Guardsman at his heels, a US Army second lieutenant, dressed in a motorcycle crash helmet and anti-skid leather, was jogging across the lobby of the Soviet delegation's HQ towards him.

'I'm Lowel.'

'Very good, sir. I have a despatch for you.'

The bike rider took an envelope from a pouch chained to his wrist and passed it over. The pink note form inside was from the US Mission Security Chief, now installed at Alupka.

BY HAND OF MESSENGER: J. LOWEL EYES ONLY
HOLDING HI-BURST RECEIVED FOR YOU FROM FBI.
SUBJECT, 'AEROFLOT'.
UNSURE LOCAL LAND LINES.
REQUEST INSTRUCTIONS FOR DISPOSITION.

Aeroflot: must be something more from the hassled boarding agent in the Grateful Dead sweatshirt, at Dulles

Airport. Lowel wondered whether to return to the Alupka Palace – then decided against.

'Bring the message to me here,' he told the despatch rider. 'I shall be with a senior official called Berov.'

'Yes sir.' The lieutenant saluted and turned on his heel.

'Hold it!' Making another on-the-spot, he wrote a message on the back of the pink form and returned it to the rider. 'Ask Mission Security to send this through, with Flash routing to SIS in London – and if he gets any reply, I want it immediately. But again, no phone. Use your wheels.'

Trailed by his jackbooted Lenin Guard, the biker lieutenant skidded leather back to his wheels. In the other direction, a second Soviet guard was posted beside the facility senior staff dining-room. Even after reform, some Russians were still more equal than others.

A preoccupied Kliment Berov was seated at a mahogany table that looked like a pair of the recreational facility's ribbon-grained doors badly glued together. Two white porcelain bowls of cold, creamed cucumber soup, pale green, rested on scarlet place mats, plus the inevitable gold hammers and sickles. The collie, Mischa, was just polishing off the last of his evening meal from a similar set-up on the carpeted floor in one corner.

'Your conversation with the First Secretary took longer than I allowed for; however, with cold soup, no matter. It has been tested but, as host, it seems only good manners that I go first.'

The small man's smile was even more mournful than usual. He raised a silver spoonful –

And survived. Lowel realized that, without meaning it to, his own hand had been waiting. He followed –

The soup was delicious, flavoured with ginger. He explained the possible significance of the FBI's message.

'But don't hold your breath. If this young man witnessed our woman, her appearance at Dulles doesn't bear the slightest resemblance to any of her other descriptions.'

'Our female chameleon.'

'That's something else we didn't think about soon enough.' He explained his fear of possible male impersonation, especially among the press. Berov scribbled a note to himself, finished his soup and rang a small brass bell positioned by his right hand on the linen tablecloth. A military steward backed in through a swinging door, pulling a trolley of covered dishes behind him. The collie gave a last lick of his own empty bowl and came over to sit beside his master. And then stared with longing blue eyes at the loaded trolley.

'Such greed!'

A reprimand from the head of the KGB scared the living hell out of Russian humans; his dog just laughed. The steward glanced uneasily, exchanged the used plates for fresh ones, and put a silver dish of butter curls and a basket of crisp rolls on the table.

'My rendezvous with destiny.' Lowel reached. But even though he grinned, *Maybe it is . . .*

He broke the roll and ate. Mischa got up and walked delicately around to sit beside him, and do some more staring. A dribble of saliva dropped from the collie's pointed chin.

'Now that is enough! Back here by me! Lie down!'

The commands were no louder than usual, no harsher, but the dog obeyed instantly. Only his blue left eye, half shut, and gleaming sideways like a whale's, still showed a secret amusement: *he doesn't mean it, man – or if he does, it ain't for long.*

As usual, the dog was right on. By the time Lowel got to the First Secretary's architectural description of Anton Chekhov's house, Berov's hand was automatically reaching down to the grey muzzle on the floor. Lowel went on to the significance in the Secretary's mind of the Swallow's Nest, and its comparison to the Dismantling Agreement.

'After the explosive events of last night, he could hardly disguise the reality of those concerns from you.' Berov ate a small piece of plain roll and spread butter on another. 'High level opinion of foreign policy must always be divided at turning points of history, and those directly involved are probably least equipped to judge dispassionately the long-term results of their actions.'

'Fortunately,' Lowel said, 'now we have satellites to do that.'

'So we do, don't we, Mischa boy?'

The collie's amused blue eye watched a scrap of buttered roll descend. The steward lifted the lids off the next silver dishes to identify, 'Duck Massandra!'

Roasted, after being skinned: then stuffed with its own boneless meat, mixed with Crimean herbs, and wine basted. The golden brown result was sliced in fine strips and reassembled – with a Mallard drake's startling beaked head and feathered neck placed at the front end. Those feathers were the last straw to dog discipline: the collie sat up, then stood, then drooled, still staring at Lowel.

Toxins act differently on a canine's central nervous system than on a human's. More slowly.

A man had to watch as his dog stood, on wavering legs . . . as those unblinking blue eyes turned in terrible slow motion . . . away from a stranger . . .

To master.

'*Mischa! My love –!*'

The brain behind the blue eyes seemed to hear the last anguish of a man's love.

Before it faded . . .

The toughest part for Lowel was restraining Berov from

his instinctive urge to cradle his dead dog in his arms. The small man's hands reached to take the grey muzzle.

'Don't! His saliva will be contaminated.' He added more gently, 'Kliment Klimentovich, we have to leave Mischa for your forensic experts.'

'Of course.'

Berov got to his feet and left the dining room without a backward glance. Lowel knew what that gesture cost him. Jacqueline, Sam Wong, the collie –

The chameleon bitch had destroyed another best friend.

He caught up to the KGB Chief at a phone in the headquarters lobby.

'Our efforts to intercept the target will continue. Alupka has already been warned to double precautions for the President. Another tracking dog is being sent immediately to Livadia. Test your theory with the woman's shirt at the palace. I shall complete matters here with my forensic department.'

The small Russian was back on the job. Lowel squeezed his shoulder in silent sympathy and felt only bone below the jacket material. A man as thin as that must be running on borrowed time.

'You will have to use my helicopter for Livadia,' Berov concluded, with a bitter note, as he left. 'The vultures of the press have gathered.'

31

Signing day:

Death watch

The media were an army camped out for the night: huge
satellite transmission trucks were its armoured brigade.
They were drawn up in a covered-wagon circle around
the main avenue of approach to Livadia, with smaller
mobile van reconnaissance units on all the side roads.
The shooting armies of the United States and Russia in
turn encircled the forces of global journalism, with real
tanks, real guns, and batteries of searchlights that swept
constantly over the mass media equipment and the palace
grounds.

Lowel looked down on the astounding scene and felt
like a moth on a pin as the white hot scalpel from the
searchlights transfixed the Red Star chopper lifting him
past the journalists' barrier. Inside the circle, Livadia
was shrouded in darkness, all the more black for the
blaze without. Only the tips of the square corner turrets,
the glass doors of the front entry, and the flanking lions
on the steps sporadically showed and disappeared as the
beams crisscrossed above them.

The helicopter set him on the lawn where the ambulance
had chewed the turf that morning. The rotors stopped: the
night was silent. He ordered the pilot to train a spotlight
on the evacuated north wing of the palace. It picked up the
row of armed Soviet guards, squinting one after another
as the sudden glare hit their eyes. Beside the sixth guard,

the French doors to the Empress's sewing-room ward were still chained shut. Lowel walked towards it.

The night shattered with a sound from hell. The hair went up on his neck. A shape hurtled through the dark against the back of his legs. He crashed to the ground. His left elbow dug into the turf; his right hit a fleshy mass that wobbled. The noise deafened. The stink of some kind of hot wet breath choked –

'*Blyadun!*' a voice bellowed in Russian. 'Whoremonger hound! Leave him, you bastard! The man is a friend!'

God help its enemies! Illuminated now by the chopper light, 150 pounds of ears, jowls, and bull's balls stood over Lowel: a bloodhound, baying and wagging its tail. Then it began to hump his knee.

'Sex mad brute pulled loose from its trainer!' The voice was Boris Strelnikov's. Berov's linebacker Deputy restrained the dog with one huge hand, and offered the other. 'Also, Forensic reports there was no poison in the rubber on the Jew.'

From that promising start, things went downhill. The guard by the French doors didn't have a key for the padlock on the chain wrapped around their handles, and by the time a pair of bolt cutters with large enough jaws was located, the principal canine actor had gone to sleep. The bloodhound's trainer, a tall, gentle Georgian, with a melancholy moustache, arrived to deliver a fresh string of apologies. Strelnikov booted the dog's ass.

Lowel showed the barely roused animal the Madras cotton shirt, which it sniffed . . . it then dragged the Georgian at the charge through the thorns of a rosebed, to a spot beside the door – where the bloodhound lifted its leg and pissed a couple of gallons on the adjacent guards.

'Present the shirt again,' the Georgian said, with a certain lack of conviction.

The dog sniffed the Lady Brooks button-down and licked Lowel's hand, with an increasing passion at both ends. He got the horny beast to follow him into the abandoned ward, where it promptly sat down in the middle of the floor and howled to go out.

A bobbing headlamp approached across the lawn. When it was close enough to compete with the bloodhound's baying, Lowel heard the double-bore rumble of a 1200 cc engine. The US Army second lieutenant biker kicked his machine onto its stand and strode in with the despatch pouch.

'Your FBI message about New York, sir. Mission says there's nothing back yet from London.'

He took the form, but couldn't read it in the room's faint illumination. He said in Russian to Strelnikov, 'There has to be electric light. Can you locate the switch?'

'Yes, but it won't help reading. The effective way to reduce fire hazard, and prevent cross-ventilation to the conference apartments, was to cut all power to the wings of the building.'

More Soviet brute-force solutions. He took the message out to the motorbike and got the rider to start the engine. In the glare of the headlamp the FBI reported:

FROM SENIOR FA DULLES:
INFORMANT PLAYFAIR NOW RECALLS:
1 RITZ HOTEL LONDON DESCRIBED INCORRECTLY.
2 TICKET CONFIRMED RITZ PARIS FINAL DESTINATION.
3 FEMALE CARRIED HUSBAND'S PART-TOUPEE.

He studied the terse Bureau-ese to decide what to do with it at this eleventh hour. André Dolmain at the French Sûreté might as well be informed. He looked at his watch: already past midnight.

'I want you to run a follow-up back to Alupka,' he said to the biker lieutenant. 'Tell mission, because of our deadline, they can use the code-phone to Paris.'

'Yes, sir. But if time is getting to be a problem, it took me forty minutes coming over. Dirt-riding through those media lines is a total son of a bitch.'

The lieutenant indicated the Red Star chopper waiting on the lawn. By air, the trip would only take five minutes, and Lowel could speak to Dolmain himself. He turned to Strelnikov. 'Tell Kliment Klimentovich I've gone to Alupka, but ask the handler to keep his dog here until I get back.'

'You're too polite,' Strelnikov grunted. 'The only thing that pair of trained assholes will produce by the morning is a truckload of shit.'

Visual intelligence, revealed by the flashing amber from the Red Star's undercarriage light, confirmed that the bloodhound hunched on the lawn was already halfway to its objective.

He had been wrong in his earlier media estimate. Within two minutes of lift-off, it was apparent that only one corps of the press had camped at Roosevelt's darkened Livadia. The other half was besieging Churchill's former quarters, in what appeared to be broad daylight, but was really a necklace of arc lights that surrounded the palace like candles on a seventy-year-old's birthday cake. A worm couldn't poke its head up through the manicured grass without throwing a shadow, and getting it riddled by cannon-fire.

The US tank commander from Bangor, Maine, had tracked his Automated Battle Center from the garden perimeter to spitting distance of the palace front door. The light colonel's turtle frame was still half in and half out of his turret, and his gaze just as alert as it had been sixteen hours earlier.

'Has there been an incident?' Lowel asked him.

'Only between me and their head garden-ah!' replied

the North-Easter, in Franklin Roosevelt's own cadences. 'I had to in-form that peasant gentleman: My ord-ahs, sir, are close pro-tection of our President!'

Lowel smiled. In spite of his own crushing tiredness and tension, there were still odd moments when it was a pleasure to meet a fellow American. He waved a salute to the colonel, passed the automated recognition procedures of both countries, and entered the building.

'The President wants to see you in his dressing-room,' said the duty officer at the mission security desk. 'The routing word was operational-immediate.'

Which meant a response faster than budget-crisis, but not slow enough to allow a conversation with Paris. He drafted his message and ordered the duty officer to read it to André Dolmain in person. There was still nothing back from London.

Outside the presidential apartments, the young naval aide was talking on the interplanetary radio of his Button Box to a nuclear submarine command somewhere in the South Pacific. US Secret Service were stacked four layers deep in the corridor leading on to the presidential bedroom door. The pair of agents making up the last layer were staring at a silver jug of hot chocolate on a tray between them.

'The man just ordered his regular nightcap,' the senior agent said uneasily to Lowel.

'Fine. I'll take it in to him.'

'What about the tasting?' said the junior agent.

The pair exchanged you-first glances. Putting your life on the line in a bullet-proof vest wasn't the same thing as volunteering for poison.

Lowel said, 'I issued orders that all bulk kitchen supplies would be tested on laboratory rats.'

'They have been,' said the senior man, 'but after this latest incident at the Soviet headquarters, our people in Washington are insisting on a rat with two legs.'

'That's out. The President has refused to allow human testing.'

He picked up the tray. The agents blocked the door.

'No sir. It can't go in.'

He stuck his finger in the silver jug and withdrew it. The bird dogs' eyes widened. He licked the finger.

The man whose life he might have spared was in front of a portrait of a boiler-suited Churchill, beside an open window. Lowel observed that he wasn't wearing his hand prosthesis which sat separately on a dressing-table.

'Churchill stood here in the nude,' said Galbraith. 'I've been re-reading his memoirs on the first conference. The old British bulldog called Air Marshal Tedder in to try out his toast to Stalin on him. The kitchen staff didn't have lemon peel for the cocktails, which Tedder mentioned. The next morning, a lemon tree was waiting by the front door in a tub. But that ain't the punch line: before Uncle Joe arrived at Livadia for a session with FDR, he had the gall to send his secret police goons on ahead to search for mikes! Under the floors, behind the walls. Sometimes this evening I've almost felt I could see the bunch of them down there on the terrace, with the lemon peel in their drinks, going into a huddle over Poland and the Nazis' unconditional surrender.'

Lowel said, 'The feeling is even stronger at Livadia.'

His friend nodded – and for a moment once again the resemblance to Bergitta was overwhelming – then, massaging the stockinged stump of his right wrist with his left hand, replied, 'I nearly went across, after sunset, but my own Secret Service people were having a new rush of blood to their heads, about something with your name on it.'

He almost explained the collie's death, and did not. Bergitta's brother had enough future anxieties to wrestle with. Instead, he offered the pot of chocolate and

337

described his meeting with the President's opposite number.

'The guy looks over his shoulder at the tsars the way I do at Washington and Jefferson, but are the two of us going to get a passing grade from history?' Galbraith took the chocolate with his good hand and pointed the truncated stump at the massed firepower below him in the garden. 'When you see what it takes merely to get our two signatures on a piece of paper – Jack, tell me: am I setting up a second Pearl Harbor, as the stone-age morons say back home?'

'In the middle of the night before the battle at Trenton,' Lowel answered, 'I don't imagine Washington felt too smart about taking on the British Empire, but that gamble didn't work out so badly.'

'Sure,' said Galbraith, 'but if Washington had lost all his chips crossing the Delaware, his fellow citizens would only have turned into a bunch of peaceloving Canadians. If I'm wrong, there's nothing but cinders.'

'You're not wrong, Dan.'

'Just morbid.' The President drank some chocolate and smiled wearily at his prosthesis on the table. 'Blame my tin barometer. Our national weather service could save a bundle on satellites with one of these.'

Lowel smiled back. 'I've got a couple of messages pending. Was there anything else?'

'Not unless you can tell me that the dead woman I hear you and Berov found on the beach this afternoon was Typhoid Mary.'

'No,' he said, 'she wasn't.'

'Which means the lady's in Yalta?'

'I can't say that either.'

'Can you say she isn't?'

'No.'

'Just my luck.' Galbraith turned to the portrait of Churchill. 'Right when I could really use it, we tear

338

down the old lion's Iron Curtain. The other side wants to start early: 08.00. See you at the table.'

He left the dressing-room and reversed through the Secret Service. The bird dogs were still shaken by the finger-licking episode but agreed they could handle the presidential morning coffee. At the mission security desk, the duty officer held up a phone. 'London just came in. Code of caller: your Sandwich Man at SIS.'

He took the receiver. 'Sandwich Man, go ahead: this is Three-Fingered Jack.'

'That name must rather turn on your more unstable callers,' said Ryder's digitalized, crisp English voice. 'First thing, speaking of sandwiches, and better late than never, Forensic found one in the chopper wreckage. No toxin.'

'They're a hundred per cent sure?'

'Afraid so. The wrapping was burnt, but the bread was whole wheat, stone-ground at the village mill. Contents, local butcher's pressed tongue.'

Not in the eye drops, not in the sandwiches, not in the condom. He had been wrong again. Wrong every time he tried to outguess her.

'It's not a complete wipe-out,' Ryder's voice continued. 'You were right about the book.'

'It was there?'

'Indirectly. The author does mention constructing one such item in your region, but not exactly where. And later he shows a drawing, but it's for a super mock-Tudor he did near High Cross, in Hampshire – our Victorian fore-bears were gung-ho on that Elizabethan Gothic sort of thing.'

'Does he show the mechanism?'

'Oh yes, no problem on that score.'

'Can you describe it?'

'Standby your Hi-Fax: I'm letting the author do that.'

The double-encoded facsimile machine at the security

desk beside him began to produce an image on its semi-translucent paper:

A Folly Of The Rich
as constructed for a Client
by
H. Hunt

The paper fed smoothly out of the machine, one line of composition at a time, until the picture being transmitted was complete. He was looking at a reproduction of an engraved architectural print for a small room: a draughtsman's symbols for dimensions, wall thickness and composition, stair risers and treads, a fireplace with two flues, the swing of doors – inwards or out – but no windows. This room was never designed to see the light of day.

'OK?' said Ryder's voice.

'Better than OK. The quality's perfect.'

'Good. Afraid I have to close with an unpleasant twist. North London says the application on your Oriental friend was both paper and tobacco. The lady's mind is smart, but not nice. If you're going hunting, one last word to the wise: careful.'

'I will be.'

Paper and tobacco. Like Crazy Glue. In bringing together both combinant halves, the methodical bitch had checked out the alternative method of applying the toxin. Sam Wong was her guinea-pig as well as her victim.

He hung up. The plan dropped out of the Hi-Fax into the bin. Centred at the bottom of the engraving, the title reproduced in script read: 'A Priest's Hole'.

For a priestess?

The almost bottomless pit of Secret Service resources air-lifted to Alupka produced a Benzedrine pill, two

340

lightweight but super-intensity torches with long-life lithium batteries, a 1,000ft roll of yellow polypropylene string with a 100lb breaking strength, two cans of spray paint in Day-glo orange, a Walkie-Talkie good for three miles, a roll of black electrical tape, a 9mm Beretta, and the toughest item – which had to draw on the even greater resources of Russia – an ice-hockey stick from the local Soviet Army team.

He swallowed the bennie and let the mission duty officer check the operation of lights, radio, and paint cans, but he checked the pistol's mechanism and the loading of the snub bullets in its spare magazines for himself.

Satisfied with his trick supplies, he had the duty officer place them in a ready bag and carry it out to Berov's Red Star chopper, still waiting patiently on the palace lawn. Now for the wetware.

He walked over to the Maine light colonel's tank parked by the fountain. A soft-faced major with a killer's chin was occupying the Battle Center's turret.

'The CO finally turned in,' said the major.

'No he didn't.' The colonel's turtle head appeared. 'I admit the thought of shut-eye had crossed my mind,' he added in his clipped phrases, down to Lowel. 'Have you fresh ord-ahs?'

'I need global communications ability in the field. Can you talk from Yalta with Nato's infrastructure?'

'Unless someone just nailed our Battle satellite.'

'They didn't,' said the major.

'How about infantry?' Lowel asked the colonel.

'We have one platoon of para boys available. I asked for a full company, but high-ah authority again deemed othah-wise.'

Captain Hawk at Defense was running his Star Wars grudge interference right to the goal line.

'A platoon is good enough,' Lowel answered. 'Your

new orders are to deploy the paras and yourself at the Livadia Palace immediately.'

'Sir, my regrets, but that ordah doesn't align with close-protecting the President.'

For what had to be the last time, he took the purple Finding from his pocket. At this moment its power was still absolute: after tomorrow . . .

He passed the document up to the turret. 'While you look at his signature, Colonel, let me just tell you: protection for this President doesn't get any closer than where we're heading.'

Livadia seemed even darker after the arc-light blaze encircling Alupka. The Red Star chopper hovered in cautiously as Berov's personal pilot tried not to end up with both of them as shish kebab, skewered on one of the palace spires –

The machine lurched. An ominous *crack* sounded outside the fuselage. A pyramid shape, blacker than the night, went by the perspex.

'Cypress!'

The pilot hit his pitch and tail rotor controls to rock the craft sideways to starboard past the tree – and almost got spiked by its twin to port. A ghostly Lenin Guard came running from the building. As the chopper came within touching distance of the ground, Lowel saw that the man was trying to wave them off, pointing at the undercarriage.

'You may have a broken strut,' he told the Soviet pilot. 'Don't put weight on it, I'll jump.'

'Very good, but what can I tell my superior you will do for transport while I must go for repair?'

'Tell him not to worry. I've already got transport on the way.'

He picked up his tricks bag and, using the hockey-stick blade through the bag's handles, lowered it to the ground.

It was further than the length of the stick by a couple of feet. He made a downward gesture. The pilot nudged the controls a fraction, then shook his head. Lowel let go of the hockey stick – praying it hit turf, not slate paving. He lowered himself past the hatch and prayed harder for . . .

Grass. He was congratulating himself on the soft landing when he tripped over the hockey stick and felt something go wrong with his ankle.

'You are all right, comrade?'

The Lenin Guard bending over him turned out to be the unit's commandant, determined to use English.

'*Spasibo*,' Lowel thanked. 'I'm fine. But you can help with my bag, over to the building.'

The ankle wasn't fine, and he was on the wrong side of the building. The chopper had put him down in front of the circular main entrance to the palace, not outside the former sewing-room in the east wing. Gritting his teeth, he walked up the steps past the lions to the recognition equipment. The red and green lasers fired.

'You too,' he said to the commandant.

'My men and I have not clearance for building interior.'

More Russian dolls within dolls. The Soviet habit of keeping the left hand ignorant of the right was great for security, until you wanted to know how to turn the goddamn light switches on!

'KGB has left message for you,' the guardsman added. 'They expect in one hour to complete all post-mortems.'

The front door closed the commandant and his sentries out.

Lowel stood alone in the darkened main rotunda and groped for one of the torches in his tricks bag. The palace was eerily silent. A few minutes more and he would imagine Princess Anastasia sleep-walking –

Was *She* already in here with him? Waiting in the blackness at the top of the stairs . . .

343

His hand found the flashlight and pressed it on. The ghosts retreated slightly. He shone the beam around the rotunda. The electrical switches were obviously placed, beside the main doors. He flicked them. The great crystal chandeliers of the tsars blazed over his head. The imperial ghosts vanished, but the figures in the conference picture once more seemed to come to life. He lit the grand staircase, the cloakrooms off the lobby, and the mezzanine landings. Berov's surveillance monitors and KGB communications desk were set up in a former butler's pantry. The video was from Roosevelt's former study: there was no audio, for privacy.

In the study itself, the silver stars on its blue wall-covering flashed and shone. But what dominated the room were the two sheets of white parchment on the small square table. Observed by the closed circuit cameras, he limped across the gleaming parquet floor to see the words waiting to make history.

'*We, the Leaders of the two Unions of American States and Soviet Republics . . .*'

Neat and neutral. The two copies of the Agreement were still under their clear vinyl-wrap, as were the two signing pens and embossed blotters. The mini high-speed shredders waited to devour them, and any other leftover executive bargaining reminders. The filigreed carbon-steel screens, with their dual voice release locks, were already drawn and fastened across the inside of the cathedral windows. As he was checking the screens, outside, working by floodlights from ladders, four more workers of Berov's limitless labour pool had just finished installing huge sheets of the special bulletproof glass used earlier on the fireplaces. The last workman gave a thumbed A-OK through the now doubly impregnable window. Lowel waved goodnight and went back to the rotunda to do something for his ankle.

The roll of electrician's tape in his bag was the only

first aid available. He sat on the bottom of the Tsar's staircase and removed his shoe and sock. The ankle was slightly swollen, but no sharp bits stuck out of it. He began to wrap the tape, then realized he might run dry before he'd used it for its main purpose.

He placed the handle of the hockey stick down between his thighs and out behind him like a tail. With the blade resting on his knees, pointing forward, he held the flashlight against it and began to wind the tape. When the blade and the light were solidly locked to each other, he bit the tape through and applied the remainder of the roll to his ankle.

Re-booted and spurred, he turned the lamp on and stood up. The ankle only felt marginally better, but the hockey light performed perfectly. By holding the stick so that his forearm and elbow supported it, he managed to keep the beam just above the floor, like a metal detector working the beach at Coney Island. He switched it off, but left every other candlepower burning in the building. Outside, when he looked back, Livadia blazed as it must have for the last waltz of a Russian emperor.

He made his way along the darkened west-wing exterior, passing and being challenged by the domino Lenin Guards stationed at the ground-floor windows. Once around the end, light shone ahead of him again from the Roosevelt study. On this journey to the past, a pair of red stone benches had Roman eagles and the word CAESAR carved into them.

He moved back into darkness. His lamp picked out rose bushes smashed down from the bloodhound's charge – barely in time to avoid a truckload of the brute's main calling card.

There was no other evidence of the dog. The guard posted by the sewing-room doors was also missing.

Lowel walked back to the sentry post closest to the

study. The guard there was being chewed out by his commandant. Lowel asked the obvious question. And got the obvious answer.

'Your tracking dog has run off, comrade. Its trainer asked my man at those next doors to help catch him. But this man has been watching for both. He swears only one owl has moved here in the garden since he came on at midnight.'

The bird hooted a corroboration from the direction of the cypresses flanking Tolstoy's path to Oreanda. To limit misunderstandings, Lowel replied in Russian. 'The principal threat won't come from the garden. So that they can see what's going on inside, have every second one of your men about-faced, to watch the interior of the building. At the slightest sign of anyone moving, sound a general alarm. And one last thing: a unit of American tanks will be arriving to join you. When they do so, show their commander where I am.'

'Yes comrade. Absolutely.'

The commandant saluted smartly, but it must be a weird turn for a man with Lenin's name on his shoulder badge to be co-operating with US Armor, on Soviet soil. More ironic was the way Russians accepted these orders for presidential safety unquestioningly from an American, while the Yanks had to have it in writing from the Finding.

He returned to the Empress's sewing-room. The French doors were still ajar, with the cut chain hanging from their brass handles. He went inside and once more sensed the curious mixture of hospital smells and layers of old paint, and something else, more delicate, but indefinable in his nostrils. He cursed the shitting bloodhound for its absence and took the Hi-Fax plan originally drafted by Henry Hunt from his tricks bag.

He placed the other flashlight on top of the bag and squatted to study the copy of the engraving. A heavy arrow, broken through its mid-section, was shown

346

running from the back of the chimney, within the priest's hole, to the front wall above the fireplace opening, which was drawn as a pyramid with its top chopped off.

He stood up and rotated the bag so that the light shone at the blocked brickwork where the fireplace had been when it kept the Empress warm. At a height of five feet above the floor, a heavy double ridge of paint, six inches apart, extended horizontally for a length of eight feet. He looked at the engraving: the broken arrow stopped at the left end of MANTEL.

Examining the left end of the double ridge of paint, he ran his hand along and felt a bump. In the light of the torch, it looked like a leftover gob of plaster.

He took out his Beretta and double-checked the pistol's action. Holding the gun in his right hand, he located the plaster bump again with his left-hand's remaining fingers, and pressed . . .

No noise alerted him. Only a cold rush of air that spilled out of a crack running vertically up the wall to a short head height from the floor. He took in the first slack on the Beretta's trigger and pressed the plaster bump harder. The crack widened to a slit – then the entire section of wall swung open on a central axis.

Nothing showed in the light that sliced into the hole on each side of the door. But the corners of the space beyond were still dark. He reached behind him and found the hockey stick. He pulled it to him and switched on the second high-intensity beam. He stood with his shoulder immediately beside the door opening and flipped the hockey-stick blade –

Nothing in the two left corners. He removed the stick, switched its light off, and withdrew from the fireplace wall until he was able to move around behind the flashlight that still rested on the tricks bag. He moved to the other side of the wall opening and repeated the procedure for its right-hand corners –

Blank.

He had been so sure. It took a moment to realize: feeling disappointment was crazy! The last thing on earth he really wanted was to find the phantom bitch within a thousand miles of Yalta.

Because his attention had been focused totally on something breathing, he hadn't noticed the inner room itself. The reversed brickwork of the sewing-room fire-place was still complete, and neatly finished with raked joints. All the other interior surfaces were covered with a crimson damask material of a crudely graphic 'nymphs and satyrs' design, woven in a tarnished thread that was once silver. Flanked by candle-sconces, an ornate Greek Orthodox crucifix, crusted with semi-precious gems, hung facing the normally hidden opening –

He saw himself!

The shock was momentary: the explanation obvious. Instead of a religious altar, a velvet-upholstered *chaise-longue*, thick with dust, was placed below the cross. At the foot of the divan, and on the ceiling, mirrors were fastened in rococo gilt frames. The last Empress's man of God performed his legendary satyr acts, not spiritual miracles, with the palace serving-maid 'nymphs' in this Mad Monk's hole.

A glass of water.

It rested beside an enamel jug, on a small table next to the divan. The glass, the couch, the cross on the wall, the candlesticks were antique – but the enamel jug was stencilled: property Livadia Sanatorium Number Three.

The skin rippled on his back. He collected the tricks bag of supplies and, using the hockey-stick handle, passed it through the room's opening. He set the weight of the bag on the floor within. Nothing happened. Cautiously, he stepped to . . .

Footprints. In the dust. Smaller than his own. The footprints led to a set of stairs, going down from the room's far corner, just as they did in Henry Hunt's engraving.

He took another step forward, and two things happened: a 60mm tank-gun fired outside, and the door began to close behind him.

32

Labyrinth

He managed to jam the hockey-stick handle into the last inch of the opening as the wall section crushed the wood to half that thickness. It was better than nothing, but not good enough; the locking mechanism had engaged within the adjacent walls.

He pushed down an irrational feeling of panic, not experienced since his first flight solo, and examined the engraving plan again. The door was triggered by floor pressure, which he had tried to allow for with the weight of his tricks bag, but Henry Hunt, or Rasputin, was smarter than that. On the plan, the inner point of the broken arrow, used to illustrate the latching system, was shown running to a spot at the back of the fireplace brickwork. Within a prudent hand's reach of the head of the *chaise-longue*, a rusted wrought-iron lever still extended from the chimney bricking. But the handle had been cut off. Recently. Only a shiny metal stub was left, too small to use, barely protruding from the mortar.

As he took that in, he heard the muffled *thump* of the tank-gun firing again. Another internal struggle between Soviet military factions, or a Super Powers start to World War Three . . .?

Speculating was pointless. He was in here. His only action could be to follow the footsteps in the dust, leading to the stairs going down from the Rasputin room in the far corner. He wrote a message of his intentions on the back of the Hi-Fax copy of the plan and pushed it into the slit above the hockey stick wedging the wall of the sanatorium ward. Some eventual rescuer would find it.

But after all his earlier work with the electrical tape, now he couldn't use the goddamn stick! He lifted the blade with the light attached in an attempt to snap the handle: the wood was too supple, and its distance from the adjacent wall wasn't far enough to bend to breaking point. He unstrapped the flashlight and let the stick-blade snap back to the floor; then he collected his tricks bag and slid it over to the corner.

There were six steps down, made of stone like the ones by the carved lions in the garden. The door at the bottom was activated by another of the iron rod arrangements, but this one was intact. When he engaged it, the door slid slowly sideways. His finger tightened on the trigger of the Beretta.

The torch showed a whitewashed brick wall, four feet away. Cursing the trapped hockey stick which could have done the checking for him, he edged up to the opening, and looked . . .

A cross passage led left and right.

He tried to orientate himself: the sanatorium ward was east of the Roosevelt study and the Rasputin room was west; the stairs were in its far left corner – which meant that left, in the passage, was south, towards the sea and the main entrance of the palace.

The footprints went north, to the right.

The paces were even, about a thirty-inch stride. That was long for a woman. He listened again. Absolute silence. He suddenly noticed: the door he had just come through had a pinprick peep-hole.

Was She watching . . .?

Before he stepped through the second doorway, he placed

his tricks bag on the sill, lengthwise, which should block half the door's travel if it was also triggered to close when weight was applied on the floor of the passage.

He put one foot across – then changed his mind and used the one without a screwed-up ankle. He shifted his weight onto the sound foot . . .

The door remained open.

The wall he had come through was made of doubled stone, three feet thick, and the door slid inside the cavity. When shut, it was meant to be hard to find. The ceiling of the passage was also whitened brick, but rounded, and low enough that when he moved forward his head brushed it. He took out one of the spray cans and painted a spot of Day-glo orange on the wall opposite the door. He tied the free end of the roll of yellow cord to the iron rod mechanism and put the rest of the roll in his Safari jacket pocket – leaving its Velcro flap undone, so that the string could unwind from the top as he moved. He put the spray can in his other pocket. The second flashlight he stuffed in his trouser pocket.

For a second time he cursed not having the hockey stick: had the lamp been strapped to it, if She wanted to shoot at his light he wouldn't have been standing with his vital organs in line with it! Now, all he could do was keep to the extreme right of the passage, and hold his arm with the beam as far as possible to his left.

He began following the footprints.

The string paid out with no problem, but after fifty paces he stopped and sprayed another Day-glo on the wall, in case. Another fifty, and the passage curved right – which was east.

He slowed – which just stopped him slamming into a closed door.

This one was conventional, of vertical planks, with massive blacksmith's hardware. The handle was a ring that lifted a latch. The latch and the hinges had been freshly oiled.

Unless She had brought a small machine shop along with her, the evidence of forethought, plus the hacksawed iron rod behind him, meant she had an ally in the palace.

He made another Day-glo dot and turned the ring handle.

The latch lifted . . .

The door moved a few inches, then stopped: the gap at the bottom was wedged with something made of cloth fabric.

He pushed the door harder –

It gave way. He was barely able to stop himself from falling through and presenting Her with a full-body target!

The space beyond was also empty. The fabric on the floor was only a grey, sanatorium woollen blanket. Beyond were a coarse flannel sheet, folded, and a pair of the uniform pyjamas worn by patients. A man's drawstring fly – but that could just be unisex, Soviet style. The pyjamas were at the base of another bricked-off opening, to his right.

Which was east again, towards the sea. Could this have been the last Tsar's windproof route for afternoon tea at his Swallow's Nest folly?

The footprints didn't go anywhere.

The last pair just stopped by the pyjamas. The tunnel dead-ended. The wall seemed to be bedrock. When he inspected it closely, miners' chisel marks and drilling grooves were still visible beneath the white paint. He turned to the left-hand wall. Where it met the end of the passage it too was made of stone, not brick. In line with his eyes was a pin-hole.

A squirt gun!

He pulled his head back, half-ashamed of his reaction. Fears and fantasies got magnified out of proportion below ground, hemmed in by darkness. A hairline crack ran up the wall on each side of the pin-hole. He stepped forward to look for an opening mechanism, and Henry Hunt almost nailed him again with the floor-pressure oldie.

He jumped sideways onto the flannel sheet, which skidded under him. By the time he was balanced, the new door was open. Again, although he had promised himself not to, his mind kept saying, *Is She –?*

When he was inside the next empty chamber, and she wasn't:

'Goddamn bitch, you must be!'

He bawled it and relieved some of the tension. The space was the foundation base of the massive central chimney of the palace. A cube of bedrock came up from the floor to meet dressed stone and then brick which was cemented into the arched ceiling. There were no openings for soot or ash dumps; the cube must be solid. He walked again, all the way around it, following her footprints until he got back to the opening by the sheet and pyjamas.

His bellow this time raised his blood pressure. He switched to deep breathing. Unless she had walked backwards in every one of her footprints, perfectly, to the Rasputin room, there had to be some other way out of this sub-chimney chamber.

He followed the footprints around the chimney base a third time, but on this circuit he examined each tread carefully. Eight of the heel marks *were* misaligned: She had stepped in them twice!

And beside the eighth doubled print was another of the pin-holed stone doors. Activation from this side was by a conventional iron rod.

He unwound his yellow string which by now had trussed the chimney base like a turkey, went back and Day-gloed the opening by the pyjamas, then ran the polypropylene in a straight point-to-point. With the Beretta and flashlight ready, he pulled down on the iron lever. This door wasn't as well fitted, or possibly the ground had shifted in one of the Crimea's frequent earthquakes. The door rumbled into its wall cavity like a subway train going up Fifth Avenue.

He eased his shoulder forward to check out the latest destination.

Day-glo orange!

His own starting mark confronted him. His yellow string and the tricks bag confirmed it: he was back at the door of Rasputin's chamber.

A thundering crash sounded inside it. Dust poured out into the passage. Odd chunks of masonry collapsed. Someone coughed, then called, 'Mist-ah Lowel?'

In Maine's unmistakable accent, the US Cavalry was here.

She wasn't.

33

04.00 hours:

Second strike

The sharp end of the US Army in Russia was parked on the Livadia lawn, with its huge, bulbous barrel snout poking through the sanatorium ward's French windows. A wrist-thick steel cable ran from a winch, mounted on the white-starred front of the massive tank, to the spot beside the last Empress's blocked-up chimney where a half-inch crack in the wall used to be. Now a ragged hole, eight feet square, revealed Rasputin's squalid secrets to the world.

'This seems to be yours,' the colonel said, as he looked in his laconic Bangor fashion at the Mad Monk's tits-and-ass wallpaper and velvet divan. 'Won't ask what you were doing with it in he-ah.'

He passed Lowel the fractured hockey stick. The water glass and jug by the divan were still intact. The winch began reeling in the cable. A giant magnesium alloy hook which tapered to a serrated needle-point had been his saviour. Behind the Maine colonel, the Lenin Guards' commandant was looking more apologetic than last time. Lowel said in Russian, 'You haven't found the dog?'

'Unfortunately, comrade, yes. In the disturbance it was run over by one of our own tanks.'

'We were the distuh-bance.' After this revelation that Maine could understand and speak the language almost as well as the natives, the colonel allowed himself a momentary turtle grin before adding in English, 'Had to end-run around the press. Heading cross-country, met one Ivan, play-acting being terrible. Knocked him out.'

Lowel said, 'I thought I was hearing World War Three.'

'Not this time round. Your little KGB pal, good man, cooled things off.'

The colonel sounded slightly sad about that lost golden opportunity and, by calmly inserting his boot in the lethal jaw of the returning hook, let the winch lift him the first half of the mountain climb to his turret.

'How about the infantry I ordered?' Lowel asked.

'Waiting over the-ah with Lenin's boys.'

The tank commander nodded towards the terrace with the Roman benches. Lowel realized he could see them, at least their outlines. Morning twilight was advancing already, faintly reflecting, in the bulletproofed windows of the Roosevelt study, the Black Sea paling from the east.

'Nato on-line Battle came through, holding Paris,' the colonel concluded as he dropped back into the familiar comfort of his steel coffin. 'Had your name. Welcome abo-ahd. Any time!'

Lowel left Paris on hold in order to deploy the group of mixed Soviet and American troops fraternizing at the Roman benches. The tank warfare didn't appear to have generated hard feelings among the sideline players: the US Airborne were in the charge of an absurdly young captain who was demonstrating his miracle microchip field-gyro compass to the Lenin's commandant.

'I want six men, three from each of you,' Lowel said. 'They'll be posted in pairs below ground, and while I'm showing the way, organize some emergency lighting.'

He led the troops back through the rubble, getting some bilingual wolf whistles at Rasputin's wallpaper – which turned to muted whispers of nervous astonishment down in the darkened tunnels. He positioned one pair of the men at each of the sliding doors, except for the point

357

of entry where the two openings faced each other. His instructions were identical in both languages.

'If you see a woman, shoot to kill.'

The Automated Battle Center tank had all the technology of the Stealths and B1, plus as much again, crammed into a location like a coal miner's, working a seam at the pit face, flat on his back. The Maine colonel, beside a laser-aided periscope in the middle, was almost able to sit upright, but his killer-jawed major and two other crewmen had to contort themselves around chain-driven machinery, super-pressured hydraulic pipes, and live ammunition. They appeared to enjoy this. The tank's crouched engineer was boiling coffee in a jerry-can on his engine block. The motor wasn't running, but temperature and humidity were still at Persian Gulf levels. The aroma from the jerry mixed with oil fuel, sweaty leather, and scorched rubber in a nauseous stench. The engineer sniffed appreciatively. The 2IC major, beside him, unwound and reluctantly went topside to fresh air to make room for Lowel, saying, 'Nato on-line, console four. Use Polaroid hard copy.'

That was the extent of the major's instruction. His position circuit mikes and phones were held up out of the way with the same nylon miracle grabbers as Lowel's Safari jacket pockets: Velcro! What would the world do without it? The Polaroid camera referred to was similarly supported and in line to snap any transient image on the Battle consoles, which were colour and split-screen. The one in front of the colonel was showing both Livadia and Alupka. From his graceful office at the Quai D'Orsay in Paris, the suavely groomed, unruffled Gallic image of André Dolmain was on the tube in front of Lowel.

'Jack, *bonjour*, but you look a little tired.'

'*Bonjour*, André. Just a bit.'

More surprising than the pictures from the outside

world was the realization that an image was being transmitted back to Paris from inside the tank. A mini-cam
bolted to the periscope standard swivelled automatically
to whichever console operator was speaking.

'I myself am just returned from the Ritz,' said Dolmain
with his ironic smile. 'Unfortunately, your lady was not at
home.'

'I wasn't expecting – you mean she had been?'

'Indeed. Also, the wig information may not have been
unrelated. A receipt was found for a costumier. Verger.
I am about to send a car to the address.'

'André, can you go along yourself? And pack a mobile
video in the car.'

'Understood,' Dolmain flicked his tapered fingers.
'Consider it done.'

The silver-haired image from France stood up, walked
to the door of its office, and was gone. Lowel said to the
tank commander, 'I want to be informed the instant Paris
comes back. Now, can we talk to Soviet Yalta HQ – their
KGB operator?'

The colonel stretched his turtle neck to dodge the
periscope and pressed a button on the fourth console.
The brick shithouse that was the back view of Boris
Strelnikov appeared.

'I have a drinking glass and jug to be tested for
prints immediately. I need Berov,' Lowel said tersely
to the Deputy.

'I shall send mobile Forensic for the glass.' Strelnikov
swivelled in a chair to face the camera. 'Kliment Klimentovich is already with you at Livadia.'

'Where? I haven't seen him.'

'Try Oreanda, in the park.'

'Out walking with Tolstoy?' While he was running
his ass into the ground, Berov had been farting around
with Byzantine politics between feuding armies. What was
needed this minute was everyday police legwork.

'While we speak,' Strelnikov added, 'another tracking brute is being flown from Odessa. Apologies for the delay, but when it arrives, if the woman's around, this bastard will sniff out one hair on her crotch.'

The Soviet HQ feed cut out. Lowel uncoiled from the major's seat – just missing losing another finger he couldn't afford to an ammunition lift. As he scaled the rungs of the turret to leave this metal hell-hole, its Maine OIC said after him, 'Couth moth-ahs at KGB. Any incoming, we'll call on your Walkie.'

After the claustrophobic interior, getting back on the ground was a relief, but the last jump from the hull did nothing good for his taped ankle. He looked in the direction of the park at Oreanda. Dawn was breaking over its ponds. Dan Galbraith and the latest master of Russia would be waking for their moment of history. There was no sign of Berov.

Or Her.

In the tunnel world below Livadia, the emergency power was rigged, the paired sentries were at their posts by the secret doors. All reports were negative. Lowel showed the peep-hole apertures to the troops and had them examine every inch of the passage walls for any others.

She couldn't disappear into thin air.

That obvious truth only made the frustration fiercer. He stared at the footprints leading away and arriving back at the bottom of the steps that led down from Rasputin's room. The mind that could think of backtracking like that in its own footsteps around the chimney must be somewhere behind the walls, waiting . . .

Not much longer.

Any moment, the show would be starting. The press flood would be sweeping up the drive from the park gates; the cameras above his head would be live. The whole world would be watching . . .

The footprints only went one way, he realized.

To his right, north, and that was the only way he had followed. The unmarked left branch of the passage had been completely ignored. His yellow polypropylene string still stretched across as a barrier: the space beyond it was still dark. The floor was smooth dust, fading into total shadow. He shone his high-intensity lamp into the blackness. The walls ran straight for about eight feet, then curved around a corner. Right, again: west, avoiding the rock of the chimney base, towards the Swallow's Nest.

He didn't know why the name kept coming back to him or why it seemed to carry greater significance than the other imperial relics. Were these passages the places Stalin's goons checked for mikes before they were all blocked off to stop the sanatorium patients – ?

But when he thought twice about it, he realized that if she had tried to jump the unmarked straight section of floor, if she hadn't smashed her head on the low brickwork of the ceiling, she would have hit the curving chimney section wall beyond. There would be footprints in the dust at that point, and there weren't. Only a fly on the wall could get around that corner.

'Chimney climbing.'

'*Sudar* – Sir?'

His spoken thought got instant bilingual response – but didn't make sense to the US Airborne and Lenin Guard sentries hanging on his every word. Only another mountaineer would know his meaning. He said to the American para, 'I'm going to try something. This way! Bring an emergency light along behind.' And added for the Russian, 'Do not look at me. Watch ahead. If you see movement, open fire.'

He ducked under the yellow string and stood facing the left wall of the passage. He placed his heels against the base of the right wall and let himself drop forward. His palms and fingertips engaged the brickwork two feet down from the curve of the ceiling so that his body was across the tunnel at a sixty-degree angle. He slid his uninjured ankle up the wall behind him. The weight increased on his fingers. He slid the taped ankle . . .

The classic chimney position. But it was normally used to move upwards through a fissure: flipping sideways was much tougher.

He slid his right leg in that direction along the wall. Immediately his body tried to collapse downward. He increased the flex tension – and stabbed his right hand off the wall in front, and out to the right . . .

He was falling.

It was only a few inches: if he had allowed for it by lifting his hand higher in advance, the drop would have been compensated. He repeated the movements with his left arm and leg.

Flip. And flex. Dripping with sweat.

He had covered two feet of lateral distance.

Four feet. The sentries were following, almost touching. Fortunately he couldn't see the looks on their faces. Flip, flex, flip –

The third time he knew he was going to hit the floor. So did the US para with the light, reaching out –

'Don't touch, goddamn you!'

He hung there, looking down at the unblemished dust on the floor . . . and agonizingly fly-walked his hands back up the wall.

Flex. Flip. At the bend in the tunnel, and still no footsteps. His weakened ankle he could manage, if he didn't think about the pain: it was having only three fingers on one hand that would finish him.

Flex . . .

Coming out of the curve he crashed to the floor, and lay gasping.

'Sir!'

'*Sudar!*'

'I'm OK. Just too old.'

Which he was. And stupid, competing for a coronary against this super-human younger woman, when all he needed to do was walk down the tunnel.

Her prints started one yard beyond his point of total collapse and led straight on along the passage, for seventy of her thirty-inch paces. They stopped at another of the planked doors with a ring latch. The door was closed. There was no peep-hole.

He waited for the American boy to bang a spike on which to hang the emergency lighting cable, then ordered the para and the Russian kid out of booby-trap range back down the tunnel. He reached out for the ring latch.

The last effect of the Benzedrine had been used up by his body for the chimney caper. His reflexes were nil. His mental processes no better. His hand had already touched the handle before he wondered if it had been poisoned.

The door opened normally.

The passage on the other side was empty. A short distance beyond, steps went upwards: the same number and construction as the ones behind for Rasputin. 'Jesus,' he thought, 'not another circle back.'

The steps were blocked at the top by solid stone, but when he got there it was just another of Henry Hunt's sliding door/iron rod/peep-hole deals. The only difference this time was that he could see through the peep-hole.

It was all the difference in the world. He was looking at the blue walls and silver stars blazing under the chandelier in the centre of Roosevelt's study.

34

The study was also empty – but Lowel's moment of elation was swiftly over. If She had access to the study, he realized, everything in it could be contaminated.

She hadn't.

The door, he discovered, had long ago been mortared closed, but recent marks at the bottom showed an attempt to scrape out the cement along the original sill. The iron rod mechanism at the top was intact but seized with rust. A bare copper wire hanging out of the wall, and a microphone diaphragm on the end of it, were corroded green. The mike was forties vintage, installed by an even greater paranoid than Lowel: Uncle Joe.

What else would she try? She wouldn't give up this close to her target. He looked through the peep-hole again into the Roosevelt study: his line of sight led directly to the vinyl-covered documents on the square table.

A laser! Could she fire it through the hole –?

'*Sudar!*'

'Sir!'

The practical young soldiers standing behind him in the passage were pointing at the last few footsteps before the base of the stone stairs. She had repeated her reversing trick from the chimney circle. Seven paces backwards was a second peep-hole. It was on the left side, viewed from the study – which was north again. He felt along the passage-brickwork for the activating lever, and found it just below the curve of the roof.

'Stand back.'

He flattened himself to the wall, checked that the sentries were both clear, tightened his grip on the Beretta, and pressed the wall lever . . .

Finally!

A form crouched in the darkness. Something gleamed.

'Come out,' he ordered. 'Hands free from the body.'

No movement. He repeated the command in Russian. Nothing.

He fired. Three shots, deafening in the tunnel. The form collapsed.

'Bring up the light,' he said to the US Airborne, 'but be careful.'

Caution was still essential. She could be faking –

'Holy shit, sir!'

The Lenin kid added to the para's astonishment: *'Sudar! Is skeleton?'*

In a Polish army officer's uniform, of the same era as the microphone. This other grim memento of Stalin had been sitting on a stool: its cap badge, a golden eagle, had done the gleaming. His three shots, all mid-torso, had knocked it sideways, but what had killed it was a shattered vertebra from a single bullet to the base of its neck, five decades earlier.

She had ignored the gruesome relic. The footprints went straight past, without any change in their thirty-inch pacing. She must be nerveless.

She was making a fool of him. Through one more wooden door and then a stone one, her footsteps brought him out into the garden at the trampled rose bed, beside the Battle Center tank, facing south: precisely the reverse of his estimated position, on the opposite side to the main entrance.

'. . . I say again, in-coming, Mist-ah Lowel.'

The radio at his belt was squawking. The masonry of the palace had been blocking the Maine colonel's transmission.

'This is Lowel,' he called back. 'I'm right beside you.'

The colonel's turtle head emerged from the turret. The tank commander stretched a long arm downward, holding something.

'From Paris. One dirty pict-cha!'

The rising sun was just above a jagged-tooth gap in the cypress trees: the mark of his helicopter's brush with death in the night. He had no trouble seeing every detail of the picture taken from the image on the Battle console screen. The Polaroid was a picture of a picture. The original in Paris had lost its head – the corner of the photo appeared to have been burned or melted – but the rest of the frontally naked, female figure was intact: flawless, except for its small white scar.

'Paris said it was found under a steam iron,' said the colonel. 'They have anothah, but when the press here flashed up, we lost our satellite signal.'

'Shut the bastards down,' he said, 'and get it back.'

He commandeered a jeep and took off for Oreanda.

He found Berov standing in the shadow of more pyramid cypresses on the west coast of the miniature Caspian Sea. The grass where the KGB Chief stood sloped gently to the water. A white church and the blackened hull of the Soviet tank destroyed by the Maine colonel were stark contrasts on the far side of the pond. The same type of giant lifting crane as the one that almost finished things back at the start, their first meeting in Moscow, was lifting the wreckage onto a transporter.

'The evidence had to be removed before the television cameras caught it,' Berov said in a tired voice. 'If you had told me you were sending American forces across country, the problem might have been avoided.'

'If I could have found you, Kliment Klimentovich, I would have told you a hell of a lot more.'

'I apologize. You have been carrying an unfair weight through the night. It was probably not an effective use of my time to cross-check all the female western journalists' dossiers myself. Or the missing one's hotel room. I would have returned sooner . . .'

Berov broke off. The cypress shadows were retreating. The morning sun struck a pile of fresh dirt at the secret policeman's small feet, and then the side of an excavation, and then grey fur on a bed of dark green cypress boughs at the bottom. The wonderful eyes were closed, but the plaited blue collar that matched them was placed beside the collie's muzzle. A scarlet card, with a gold hammer and sickle:

Mischa my love . . .

In memory. The closing of a circle. Like Bergitta's cornflowers on top of a mountain.

The animal's lifelong partner picked up a handful of dirt, knelt, and spread it gently over the beautiful body. Lowel felt a stabbing guilt replace his earlier annoyance.

'The gardeners of Oreanda will do the rest,' said Berov. 'The history of the world must not be kept waiting any longer for a mere dog.'

The tempo of events accelerated as they returned in the jeep via Tolstoy's Walk to the palace. He told Berov of the photograph from Paris and his night-long succession of blind leads and dead-ends in the tunnels: especially the last two that gave access from the palace exterior directly to the Roosevelt study.

The KGB man nodded, but his first response at Livadia was to order the retreat of the US Battle Center.

367

'The cause of world peace would not be advanced by the sight of an American sixty-calibre gun sticking into the ward of a Russian sanatorium,' Berov told the colonel. 'Join your other forces, south of the lawn, behind the trees.'

'Wait one,' Lowel said. 'I need to keep direct communication.' He asked the tank's commander, 'Do you have a field portable remote you can assign me?'

'My 2IC, on Battle-Pak.'

The Maine colonel called a command down his conning-tower. The baby-faced major with the killer's jaw emerged from a side-hatch, lugging what looked like a larger version of the nuclear warfare Button Box. The tank's engine roared. Clouds of exhaust and dust from the broken Monk's Hole filled the sanatorium ward. At the same moment that the massive tracks clanked backwards, a crew of labourers arrived to hide the evidence with a flatbed load of turf.

A mobile forensic lab was right behind it. Lowel led the senior Soviet technician through the choking cloud to the jug and drinking glass. 'I left the stuff in place, and no one's touched anything. Whatever you can get: make it immediate.'

Berov had followed. He looked at the Rasputin furnishings with interest, mixed with a professional policeman's contempt for human weakness.

'How we needed our Revolution,' he remarked drily. 'Show me your tunnels.'

The yellow polypropylene was still in place. They followed its route swiftly, but with the KGB Chief observing closely, through the first wooden door to the pyjamas.

'These should go also to Forensic.' Berov signalled their immediate removal via the closest Lenin Guard.

The backtracking around the chimney base slowed their progress: Berov examined the walls of the foundation with even more care.

'An opening seems logical,' Lowel said, 'but I looked already. No joy.'

'There seldom is in my work. If the chimney had been used, there would be some trace of soot on the walls or floor. Let us continue.'

They followed the string back to the starting place, which produced a faint hint of Berov's familiar mournful smile. Lowel led the way into the left-hand tunnel without describing his middle-aged climbing exploits. 'We picked the tracks up again here,' he said, 'after the bend in the passage.'

'And this leads straight to the Roosevelt study. So we must now be passing directly beneath the conference hall.'

Berov's sense of direction was better than his own. At the top of the steps, the small policeman had to stand on tiptoe to look through the peep-hole. Lowel mentioned his irrational fear about a laser weapon.

'Not so irrational. After establishing a given *modus operandi*, a skilled criminal might well employ a different weapon for the final kill – but the opportunity will no longer be available at this venue.' Berov summoned another of the Soviet guards to him and showed the iron rod mechanism. 'Bring an engineer immediately, with an acetylene torch to burn it off. And that.'

The man saluted and left at the double. *That* was the Stalinist microphone hanging out of the wall. Berov made no further allusion to it: the KGB had its own embarrassments. When they came to the Polish soldier's skeleton, he merely remarked, 'This day must have a second honourable burial.'

Outside in the rose garden, he walked across to the landscapers' foreman and gave an order. A small truck filled with black Ukrainian topsoil reversed across the slate paving of the terrace. The load was dumped: seven tons of dirt blocked the last of the secret stone doors. No access.

The radio at Lowel's waist squawked, 'Battle Remote: Alupka reports the President is leaving.'

At the same instant, two KGB gunships appeared over the roof of the palace. Berov said, 'The Secretary's car is arriving. I must be with him.'

The last rolls of turf were laid to hide the tank tracks; the last of the labourers threw rakes and shovels in the dumptruck; the gunships circled away towards Yalta; the Soviet mobile forensic unit and the US Battle Center were discreetly screened behind the cypresses. Except for the baby-faced major with his communications backpack, standing in a group of flowering shrubs beside the French doors to the sanatorium ward that used to be a sewing-room, Lowel was alone in the peace of the south garden.

She could not have gone to such efforts, worldwide, for nothing.

He gazed around him at the beauty of Livadia and tried to think what was missing. The bulletproof panels of glass shielding the windows of the Roosevelt study were visible evidence of the building's physical security. The media would not be allowed on the premises until the two leaders were safely behind the doors and locked filigree screens that barricaded the interior approach to their signing.

And there were no women.

Not in the journalists, not in the landscapers, not in the military units, not in the police, not in the cooks and private staffs. Nor any male impersonators. With typical Russian crudeness, the Soviet medical teams had conducted mass inspections by the quickest possible method: pulling down zippers.

Then where was She?

He had just started to walk around to the front of the building and wait there for Galbraith, when the new tracking-dog arrived. The animal was an Alsatian, with a wolf's slink and a saddle marking on its back. The tall Georgian trainer, with the melancholy moustache, was on the other end of the animal's harness, still apologizing for the night's fiasco.

'Forget it. Stick with me.' Lowel crossed the lawn to the mobile forensic lab parked among the trees.

'We have nothing positive yet from the drinking jug,' said the senior lab technician; 'however, your animal reminds: here are our analysis results for Comrade Berov's dog.'

The man passed over a computer print-out. Lowel stuffed it in a Safari pocket and told the Alsatian's trainer, 'Forensic has a pair of pyjamas. Show them to your tracker, and see what happens.'

Outside the mobile lab, the KGB gunships were back, and this time they stayed, keeping a tight circle. He signalled to the Battle-Pak major to join him, and set off to find the action.

He heard it first: 10,000 journalists screaming in a hundred languages, louder than the double drumming of chopper rotors. When he passed the north-east end of the building he saw the reporters. The cordons of American and Soviet troops had forced the media apart, back from their quarry to both northern corners of the palace. Only the privileged few had invitations to the conference room; the rest of the press mob was howling for blood.

Daniel Galbraith's helicopter arrival boosted the scene to a feeding frenzy.

With the major and his Battle-Pak running interference, Lowel tried to break through, but the journalists' surge made that temporarily impossible. He caught a glimpse of the President's head, taller than any others, at the top of the steps.

'Battle Remote: Cent-ah!' The Maine colonel's voice

came over the pack set beside him. 'We have Paris. Stand by visu-ahl!'

Suddenly, he and the major were again in the open. The media herd was stampeding for the steps. The leaders were inside! The by-invitation-onlys were being let in one at a time past the laser recognition system at the palace doors. The crowd milled outside them in frustration.

'Battle Center,' the major replied, 'this is Remote: getting your picture.'

The six-inch flat screen on the Battle-Pak showed a colour generation signal. The digital image formed from the top down, like the Hi-Fax engraving, a line at a time.

It was another photograph with a burned corner. Again with the face missing – but the hair wasn't! The head was in two-thirds profile: its Prince Valiant bangs and brazen dye-job set off a bomb even before the padded shoulders, French cuffs, and pimp's pants appeared. Kolinski, king of the singles bars, met Her in Paris! Or worse –

Impersonation. She is Kolinski.

'Call Secret Service,' he ordered the major, and when they came on: 'This is Lowel. Have you seen the interpreter?'

'Affirmative.'

'What was he wearing?'

'A pair of those stretch cock-huggers. Bright green.'

'To accompany the President?'

'Hell no. He was jogging.'

The Alsatian lunged around the corner. The Georgian trainer was hanging on for grim death.

'He get scent near soil pile,' the trainer shouted in his accented Russian. 'So hot, must be recent.'

The dog charged on, ignoring the mass of flash-snapping journalists. Lowel ran after it, equally oblivious. The animal veered left, heading towards the Black Sea. Down into a garden made from a quarry. Butterflies on a bush. A pool, emptying to a trickling stream. In the distance, the spiked tower of the Swallow's Nest. In front, a small thatched summer-house. A single path. One door.

The Alsatian leapt up onto the porch. Scrabbling, whining. The Georgian yanked at the harness. Lowel pulled his Beretta and yelled, 'Stay aside!'

He smashed the door full strength with his foot. The panel shattered. The door flew open. The dog got loose and lunged again, worrying and growling at something on the floor.

Green spandex cock-huggers ... Not the jacket and pants from the photograph. Lowel found himself staring at a male body that wore Danskins, topline Adidas runners, a head sweatband. A hairpiece. The purple tinted glasses were missing, but the corpse was Kolinski's.

'Call KGB,' he ordered the major. 'Get me Berov!'

He got Strelnikov.

'Why not Berov?' he yelled into the Battle-Pak.

'Private. There is no audio link with the Roosevelt study.'

'Send a messenger.'

'The doors are closed.'

'They've started signing? But I have to be in there!'

'Not possible. The system is activated.'

The dog was panting, exhausted from its excitement. The Battle-Pak major and the Georgian looked at him for some kind of explanation. The commandant of the Lenin Guards assigned for sentry duty drove up in a Fiat-style jeep.

'You must have seen something,' Lowel shouted at the Russian. 'Goddamn it, you had fifty men. The place was nothing but a blaze of light.'

'No one moved inside all night.' The commandant's face was pallid with shock. 'We watched as ordered. Only the American interpreter arrived, thirty minutes ago, walking on the path from the Swallow's Nest. To double-check supplies in advance. For five minutes only, then he left. I heard his voice myself. The system accepted. I saw the lasers activate. The same exactly, as just now, when he returned to be ready before the two leaders entered.'

'*Before?*' Lowel said. 'Sweet Holy Jesus Christ!'

He was locked out. *She* was inside.

35

The two-minute trip in the Fiat jeep, back to the palace, took a thousand years: a millennium for Lowel to confront his previous tunnel vision. His complete attention had been focused wherever *She* wanted it directed. Inside the building; underneath the building; out on Tolstoy's south side of the building. Anywhere but the north side, wide open, in broad daylight, at the last of the Tsar's follies: the path from the Swallow's Nest.

The Fiat's horn blasted. The Lenin commandant kept his foot to the floor, the journalists' flood held firm, wavered – then somehow parted: the jeep roared through, following the driveway's curve on two wheels, tyres screaming.

The brakes slammed beside the carved stone lions. Lowel jumped out while the vehicle was still moving. That was the moment he realized he had kicked in the summer-house door with his taped ankle.

'I'm not going to make these stairs without your shoulder,' he said to the US major carrying the Battle-Pak. The Lenin Guards' commandant went ahead, three steps at a time. Lowel followed at his cripple's run: past the first Churchill lion, the second, the third; at the top, the Soviet commandant already had the front door open.

Inside the rotunda, Lowel stood for a moment, gasping. Five hundred invited heads and twenty global cameras were trained in the other direction. On history, taking place behind the doors to the study.

Even if he ignored the cameras and booted a path over the journalists' heads, the study doors were locked. And the steel filigree screens. Only his own voice and Berov's could open them..

Berov. The other half of their Allied blindness. Every jigsaw piece of added KGB security – the screens, the locks, the bulletproof glass on the fireplaces and windows – that had been meant to stop Her getting in, now stopped her two targets, the leaders, getting *out*.

But Galbraith must have noticed.

If *She* was now understudying the ham interpreter, Kolinski, nobody could be that perfect –

She had been. Every step.

'Clear the building,' he said to the Lenin commandant. 'Not using the PA. Pull a quiet bomb scare. Everybody out – except us,' he added to the Battle-Pak major.

'Whatever you say.'

'KGB Control, the mezzanine.'

Up another set of stairs. Using an ankle that felt like broken glass.

In the former butler's pantry, Strelnikov was watching the two study monitors.

'Are the leaders all right?'

'Of course.' The KGB Deputy looked up calmly. 'We had a moment of excitement before your side told us about the switch.'

'The interpreter!' He pushed past the Russian's massive shoulder.

'The interpreter is fine –' Strelnikov shrugged contemptuously – 'for a bum fucker. The change was your President's end-of-the-world man.'

A man who had no right to be there: the young naval

aide, with the nuclear communications Button Box.

The aide was sitting with it, on what would have been Lowel's own chair – if he had been where he should have been, at Galbraith's side in the Roosevelt study . . . instead of helplessly stuck on the wrong side of the looking-glass.

The First Secretary was speaking, the left-hand monitor in the pantry showed him, but with the privacy restriction no sound of his words came through to the pantry. Dan Galbraith was on the right-hand tube. The interpreter, somewhere in the middle –

Lowel was looking right at him.

At Her?

The impossible question . . . the interpreter was situated at an angle to both leaders: only the padded shoulders, Prince Valiant side bangs, rear profile, and theatrical false gestures were caught by the cameras.

'Close-up!' he ordered Strelnikov.

'We installed fixed monitors. With this Administration, we understood America's Hollywood days of playing to the cameras were over.'

Was Strelnikov part of it?

But Dan Galbraith might have made that last Hollywood crack himself. The President was smiling. Now the First Secretary. Both smiling. They had agreed to the new global game rules and penalty clauses.

There was only the last play. The signing.

But the whole preceding ten days of Her astonishing organizational skill and carnage had been to prevent this process. To stop the pull-back from thermonuclear disaster . . .

The Button Box aide!

Was *he* an agent? A mere kid, five years out of Annapolis, who played radio games like talking for fun last night to a sub in the South Pacific . . .?

377

The Box could talk! Even though all other communication was severed with the study, Lowel realized, the aide's radio link was still accessible.

'On your Battle-Pak,' he shouted at the major. 'Using Nuclear Emergency, get me through to the President's aide.'

'Without an Alert State Red, I can't do that from a regional command.'

'So call one.'

'Call Nuclear Alert Maximum?' Strelnikov suddenly entered the conversation.

The US officer lost his baby-face. 'Only the President can authorize –'

'If you don't make that call, Major, we won't have a President.'

The Finding had not been used for a last time: this was the last time. Lowel flipped his Velcro pocket flap – and found himself looking at a lab print-out in Cyrillic: 'Collie post-mortem. No presence of Viscumin . . .'

He dropped the now useless canine report and located the vital purple-stamped document. 'Alert State Red, Major. Then call up the aide. Got it?'

'Yes, sir.'

'*Nyet!* Yanki First-Strike launch bastards!' Strelnikov lunged to his feet.

'Sit down!' Lowel's Beretta between the Deputy's shoulder blades got through before the Russian words. 'No one is launching anything. It's for communications only: the strike threat is in there. The study.'

He watched the US major spin the dials on his Battle-Pak . . . and the Christmas-tree nuclear warfare lights start flashing . . . and the two leaders of the world about to write their names for history . . . the first time, on the monitors in front of him.

And a killer in the middle.

* * *

But how was She going to kill them? All Lowel could do now, to beat her, was to try and see things from her feminine perspective: to use her weapons. She preyed on human nature, analysed weaknesses, detected patterns of behaviour – in this case, despised male.

On the monitor, Berov and the interpreter had finished stripping the sterile wraps from the pens and documents. The vinyl waste went into the shredders.

The toxin had to be on something both leaders would touch. But they must touch it together: if one showed symptoms before the other –

'Washington doesn't like it!'

The Battle-Pak was glowing orange.

'They don't have to like, Major: just obey a lawful command.'

Could it be the pens?

The President picked his up first: holding it with difficulty, in his gloved dummy, while his good hand removed the cap. The Secretary waited politely: a man branded with the mark of the devil has his own personal defect . . .

The ink?

The leaders' hands would blot and ruin the signatures if they touched them. So maybe with nib pressure, he thought, the ink might squirt – but relying on two separate physical mechanisms to work perfectly, in unison . . .?

'Washington is red! We can call.'

'*Dermo!*' Shit! roared a still disbelieving Strelnikov. The huge Russian was eyeballing the major and the Battle-Pak for a weak point.

'Don't try, Boris.'

Lowel gave another jab of the Beretta. If the Deputy's patriotic outrage was an act, it rated an Oscar. On screen, the manicured fingers of the interpreter's right hand were going through a habitual Oval Office routine: holding the document steady on the blotter for Daniel Galbraith to sign with his left hand, while the useless arm hung down at his side.

The first pair of signatures were drawn . . . On paper. The toxin could be in the treaty documents themselves!

But if it was, both Her targets should be dead. One drop of the combinant liquid contained enough super-absorbing nerve gas molecules to spread and bond with every single cellulose fibre.

On the monitors, via Berov and the interpreter, the leaders exchanged manuscripts, for their second signatures. The young naval aide suddenly went ghost white. The kid had seen –

On his nuclear Button Box: the winking lights of Armageddon.

Lowel replaced the dog-eared Finding, absent-mindedly, in his Safari pocket. He watched the young naval aide pick up the Button Box's radio receiver as though it were a Black Mamba.

The major said, 'You're through!'

He seized the Battle-Pak transmitter. The second signatures were being written. Dan Galbraith's, with an extra flourish . . .

'Hey, what is this?'

The naval aide's voice in his ear was on the way to hysterical. Lowel snapped shut the Velcro grabbers on his pocket. On screen, the leaders passed the used blotters to their intermediaries for disposal in the shredders: Galbraith with his left hand, the Secretary with his right.

'Mr Lowel?'

The interpreter heard the name. The Prince Valiant wigged head swivelled sharply to the winking Armageddon lights. So did Berov's . . .

But if *She* was playing Prince Valiant – letting herself be locked in the study meant suicide, totally against her character.

Another way out.

There could be a Rasputin secret door in every wall of the study. On the monitor, Berov's crumpled blotter had stuck to the metallic side of the shredder, glued there with static, like brushing hair –

Collie post-mortem. No Viscumin . . .

The delayed fuse of the forensic report exploded in his brain. But the lab's words could not possibly mean Berov was involved. Poison his beloved Mischa?

Lowel grabbed the discarded lab print-out. The rest of it said, 'Animal died from strychnine, in butter, with heavy tranquillizer sedation.'

In butter, which neither he nor Berov used. So was it a mercy killing? By a pet's master, who had abandoned cancer chemotherapy. By an old-style Communist, who knew his own death was inevitable –?

Disregard the dog poisoning, Lowel told himself. Concentrate on Her method: the present application of the toxin. Looked at from her 'reversed' perspective – as a woman, down there on the field, interpreting was like refereeing, between two male team captains at the end of a Superbowl game. Win, lose, or draw, her work was over. The score was on the board. The teams were ready to go home. To solve her riddle, what was the last thing that happened in a game . . .?

'Hang on to the President!' he shouted at the aide, through the Armageddon line. '*They mustn't shake hands.*'

Like watching Ruby shooting Oswald, after Kennedy . . . was how the technician at Paracel-Tech had described that first taped killing. This was another of those timeless television moments. There was nothing more that Lowel could do but watch the monitors, and pray . . .

Part of the riddle, he had realized too late, was that it could not be the treaty documents – after only the first signatures, everybody touched them: it had to be the blotters. They were kept segregated by each side to the end: like the Crazy Glue analogy, except that the sequence of left and right hand movements through the signing process didn't fit the biological. The final solution to the toxin riddle must be that the two combinant-halves making up her fatal poison were more like the Velcro on his pocket flaps: no reaction could occur until the hook molecule of one contaminated skin surface grabbed the chemical loop of the other.

Man to man. Palm to palm.

On the monitor, in the Roosevelt study, the young naval aide was shouting silently, in a room full of history's ghosts. F.D.R.'s successor, Galbraith, half turned –

'Good boy!' Lowel yelled from the pantry sidelines.

The young aide had chucked a career, and grabbed his Commander-in-Chief by Galbraith's undamaged left arm – at the same instant, the Soviet First Secretary, making the automatic mistake, reached to pump the American President's dummy gloved right.

'Thank God your Cong pals in the delta blew off his other one,' Lowel said to the atheist Strelnikov. And via the Battle-Pak to the Button Box aide: 'No one move. I'll be there.'

He smashed in through the bulletproofed windows and steel filigree screens with one swipe of the Battle Center tank's massive barrel; on the rose-bed side of the palace, away from the oblivious press cleared from the conference room.

From the window ledge, the tableau scene was still frozen inside the study. The two leaders' hands only inches apart. Berov stood to the left, ice calm. And on the right –

Her.

The face turned. It could not be Kolinski, and yet . . .

Lowel saw the tinted glasses, the moustache, the supercilious mouth under it even at this moment trying to brazen things out with a ham smile. An impossible performance. He levelled the Beretta –

She broke, and dived forward. He started to squeeze the trigger, but Berov was between them. The Russian reached with a frail hand to stop the target – and got a kangaroo kick to the jaw like the one that flattened Lowel on the London roof. The KGB Chief's falling body let her get by to reach the fireplace, behind the Soviet leader. She pressed frantically with both hands along the moulding on the mantelpiece.

'If you're trying for that way out,' Lowel said, 'you can slow right down. The door mechanism has been destroyed.'

He took one pace sideways to clear the line of sight. She suddenly swung towards him – and grabbed the First Secretary to use for a shield.

Lowel fired.

A wing shot, shattering her left elbow. Maximum pain. She screamed and released the Russian leader. Her right hand whipped in an arc across her body to clutch the wound . . .

Halfway there, one finger brushed the blotter that was still adhering to the side of the Soviet shredder. Skin touched skin.

The toxin struck the central nervous system of a poisoner with the same implacable speed and effect that it had for all her victims.

The forensic unit arrived for decontamination. The two world leaders held their half-poisoned hands out, like obedient children, for scrubbing. The red Christmas-tree alert lights on the nuclear Button Box went back through orange. The first tight smiles began to reappear on the survivors' faces. A medical team administered aid to Berov. He was conscious, but his jaw had been fractured. As the small Russian was removed by stretcher, through the windows, his lips managed to curve with their usual amusement at human frailty.

Strelnikov came in the other way with the acetylene torch crew to burn off the remaining voice lock. Lowel, as one of the walking wounded, pointed at the young naval aide, who had grown a lot older, and said to the President, being scrubbed, 'I didn't authorize him. What the hell was he doing here?'

'Executive privilege. Not even for my oldest friend would I lock myself in a cage, in Soviet Russia, and leave the Button outside.' Daniel Galbraith made an effort to stretch the smile to his familiar grin. 'The Cold War crowd back on the Hill would finish the impeachment proceedings our side started with Nixon.'

The master of Soviet Russia looked at the American President, at America's communications link that could have fried the world, at the Byzantine filigreed steel that would have locked them into this graceful prison while it did so. The First Secretary said in perfect English, 'What history needs now, gentlemen, is a little *glasnost*.'

36

Forenoon:

Post-mortem

After the nuclear light on the Box was back to green, and civilization got its second chance as the treaty was signed in front of the global cameras, Lowel returned with the forensic team to inspect the body lying on the floor in the Roosevelt study.

He looked at its interpreter's costume: the padded football shoulders, the high-hipped 42nd Street pants; shirt, tie, cufflinks – engraved V and K – the pimp's pointed alligator shoes. Like the Polaroid picture from Paris, everything checked out except the face.

It was turned towards the floor. One of the neoprene-clad forensic team pushed the prominent buttocks and rolled the body over. The tinted glasses fell off. So did the false macho moustache. The dead mouth sneered. The open eyes still showed a final contempt.

The forensic expert, protected by heavy double gauntlets, grasped the grotesque Prince Valiant head: its absurd gold dye-job came off as a full wig.

Lowel recognized the shaved hairstyle underneath. It had belonged to the female cab driver from the crane incident in Moscow.

The forensic expert disagreed. Gesturing at the expensively tailored, right-dressed bulge of the crotch, he told his partner: 'Androgynous facial characteristics, but male.'

'Don't bet on it,' said Lowel.

The technician shrugged and yanked the zipper. The briefs on the corpse were Calvin Kleins. The sexual organs they contained, 'Do look smaller than average, comrade, from outside, but indisputably masculine.'

'Just keep going.'

The technician cut one elastic leg band and exposed foam rubber, shaped to order. The man whistled in surprise. Lowel was staring again at the face. He was spared his worst nightmare: the phantom he had tracked across the world – *She* – was not Jacky.

But how could the recognition system have believed She was Kolinski?

The second forensic expert had removed the jacket and was working on the shirt. As the man said, 'Chest padding,' and revealed a specially built-up corset brassière, a mini Walkman recorder fell out of a pocket.

'Hit the play button.'

The technician obeyed. A high-pitched voice yapped: 'Victor Kolinski wants *in* . . .!'

And solved that half of the recognition puzzle. The technician said, 'She was also carrying this.'

A surgical rubber glove. The senior man examined the corpse's right-hand fingerprints, calibrating them against a photo set. 'Taken from the drinking jug you provided,' he said to Lowel. 'Observe: the pattern match is exact, yet the originals on the summer-house body are three microns smaller.' The man held the surgical glove under a magnifying light. 'Right hand also. The jug prints were applied with these. The cadaver's own prints would have been lifted from some personal item with a smooth surface – a soap dish, for example. Then the prints were transferred to the glove's finger and thumb tips, by a reverse-positive process. There are certain spray fixatives now available – it's the same principle as pouring and stripping a ceramic's latex mould. In miniature. Very clever.'

It had certainly been smart enough to fool the moron machine guarding the palace front door. And the bigger fool, Lowel himself, who had pursued the triple-bluffing mind responsible.

The pictures from Paris that he thought had been such brilliant, last-minute lucky breaks which he'd deserved after all his slogging . . . the Polaroids and their randomly burned-off corners were intentional. So was the wig she'd shown to the Aeroflot boarding clerk, naming the Ritz Hotel – before she left a costumier's receipt for André Dolmain, sanatorium pyjamas for the Alsatian, and the green Danskins on the pathetic remains of male vanity lying back in the summer-house. Her contemptuous throw-away evidence of how easy it all was.

But she'd lost. At a terrible price, he had won.

As part of the wind-up, the FBI picked this moment to come through on Hi-Fax with a Castilio close-out: 'Toxin Compound A found on eye-drops label. Compound B in tabloid newsprint.' Which just left Powys and his pilot, Teddy Campbell, unproven for cause of death. One drop on the red dragon sandwich-box and another on the doilies could account for that.

'This is all.' The Soviet forensic expert had finished cutting off and discarding the rest of the Calvin Klein underwear. 'Abdomen unblemished. Never pregnant. No further distinguishing marks.'

No scar.

Except in Murphy's rigged biography, there never had been. International Hallowe'en was over.

He limped on his swollen ankle out of the Roosevelt study and the Palace of Livadia, along the Oreanda path flanked with blue Yalta poppies, once followed by Tolstoy. Just beyond the collie's grave, by the Caspian Pond, the two leaders were having their pictures taken for the millionth time to reassure the world.

Daniel Galbraith waved him over, mentioned gratitude and anteing up a special Medal of Honor. The First Secretary sweetened the pot with the gold star for a new Hero of Leningrad.

Lowel smiled as expected and went back to drop one of the blue poppies on the grave in lieu of a gold star: for Mischa, and Bergitta, Sam Wong, and Jacqueline . . .

37

Sunset:

Switzerland

The manager of a small Swiss hotel watched the latest
return of a favourite guest. That was how he always
referred to her in his dealings with the hotel staff. She
epitomized everything the establishment stood for, he
told them: elegance, understatement, reliability, complete
reserve, money.

Of course, to have those attributes, the last item really came first, but that would not *be* elegant. There was
enough shit in the rest of the hospitality business, the
manager reminded the staff: 'With us, money is never
mentioned – and we do not take cards!'

The favourite guest paused as usual at his desk located
beside the only television set on the premises. 'But only
for special occasions, Madame,' he was quick to reassure
her. 'For watching catastrophe, you understand. Or history in the making, such as this morning's momentous
treaty signing at Yalta.'

'I understand. My packet of letters, please.'

The voice, the manager always told the staff! Listen
to the guest's voice before you leap to conclusions about
appearance. Many of the hotel's otherwise perfect guests
carried understatement in their clothes to such a point
that it put the boot to elegance. Her voice conveyed it.
The manager opened the safe in his office.

'Your letters, Madame.'

On a silver tray. Four of them, bound together with

389

a red ribbon.

'Do you have a pair of scissors, by any chance?'

'Certainly, Madame. Allow me.'

He snipped the ribbon and watched surreptitiously as she scanned the addresses: Washington, Moscow, London, Paris. She hesitated for a moment with the American letter, then asked for a new envelope, changed the name from something that seemed to begin with an 'M', to what might have been an 'S', banded all four letters with an 'out of town' wrapper so that he could no longer see any writing, and returned the bundle to him.

'For tonight's post, please. And if you could be kind enough to arrange my conference call?'

'Of course, Madame. At once.'

It was a familiar ritual. After every return to the hotel, following the letters routine, his favourite guest always asked the same question. The manager always saw to it himself. That was the meaning of reliability. Although greatly tempted, he had never been foolish enough to actually open a letter . . .

Upstairs in her suite, she gazed from a latticed window at the sunset beauty of the Swiss countryside. Behind the green valley meadows sloping south to the blue Brienzer See, the Alps shut out the world beyond the borders of this neutral land. Yet even here, death intruded. She stared at the black cliff of the Eiger, the mountaineers' North Wall, where the roped bodies of men sometimes hung all winter. Like frozen chrysalises in a spider's larder.

Waiting like this for the telephone to ring was always a curious anti-climax to her missions. She stripped, showered, and changed into an embroidered Japanese silk kimono. The light from the dying sun turned the small pubic scar, left from the childhood removal of a mole, from its normal silver-white to a golden sheen. Her eyes took in again the marvellous view beyond the window. The mountain beside the man-killing Eiger was named the Jungfrau. Virginal innocence, confronting brute strength.

The inspection of her own trained body made her think of the other, so physically similar. Too bad the woman Moscow provided for the last substitution had been a better actress than an agent! A true professional would have found ample opportunity to break out after a successful conclusion to the operation. The substitute must have been too caught up in the part: that slime Kolinski, with his ham introductions and small talk –

The phone!

She picked up the receiver. 'Your conference call, Madame.'

'I'm connected to all parties?'

'But certainly, Madame. Those were your instructions.'

By now she could scarcely endure the management creep's crawling discretion, or the time it took him to get off the line. But if he had not been so discreet, considering the unusual pleasures he demanded of the temporary help at the height of the skiing season, then the solid Swiss burghers – or herself, if she should ever find from her special security precautions that he had tampered with one of her envelopes! – would long ago have strung the little squirt up like one of those corpses opposite.

Click.

The man was gone. But it was still a male world, she reflected: a woman could not always win, no matter how skilled. Never look back. Try harder in future.

Anticipating the quadruple reactions and emotions from her disappointed Four Power clients on the other ends of the line, a sardonic smile lit her face. Men promise the earth beforehand, but they never like paying after the event. If the cash wasn't in her bank account by noon tomorrow, then opening her letters would remind the gentlemen of their obligations to a lady, in a novel fashion.